THE DOOR OF
NO RETURN

THE DOOR OF NO RETURN

SARAH MUSSI

Margaret K. McElderry Books
NEW YORK • LONDON • TORONTO • SYDNEY

Margaret K. McElderry Books
An imprint of Simon & Schuster Children's Publishing Division
1230 Avenue of the Americas, New York, New York 10020

First published in Great Britain in 2007
by Hodder Children's Books
First U.S. edition, 2008

The text for this book is set in Bembo.
Manufactured in the United States of America
2 4 6 8 10 9 7 5 3 1
Library of Congress Cataloging-in-Publication Data
Mussi, Sarah.
The door of no return / Sarah Mussi.—1st U.S. ed.
p. cm.
Summary: Sixteen-year-old Zac never believed his grandfather's tales about their
enslaved ancestors being descended from an African king, but when his grandfather
is murdered and the villains come after Zac, he sets out for Ghana, Africa, to find
King Baktu's long-lost treasure before the murderers do.
ISBN-13: 978-1-4169-1550-8 (hardcover)
ISBN-10: 1-4169-1550-8 (hardcover)
[1. Adventure and adventurers—Fiction. 2. Buried treasure—Fiction.
3. Blacks—England—Fiction. 4. Murder—Fiction. 5. Foster home care—Fiction.
6. Slavery—Fiction. 7. England—Fiction. 8. Ghana—Fiction.] I. Title.
PZ7.M97272Doo 2008   [Fic]—dc22
2007018670

This edition is dedicated to the year 2008,
a significant and historic year that marks
the bicentenary of the banning of the
importation of slaves to America.

Sɛ wo werɛ fi na wosan kɔfa a, yenkyi
May we learn from the past
Sankofa ~ traditional Adinkra wisdom
Ghana

Caruthers & Ambrose

LEGAL PRACTITIONERS, CONSULTANTS

364 London Road
Gloucester
GL49 DDF
Tel/Fax: 01442 564789

Beamish, Ludgate & Perkins
226 Camberwell New Road
London SE5 9JK

Dear Messrs Beamish, Ludgate & Perkins

RE: SUIT NO. MISC 991/200
ZACHARIAH BAXTER & OTHERS
VS.
HAROLD REEVES, INGLEWORTH & OTHERS
in the FIRST INST. & THE STATE in the SECOND INST.

Please find enclosed the statement of my foster son, Zachariah Baxter. I asked him to write the story down exactly as he related it to us. The police had it typed up and used it in preparing their case against Reeves and others (criminal charges). Attached also is all his supporting evidence.

I'd like you to read it carefully and extract what you need for the breach of contract petition and compensation claim against the State. We may have to take it to the Court of Human Rights. If so, I am happy to advise; it being, as you know, my area of speciality.

Of course, the bond itself will form the basis of the case, with the other artifacts and records, which you already have, but Zac is prepared to take the stand.

Let me know if you need clarification on any parts of his story.

Yours sincerely,

Bernard Caruthers

Bernard Caruthers

Form MG 11

Witness Statement
(CJ Act 1967, s. 9; MC Act 1980, ss. 5A(3) (a) and 5B; MC Rules 1981, r. 70)

Statement of....*ZAC   BAXTER*..

Age if under 18 ......*16*...... (if over 18 insert "over")

Occupation .*STUDENT*...

This statement (consisting of ..*3*...*PARTS* ~~page(s)~~ each page signed by me) is true to the best of my knowledge and belief and I make it knowingly, if it is tendered in evidence, I shall be liable to prosecution if I have wilfully stated in it anything which I know to be false or do not believe to be true.

Signature *ZAC   BAXTER*. Date.*NOVEMBER   5TH*.. *DJ Hesketh*

Statement

The diaries—what is left of them—sit here in front of me. Three hundred years of history. When I am done with this account, I'll add it to the pile. I doubt if that will be the end of the matter, but I know Pops would like it.

After all, it started with him and the diaries.

PART ONE

Gloucester, England

The Lost Prince

I knew something was wrong the minute I shut the door of number 13, Arrowsmith House, Tuffley. I'd lived there as long as I could remember. What I didn't know was I'd just closed the door on that part of my life.

We were late. Pops had insisted on wearing his kente cloth. He didn't really know how to tie it, and he had to get his coat over the top of the whole thing, so we'd been fussing in the front hall for ten minutes. It was cold outside, bitterly cold, and with only two days to go, I was hoping for a white Christmas.

I think it was because I was inspecting the patch of grass at the front, to see if it was snow or frost, that I noticed the footsteps. Someone had been standing there for a while. The frozen grass was broken and crushed; there were patterns of pale steps pacing along the front of the flat, up and down.

For some reason I felt a flash of anger. Someone was taking liberties. I scanned the parking lot and thought I saw a shape, a woman—sort of ageless with a blank gray face.

"We'll dazzle them tonight, eh, Zac?" said Pops.

I didn't reassure him. That woman's gray look had unsettled me. Instead I took his arm and glanced the length of the housing estate. It looked safe. Fairy lights twinkled in windows—but people get angry at Christmas. Angry for all the things they want and can't have. So I wasn't taking any chances.

"When I get to the part about the Lost Prince, you show them your back."

My back is stunningly fit like the rest of me, but that was not why Pops wanted to show it off. A cat ran out from under a car and I jumped.

Pops chuckled; I was not in a mood to humor him. "It's cold," I said. "I don't really want to." To tell you the truth, I didn't want to go at all.

The Cormantin Club was Pops's baby. He was the founding member, Big Chief, the soul of the whole thing. That's Pops for you. Really the Cormantin Club was just a bunch of old black folks harking back to the days of slavery and drinking. After a few glasses they tried to outdo each other with wild tales. Pops's were always the wildest.

"They can't disprove me today, 'cause I got the diaries." He clutched the plastic bag up to his chest.

I remember that bag.

"I'm going to read them the dying words of King Baktu." Pops stopped and flung out his hand. Funny the things you remember. His outstretched arm, the plastic bag, and that feeling that something was wrong.

"Until my son, the Lost Prince—get it, that's you—comes back through the Door of No Return and claims his ransom, my soul will never rest in the land of my ancestors. That'll shut the old buggers up."

"But Pops, *you* wrote that bit in *your* diary."

"But that's what he said, son, so it doesn't matter which diary it's wrote in."

I'd got him a briefcase for Christmas. I figured he needed it!

That's when I noticed the two shadows up ahead. I shivered. A cloud passed over the moon like a hand across a face. The pavements darkened. Only the orange glare of the streetlights glittered on the frost.

"Then when they see the tribal marks . . ."

"Let's cross over."

It was always the same old story. Pops told it over and over, as if nobody had heard it before. That him and me were the last descendants of King Baktu, that King Baktu's chosen son and heir, our great-times-whatever-grandfather, had been stolen away as a child by slavers, that a king's ransom had been raised, but the treasure and the child were lost. It was true that we did have scar marks on our backs. But I know for certain that mine had been put there by Pops.

I suppose he was trying to feel important about something. Living on a Gloucester housing estate needed bigging up a bit.

The two shadows waited, half hidden behind some

large waste bins. As we crossed over, they came forward. I can't remember much about either of them, other than a glimpse of royal blue tracksuit with white stripes. What I do remember was that woman's blank face flashing into my brain. I began to feel very edgy. Despite the cold I broke out in a slight sweat. I moved Pops to the inside so I was between him and the street. I tightened my features into a really mean screwface. I thought I was tough. What was I thinking? Why couldn't I have done more?

It happened very fast. Suddenly one of the shadows came running straight at me, yelling something about a stabbing, about needing help. The other one staggered into the street, screaming. I looked at one, then the other. My jaw dropped. I should never have hesitated. The next thing I knew, I was flat on my back with my head exploding. I heard Pops scream. I saw the other shadow sprint forward and grab the plastic bag. I heard the dull *thwack* of Pops's skull hitting the pavement. Then they were gone.

I can't remember reaching Pops; I thought stupidly that he must have arranged it all as a bit of drama. My head hurt so much I couldn't think straight. I think I was bleeding.

Pops looked so small lying there—crumpled, like a bundle of discarded rags. In his hand was part of a diary and shreds of bag. He wasn't moving.

Everything was going to be okay. I shook him a little and then remembered not to. I pulled out my mobile. Funny how I'd always wanted to dial 999.

"Pops, it's going to be okay."

"No," he said, "it's not."

He was speaking—so of course it was going to be okay.

"They've got the diaries, but they haven't got the map."

"Just hold on, the police are coming."

"Look in my pocket." His hand fluttered. I tore aside the kente. I looked in the breast pocket of his overcoat and pulled out one slim volume.

"That's the one they wanted." His voice was so old and tired. An ache started somewhere in the back of my throat. I looked helplessly around.

That was when I saw the woman with the blank gray face again; she was right behind us. Far too close.

"Don't let them get it," he said, and pressed the last diary toward me.

I took off my jacket and covered him. I sat down and cradled his head. I thought, if that woman comes any closer I'll smack her so hard she'll be the one who needs the ambulance. Somebody leaned out of an upstairs window and started shouting something.

"You've got to promise me, Zac, to go back and get the treasure."

My heart was thudding. My head hurt. The tightness in my throat was choking me. But I didn't want the woman to see the diary, so I let go of Pops's hand and stuffed it inside my hoody. She was weird. She just stood there, not offering to help, not doing anything! Just standing there pushing back the cuticles of her left hand with that blank gray face.

9

"They haven't got the map," said Pops again. "It never was in the diaries."

I didn't want her to hear what he was saying either.

"The map is the secret, see."

"Try to stay quiet."

"They haven't got it."

The woman moved closer. Pops's hand clutched at mine. "Zac, promise . . ."

I played along. "Who's got it then?"

"You have."

The Police Station

The ambulance came. I wanted to help, but they looked at my head and made me sit down while they made Pops comfy. Then the older guy came over to check me. The other put a silver blanket on Pops and went back to the cab for something. I saw the woman move toward Pops and I shouted. The older guy calmed me. I gripped his arm and told him that the woman was nothing to do with us.

"She's a witness, though, mate," he said.

Then more people and the police arrived, and it all got mad. They wouldn't let me go to the hospital. They wouldn't let me give Pops the funky we-can-beat-this handshake. I ended up at the station making statements, seeing social workers, I don't know.

At first I didn't think it was odd that the woman ended up in the police station as well. I supposed the ambulance guy was right and she was simply making a statement too. I was worried about Pops. I was wondering what he meant about the map. I was angry with myself. I was thinking about how I was going to find those brothers and pulp them. But still, she gave me the creeps and instinctively I checked that the diary was safe.

At some point a lady came in. She said, "Sit down, Zac. This is going to be hard for you."

I was already sitting.

"You have to be very brave."

I waited. It's funny how some minutes seem long.

"We've just got word from the hospital. Is there anyone we can phone for you?"

I shook my head. It had always been just me and Pops.

"Your grandfather was declared dead on arrival. I'm sorry."

I remember thinking—strange—we certainly are going to show the "old buggers" now.

I think I smiled. Then felt that I shouldn't smile. It wasn't true anyway. It was all a mistake. He'd been talking to me before the ambulance came.

"I'm sorry," she said again.

"You're lying," I said. "I want to see him."

"We don't want you to go home alone. If there's no one we can call, I'd like you to stay here until we can fix something up."

"Where's Pops?" I said.

"He's dead, Zac. You've got to be very strong."

I made for the door. The lady said, "You'll need a few minutes alone. I'll make you some tea. Do you take sugar?"

I waited until she'd left, then I left too. I was going to the hospital, even if I had to walk. I took the stairs to the ground floor and I was just about to go out when I saw that gray-faced woman again. She was standing inside the main door making a phone call: ". . . Stage one, objective one . . . It can't be helped at present. . . . Objective two in progress . . . Objective three completed. . . . The boy has it. . . . Another objective three? . . . Well, he's already in the system. You'll have to pull strings on your end. . . . Yes . . . Yes . . ."

Click.

I belted back up the stairs. I asked for the toilet. I bolted myself in a cubicle and sat on the loo seat shivering. "*. . . Objective three completed. . . . The boy has it. . . . Another objective three? . . . Well, he's already in the system. . . .*" Didn't sound like a call you'd make when you'd just witnessed a mugging. I don't know what it sounded like, but the words "*the boy has it*" were pretty clear. There was only one boy around and there was only one thing he'd got. And right now I was pulling it out of my hoody and opening it up.

Pops's last diary, the one he'd said *they* wanted, was written in a foreign language.

Unreadable.

I didn't know what to do, but I couldn't stay in the toilet forever, so I went back to the interviewing room.

Ms. Shaw, the lady with the tea, was there. She puckered up her lips in that I-feel-sorry-for-you way that adults do, then she said, "Did your grandfather give you anything before he died that might be a clue as to why he was attacked?"

I thought that was a very odd question. It made me feel very suspicious. Ms. Shaw was nodding away, as if to reassure me, but I could tell she was looking at someone else. I glanced round. I'll give you one guess who was standing in the corridor outside. Yep, through the glass door behind me was that woman again. She was just standing there with her blank face looking in on us—just like she'd done on the street.

"Who's she?" I said.

"I don't know, Zac," said Ms. Shaw. "She's—I really can't . . . They don't tell me anything." She smiled as if she'd like to be more cooperative.

I hate tea, but I drank that one. My brain had just added up 2+2. I'm not stupid.

They made 4.

"She wants to help with the attack," continued Ms. Shaw.

I spluttered the tea. She helped all right, I thought. She really helped a lot.

It was a good job I did not find out the truth about that woman then. I might have given up. I might just have walked out, handed her the diary, and said, "I'm ready for my objective three. Please make it as painless as possible."

Pops used to say, "*Ignorance is bliss.*" That might be an exaggeration, but right then it probably saved my life.

December 23

I stayed in the police station that night. Oh, they tried to get me into emergency care, but it was the night before Christmas Eve. People were wrapping presents, eating mince pies. Ms. Shaw had her own family to get back to. I don't want to talk about it.

I didn't sleep. I sat on the corner of the bed and watched the door. Every hour or so a guard strolled by. I didn't see the woman, though. I gave up biting my nails when I was ten, but that night I cheated.

I thought about Pops. I thought about the mugging. I thought about that woman. Who was she? Why had she been watching our flat? Was she connected to the muggers? And what was she up to in the police station?

My head hurt and I had a pain deep in my chest that hadn't been there before. The words "*declared dead on arrival*" kept swimming up into my ears. Pops couldn't be dead. He was too colorful to die. He couldn't be dead: It was Christmas. I didn't care if he never used the briefcase; I would even carry his plastic bag for him. I'd show his old blokes at the club my back. I'd believe in his stories. Yes, we'd go to Africa. We'd rest beneath rustling palms and hunt for his treasure. . . . Look, I'd even turn my music down. What was going to happen to me? Where had they put him? I was all alone now in a big unfriendly world.

The next morning they brought me beans on toast for breakfast, but I wasn't hungry. One of the policemen was reading the newspaper. It was the Christmas Eve edition. He showed it to me. I think that was when I really believed. I kept it. Here it is. I'll stick it in.

OLD GOLD-COASTER DIES IN BRUTAL MUGGING

Popular pensioner Samuel Baxter died late last night as another victim of street crime in Gloucester. He was attacked by two assailants outside his home in Tuffley. They only got away with some personal papers, but left their victim dying. Mr. Baxter, 85, was well known in the area for founding the Cormantin Club. He was actively involved in seeking sponsors to fund his Return to Africa venture. Mr. Baxter believed that he was the inheritor of a vast fortune in gold

dust raised by one of his distant ancestors. He had traced his history and said
he knew where the treasure was buried.
In a recent interview with the *Daily Echo*
one month ago, Mr. Baxter said, "I have
tangible evidence of where the treasure
is. In 1701 my ancestor was sold as a
slave from Cape Coast. All I want is for
members of the black community to
come forward and sponsor my club to
mount an expedition to retrieve the
gold. Until the West pays the descendants of slavery due compensation, our
community needs every penny it can get."

Mr. Baxter leaves behind a teenage
grandson. The police are now treating
the assault as a murder inquiry.

"It *was* murder!" I told the policeman. "He was alive
and somebody killed him in the ambulance." Then I
paused. I'd remembered something. When I'd been sitting
on the curb, when that woman had gone over to Pops, in
that split second when the ambulance guy had spoken,
I'd heard a second dull *thwack*. A second crunch of bone
hitting paving stone. Or had I?

"That woman did it," I said. "She killed him."

"You've been through a lot, kid," said the policeman.

"I've remembered something," I said. "I want to change my statement."

"Sometimes it's like that," he said. "Stress."

I think I made a bit of a fuss, but they wouldn't allow me to change anything. I demanded to know who the woman was. "I want her name—the one who made the witness statement."

Eventually a policeman went to check. He came back shaking his head. "No witnesses," he said. "Only you."

I stopped making a fuss. I went cold all over.

Even though I don't have asthma, I couldn't breathe. In my mind I saw her crouching over Pops, whispering, "Are you okay?" Then dragging his poor, old, beloved head up with her cuticled nails and slamming it back down on the pavement.

Writing that makes me very, very scared. I may never prove it and I may never get even, but, like King Baktu, my soul will never rest until I do.

Bernard says justice is the best revenge. He likes to quote. He says, "*The wheels of justice grind slow, but they grind exceedingly fine.*" I'm sure hoping they are going to grind right over her. Bernard says it's best to record everything. He says my "insights are important." He says to attach all the documents I've collected, so that the barrister can create a case out of it. I'll take the stand as well if necessary. I was scared once, but I'm not anymore. You see, this is all part of the justice, part of the revenge, and part of my pledge to Pops. He wanted a court case and he'll get it. I'll make sure he does, if that's the last thing I do.

Talking of diaries, I did ask my social worker, Ms. Shaw, if I could have the pages that Pops had held on to.

"As soon as the inquest is over, I promise you."

I asked her if I could go home now. I wanted to be alone in the flat. I don't know, but I still felt ill. I wanted to curl up in Pops's bed, like when I was small. I wanted to look at his picture, because for some silly reason I couldn't remember what he looked like.

"Sit down, Zac," she said. "There's something I need to tell you. Try to be strong."

I sat down.

"Last night your home was broken into. It seems with all the upheaval going on, we forgot to send an officer to check on your flat."

?

"Za-ac?"

"What did they take?"

"Well, it's quite extraordinary: Everything except the carpets is gone."

I looked at her. Boy, she had to be making that up.

"We are not connecting it to the attack at the moment, but it does seem strange. . . ."

Strange? My CDs, my clothes, Pops's papers, my sound system, his drums, his bed with the quilted cover. I think at that point I put my head down on the table.

"We know your grandfather was involved in a bid to

return to Africa. . . . Had he collected any sponsorship money? Did he keep it in the flat?"

"No. That buried gold was just an old story—nobody believed it." Even I didn't. But you know how it is—it kept him going somehow; it was his dream. Everyone needs a dream. And it was kind of fun to help him make his plans.

"We'll need you to make an inventory of the flat—but not now, not until you're ready. Do you know if your grandfather had any insurance?"

I shook my head.

"I've arranged for you to go to a foster home. They're nice people. They know all about what's happened. Try to be strong."

When I look back now, I can see how un-strong I was. Boy, I didn't have a clue. I was adding 2+2 and getting 4. Duh! I didn't imagine anyone could take Pops seriously. What—seriously enough to kill him?

Did I say I was all alone in a big unfriendly world? I was about to find out just how unfriendly it could get.

Christmas Eve

Ms. Shaw gave me my bus fare, an address, an overnight pack, and her mobile phone number. She told me to "be strong" a few more times, and said although it wasn't normal procedure, she was invited somewhere for Christmas and wasn't paid overtime.

When I left the police station, it was snowing, but I didn't care about a white Christmas anymore. I walked into Gloucester and waited for the bus. Somewhere "Jingle Bells" was playing and the afternoon smelled faintly of charcoal and doughnuts. As I waited, I scanned every face. That woman knew I had the diary, and part of me was expecting her to show up.

I must have been in a weird state, because I can remember every detail about that bus stop: the ad for Levi's jeans, the red plastic seating, the snow, the feeling of disbelief—this couldn't be happening. . . . Pretty soon, a woman joined me. I could see straightaway that she wasn't the one I was looking for—but I became edgy all the same.

This woman was quite plain with dark hair, and I could have sworn she was shorter. But there was something—a feeling, a tingling down my spine and a sudden dread that gripped my stomach. I tried to tell myself it was nerves, imagination, that soon I'd be believing every woman was a murderer, but as I clutched the diary to me the feeling wouldn't go away.

The bus came and I got on. She got on too. I went upstairs. She went upstairs. There were loads of empty seats, but I sat down next to an old bloke. I didn't want her to sit next to me, to trap me against the window. She sat opposite. I kept telling myself to get real, to stop the paranoia.

It was no use.

My heart was thudding so hard the front of my jacket shook. I glanced across at her. Not the same woman. Even so, the skin at the base of my neck started to crawl. Her face was weirdly washed-out. I started to panic. She turned her head toward me. She did not smile. Her eyes were blank and pale—like a lizard's. She looked straight at me and started pushing back the cuticles of her left hand.

A wave of nausea spiraled from my stomach to my mouth. I lurched forward as if the bus had suddenly braked. I clamped my hand across my face. I felt sick.

The bus stopped.

I got off. She got off.

I ran.

I was the fastest sprinter in Key Stage 4, and she didn't

look like Kelly Holmes, but I wasn't taking any chances. I ran and ran until my chest hurt and my legs were weak. And that's how I arrived at my foster home. Out of breath, scared stupid, with a welfare pack of emergency items that I was ashamed of, and a bad attitude I wasn't.

My New Year's Resolution

I think that was probably the worst Christmas my foster parents ever had. I don't apologize. It's just how things were. They were white. They couldn't help that, but they didn't understand. It was bedtime at ten and brush your teeth, all over again—as if I didn't know! My room was middle-class magnolia with brocade curtains.

I guess it wasn't home.

The incident on the bus had shaken me so badly that for the rest of the holidays, I stayed locked in my room and refused to come out. I had terrible nightmares. I would barely talk to my foster parents, and I didn't like talking to Ms. Shaw. I answered everybody's questions with shrugs. I sat by my window and watched the road. That woman was out there somewhere, out there waiting for me to make a false move.

Of course, I looked for answers in Pops's old diary. But as it was written in another language, I didn't get them. During those long hours at the window, I scoured through it anyway. It read *Los Eventos de Cabo Corso em*

1701.[1] I remember the opening words: *"Chamo-me Bartolomeu . . ."*[2]

Whatever was so important about it beat me. But I tried—I tried to imagine what it might say. And you can be sure nothing went up or down that road without me seeing it.

Later, much later—at a very different window, watching a very different road, alongside which tall palms swayed by the Great Atlantic Ocean—I thought back to how I searched those streets for an answer—how slow I'd been—how the best I could come up with was that the muggers must be after the buried treasure, and probably believed the diaries would lead them to it. Back then, that seemed crazy. Wasn't Gloucester in the twenty-first century, not *The Pirates of the Caribbean*? Nobody (except Pops) seriously believed in buried treasure. A plastic bag full of old diaries, with no map—which might or might not contain hints about a pile of gold dust, buried three hundred years ago somewhere in Africa—was not a convincing motive for murder.

Murder. It's hard even now to write that. Pops murdered.

Will I ever forget that frosty night? Will I ever stop going over and over it, trying to find a way to make it come out differently? Why *hadn't* I promised to go back and get the treasure? He was dying. Even if I didn't believe in it, I should have promised. It was his dream; it kept him going.

1. The Events of Cabo Corso in 1701.
2. I am called Bartholomew.

It wasn't logical, but I kept thinking that if I'd promised, he might not have died. I couldn't forgive myself. You see, a promise that you *don't* make, that you should have, is more powerful than one you do. You can't keep an un-promise and you can't break it. So even if there was no treasure—and that would make my task impossible—as I sat there at that window, I promised and *promised* him I'd do everything I could to finish what he'd started.

It was just that I didn't know where to start.

Winter

I had to start somewhere and I had to come out of my room to do it. And by February, I woke up to the fact that no one was going do it for me. Ms. Shaw thought I should "adjust," but I wasn't doing too well, so she was often very blunt. My foster mother took my side. She didn't try to make me talk, and I didn't need to tell her how scared I was. She let me keep those brocade curtains nearly drawn all day and the door locked. She'd just sit very quietly when I dared to come into the lounge. I found being around her was okay, and now I was out of my room I might as well go a bit farther.

Before long I was going out with the same determination that I'd stayed in. In my mind I switched the rules. I was now the hunter and *they* were the hunted. Night after night, I'd comb the streets looking for that woman, looking for the muggers, looking for any way to get even. It was cold and it was dark, but that suited my mood. I went back to Arrowsmith House and prowled the estate. I peered through the windows of number 13, hid behind the waste bins, and came home silent and haunted. Ms. Shaw said I was "acting out," but my foster mother just sat up waiting for me. Whatever time I came, she'd be there with her worried smile ready to make me some toast, or warm up my dinner. And so slowly, very slowly, I began to trust her. I began to look forward to coming home.

After the staying in and the going out, what bugged me next was that I hadn't given Pops his Christmas present.

I started visiting the graveyard—at first on Sundays, but soon it became a daily obsession. I'd sit there and look at the mound. There was no gravestone. You'd have thought the Cormantin Club might have arranged that, but they just carried on with their meetings. Always talking—never doing. Maybe it was the lost briefcase, maybe it was Pops's tale of buried treasure that first got me burying little gifts to him. Maybe I wanted to make it all come true in a different way. Whatever change I had in my pocket, I'd dig into the mound. It began with coins, but soon I was burying other stuff. It was a dark time. I don't want to go into it much. Once I had quite a struggle to get a Rolex watch ten inches deep. The sexton told me that the soil there was all clay— that it preserved the bodies, and six feet down, dead people lay staring upward as perfect as the day they died.

I got the idea that Pops was watching me. Far from being spooked, I liked it. Nobody else gave a damn about me anyway. Then on the evening of St. Valentine's Day something changed my mind.

St. Valentine's Day

It was another cold evening, not unlike the night we were attacked. A chill frost lay everywhere. I was about to leave when the phone rang. I picked up the receiver and said, "Hello, this is the Caruthers Crew." Nobody answered. The line clicked. I hate that. It makes me paranoid.

Outside, for some reason two streetlamps had failed. Inky blackness shrouded the sidewalks. I didn't like that, either. My foster parents live in a posh suburb where streetlights don't go out. I stood for a long time on the doorstep scoping the street. Then I saw them—under the bridge where the grove turned into Malvern Road: two shadows.

A familiar dread gripped my stomach. I should have stayed in, but because I'd missed Christmas, I was set on giving Pops a Valentine present. I zipped up my hoody and played with the gold ring I'd got inside my pocket. Yes, it was a ring I'd stolen. I can say that now, because I've apologized to my foster mother; but at the time, I only thought: It's real gold—that's what Pops wants. As I rolled the ring,

I clenched my fist trying to convince myself I was not the kind who'd hesitate twice.

When I got to the bridge, my heart was beating fast, but the shadows—if they had been there—were gone. In a way, I was disappointed. They'd tricked me again. But I did not go back.

I got two blocks from our house to where the number 37 bus stopped. A bitter wind started. The tarmac shone in cold orange patches under the streetlights. Something was still very wrong. You could almost smell it on the frosty air. I wriggled my feet and paced a little down the deserted sidewalk—waiting for the bus—up and down.

At the end of the street a woman appeared. She must have been old, because she kept stopping to balance her shopping bags on the footpath. I watched her every movement, daring her to be the woman I was looking for. I stamped my feet so that they echoed down the street. I began to flick the ring over and over again in my pocket. I clenched and unclenched my fist for real. I was ready.

The old lady bent herself against the wind and hesitated in such a weary way, as if she was frightened of shadows too. She glanced at me uneasily. I thought of Pops and stopped stamping. I guess she was more scared of me than I was of her. She shouldn't have been out. Streets aren't safe for old folks.

At that point two school friends passed me on their bikes. I stuck my nose into my collar and pretended I didn't know them. They saw me anyway.

"Wha'happen, bro?" said Maggot.

My nose was running slightly, so I sniffed into the drawstring of the hood. "Boy, am I cold," I said.

He braked and skidded to a stop. "Where you going?"

Opoku stopped too.

"Nowhere." I'd been blanking my friends for a while. I told myself it was because they smiled too much, but really, I couldn't stand myself around them. They reminded me that life went on.

"Furthermore, you are not going nowhere," said Maggot.

"We are all going somewhere," said Opoku. "Life's a journey. You will go on a long journey, Zac Baxter, to a distant land." Opoku is from Ghana and pretends he's got juju powers.

"Any land after a long journey is distant," I pointed out.

"I see gold and . . . shadows . . ."

I knew he was pulling my leg about Pops's Return to Africa plan, but the shadows bit was weird.

"I'm going to see Pops," I said.

Opoku looked embarrassed, but Maggot tossed his head and laughed. "You need to get a grip, Zac. Right now you're sad, the saddest I know."

"I don't need that," I said. "Allow it."

"Nuff said then." Maggot pedaled down hard and shot off. Opoku followed.

Later, much later—in a distant land, after a long journey, in the heat of a tropical night, where fireflies flickered at the edge of a great rain forest—I thought about those predictions of Opoku's, and since then I've kept an open mind on juju.

It was a pity I didn't have an open mind a lot sooner.

The old lady was nearer. Much nearer. She had sort of crept up on me while I was talking to Maggot and Opoku. I glared at her, real screwfaced. She turned to cross the road, like I was going to mug her. Then she seemed to slip. She screamed. What made me jump across to help her? She screamed again, and before I knew anything, somebody grabbed me from behind, yelling stuff. A hand clamped over my mouth, an arm went around my throat. I started to panic. My feet were jerked out from under me. I couldn't breathe. I fell facedown, hitting the road, struggling. This was it. I'd missed my chance. They were going to kill me.

My nose was pressed on the cold tarmac. I felt a weight on my back. The ring hand was trapped beneath my body, but I wasn't as skinny as I am now, and I thrust my elbow backward with whatever force I could. I must have hit him somewhere, for suddenly the weight lessened and I could drag my hand free. I grabbed at him and must have caught his ankle because abruptly he tripped and fell, smashing what I guess was his knee against the curb.

He swore, jumped up. I rolled over. The old lady was on her feet. She sprinted off down the road. He tried to sprint too, holding his leg and cursing.

I guess she was a lot younger than she looked. I guess she was a lot less female, too.

I sat up. My legs were shaking, but I was on my feet as

well and sprinting after them. This was what I'd been waiting for. All those evenings. I was still in with a chance. I was going to catch at least one of them. Bernard may say *"justice is the best revenge,"* but any revenge will do when you've had your life stolen. But it was no use. They simply vanished at the corner.

Trembling, I stopped and leaned over a garden wall. My breath came in bursts of white smoke and my heart was banging. I felt for the ring in my pocket, stupidly not knowing if I was still going to see Pops. The number 37 bus chugged past. Freezing rain started to pelt down. I think I was sick. I'm not sure.

Inside my pocket was something else. I pulled it out. A new Nokia, the latest model.

?

I looked at it, blank. What was a new mobile doing in my pocket? For a moment I thought I'd lost it. Had I mugged the old lady? Had I nicked her phone? Had I imagined she was attacking me when I was attacking her? Maggot's words echoed in my head. *"You're sad, the saddest I know."*

But old ladies don't have lush mobiles. They can't even use predictive text. I leaned over the wall again, confused. Sense began to return. What was I doing? What was going on? I pushed the phone into the low privet hedge thinking I'd go back for it, if this wasn't all a nightmare. I hadn't mugged her—had I? Look, I didn't even want the phone. I pushed it in farther. I'd heard of people who relive crimes, unable to move on. Was I that sick?

I turned to go home and made the first block before I heard the police siren. Boy, was I glad. I wanted to get in and hear my foster father, Bernard's, deep voice, have my foster mother, Marion, say, "Oh, Zac." I chose a bright patch of street and waited. Maggot and Opoku must have seen what happened, must have phoned the police. They must be on their way to help.

I was quite wrong. Suddenly it was, "Up against the van . . . Hands behind your back . . . Where do you live?" And, "Empty your pockets." One of them kicked my legs wide and started to search me. The other started reading me my rights. I was so shocked my veins actually felt weak.

"Whassup?" I said. "Hey, whadda'you doing?"

"Shut up."

They found the ring, and I shut up.

If there had been any sympathy from last Christmas at the station for me, it had evaporated. I cooperated with them as best I could, but I was puzzled . . . if they hadn't come to help me—then who had called them? They didn't seem to believe anything I said, and rang my foster parents. They kept asking me where I was going and where I'd got a gold ring from. I decided not to tell them about me and Pops, the phone or the presents. I tried instead to tell them about the bus woman—flat-faced, blank lizard eyes—and the muggers—two, one definitely white—the woman who might actually not be a woman . . . and how they were the same people as last Christmas. Fat chance. To them, I was another problem kid wandering the streets with a suspected stolen ring and an antisocial attitude.

It didn't look good.

Anyway—I'll put it like that, but at the time I had a creepy feeling that they knew all about the blank-faced woman. It was like they'd signed the Official Secrets Act or something, and the mention of her made them close ranks.

My foster mother, Marion, was great, though. I could tell it was hard for her. She was sniffing and her voice wobbled. I couldn't see her, but I heard her say, "It's my ring; it was my mother's. I gave it to Zac. He has nothing, you see. Nothing from his mother." I kept inspecting the floor. I hadn't thought about Marion when I'd taken the ring. I did now; and I felt terrible.

My foster father, Bernard, said, "That's right, we can verify it." When I heard him say that, I felt even worse. He was a human rights lawyer—like, really straight. He didn't lie easily. A thick feeling started to suffocate me behind my nose. They must be feeling so disappointed. They wouldn't want me anymore. I couldn't blame them. I'd stolen from them.

The policeman didn't look like he was going to take anybody's word for anything. He made them write it all out and asked them to produce a receipt. Then he said that there was another complaint against me, which wasn't so simple. It took a very long time and I ended up being charged with robbery and released on bail.

On the way home, I didn't need to be told to shut up.

I don't think I could have spoken anyway. My voice was choked deep down in my chest. At any moment I was expecting them to say, "Listen, Zac, maybe this fostering isn't working out. Perhaps it's time to rethink."

To make it worse, I was certain we were being followed. A green Fiat Brava had been tailing us all down the ring road. I wanted to tell them, but what was the point if it wasn't working out?

"Why?" Marion kept saying, as she shoved her hair repeatedly behind her ear. "Why, Zac? Tell us why—we wanted so much to help you."

Notice the past tense.

"This is serious," said my foster father. "There was a lady in the charge office who identified you as having attacked her; she said you'd stolen her phone. You've got to be straight with us. No more stupidity. Did you?"

I hunched my shoulders, kept my head low, and shrugged. Once you're a thief on one count, it's difficult to deny a second. The smell of new car made me feel slightly sick. I pressed my forehead against the side glass. I wanted to ask him about that lady, what she looked like; but I figured it wasn't the right time.

"You'll tell us, won't you, Zac? Leave him for now, Bernard. He'll tell us."

Future tense. I crossed my fingers.

After we'd reached the house, and we'd sat silent in the front room, I found my voice. "If you think I mugged someone, where's the phone then?"

"You can drop that tone," said my foster father. He stood in front of the Victorian fireplace, pulling at his beard and staring straight at me from under his bushy eyebrows.

Truly I was puzzled. I think Marion saw it, 'cause she said, "We know you wouldn't attack anyone. There was no phone on you. Maybe she made a mistake. But why did you take my ring? It was my mother's. . . ." She started to cry.

Bernard crossed the room and put his arm around her plump shoulder. "Here's the ring, Marion. Let's stay calm. We can work through this as a family."

A ray of hope.

I wanted to say something that would make Marion forgive me. I wanted a signed contract from Bernard about working through it as a family. And I still wanted to ask about that woman—but instead I crossed to the bay window and peeked out onto the street. A green Fiat Brava was parked opposite.

"Well?" said Bernard.

I think I twitched a bit. He came over to me and pulled me round so that I faced him square on.

"Well, Zac?"

I mumbled some line then about wanting something of theirs, about needing their love, about losing everything I'd ever had. I said sorry enough times.

He let me babble on until I'd seriously repeated myself. "I don't doubt all that is true," he said, "but it is only part of the truth." He raised those bushy eyebrows and looked right through me. "I think you had better tell us everything."

Something inside me cracked. Standing there face-to-face was too much. He was so solid, so overwhelming. I'd been living with shadows for too long. It was time I chose which world I belonged to.

I told them everything.

I told them about the woman, about the bus ride, and about the diaries. I told them about the last attack, and how I was sure that even the woman at the station must be the same one. I told them about the weird phone calls and the streetlights—the only thing I didn't mention was the phone. I guess I knew I'd go back for it.

Marion wiped her eyes and smiled, that kind, plump smile. She came over and put her arms round me. "You poor, poor darling," she said.

Bernard nodded thoughtfully. He went to the window and looked out at the streetlights and the Fiat Brava. Then he made a long phone call.

"Of course," Marion said, "a gold ring. It's a symbol. A token—it seals a promise. It's a way of showing how faithful you'll be."

I hadn't really thought of it like that, but now she'd pointed it out, that's what it had been. A token of my promise to Pops.

"It is binding when you give someone a ring . . . Yes . . . Valentine's Day, when we prove our love. I understand, Zac. You must have the ring and you must give it to your grandfather. But not tonight—I'd be too anxious to let you out again. Here." She pressed the ring into my hand.

"It's a symbol of my love too. There—you have it: I can't think of anyone I love more."

Bernard raised his eyebrows in a funny, surprised way, and said, "I see."

Then we all laughed a bit and cried a bit too.

There was no talk of "rethinking." Bernard and Marion stuck by me, but I still got eighty hours' community service. I had no alibi. The woman wouldn't drop the charges, she didn't appear in court under the witness protection scheme, but the magistrate seemed only too happy to agree with everything she'd said. It wasn't worth fighting. Even Bernard agreed. So that put a stop to my weekend activities, but you know the whole thing puzzled me. Why would anyone want Pops dead? Why would anyone attack me, plant a mobile—a nice mobile (yes, I went back for it; after all, I was doing the hours, wasn't I?)—and then accuse *me* of attacking them? Why would anyone steal the entire contents of my house? It didn't make sense. Nobody can hate you that much. I thought about the flat-faced woman and her phone call: "... *stage one, objective one* ..." It made sense to her. ... Everything must have been calculated. And if it wasn't personal then it must have been about getting the diaries. And that conclusion was the only thing that cheered me up.

Because it was too bad for them—you see, the one they wanted most, I still had.

Chamo-me Bartolomeu

It was obvious that I needed to translate the diary. I smiled at it for a day or two, but being charming isn't one of the talents you need to be a translator, so in the end I asked Marion to help. She didn't know what *Cabo Corso* meant, but she thought the encyclopedia might. It did. I got it up on the CD-ROM. Here's what it said.

> . . . town in the center of the seaboard of Ghana. It lies on a low promontory jutting into the Gulf of Guinea (Atlantic Ocean) and is about 75 miles southwest of the Ghanaian capital of Accra. In the fifteenth century, the Portuguese established a post on the site, and in the sixteenth century, the British arrived. The town, one of the country's oldest, grew around Cape Coast Castle, built by the Swedes in 1655 and taken over by the British in 1663 . . .

So Cabo Corso was in Ghana—and Portuguese. Marion got dead excited. She was doing evening classes in Spanish and was saving up for a time-share in Barcelona. Even though Spanish is not Portuguese, with the help of her guidebook called *Everything for Travelers to the Iberian Peninsula*, we translated this:

THE EVENTS AT CABO CORSO OF 1701

Chamo-me Bartolomeu = I am called Bartholomew. This name prestigiously [?] very good [maybe excellent] was given to me by Senhor [Mr.] Dias who my father God in became. [O pai o Deus might mean God the Father, or maybe means: His name was Bartholomew and that was the same name as his godfather—who was also called Senhor Dias?]

I write my pen to this account—day [something we couldn't work out] year of 1713 in the land Montegos, Jamaica, where I am a slave.

The next evening, Marion phoned her Spanish teacher, who phoned up her sister's husband, who was from Brazil, and then we got this:

My sad adventures I will unfold from my country and people in Africa. I am a O hene—prince [?] there and this alone gives me strength to bear the misfortunes I have seen. I will start from the day of my tortures in the great white Prisão, Castle of the English.

I had gone to the bush to search for small beef when I heard the dogs. My mother had warned me— she had said, "Beware the White Death, for he hunts with dogs for bad children."

I was afraid.

A shiver ran over me. The first Baxter ancestor sent into slavery had written those words! Bartholomew was the Lost Prince! His hand had touched that paper. It made me go cold all over.

Had it really happened? Had the English rounded up kids with dogs? When you read about slavery in history books it's like reading about a past that happened to someone else. Not you. Not your grandfathers.

It took the edge off my excitement.

And how come an African prince could write Portuguese? It was not just amazing; it was AMAZING. This diary might hold the key to the treasure, to Pops's murder, and—with Marion's help—I was about to solve it!

Good Friday

It was around that time the nightmares got worse. I'd wake in the middle of the night convinced that I'd been to some flat open place, where the sea crashed on one side and a gigantic rain forest rose on the other. I'd look down that beach and see in the distance a white fort. Turrets rose on each of its corners and huge steps shone in silhouette against a rolling gray sky. It was always night and I was always terribly afraid. Then I'd scream and wake up sweating.

Ms. Shaw wanted me to get counseling. What I wanted to get was the remaining pages that Pops had hung on to. So I played along with her and she played along with me. By March, she'd finally got them back from the police. She promised to let me have them before Easter.

Don't think because of the ring incident I'd stopped visiting the grave. I hadn't. I just didn't steal anymore. I kept up with the coins, and because I wanted to give him valuable things, I'd write words on paper, like "diamonds," and "ivory." Then I'd fold them round the coins and push them in. I'd write him little letters, too. Maybe Maggot was right. Maybe it was pretty sad.

The day after I got the lost pages back, I sorted through my coins. I'd told Marion that I was collecting them, and she'd got all her friends, the "good ladies of Cheltenham," to give her the remnants of their foreign holidays. I had an American quarter, a few defunct French francs, a bunch of old drachmas, ten kroner; I even had one forint. I packed them in a twist of paper and picked up the sealed envelope with the pages in it. I'd planned an Easter ceremony. I'd give him the coins and then open the envelope and read to him.

It was a fine spring morning. Too fine. Puffy white clouds and a blue sky couldn't drive away a certain frosty feeling. I stood on the front steps of my foster home and tried to pinpoint just what was unsettling about it. Nothing obvious, only a spiral of fear that wound itself into my stomach. Risking everything, I set out for the graveyard.

As I did my gangsta step down the footpath, I kept my lush Mobz at the ready (it was a really cool one—did videos, infrared, Bluetooth, e-mail, the lot). I was on a mission. Ceremony for Pops, proof for Bernard. You see, after Bernard's mysterious phone call to complain about the house being watched, I hadn't seen the Fiat again, but following his advice, I'd started collecting evidence. Whenever I could, I clocked stray people: on the street, in shops, in the park—you name it. Cars too. I'd get their license plates, and add location and date. All of it *clickity-clock* into my Nokia.

I still wasn't quite clear who I was up against, though. I'd tried asking Bernard who he suspected, who he'd called. . . . But he'd only nodded and said, "A little knowledge is a dangerous thing, Zac. I will tell you everything when I know the truth." *Like maybe in a hundred years!* I thought.

His worried look, however, had warned me to stay on guard. So when on my way into the churchyard I passed a thin-looking group on their way out, I was ready. There were two men, both of indifferent age and average height. One was black, the other white. They could have been the muggers. There was a woman with them. She could have been *the* woman, but it was hard to be sure. With the phone, I got all three of them.

I wasn't taking chances, either, so I loitered around until I saw them get into an old Volvo and drive off. *Click-clock.* License plate: C171 TPL.

That morning All Saints' church was lit in stripes of sunlight; late crocuses grew in little crowds under the hedges and beside the railings. I picked a few. The golden ones. Then I made my way to the low mound at the far end, by the dry-stone wall. I checked behind me and sat down on a marble grave. For a while I looked enviously at all the headstones and composed an imaginary one for Pops. It read:

Samuel Baxter
born 1920
R.I.P.

HERE LIE THE BONES
OF SAMUEL B.
WHOSE GOLDEN WORTH
HAS NO MEASURE,
BUT NOW HIS SPIRIT
IS SET FREE
TO FIND, AT LAST,
HIS BURIED TREASURE.

I laid the crocuses in a little bunch where I figured his head was, and then I set about pushing in the coins. When that was done, I sat down again and opened the envelope.

Far away I heard a car arrive and then the tread of steps on gravel. I slid off the grave and hid. Two figures wavered between the yew trees, heading for the church. A man and a woman—indifferent age, average height. The spiral of fear tightened.

I stayed put until I was sure they'd gone into the church, then I continued with my ceremony.

Okay.

Inside the envelope there weren't many pages, maybe ten or so. They were written in English—sort of. They seemed to be from one of the later set of Baxter grandfathers. The writing was dead slopey and very curled. The *s*'s looked like *f*'s and it was pretty difficult to read. In fact, after a few lines of something about waves, I gave up and flicked through the rest. There was one entry, though, that looked interesting. Here's what it said. I know it off by heart.

1844   My Seventh Birthday
I was afraid. When they broke the glass, my heart was pounding so hard I thought I'd faint, but even though it hurt, I was really happy. The last bits were the worst, because my back was bleeding a lot and Daddy kept wiping it. But Grandpa said it was a really good copy, and that cheered me up. When all the cutting was finished, they told me the secret. I can't tell you, because I promised not to—until I die.

Supposing my math was correct, the grandpa mentioned in that extract must have been the grandchild of Bartholomew. If that was true, then there really was a lost prince and we really *were* his descendants. Pops had been telling the truth all along!

Stunned, I reread the extract.

You see, it was almost exactly what Pops had done to me. Except he'd copied a photo of his own back, and used a razor blade. I wriggled my shoulders, so that I could feel the scars against my T-shirt. Then suddenly I jumped to my feet. You see, it struck me that if the tribal marks had been accurately passed down, then there was no reason to disbelieve the rest of the story. Boy, how I wished I'd listened more closely. I ran through the bits I could remember. The Lost Prince, a ransom paid, the treasure buried, the prince sent into slavery, about six generations of Baktus. Then I saw it—Baktu changed to Baxter! Whoa! Pops had really been onto something.

There actually was a pile of treasure. A vast fortune lay waiting for me! If I found it I'd be rich. Make that *very* rich. Make that *very, very* rich. Make that so *mega, totally, totally, mega, mega* rich . . . Whoa, I felt dizzy! I'd better try to understand the pages (you know!), I'd better work harder at the diary. I'd better find that mystery map. 'Cause boy, was I ready! I was going to swing right through those jungles and dig up all that lovely gold. . . .

As if by a sixth sense, I felt the church door open and that strange blank couple turn to my end of the churchyard. Quick as a flash, I darted a dozen graves away. From behind a large tombstone, I saw them walk right up to Pops's mound. They stood there for a while looking at the unmarked graves. My excitement evaporated. My heart started pounding. A knot of fear traveled into my throat. The woman walked up to my little bunch of crocuses and picked them up. Then with the thin heel of her shoe she stamped a ring of small holes into the grave. She scrunched up the crocuses and tossed them down. Then they left.

I sagged against the tombstone, trembling. It had been them. I'd been right. They were working together. That woman was one of them!

I was shaking so much you'd have thought I'd got fever. Cold sweat broke out across my forehead and my palms went clammy. Why had she marked Pops's grave like that? What horrible objective were they planning next? I thought of the clay that preserved everything and Pops lying down there. . . . I thought of mountains of buried gold. I thought I was going to be sick.

After a very, v-e-r-y long time, I came out from behind that tombstone. I went to the ring of holes and I pinched them shut. I teased the grass back. I smoothed Pops's grave so that even the coin holes were gone. Then I got a brain wave. I picked up a twig and punched a ring of holes into the next grave mound beside Pops. I collected the crushed crocuses and moved them over as well. I don't know why I did it. I guess I wanted to spoil their next objective—whatever it was.

As it turned out, that simple action bought me time—not enough, of course, but even a few days can help when time is running out.

It was as I left the churchyard, as I was going through the lych-gate, that I remembered the Cormantin Club and Uncle Fidelis (no real relation). Pops had once told me that "Fidelis" meant faithful—but it was more like *un*faithful, as far as Uncle Fidelis was concerned.

He was the one who kept bugging Pops, who said that Pops talked a load of bull, and that he needed a lot more evidence than the word of a "daft old bugger," before he "uprooted" himself on any Return to Africa venture. Pops had got into a pretty straight face-to-face with him. I remembered. Pops returning home, pushing away his cup of tea, cursing, pouring himself a gin and pushing that away. Uncle Fidelis had really got to him. I'd hovered around, trying to watch the football on telly. I remember Pops saying how he'd "bloody well prove Fidelis wrong." How he'd marched into his room, rooted around, and left. He was away a good hour and a half, and when he'd returned, he seemed satisfied.

"Give him something to read. Do him good. Illiterate old fool," he'd mumbled.

At the time I'd just said, "Yep, you're right, show respect." But now it struck me that Pops had given him something. Some evidence. And if I remembered correctly, after that, Uncle Fidelis had lived up to his name—extra.

It was about time I paid Old Faithful a visit.

Easter Weekend

I didn't know Uncle Fidelis's exact address, but I knew where I could find him. I'd pay the Cormantin Club a surprise visit. They met in the annex room of the Jamaica Meeting House, next to the billiard room, every Tuesday night. I was excited. At last I was onto something.

Over the Easter weekend I tried to remember exactly what had happened after Uncle Fidelis had done a U-turn. I remembered that he and Pops had worked on a radio interview. It wasn't with a mainstream broadcaster like the BBC. That had annoyed them. They'd argued about that. On one occasion Uncle had come round to our home in Arrowsmith House. Wimbledon was on, and the mixed doubles were slow, so I started listening to the two of them. There's something about a good row that makes you tune in.

"What's the point of going on air if nobody's going to listen?" said Fidelis.

"Oh, they'll be listening all right," said Pops, "and when they hear we've dug up the accounts of all the goings-on—that'll set the cat among the pigeons."

"You're daft," said Fidelis, "nobody listens to FM Shurdington." He tugged the brown CLIPPERS fitted cap he always wore till it was stuck sideways—a fashion about as ancient as him.

"Daft—is that it? We'll see who the daft one is when the money starts rolling in," returned Pops.

"I won't have anything to do with it, Sammy, makes the venture risky. If we're going to get sponsors, we need prime time and so much exposure they won't dare come for us."

"You're the daft one—"

"No, you listen to me, maybe you bin in this country too damn long and you forgot what they do to folks who fight back. If you want to start shoutin' about suing the whole damn British government for compensation, you don't start tickling them with FM Shurdington. They slap you down like a mosquito—straight. You wouldn't know what hit you, and then what you goin' to do?"

"Got to start somewhere. If we don't start—nobody's going to get nothing."

"That's the point. You don't get it, Sam, you stirrin' up a damn hornets' nest and you ain't even got the bond as evidence yet, you ain't got the gold to pay for the court case; all you got is a bunch of old papers, a map you won't show no one, and a big mouth. . . ."

"And I'm going to use me big mouth to get sponsors and air me views."

And so they'd carried on. I turned back to the tennis. I didn't know the conversation mattered. In fact the only reason I remembered any of it was that odd phrase: "*cat among the pigeons.*"

Now it struck me just what this was all about.

A totally mega fortune in gold dust was only the kick-off! This was about Pops's dream of compensating the entire black community of Britain for four hundred years of slavery. This was about taking on the whole nation. This was about a compensation claim for so much money that I started to feel giddy. . . .

Think about it—why would anyone bother with Pops if there were nothing in it? Why would Uncle Fidelis bother, to start with? ('Cause, boy, he was one lazy old bugger.) Think about it! Phone calls that cut off, street-lamps that fail, unmarked cars that follow, police that don't want to get involved, the constant feeling of being watched—what does that add up to? I'll tell you—24-7 Big Brother—and not the TV show, either!

With a horrible clarity things began to make sense.

I ran my hand across my face. I tried to smile. Pops's wild imagination? Nobody could really have enough evidence to take on the government—could they?

Because boy, that was no ordinary cat. But the more I thought about it, the more I realized how very possible it might be—and the more possible it got, the more I worried about the pigeons.

Easter Holidays

On Easter Monday I had another of the terrifying dreams. I awoke, as usual, sweating. Marion was there. She looked at me, her eyes wide. "Oh, Zac," she said. "Oh, Zac." In the morning she rang Ms. Shaw, but—as luck would have it—Ms. Shaw was already on her way round. It was the beginning of the holidays. I remember that.

For some time Marion, Bernard, and Ms. Shaw sat in the front room with the door closed. When they called me in, I stood next to the bay window and looked at them. Marion was crying. Bernard was angry. Ms. Shaw was fidgeting with her handbag.

"I don't know how to tell you this, Zac," she started. "I'm at a loss for words. I don't want you to think that this has got anything to do with your foster family—or you for that matter—but . . . well, you see . . . actually you've been getting on a bit better, and I was very pleased with the way things were shaping up . . . but—"

"Just tell the boy," snapped Bernard. I could see he was about to lose it. "But we'll fight it. I want you to know that." He slapped his thigh, as if he'd like to slap her.

"Well, this morning I got a memo from my boss—*the boss*—and well, basically, the state thinks that you've been misplaced in your foster home. It's got nothing to do with you; I want you to understand . . . But we just feel you'll be better off with a black family. It's the policy, you see. I thought that as there was no available family ready to take you, you could stay here. . . . I felt that that was better than a state home. I argued with my boss. Believe me, I did."

I was stunned. Somehow I'd got used to the magnolia and the bedtime curfew. They were part of my life now. "But I'm okay here," I said. "I mean—I like it. I like my new mum and Mr. Bernard."

"And I know they like you," she said warmly, as if that meant anything. "But last Christmas was one thing; your grandfather had—well . . . and it was a fair decision, under the circumstances, but for the long term . . ."

"Can't you tell them I like it? I'm okay." Surely if I liked it they could have no objection?

"It's not policy," she said flatly.

A nasty thought pinched me—just whose policy was it?

Marion rushed out of the room. Bernard sat there as if he were going to fossilize. "Tell him," he said.

"We've got your order to move. We've all got to be very strong about it."

"Where? When?"

"Today. To a state home."

"*Today?*"

"I'm afraid so. Right now, in fact."

I looked wildly at Bernard, at her. I think I sat down on the floor. "I won't."

"You have to," she said. "We'll try to get another family for you before the end of the holidays, so that you can stay at the same school. I promise that."

"Why, where am I going?"

"Near Cirencester—in the hills. You'll like that, won't you? Plenty of fresh air."

Bernard snorted. "And you think that is the best thing for Zac?"

"It's what the County Council thinks. I don't have a voice there, I'm afraid."

If air can smell of finality, the air in that front room sure stank of it. And it was a fishy smell, too.

Consider the facts:

- Bernard makes inquiries to a mysterious number about a Fiat Brava, streetlights, and the phone being tapped.
- Suddenly no Fiat Brava, totally bright streets, no more weird calls.
- Suddenly Bernard and Marion are no longer suitable foster parents.
- Suddenly Zac must be moved to a children's home.
- Guess who controls the streetlights, phones, police, children's home, and Ms. Shaw?

- Guess who sets the policies?
- 2+2 are now making 22.

Well? What d'you reckon?

"I'll leave you to pack and say good-bye. I'll be back at two." Ms. Shaw got up and left.

Mr. Bernard came over to me. He put his arm around my shoulder and helped me up. "Zac," he said, "I want you to know that I've never had a son. We—I mean Marion and I—can't, but if I had a boy, I'd want him to be you. I'll fight the Council on this decision. I don't know, but since you came here . . . well . . . it just feels . . . well . . . But for now we must abide by the rules. Rules are important even if they don't always make sense. We can work through this as a family. Come and visit us—they can't stop you from doing that. . . . This is your home. Soon you'll be sixteen, I'll find out when you can make a decision for yourself." He choked, and put his arms round me and hugged me. Hard.

I held on to him for dear life. "It's a setup," I said. "Don't let them take me away."

"I have some influence," said Bernard. "I'm investigating your story—but things take time. At the moment there is very little evidence that we can use to insist on a full inquiry. Be patient, Zac, and be very, very careful."

I didn't trust myself to speak, so I nodded and twisted my chin a bit, and tried to give him a funky we-can-beat-this smile. Then I rushed upstairs and flung myself face-down on the bed.

SGCCCH

By six o'clock I was sitting in the common room of Syde Gloucestershire County Council Community Home.

Home?

They should think of another word.

Just when I'd found a family, just when I was onto something, just when everything might have worked out, I was in the middle of hillsides and eight miles from everything I'd ever known.

Sometimes, even if you're totally fit, you can feel sorry for yourself. My chest hurt, my eyes hurt, and there was a big lump in my throat. My right hand was okay, though, so I punched the common-room wall.

One part of me said "Give up," another—the Cormantin streak, I guess—said "Fight." I tried to phone Uncle Fidelis at the Meeting House. It was unlisted. I tried to phone Bernard. I got a series of suspicious clicks and then the answering machine. I even tried to beg Ms. Shaw, but she couldn't discuss anything; *she* was on her way home—and that was that.

Well, Bernard phoned me back. He said pretty much the same things. Things I didn't want to hear. You know: Play by the rules. I'll do my best. It may take some time.

Time.

There wasn't enough time left! Today was Tuesday— Cormantin Club meeting night. Even if I'd trekked to the nearest bus stop, there was no way I could get into Gloucester and back before nine. It sucked. I'd have to wait another week. (One long week, during which—I have to tell you—there was no mention of any other family, black or white.)

Boy, that's funny—because getting in and out of that home before curfew hour was the least of my worries. I should have been worrying about how I'd ended up there, not to mention *panicking* that my enemies had outfoxed me.

'Cause they had. They'd run me to ground. And were closing in for the kill.

I was glad, at least, that Ashley was in my room. He was the only person who made me smile. "Welcome to the funnest place in the Cotswolds," he said. "When the pace gets too hot, mush, you can talk to me. I can help chill the excitement. Right? And if Susie gives you problems—hey, I'm your man, Stan." He gave me the high five and showed me where the toilet was. He was a true Gloucestershire Chav, but his spirit was Cormantin.

Grandpa once told me, "*The Cormantins were the black gold of Ghana!*" He'd crinkle up his eyes, until right in the center a spot of fire shone out. *"Infinitely more precious than the yellow type, famed for their daring, reckless, and stubborn natures!"* He had a way of telling things; his voice pulled you into that mysterious place where the past burnt brighter than any pale present, and you hungered to be there, where "brave deeds and terrible sacrifices" made life worth living. *"The Cormantins were at the center of the Jamaican slave revolts—such mutinous acts!"* Then his voice would dip and leave you to imagine "mutinous acts" and long to do them. *"And from 1650 to 1850 over seven million of them were sold from the Slave Coast."* And I'd wonder what it must be like to be "sold from the Slave Coast," and in my head I would escape and be Cormantin and daring.

Do you think character traits can be inherited? I'm sure it was my stubborn Cormantin nature that helped me through that week, encouraged me to plan mutinous acts, dared me to escape and recklessly visit Uncle Fidelis— whether I got back by nine o'clock or not.

Mutinous Acts

This was my daring plan:

1. scope the village
2. suss the home
3. search for the bus stop.

These were the results.

First off, Syde village was a dead end in more ways than two; if you ever get the chance, don't bother going there. One of the kids had sprayed on the front wall, "*Stay in and do your homework—it's more exciting.*"

Next, SGCCC Home was worse. I'd been there five minutes and I'd worked it out. Breakfast at 7:30 a.m., followed by zero till lunch, more zero till supper, then nothing.

I'm not kidding.

Last, the M4 link to the M5 (called the Ermine Way) ran near Syde—straight from Cirencester to Gloucester! Better still, a country bus pulled off it at an old inn called the Highwayman every afternoon at 3:15 p.m.

I planned on leaving right after lunch. I'd pretend to have a headache. I'd do the pillows-in-my-bed scam and hope my absence would go unnoticed (highly likely during Susie's shift). There was only one problem: The other two kids in my room might tell. I wasn't worried about Ashley. He was cool—from day one he'd been okay. "I'm bored stupid," I told him. "I'm going into town for some action."

"Right, I'll cover your back, Zac," he said.

That left Dave, a little twerp who would wreck anything if he could. God must have been on my side, because at breakfast Dave got a phone call. His aunt and uncle were driving down from Birmingham to take him out.

I was set.

Two thirty p.m. saw me walking fast up the lane toward the Ermine Way. It was a bit narrow and hedged in, and I was worried that one of the care workers on the afternoon shift might stop with questions I didn't want to answer. I was more worried by the helicopter that suddenly swooped up from the direction of Cheltenham.

One large, gray, unmarked helicopter. Not much more noticeable than the Empire State Building. *Nice try,* I said to myself. *That helicopter must be on a rescue mission. Not.*

Boy, if they thought I was that stupid, they'd seriously underestimated me.

2+2 = 444,444,444 − 444,444,440. Check it out.

Before I was spotted, I cut into a field and hid behind a hedge. I'd have to go cross-country now. My heart was thumping. I broke out in a sweat. Forty-five minutes across unknown territory. What if they had heat sensors in the helicopter?

I skirted the field until I reached woodland, but I'd hardly got through the first few trees before I saw two figures. They were staked out opposite the boundary walls of a country estate. They probably thought they were well hidden, and if the helicopter hadn't freaked me out, I guess I wouldn't have seen them. I started to chew my tongue. What was I going to do?

To get to the Highwayman, I needed to cross that estate, and if I didn't get going soon I'd miss my bus. I took a risk. When a dip in the landscape hid them briefly from view, I sprinted to the boundary wall. The graying limestone had toppled in places, and I was soon over it and into cover. I was choking for breath, but I kept on running. If they'd seen me, they'd have to catch me now.

My heart was pounding. Damp from the grass soaked into my sneakers. I pushed myself faster.

The park was big—very big. There were cows. I kept away from them. (I wasn't used to country life and cows could mean bulls.) Overhead the helicopter whirred like a pneumatic drill. Perhaps dodging the cows was a mistake. I wondered if on a heat sensor cows look like boys.

A sharp wind bit through my jacket. My sweat turned cold against me. My lungs were burning, but I blundered on, zigzagging between trees and stumbling on clumps of grass, in the direction I thought the Highwayman was. Something like rain clouds gathered. I began to get very scared because

I realized after ten minutes or so that if the wall extended all round the estate I'd have to get back over it again.

Think about something else, I told myself. Try to focus. Uncle Fidelis. Pops's records—he'd researched the English Chartered Company of Royal Adventurers. He'd sent for copies from a registry in Jamaica. Were these the things he'd given Fidelis? What about the map? I needed to give *that* a serious dose of Zac Baxter IQ because, despite Pops's dying words, I didn't have it.

Even if Fidelis had everything, how could I find the gold? Let's say I got money from somewhere, could buy a ticket—how could I get to Ghana? I didn't have a passport.

I'd remembered one of Pops's sayings: "*Where there's a will there's a way, and when there's no way there's always excuses.*" I'd add, "*and lazy old buggers.*" We'd laugh.

There had to be a way.

I mean, I was the last descendant of the King of the Baktus. It was up to me, wasn't it, to find a way?

Ahead was dense bramble. I swerved right and forced my legs faster. Why were they watching Syde today? Why the helicopter? Did they know I would try to contact Uncle Fidelis? Or were they out there every day—just in case? I'd gone too far into the estate. I started to worry about missing the bus.

Stop being negative, I told myself. You'll get a passport. You'll make the bus. Keep running. You'll get to Ghana— after all, it's just a country that lies three thousand miles down the Prime Meridian. And some Chinese bod said: "*The journey of a thousand miles*" (or three in my case) "*starts with the first step.*" Yep, I made up a little ditty to encourage myself, it went like this: *Zac is coming, better look out—get your cook out—sweet potatoes with tomatoes—Ghana's waiting—no hesitating—vast savannahs—big bananas—tropical sunsets—that's how the fun gets* . . . Yep, from now on every move I made was leading me closer to those palm green shores. . . . I was gonna do it! Goddamn it! I was gonna dig up that crazee gold!

The helicopter circled off, but I kept on running. I'd got a good start on the two figures. But there were usually three. I mustn't slow down. I still had one to locate. He could be anywhere.

Rain started to spatter the leaves, my knees felt weak, and my mouth was so dry I could have drunk up the river Niger. Mobz said it was already 3:10. I could hear traffic and I could see the gray limestone wall winding back toward me. Five mins to get to the bus. Still no Enemy 3. Maybe he was the one flying the helicopter. Risking everything, I struck out into the open and sprinted.

Problem. Either I cut left and scrambled back over the wall, or I went straight toward a distant gatehouse. More fields and bulls, with little cover between the large conker trees, wasn't tempting; but I didn't want any Trespassers-Will-Be-Prosecuted rubbish either.

I chose.

Badly.

I clambered over the ten-foot wall, and bumped straight into Enemy 3.

Enter and Exit Uncle Fidelis

E3 reacted like a goalkeeper to a penalty shot and dived straight at me. I imagined the headlines: BOY ALL ALONE IN OPEN COUNTRY. BOY AWOL FROM JUVENILE HOME. BOY TRESPASSING ON PRIVATE PROPERTY. BODY SADLY FOUND IN DITCH. BODY BADLY DECOMPOSED. BULL-FIGHTING SUSPECTED. DEATH BY MISADVENTURE. QUIET CREMATION. NO FAMILY.

Like I said, I'm fit, good-looking, and the Intermediate Boys' Sports Award champion. So despite a loyal curdling of blood in the pit of my stomach, I gave him a display of my talents. First I introduced him to Mr. Right Foot, a superb Zacaldinho tackle. Second I introduced him to Mr. Left Foot, a well-placed Zacaldo free kick, and last I introduced him to a great coordination of Mr. Right and Left Foot together—doing the hundred-meter Zacce Owens sprint.

It was just as well I ran. By the time I got to the Highwayman, the country bus was pulling out. Once I was safely on the backseat, I allowed myself some time out to breathe and do the nervous wreck thing, but I had to cut the trembling short because the helicopter was now shadowing the bus. I got out Mobz and took some bad pics of it and then tried to make an emergency plan.

By four o'clock I was in Gloucester town center with a daring new scheme. The helicopter had disappeared, but I was not fooled. Even an idiot like Dave, my less than friendly roommate, could look up a Gloucestershire Stagecoach timetable.

As I got off the bus, I Nokiad every face. Then I walked into a large department store which I knew had three exits. Before they had time to get a guy on each, I tipped over a display and, in the confusion that followed, dashed through the shop and out again.

Neat, eh?

I was pretty sure I'd lost them, but I still had two hours to kill before the Cormantin Club, so naturally I set out for the graveyard.

On my way I tried to work out exactly what they were up to. I figured they'd kill me if they could, but they weren't in a hurry. After all, they'd had plenty of time to come up with a convincingly fatal accident. Why? 1) They wanted Bartholomew's diary. 2) They wanted the map. Right, they couldn't search Bernard's house, and he was asking too many questions—so move me to SGCCCH. Good. Search my stuff there when I am at school. Ahhh! It was Easter holidays. So watch the home and see if I go out. If I do, catch me—search me—dispatch me—collect all my belongings. Perfect. Lucky I had the diary with me! I shuddered. The talent show by the estate walls had been a narrow escape. I'd better be a lot more careful.

All Saints' churchyard was deserted. That was worrying. (BOY HAS ACCIDENT WHILE ALL ALONE IN GRAVEYARD?) All the same I slunk in and headed for the far end. There in the late afternoon sun was the mound. Right next to it was a huge pile of dirt. Pops's next-door neighbor had been dug up. Yep, the grave which I'd transferred the small ring of holes to was now a six-foot-long, three-foot-wide trench. You could see the coffin at the bottom. I could even read the name on the plaque: Penelope Hannah Mustoe.

I didn't like it. You might think I'm suspicious, but I kept thinking it had something to do with the holes. I tried to think of a happier reason. Maybe relatives were measuring it up for a tombstone. But the happier reasoning part of my brain was not happy either. Suddenly I didn't feel too comfortable in that graveyard. I had a horrid feeling that if *they* found me there, I might just end up helping them refill the hole. I didn't think it would matter too much if I arrived early at the Meeting House. The tombstone idea was nice, but not convincing. I wished there was a stone for Pops. Maybe I'd mention that to Uncle Fidelis. Maybe I'd better go straightaway and do just that.

I congratulated myself on being a lot more careful. I sent Ashley a victory text: *Made my getaway soon b chillin*

at da Jamaica club like u sed wtch my bac mush njoy syde
ha ha—z.

It was a pity I wasn't watching my front.

Twenty-five minutes later saw me sneaking down the tarmac siding to the Jamaica Meeting House. On one side was a breakers' yard; on the other spare parts warehouses and MOT workshops were set round an open parking space. At the end of the cul-de-sac were the corrugated gates that led to the Meeting House.

A new black Golf kept driving up and down, screeching to a halt at the parking space, backing a three-point spin and cruising up again. I had to keep dodging behind salvage. I thought about Nokiaing it, but when I saw who was driving, I decided not to. Drug dealers. You could tell by the bling thing (and in case you don't know—gangstas don't like nosy people). I got inside and found Uncle Fidelis.

"Zac," he said, "what you doin' here? Not up to anything?"

"Not yet."

"How you bin? Getting along okay?"

"I came to see you."

"Well, if it's a fiver you're after . . ."

"No, but if you want to give me a five—that's fine."

"What then?"

"Can we sit somewhere?"

Uncle Fidelis led me into the bar. They didn't care there

if I was underage, so when he offered me a drink, I said, "Red Stripe."

The bar was shabby. Torn seats, tatty carpets, scratched tables, stained beer mats, and it stunk of cigarettes.

"Spit it out," Uncle Fidelis said, tugging his cap sideways.

I took a swig out of my can and looked at him. "Pops gave you some of his papers—it's a long story, but I'm really hoping you've still got them."

Uncle Fidelis shuffled his feet on the floor. "I don't think you should get mixed up in that, Zac. Your Pops didn't know what he was up against, probably never even read them."

That was a bit steep coming from him.

"But have you got anything?"

"Yes," he said slowly, "I've got a copy of everything, including some of the diaries—at least they're with me nephew in London."

"I want them—everything. You see, I promised Pops I'd finish the job." It was the truth. Palm fronds and coconuts. Sweet potatoes with tomatoes.

"Lodge it, son, you've got your whole life ahead. Let it stay buried with your Pops."

"What life?" I told him some of the things that had happened since Pops died.

He looked upset. "It's more than just his old story. This one's big. We don't stand a chance. Once, when I thought we might get backing—but not now. What worries me is what they'll do if we carry on meddlin'."

So the Cormantin Crew had shelved Pops's big compensation plan; so much for "reckless stubborn natures." I scratched my head and swigged the beer can. He carried on shuffling his feet and puckering up his lips, in a restless kind of way. "Big," he said again, "damn big . . ."

"Who are *they*?"

"What kind of a question is that?" he hissed as if I'd sworn in church or something.

"You know what I mean," I said. "Here—scope these." I clicked through my collection of photos stored on my phone.

Suddenly he looked scared. If black folks can go pale, he turned a nasty yellow. All the blood drained from his face. He glanced round that shabby bar and put his head down.

"They're everywhere," he whispered into the side of my neck, as he pretended to pick a bit of fluff off my hoody. "They can do anything." His baseball cap knocked my ear. "Princess Diana is dead. Ask yourself why they haven't found Bin Laden? Who did Sam think he was? I'll tell you who he damn well was—a bloody fool! If you don't believe me, I'll show you a note he wrote. It's in the club files."

I nodded. He shuffled out to get it. After a few minutes he brought a sheet back and gave it to me.

Fidelis,

If you think it best, get a lawyer involved. Mind you, I haven't got anything to pay him with. You'll have to offer some percentage— make it small. I can't imagine after three hundred years they'll

still be up to their old tricks, and I'm too old to be frightened by
a bunch of pen-pushers.

If you think Raphael will take it on, I'm easy with that,
although nothing is going to happen to us, and we are not being
followed to and from every club meeting. You're getting old and
paranoid. I don't think they're onto us at all, and even if they
were, I haven't forgotten all my old fighting tricks! Anyway take
whatever precautions make you feel better. I still think you're
being a Rodney.
Sam.

I swallowed the rest of my beer in one go. Then I
repeated my question more softly but with a new insistent
note. "Which ones?" I said, and slowly clicked through
my photos a second time. "You recognized someone,
didn't you?"

He shook his head and tightened his lip. "Could be
anyone, son. The past is full of people's skeletons."

And with that weird remark, he turned away from me
and began picking up his old briefcase. I could see he wasn't
going to say any more. I abandoned the request for the
headstone that I'd decided to sting him with, after seeing
Penelope Hannah Mustoe's dug-up grave, and went for
the papers.

"They're mine," I said, "all Pops's papers are mine."

"I tell you what," he said, "I'll ask Raphael to make a
copy. I'll get him to send them to you. Write your new
address down." He wiped his mouth with the back of his

hand, glanced hurriedly round the bar, and took a pen out of his pocket. He passed it to me. "Meeting will be starting soon, so I'll get along inside and set the chairs out. You stayin'?"

There was something—I don't know—like he was fobbing me off. Uncle Unfaithful again?

"No," I said, as I scribbled the Syde GCCCH address on a beer mat. "I've got to get back to the home."

Suddenly his voice dropped. He hooded his eyes and narrowed his lips. "Try to forget about it. Don't want any more accidents."

He was right. I didn't want any more "accidents" either.

"You *don't* have the map, do you? Sam always said he had it and nobody could take it away from him. Then he started saying *you* had it. Silly old fool, he thought that was funny, but the joke was on him. He should have shut up."

I swallowed hard. Even though he was right about Pops, it wasn't easy to take.

"I ain't got anything, Uncle; as you see me now, this is about all I own."

"Good," said Uncle Fidelis, "then there's no reason for anyone to come after you."

I didn't correct him. "You could increase my estate by that fiver though, if you wanted. . . ."

Uncle Fidelis relaxed and stuck his hand in his pocket. He pulled out a crumpled twenty. "Here, get a cab home. Forget the whole damn thing, you be glad they'll leave you alone."

I took the money. I got the cab. I thought about forgetting "the whole damn thing," but as for being left alone—that's what he thought.

For *they*—whoever *they* were—had other plans for both of us.

Cat Among the Pigeons

I never saw Uncle Fidelis again. The next evening there was a small column in the local press. I might have missed it, if Ashley hadn't shown me. He was one of those kids who'll read anything. We were sitting in the common room, thinking about a game of darts. While I was trying to straighten the feathers on the few that weren't busted, he was reading the paper.

"Look at this, Chris," he hissed, and shoved the article under my nose. "Wasn't that where you went yesterday?"

I frowned at him. So far I'd got away with it. I put the paper down on a side table until the care worker went out to make coffee.

"Stupid," I said, "d'you want me to get nicked?"

"But look at it," he said.

I picked up the paper and read the article. It was only one paragraph long and was squeezed in between an advert for mobile phones and the sports pages.

DREAD BUSINESS AT THE DREAD CLUB

The body of an unidentified elderly black male was discovered early this morning in a breakers' yard next to the Jamaica Meeting House. He was stabbed repeatedly with a common steak knife, which was found next to the body. There seems to have been no motive for the attack. The police have little to go on other than a beer mat, clutched in the dead man's hand. When interviewing Mr. Tyson, who works behind the bar at the Meeting House, he said, "I can't tell if it was a mat from this bar or not. I don't remember serving anyone of that description. In this job it doesn't pay to have good eyesight."

Is this the work of the Yardies? Has gangland killing started in the peaceful hills of Gloucestershire?

I lost the game of darts. I didn't eat any supper. I kept away from the windows and didn't stay long in any room on my own. I thought the doorbell would go and the police would arrive any minute. There couldn't be two elderly gentlemen with beer mats in their hands on a Tuesday night. I remembered the lady and the mobile phone incident; how my attackers had thrown me on the cold road; how the police hadn't believed me and all those long community service hours. I searched my room, went through my stuff. Nobody was going to plant anything on me. Nobody was going to find the diary. I thought about the helicopter and Penelope Hannah Mustoe, and started shivering. Then I felt bad about Uncle Fidelis. I prayed it wasn't him. I knew it was. Part of me wanted to find out, part of me didn't. But why kill him? What had he not told me? And why yesterday, when I'd been there? Was it my fault? Did they know I was there? How had they followed me? I took out the note Uncle Fidelis had given me and reread it for the umpteenth time. I thought about "accidents." I thought about the past and all the skeletons. I thought about paranoia. I thought about conspiracy theories. I cut out the newspaper report and I hid everything including *Chamome* inside a filing cabinet in the study room.

It had to be Uncle lying dead in that breakers' yard. Didn't it?

There could be no mistake. This was no gangland killing. They were not the Yardies. Yardies weren't interested in a two-bit, run-down place like the Meeting House. This was to do with me, with King Baktu, with the gold, with the compensation, and with the diaries—yep, the diaries that I'd probably never get to see.

I didn't sleep well. I had bad dreams. I was outside the white castle. It rose huge in front of me, glowing strange and pale. The sea was at my back, crashing on rocks, and in front of me on the open parapet of the castle was a row of fifteen cannons. Behind them a double-sided staircase ascended to a vast squat block of white stone, flanked by turrets on either side. I could hear whispering. Someone was pushing me forward toward the cannons. I stumbled. My legs wouldn't move. I couldn't move. I realized they were shackled together with iron chains. I screamed. I awoke screaming.

No Marion. No soft smile. No "Oh, Zac."

The next morning the post arrived and so did the police. They had a search warrant. They took me into a side room and asked me over and over where I'd been on Tuesday the twelfth of April between 6:00 and 10:30 p.m. Of course I lied. They didn't mention Uncle Fidelis, and even though I asked them why they were there, they didn't tell me. They searched my room and found nothing. They interviewed Susie the care worker, who told them the story about the headache and being in bed. They asked to see Dave and Ashley, but Dave couldn't tell them anything, and Ashley backed me up. They didn't look very happy, but they went away.

Ashley came upstairs and found me. "Better tell me all, Paul," he said.

"Nope," I answered. "You don't want to get involved

in this." (You know, I was beginning to sound like Uncle Fidelis.)

"I am anyway. I covered for you."

"Thanks," I said, "but it's better you don't know."

"What about this then, mush?" Ashley chucked a magazine at me.

"What?"

It was one of those marketing mags that come in a plastic slip. I picked it up. It was addressed to me, but someone had opened it.

"I opened it," said Ashley. Like I said, he was the kind of kid who'll read anything.

"I dunno," I said, "what is it?"

"Open it."

I opened it and from between the pages slipped a letter. Here it is. We read it together, Ashley and me.

Dear Zac,

I got a phone call on Tuesday night from Fidelis. He asked me to photocopy a set of diaries in my possession for you. However, I am being very cautious.

"Why is he being so cautious?" said Ashley.

"Who knows," I said. "Aliens? Killer tomatoes?"

"Uh?"

Sometimes Ashley is a bit slow.

You will wonder why I have concealed this letter in an innocuous magazine. That is because I have reason to believe that your mail may be being intercepted. Certainly, it would not be safe to send even photocopies of the documents to you at the moment. I will keep them safe, so that at a later date you may retrieve them.

"What documents?" said Ashley.

"The diaries," I said.

"But why all the 'innocuous magazine' stuff?"

"Because of . . . Look, let's read it, okay?"

"Seems a bit over the top."

I have studied the documents, and the gist of the matter seems to be this: One Bartholomew Baktu in 1701 was taken at the age of seven, captured, and held at Cape Coast Castle in the Gold Coast, now Ghana. His father was a local chief, a King Baktu, and he sent an ambassador named Dias to bargain for Bartholomew's release. At the time an envoy from the British government was in the castle. He was called Durward. He received Dias, the ambassador, and struck a deal, recorded in a bond. The deal offered the permanent ceding of the cape known as Cabo Corso to the British Crown, and an ex-gratia payment of 15,360 dambas of gold dust, from King Baktu for the release of Bartholomew and for the immunity of his Baktu people from capture, deportation, and slavery.

"What's an 'ambassador,' an 'envoy,' 'ceding,' and 'ex-gratia' for Christ's sake, Jake?" said Ashley. "Let alone a 'damba'?"

"Dunno," I said, "it sounds like some kind of legal stuff." I reread the paragraph again and explained that I thought it was like a ransom. "You know—you pay up and we'll let the kid go." But the name "Bartholomew" struck me. Wasn't it the same Bartholomew whose diary I was struggling to translate?

You should know that the bond they struck and recorded is as interesting as the gold. If it truly exists, it may very well be the first verifiable document that details in writing a contract between a local chief and the British government concerning the exchange of lands for the British Crown in return for the freedom of an African slave and safety from capture and deportation for a whole coastal region. If it could be proved by documentation— say birth certificates, etc., transportation dockets, sales receipts, these diaries, of course—and genetic profiling that such a contract had been broken, it would pave the way for a court case that might very well set a staggering precedent. It is for this reason that you are particularly vulnerable.

"I got it, Kit! You are the living proof that the British government broke a legal contract with your ancestors, because you are here and you wouldn't be if they had kept their side of the bond!"

"And," I said, "if I took them to court and won compensation then that means . . ."

"Everybody who feels they got a case will try for compensation too."

"Like all the uncles and cousins and sisters and . . ."

"Everyone with any genetic link at all."

I think my mouth sagged a bit. I was fast reevaluating my opinion of Pops.

Ashley grabbed the letter and carried on reading.

It seems the gold was paid, but for some reason there is no record of it ever being transferred into the coffers of the British government, although the Cape was annexed and became British Crown property straightaway. The boy was definitely transported, sold into slavery. One of the diaries states the gold was buried and nobody received any benefit from it.

"They stole the gold," said Ashley, "they stole it and still sold the boy. That's what they did—right, mush?"

"Wrong," I said, "that's what all this is about. The gold was lost."

"Wow, this is real! This *is* really real, isn't it—right?"

"Bit too real," I said.

"It's like *Treasure Island*, like *King Solomon's Mines*, like *Roots*. Wow!" Ashley raced over to the door to check no one was listening. He pulled the curtains to, which was hardly necessary as we were on the second floor. "This is scary, Mary," he said.

But he wasn't half as scared as I was.

Of course the loss of the gold is fascinating, but legally, as it was an ex-gratia payment, it would in no way compromise the validity of the bond. However, currently of course, both the gold and the bond are missing and it is to that end your grandfather, who firmly believed he knew of their whereabouts, set up the Cormantin Club—and thus my involvement.

"Wow!" said Ashley.

"'Ex-gratia' must mean like a big extra present," I said.

"Bow-wow! Wish I got presents like that," said Ashley.

What I don't have is a manuscript written in Old Portuguese by the said Bartholomew Baktu, so the full story is lost. Your ancestor, Bartholomew, the Prince, had received some education, prior to his capture, from Dias, the Portuguese trader and same ambassador from King Baktu. The inventory I have definitely points to the existence of this early account. It may contain his version of the events. The ones I am holding for you were written many years later, by various descendants of Bartholomew; and so details of the lost gold are not recorded. There is, for example, no map as to its exact location. All I have been able to find on that point was written in 1787 by one Emmanuel Baktu, I quote: "The gold waits for me, while I slave my life away, a rich man in chains. But of this I can write no more. It is a secret that I cannot tell— for I have sworn not to until I die."

"I've got it," I said.

"You have? Right . . . You've got what?"

"Bartholomew's diary."

Ashley stared at me, a smile all over his face.

Seeing as you are still alive at this moment (I'm sorry to sound so blunt), I think you may well be the key to this mystery. I enclose my mobile phone details and ask you to regularly update me. (5550194738)

I believe the diaries are genuine. However, any event of such antiquity would have to be verified against state records. Presently I am in the process of procuring these with, I might say, some success—in fact many of the details I enclose are from the accounts of the Royal African Company, who developed the Guinea trade in slaves and gold.

"What accounts?" said Ashley.

"Accounts that my Pops was looking into."

"So it's all true?"

Sometimes there is too much truth. Up until then I'd half convinced myself that Bartholomew might have escaped. Somehow. After all—I mean, I would have. I'd have hid—you know, when they gave out the food or something—and waited all crouched up in a dark place until everyone had gone away and I was really sure that I was safe. And then I'd have run for it and got away.

Bartholomew was my ancestor. He was sent into slavery. He lived and died in Jamaica, and I was sitting here in England. He did not escape—that was the truth.

Try to remember anything passed down to you via your grandfather—a song, saying, or riddle that might be a clue to the secret location of the gold and the bond, which I presume will be concealed somewhere together.

Take care. I think the key to your survival depends on not allowing any clue you remember to fall into the ruthless hands of those who have already done your (and my) family great wrong. PLEASE MEMORIZE MY NUMBER AND DESTROY THIS LETTER IMMEDIATELY.

Yours sincerely,

Raphael D. Esq.

(Legal Practitioner, Consultant & Notary Public)

"Now are you going to tell me?" said Ashley.

In a way it was a relief to tell. But as I told, Ashley's smile faded. He sat for a long time and seemed to be thinking. He asked a few questions, which I answered. Much as I *hadn't* wanted him to get involved, suddenly I was scared he wouldn't. I felt so very much on my own— even telling helped. I crossed my fingers. I needed a friend.

"Right, mush," said Ashley, "you've got to figure out the clue to the gold—and by the way, I expect a percentage."

I laughed. "Looks like I won't be around much longer to collect it."

"Wrong," said Ashley. "Let's phone Raphael right now. You see, Zac, you've got to go for this. Things come up and turn your life upside down, but you've got to be the man, Stan. Like the police coming and asking me stuff. It wasn't the time to get scared—I mean, *I* had a choice; but right now it looks like *you* haven't. You've got to phone him up and then you've got to find that gold."

I punched in 5550194738. Raphael answered. I told him who I was and, Ashley-style, plunged straight in.

"Who is it," I said, "who's after me?"

"I don't have names yet, but they're powerful."

"Powerful? Like who?"

"Work it out, Zac, *cui bono*? Ask yourself who loses if you find the bond? It's obvious, the British government, of course! Fifteen thousand dambas is a lot of gold. You've got to realize that wealth is power. And that gold would make you very powerful." He paused and then said quite deliberately, "If for half a minute it was suspected by the government that there was enough evidence: for example in the form of a legal bond, like the Baktu bond struck with the Crown agent, with supporting documents, like the evidence your grandfather collected, plus a powerful plaintiff like you with enough funds like all the gold to bring a case to court—well . . ." He fell silent. "If you were out of the way it would be unlikely to get anywhere. . . ." He paused again. "But the British government would need to eliminate the bond first—they know only too well how old legal obligations come back to haunt. . . ."

"But I don't know where the gold or the bond are."

"I think they believe you do. Haven't you got any idea?"

"No. Sometimes I think there's something, but I dunno."

"Keep working then. I'll keep working this end—but I've got an idea if they do pin something on you."

"Yeah?"

"There's been a number of cases recently where young offenders from adolescent rehab centers have volunteered for humanitarian service overseas. There was a case last week of a boy in Devon who distributed aid to the Palestinians. He spent three weeks in the Gaza strip. I've got contacts in Ghana—missionaries doing health care. It's a possibility. . . . Meanwhile, keep out of trouble—but if trouble comes to meet you, phone me. I'll act as your defense barrister."

"Go to Ghana?"

"Be sensible, Zac. That's a last resort. Don't fool around with these people. We'd better get off the phone—you never know. . . . Look, text me if you remember anything. I can't promise, but with a map—I could try to finance a trip. . . ."

"Yeah!"

"Keep working at it."

"I'm sorry about Uncle Fidelis."

"That's what I mean. Be smart. Stay out of trouble—and destroy my letter."

You can't imagine how much that conversation bucked us up. We didn't destroy the letter, though. But just in case anyone found it, Ashley and I cut it up into strips, like they do at school with poems that need resequencing. I kept half of the strips and Ashley kept the other. We reckoned that would baffle them—if they stole my stuff a second time.

"Right," said Ashley, "let's get to work—first the clue to the map, second a list of things you'll need to know when you go to Ghana." (My list: 1. Where to get a Zinger Tower with supersize chips. 2. How to find out whether Chelsea won their match in the Premiership. 3. If somebody would be willing to lend me their MP3 player . . .) Ashley gave me a withering look. "And third—let's try to translate the rest of your manuscript."

I grinned.

"Right, first—clue to the map. Think hard. Did your grandfather ever say anything—you know, *anything*?"

I shook my head. There was only that something locked away, nothing probably.

"What about your grandfather's diaries?"

"They were stolen when we were attacked."

"Pity," said Ashley. He'd got himself a pencil and a sheet of rough paper and was sitting cross-legged on the floor. "Wait."

I ran downstairs and got Bartholomew's diary. I read him what Marion and I'd done, and told him about the nightmares. He didn't laugh. He said, "You know, Joe, I read somewhere about the unconscious. It's a sort of knowledge that the mind has—it can be tuned in to lots of memories. Maybe that's what's happening! Maybe you are remembering the clue to the map, but only when you're asleep. What d'you think, mush?"

"A sort of amnesia?" I said.

"No," he said, "it's unfinished biz, Liz. There's something stopping you from remembering when you wake up, but it's prompting you when you fall asleep. You know—the force is strong in you, but you don't know it." He made a *Star Wars* voice. "May the force be with you, Zac Baxter!"

I laughed.

We made a plan: We'd copy the diary on the scanner and e-mail it with everything else that was to do with the gold to a new Hotmail account. Then we'd keep the original diary in a secret location (which is where it still is, so I'm not going to tell you). If something happened to me, Ashley would have to carry on with the mission. I told him the only person I trusted was Bernard, so if I got murked, he was to phone him. I think he liked it—being in the know. I don't think anyone had ever trusted him with anything like that before.

Then we got down to clue-cracking.

I went over Pops's last words with him, "*They've got the diaries, but they haven't got the map. . . . You've got to promise me, Zac, to go back and get the treasure. . . . They haven't got the map. . . . It never was in the diaries. . . . The map is the secret, see. . . . They haven't got it. . . . Zac, promise. . . . You have.*"

"But how can I have the map?" I said. "I've got nothing. Everything of mine was stolen."

"You realize Ms. Shaw was wrong about the robbery, mush—the two events *are* connected. They took the things from your flat to look for the map. Try to remember all the stuff you had. Try to remember if there was anything *particular* that your Pops gave you."

"Okay."

"Right, let's make a list," said Ashley.

In my mind I walked back through the door of 13 Arrowsmith House and saw once again the cluttered hall, the scuffed red carpet, and the kitchen door beyond. My throat went dry as I scanned the walls. There was the grubby light switch and the brown photographs in their thin gold frames. I didn't think I could look in his bedroom. His quilt might still be there, his cloth cap hanging on the bedpost. . . . Something in my chest grew tight.

"There's nothing in the stuff from the flat," I said.

"Ah—but how can you be sure?"

I sighed. "Because if there had been, they would have found it—in which case, by now I would be dead."

We stayed in our bedroom till suppertime anyway, but the list was embarrassingly short.

There were only two things that Pops had given me that were originally his:

1) An entry ticket to Bob Marley's home in Kingston, Jamaica.
2) A picture of Cape Coast Castle in Ghana.

I shuddered as I remembered the picture. For the first time, I realized Cape Coast Castle was the white fort I saw in my nightmares.

Dias the Navigator

Over the last week of the Easter holidays, Ashley and I carried on with the second part of our research—the trip to Ghana. I tried to sneak in a mention of safari trips and the Zinger Tower, but Ash was having none of it.

"Listen, Zed, you've gotta get real. If Raphael can get you there, you gotta be ready, right?" He marched into the study and announced, "Everybody out. Zed and me got a school project; you are welcome to the TV room." Everybody there (only Susie, the care shift worker, chatting on MSN) obediently left. "Right, mush, what we need is information, and that means reading."

We took over the computer and started to search the Internet. We typed in "Ghana" and picked up the trail from there. I found out that Ghana was once called the Gold Coast, before that it was called the Slave Coast, and before that it was called the White Man's Grave, and before all that it was called Guinea, and furthest back of all it was called Ghana. Which only goes to show that things catch up on you in the end. It was called the White Man's Grave because the average life span of a white man there was four days to three months, although some lived for much longer. How long the slaves lived for was another matter, which depended, I suppose, on whether they tried to hide gold dust or escape. Average life expectancy was a question still very much on my mind.

After a while Ashley thought task three—translating the diary—might be more helpful. And I agreed. After a great start with Marion, the translating hadn't been going well. Mostly because I wouldn't let the diary out of my sight and I didn't want it photocopied. To tell you the truth I hadn't been keen on using the Spanish teacher's Brazilian brother-in-law, either. I didn't trust the phone. You know! The contents of that diary might be all that stood between me and a slot next to Pops.

Anyway, Ash found a website called "Languaphone Learning," which allowed you a taster course, with a Portuguese-to-English glossary, before you had to cough up (£29.00) for a full online thing. He downloaded it onto the computer, punched up the scanned diary, and started (very slowly) to translate.

I carried on finding out stuff about Ghana. It was compulsive, like picking a scab. I'd uncover fragments of things that seemed, like jigsaw pieces, to belong somewhere. The name of a place, a person, an entry in the encyclopedia. Then I discovered Bartolomeu Dias.

Born 1450.

Died May 29, 1500, at sea, near Cape of Good Hope.

Dias, Bartolomeu Portuguese navigator and explorer who led the first European expedition to round the Cape of Good Hope (1488). He is usually considered to be the greatest of the Portuguese pioneers who explored the Atlantic during the fifteenth century, which led to Portugal's trade with Guinea and the exploration of the western coast of Africa. Bartolomeu Dias accompanied Vasco da Gama's celebrated voyage of 1497 as far as Mina.

Imagine that! Finding the names "Bartolomeu," and "Dias," and "Cape," and "Guinea," and "Africa" all under one heading. I caught my breath, tried to stop myself doing a cartwheel or something. Of course, as Ashley pointed out, "He was there two hundred and fifty years too early, mush," but whatever—hey, what's a couple of hundred years? I'd found one more piece of the puzzle.

I read and reread it, until it was fixed in my head. I knew one day I'd get the whole picture. It was locked away somehow there in the past—but it was *my* past, and little by little, the door was opening.

There was really no stopping Ashley. The next day, (after telling *me* to "get real"!) he drew up his own list called "What You REALISTICALLY Cannot Live Without in Ghana," which included: snakebite kit, cigarette lighter which can spark in a monsoon, Neat Deet (for lepidopterists), a waterproof flashlight, emergency high protein capsules, Swiss Army knife, wristwatch, and an instruction manual on how to find water in the wild, from dousing to splicing the traveler's palm.

I tried to slow him down and mentioned that my friend Opoku from Ghana had said, "All you need is money, 'cause you can buy everything else when you get there."

"Look, mush," said Ash, "Africa is full of green mambas, elephants, and mosquitoes, everyone knows that—you might have to swim crocodile-infested rivers, build your hut, and live on grubs and berries. Just pack, Jack, and start taking your quinine now."

I didn't fancy the grubs much, but I remembered there was a pile of strawberries in the fridge and thought I better get into practice.

It was while we were down in the kitchen that we first noticed the camera. I mean, SGCCCH has CCTV on the outside, but this camera was on the inside. It was pointing at the fridge. Apart from the strawberries, I didn't think that last night's leftover curry really needed that kind of security.

Ash looked very worried. "That's new, Sue," he said, "that is so new it's hardly out of its bubble wrap."

"The fridge is under surveillance," I said. "Somebody has nicked the banana-flavored yogurt once too often."

Ashley grabbed my elbow and led me outside across the lawn and behind the compost heap. He checked his mobile. "Right, no signal. We're safe. Listen, mush, that camera wasn't there yesterday. And it's not just pointing at the fridge—it's covering the back door, too. That means every time we go in or out they'll know. What do you bet they bugged the whole place? We must never talk openly again. We must exit and enter through the garage. We must change the hiding place and put a new password on the computer. Just in case. And from now on we'll have to talk in Gibberish. Wovagot dovago yovagou savagay, Jay?"

I didn't say anything 'cause I didn't know Gibberish.

"It's as simple as a pimple," said Ash. "Just add ovago or avaga after every syllable or before every vowel as you want, but change it sometimes. Let's check the place for cameras, turn the electricity off, and hide the stuff, Macduff. After that we'll work out who's the inside man, eh Jan?"

There were four cameras: one on the front door, one on the back, one in the study, and one in the common room. They must have been put up in the night, because they'd moved the darts scoreboard and our last game of 201 had plaster dust sticking to the chalk. Ash said, "You outwitted them on the Uncle Fidelis plan, so now they mean business."

I nodded glumly. Gibberish and more looking over my shoulder was depressing.

"Next thing you know, they'll tag you, too, Blue," said Ash, his eyes growing wilder by the minute. "We better check all your shoes in case there's a bleeping device in the heels."

After we'd checked the shoes, put a towel over the study camera ('cause you can't use a computer without power), and blown the main fuse, Ashley got really serious.

"I've worked out that it must be Susie or Kevin," said Ash. "They were the only two on duty last night. But I think your Ms. Shaw is well dodgy."

"She's not mine," I pointed out, "and Susie can hardly do up her own shoelaces, so I don't think she could wire a surveillance system."

"Yeah, Kevin has trouble with bin bags," said Ashley, "but all they had to do was let someone smarter in, Lynne! At a push they might be able to unlock the back door— or . . . ?"

"So the inside man is an outside man?"

Ashley sat down trying to work that one out, while I tried to think of an alternative to Gibberish. He won. "Savagay wovagot yovagou lavagike, Mike, but one of them knows what's going on."

Summer Term

Well, those times at least were fun. But soon the holidays ended and I was sent back to my old school in Gloucester. I was surprised. I'd imagined that I'd have to start over again at Ashley's school. I'd even quite liked the idea, but no—I left Syde at 7:30 a.m. in a special minibus laid on for me, and arrived at Oxstalls by 8:15. And just like before I got into school early and hung around in the school yard with Opoku, Maggot, and Lee.

Life seemed to go on as normal. Normal? I think I'd lost track of what normal was. Somehow in my mind it was linked to Bernard and Marion and the color magnolia. Sometimes I'd shut my eyes and try to imagine the immense security of Bernard, the smell of their house, the regular reliable feeling of bedtime at ten.

When Ashley wasn't with me, Bartholomew kept me company. I drew a picture of him in art and I carried it around. I started talking to him, telling him how sorry I was that he hadn't been rescued, how I'd come back and escape with him all over again. Stupid stuff, really. But you see, he needed me, and that kept me going. He was just a kid. He didn't have anyone to stick up for him. I'd feel his hand reach out and hold mine in the dead of night, and when I awoke I'd find my two hands locked together.

I think I needed Bartholomew too. I didn't want to go on about it to Ashley, but I was very scared. You see, Bartholomew understood about fear. You can tell yourself you're okay, that you've covered every angle, but it's not true. The fear can swallow you at any time. Right in the middle of a math lesson it can come back. It stays in your head.

Battling with fear is exhausting. At the end of each day I sank into the sofa in the common room and let Ashley take over. Then there was the night and the nightmares, and then the next day all over again.

On one of those evenings when Ashley had taken over, he said, "IvagI thivagink I'vagime bevageivaging followed too, Sue. There's been this flavagat favagaced wovagomavagan outside school evagerevagy afternoon."

I sat up, shocked. And not because I'd got the hang of Gibberish. Quickly we snuck out through the garage and regrouped behind the compost heap.

"Hope you're just jealous," I said.

Ashley shook his head. "She's there every day. But I've got a plan, Stan. I took mug shots and I e-mailed them to our address."

"Right," I said, "now she can watch us on the Internet, too."

"Wrong, Mr. Wong. You e-mail your snaps and we'll do some comparing."

So we went back inside, hung the towel over the CCTV camera, turned the volume on the computer up high until any bugging device was well zinging—and then I downloaded all my pics onto the computer.

Ash said, "I saw this really interesting documentary on the Russian royal family. It was about whether Princess Anastasia had survived and was buried in South Africa."

"Sounds totally absorbing," I said.

"We can do the same, mush."

"Ahhh," I said, "I may have royal blood, but it's not Russian."

Ashley didn't bat an eyelid. "They had to find out if the South African skull was hers. You overlay one face on another—then you measure the distance between the eyes, right at the bony bridge of the nose. Then you measure the nose. Then you get the truth, Ruth!"

Ashley came up with an enlargement and identification formula. It was something like this:

X (exact enlarged size) = R (the area covered by the face in a 6 x 8 inch rectangle) − Y (the area not covered by the face, providing it's a full-frontal pic). N measurements = N1 (E1 to E2) divided by 2 then measured on the perpendicular to tip of nose = N2

It seemed to work, so we enlarged the photos and started comparing faces. The result was staggering.

"Bow-wovagow!" said Ash.

From twenty different pictures of women who looked quite different, fourteen of them had identical nose measurements—including the flat-faced woman watching Ashley. It was spooky. Sometimes she was plump and old, sometimes thin and young, long hair, short hair, big teeth, pimples, makeup, you name it—she was the same woman.

"These are pro-fessionals!" said Ash.

I wasn't so impressed. Boy! She must have been following me all the time! Being outsmarted on a daily basis is not good for your self-esteem. My temper was intact, though, so I used it to chuck the yucca plant at the CCTV camera.

I missed.

The begonias did the trick. The CCTV camera snapped off the wall.

"Pity we didn't think of it before," said Ashley.

We did a little basketball practice on the other cameras as well, and I think our team won.

It was important that we stayed ahead—so Ashley and I went into overtime. We checked out the other enemies:

	Score
IC1 (that's police code for white male) =	3/10
IC3 (that's police code for black male) =	0/10

I sent the matches to Raphael: *Dese r da peeps watchin us. Plse check out if poss. No news yt on clue 2 map—z.* He texted me back: *Nice work u take care—Am on 2 sumting but need a bit more time—will txt u soon—r.* I replied: *Have as long as u like. Will prob c u in da afterlife.*

As it turned out, I didn't have that long. Things were about to seriously fast-forward.

Outsmarted

It was the same day that I visited Pops for the last time, that I got the expected text from Raphael. It was May and the woods of Leckington Park were bursting with bluebells. They looked so harmless. Beautiful Britain.

Summer was coming. I was on the minibus going to school. I'd planned that now the evenings were lighter I'd visit Pops a bit more. I'd found out that there were later buses. I'd even gone through Susie's super sign-out sheet. And Ashley and I had translated a good chunk of Bartholomew's diary.

That morning I had the translations with me. After school I was going to read them to Pops. I was feeling good. It was more than that—I was feeling hopeful. Sometimes in that strange land before I woke up I saw the door to my past swing open—I was on the verge of remembering something.

Mobz buzzed twice in my pocket. I sneaked it out to read the message: *Breakthrough i've verified the story, hard evidence in hand also sum interesting matches on yr villains something is up b wary—r.* I sent a text back: *Goin 2 c Pops 2day almost feel I mite b able 2 crack da map ting—z.*

Boy, was I excited. The whole day at school I was restless. I couldn't wait to get to the graveyard. I'd read to Pops, and then I'd got something to give him. A two-hundred-cedi coin shaped like a fifty-pence piece! Real Ghana money! I'd swapped it (plus a complete lesson on How to Speak Pidgin English) for my free lunch with Opoku a few days back (and I must say Pidgin is a lot easier than Gibberish). I wondered what "hard evidence" Raphael had. And I guess I was secretly hoping that being with Pops in the graveyard would unlock the door.

As soon as school was over I walked into Gloucester. Maybe I was too excited, because I didn't bother to check the corners of the street very often. Raphael had told me to be wary, so I took a roundabout route. I waited in front of a level crossing and zipped over after the barriers went down. That was wary enough for me.

The churchyard was beautiful. Really big dandelions clung to the edges of the paths and all the trees were in leaf. Pops's mound, though still low and unmarked, was covered with straggling pink flowers. Penelope Hannah Mustoe's mound was back to normal (though no tombstone!). I checked both mounds well. There weren't any marks on them. By dodging from headstone to headstone I checked out the graveyard. There was one old woman tending a grave, who could have been *the* woman, but she scuttled off with a weird look on her face pretty soon after I saw her. I watched her retreat to the Church Road traffic lights, and figured she'd gone. I wedged the church door open with a rock and cautiously stuck my head in. Empty.

Satisfied, I sat down. I told Pops the news from Raphael and all the things I'd done for the last month. I told him about our plan (Ashley was buying and selling on eBay, and I'd saved thirty quid—when we needed the rest, we were going to ask Bernard to help). I asked him questions like "What is the secret?" and "Where is the map?" Of course he didn't answer, I wasn't expecting him to—well, not right away. I did a really good backflip for him, and told him that I was definitely going to Ghana to get the treasure.

Then I settled down and read him our translations. This was as far as *I'd* got:

> fear me made (perna) shake ~~wisdom~~ my people water O rio. Shame Prince not fear. I ran. Hide forest safe dogs running. White Death. Enemies begging (a gravata) shackled Cape, Fort, blood footsteps. Mother hut sticks fire, angry no fire not cry, because a prince.
>
> Tell of capture? Buzzards brother, Akonor(?), hands walk.

Ashley had laughed at that and said, "You gotta make it flow, Joe. Y'know!" And I seriously think—although his version might not be dead accurate—it was masses better. Here it is:

> When the fear came upon me it made my legs shake, quiver, and tremble—and all the wisdom of my people

rushed out of me like the waters of a great flowing river. I was ashamed, for a prince may never be afraid. I ran. Now I know if I had only hidden myself in the forest I would have been safe, but what is the good of knowing this now? The dogs smelled my running straightaway and gave chase. Their baying made me run faster, but you cannot run before the hounds of the White Death. I ran into the hands of my enemies and fell upon my knees begging, pleading, beseeching them to save me. For answer, they put iron upon my legs and upon my hands and joined me with others whom I now saw were shackled, chained, and manacled together upon the long beach, which stretches beyond the cape.

For many hours we marched upon the shifting sands toward the white fort. The iron ate deep into my flesh and my blood fell into my footsteps. I thought of my mother's hut and of the sticks I should have carried back to light the evening fire. I thought of how angry she would be without her fire and without the small beef I should have brought to her. And water slid from my eyes, but I did not weep, because a prince may never weep.

What shall I tell you of those hours of my capture? I prayed that the buzzards above and the spirits of the forest would tell my brother Akonor of my plight. Ah, Akonor, where are you now? On I walked toward the fort. The white turrets were much bigger and the sea was rough. Huge waves slammed next to me. The others with me said nothing, but I could feel their breath on my neck and the touch of their hands against my back. I was too scared to turn round and look into their faces. I kept on walking.

Ashley had done well. He caught the spirit of the thing. I guess that's what reading does for you. It gives you imagination. Even if Bartholomew hadn't quite put it that way, I felt sure he'd approve.

I sat and thought of Bartholomew. I clasped my hands together like we did at night and told him that even if Akonor didn't save him, I would. I told him that time didn't mean anything, that stories go on and on and that nothing is ever over. I told him that as long as I was alive, he was too. I know that sounds crazy, but you don't understand. You'd have to sit there like I did beside Pops's mound, and know you were the last in the long line of Baktus and that it was all left to you. You can't escape your history, you see. Well, I couldn't—even if I wanted to.

Sitting there on that bright May evening thinking of Bartholomew, I began for the first time to understand Pops's obsession with the diaries. I felt it connected us. Like him, I now had something to live for. And it wasn't just about me, either. It wasn't just about doing it for Pops. You'll laugh if I say it was sort of bigger than the two of us—sort of for mankind. I mean if all the injustices caused by slavery could be paid for, it would settle something. I think people would feel a lot better. I heard Bernard say, "Human rights is not just about victims; everybody suffers when the human spirit is abused; it debases the whole race, and it is for everyone's benefit that we fight for justice."

It was at that point (I was kinda humming a Zac Marley reggae beat for Pops) when I got another text from Raphael. It's sometimes crazy, isn't it? Like telepathy. There I was thinking about slavery and Pops and justice and I get this: *Yep—got it—hard evidence THE BOND EXISTS follwd up SBs notes & it is in records of the Royal African Company only a copy nt signed but there—this is damn big. Where r u? r.*

Boy, it would have taken an industrial cleaning machine to wipe the smile off my face. I sent a text right back: *Gr8 dats heavy man—im in churchyard wit pops—z.*

I was in such a good mood that I thought I'd pop round and see Marion and Bernard. I was going to surprise them and say, "Guess what? We're in business. There's a bond, and that means Pops was right. If I can find it, will you help me? Will you lend me the money?"

I got round there with about three-quarters of an hour to spare before the 5:45 bus. Marion was in, and she was so pleased to see me that I forgot all about the time.

"I've done more translations," I said.

"Can I read them?"

"Sure." I passed her our efforts.

"How awful." She sat down. "Oh Zac, how awful for poor Bartholomew."

"Ashley did most of it," I said. "I wish you'd been there to help."

"I'd love to help, you know that—just ring me, anytime."

I shook my head. "Phone lines," I said. Then I added, "I've scanned it all onto an e-mail message account. I could come round after school—if that's okay?"

We made a plan for tomorrow evening.

At 5:30 Bernard still wasn't back from work. I wanted to tell him (in particular) about the bond, so I was saving my news. I guess I was nervous, too—about asking for possibly a very large sum of money. While we waited, I ate a whole lot of leftovers that Marion fixed for me. She sat and watched as I ate, her plump hands clasped together, her round eyes drinking me down. I don't know what we talked about—the garden maybe, the summer. She told me that she was hoping Bernard might have found a way through the system and they might be able to take me on holiday to the Algarve.

"Don't get too excited," she said, "in case."

I got excited anyway.

I didn't want to leave. I know that. I dragged out the time, using Bernard as an excuse. Waiting for him to come. I made Marion promise never to change my room. I told her I'd found a friend, that Ashley was okay. She got so worried about me that I stopped telling her anything else. I stayed there too long. I ate too many cakes. I followed her from the garden, to the kitchen, to the front room, unable to break away. She took my hand and told me she missed me. I didn't tell her I'd missed my bus. By the time I left, Bernard still wasn't home, and I still hadn't shared my news. What I did have was ten minutes to get to the city center to catch the last bus. I missed that one too.

I walked eight miles home. It was long. The moon was old—yellow and waning—and the trees stretched strange fingers out at me. But for all that, I wasn't scared. I guess I was still excited about Raphael's text, but it was more than that. I knew the three enemies weren't around. There was a calmness in the air; all the little crickets and things sounded relaxed. I checked (of course) and dodged into the bushes when I saw headlights, but there was really no need. At last, I thought (foolishly), I've outwitted them.

I got in around midnight; Susie wasn't hard to manage. I sent a text to Raphael and told him I was knackered, but all was v. cool.

Ash did a victory circuit of the bedroom when I showed him Raphael's text. "Wow-bovagow!"

Dave mumbled, "Oh shut up, you morons."

But that didn't bother Ash. "Start to pack, Jack. You'll need T-shirts, shorts, boxers, jeans, sneakers, towels, washing stuff, needle and thread, toenail clippers, comb, pen, paper, some light reading . . ."

"Needle and thread?" I said.

"In case you're attacked by a lion in your tent and he rips your mosquito net, mush."

I threw a pillow at him and we started giggling.

It was a good night and I slept well.

So when I came downstairs the next morning, I had no idea why the police were waiting.

Gloucester Juvenile Detention Center

This is what happened.

They searched me, and my stuff. They read me my rights, handcuffed me, and escorted me to the waiting van. At the station they asked me repeatedly about my visit to the graveyard. Then they put me in the cells.

This time there was no Bernard and Marion to speak up for me. I didn't even get a visit from Ms. Shaw. I spent the whole day in the police cells. The food was awful— cheap chips and nasty burgers, microwaved into oblivion; the bed—a roll of foam on a built-in slab. I couldn't wash or clean my teeth. I had one call. I phoned Raphael.

The next morning I appeared before the magistrate at a juvenile court. I was assigned a defense duty solicitor who asked me to milk the story of being an orphan—it appeared Raphael was stuck somewhere on the M40. When I heard that, my heart sank and I wished I'd phoned Bernard. They'd taken Mobz off me, so I had to send Ash an imaginary text: *4get da needle n thread Fred chevageck da divagiavagarravagy is savagafe. Contact B.* And his reply: *Right, da divagiavagarravagy is savagafe dn't reveal its place even unda torture. Will call B n make a plan, Stan.*

I was charged with a misdemeanor, vandalism—namely desecrating church property—and unlawfully digging up a grave on the evening of the seventh of May at All Saints' churchyard. The case was adjourned pending committal (for some reason the magistrate thought my case might need to go before the Crown Court). Bail was denied. There was no one to apply for a bail bond, that's why. There was no one to stand surety for me. No gold. I was sent to a juvenile remand home, a pretrial detention center, while the police collected their statements. They warned me this would take time, as there was no victim.

It was funny, being there. I lay awake at night and thought of Bartholomew. Him in the dungeons of Cape Coast Castle and me in Gloucester Juvenile Detention Center. Three hundred years apart.

Later, much later, by the light from a kerosene lamp, under a vast starlit sky, I heard this bit of the diary, and I realized I'd had it easy.

All around me were dim walls. It was forever night. The ceaseless turn of the sun in its heavens was as a foreign land to me. With each round of sleep and waiting, my hope faded and my strength deserted me. Some of the children said, "We will be eaten by the White Death." Others, "We will be taken out upon the seas and fed to Mammy Water." I knew not what was to become of me, but it seemed that I remembered my teacher, Senhor Dias, say from another world, another life, "Beyond the seas there is a different place, great, and fair to look upon. That is where they take your people, to build that land."

But I did not want to go there.

There was a silence in those slave chambers that could not be broken. No, not even by the weeping of the children. Such silence roused even the British agent newly visiting, and on one day we were marched out of the chambers into the sunlight. That blinding light was darker than even the dimness of our cells, for we could not open our eyes against it—so unaccustomed to the light was our frail sight. During that day, the guards broke holes from our cells through to the female dungeons, so that the children could hold their mothers' hands through three feet of solid stone. The women were charged to keep the silence so that the British agent could sleep undisturbed. There was no hand for me to hold through the darkness of that eternal night.

Then one morning I alone was called out of the labyrinth. Fearfully I stumbled up the chute into the vast forecourt of Cape Coast Castle. My heart was a rebel inside my thin rib cage for it shouted with joy to hear the waves breaking upon the shore. Shielding my weak eyes, I was marched out through the iron gates of the castle down to the water's edge, where I entered the long boat of the English and was rowed down the coast until we barked upon the shore not far from the settlement of Cabo Corso.

Imagine my joy at seeing there upon the beach my uncle and teacher, Senhor Dias. How he stood there, tall and proud, his long shadow reaching down around him, and even though a prince may not weep, I wept to see him there.

"Come," he said, and embraced me before the Englishmen and whispered into my gray cheeks, "Courage, Bartholomew, courage, we have come for you."

Then from the shadows of my dimmed vision I saw behind him fifteen of my brothers, and among them my best beloved, Akonor.

Ah, Akonor, until I die I shall never forget you. This life is but a shadow of things to come, but there in the future, they shall know of you.

I tried to run to Akonor, but the shackles on my legs held me, and the English laughed as I fell upon the sand.

"Enough," demanded Senhor Dias, "we have here the gold and the bond for his release."

Raphael convened a hearing—after the weekend, three days later. I appeared back before my magistrate, Ms. Bowdich, and—imagine my joy—Mr. Bernard was there. How tall he stood! Boy, I could have cried! He put up bail for me—one thousand pounds! I don't know how he did it; after all, he wasn't even a relative. He hugged me hard outside Gloucester courts. Raphael shook my hand—he was a small wiry black guy, nothing like I'd imagined. We all linked arms before I returned to Syde. I told them over and over, "I didn't do it."

They nodded.

"Courage, Zac. It's not a serious thing," said Bernard, stroking my head.

"I warned you," said Raphael.

"I just wish I'd known sooner," said Bernard. "I'd never have let them put you in custody."

"I'm sorry about the M40, it wasn't my fault," said Raphael.

"We can get you off. Don't you worry," said Bernard.

"We?" said Raphael.

"The prosecution have got me to reckon with. It's a ridiculous charge. I only wish I'd got home that evening. I blame myself," said Bernard.

"Can I speak to my client alone?" said Raphael.

"I'll be in the car," said Bernard.

"I didn't do it," I said.

"Listen, Zac, you've got to change your plea."

That was when he confronted me with the evidence: the quantity of coins, the Rolex, the BMW car keys, the ring, my little notes and letters I'd written to Pops. It was quite obvious that I'd been digging away at his grave for some time.

"This is hopeless, Zac. It's overwhelming circumstantial evidence. It shows you've been systematically obsessed with the grave."

I stopped and stuck my hands in my pocket. "Doesn't mean I dug him up," I muttered.

"No, but it doesn't mean you didn't. After all, someone did, and you've got no alibi."

"You know who it was," I said. "*They* planned this. They already dug up Penelope Hannah Mustoe with their first go."

"No proof," said Raphael.

"I was set up," I said.

"And there's still no alibi."

"I was walking home."

"Alone," said Raphael.

"So?" I said.

"There's a witness. I'll get a copy of his statement, but the police seemed very pleased with him. He described you very accurately."

Then he showed me the photos.

"I didn't do it. Why would I unearth his coffin? That's sick." Actually I felt sick, seeing his coffin lying like that at the bottom of the hole.

"If you plead guilty, the most you'll get is six months; they'll knock a third off for the plea and you'll only have to do half. I'll argue for a community service term. I've been on to the people in Ghana; I'm pretty sure I can swing it, if you agree to volunteer. Be clever, go for this settlement—after all, it's not your first offense, is it?"

I would have gone for a settlement, but burying coins is not a crime, so I refused. "I'll volunteer for Ghana okay, but I didn't do it."

Raphael shook his head. "Kid, you're one stubborn character. Well, I'll do my best, but I warn you, it doesn't look good. You may end up in Ghana for a lot longer and have more community hours when you come back."

"Whatever," I said. "I didn't dig Pops up."

Raphael smiled at me. "Well, if you didn't do it, then you must plead not guilty. I know there's a lot more to this case, but I warned you. You've left yourself wide open for this one." He looked at the photos again and shook his head.

"But Raphael," I said, "if I go to Ghana, I still don't know where the treasure is. So what do I do?"

"I told you; I've got some hard evidence. I'm not going to talk about it here. . . ." He glanced toward Bernard sitting in his car. "And I've still got to do more research, but if you have to go—and we haven't lost the case yet—Look, I'm a barrister, I don't talk in 'ifs' and 'maybes.' Let's take it a step at a time: first, the case; second, I need to get you as near as possible to—"

"To Cabo Corso," I said.

He looked at me, surprised. "I think you know a lot more than you let on, kid."

I smiled. Suddenly I longed to be found guilty, longed to be sent to Ghana—when I got there I was sure I would remember everything. And just as suddenly I became afraid—afraid that I wouldn't go, afraid that I would.

You know, I was so stupid. If I'd thought about it—of course I was going to Ghana. Not because I wanted it, but because *they* did. This was exactly what they'd been angling for all along. They needed to find the bond and destroy it so that they'd be in the clear. Why not let me show them the way? Then they needed to get my diary and get rid of me. Any nice lonely spot—like Ghana—would do. And what better way than to send me over there in handcuffs? (Remind you of someone else sent off in chains?) Do you think a rural magistrate presented them with any problems? On the contrary, that would be the easy part.

I shook Raphael's hand and he stood watching as I turned to go.

Bernard drove me back to Syde. He didn't say much. I didn't say much either. I didn't tell him about the bond breakthrough. It just wasn't the right time. It wasn't the right time to ask for more money, either. All I did say was: "It's *them*, you know, it must be."

Bernard nodded. He looked thoughtful—no, worried. But, as I got out of the car, he gripped my shoulder. "Raphael's your barrister, and I'm sure he'll do his best, but I want you to know I'm here. I'm taking all this very seriously, but thorough investigations take time—if you're not happy about anything, call me. I'll always be on your side. I think you've got a good friend in Ashley."

I nodded, and forgot to say thanks.

Ashley had been as good as his word; he'd called Bernard. I increased his percentage.

Not Guilty

On the eleventh of July I reappeared before Gloucester Juvenile Court. The magistrate was the same woman. She had a small gold crucifix around her throat. She said at one point that she had kids too. Halfway through the hearing she remarked that the attack on my grandfather had occurred two days before Christmas and that was to be noted.

I entered a plea of not guilty. But no one seemed to note that.

The courtroom was well weird. It looked like something out of those dramas on Channel Four. Dark stained wood everywhere, a bit like church. I was very tense—I felt my hair looked messy and I kept trying to pat it down. Ms. Bowdich was sitting at a bench high up in the front and I had to call her "Your Honor," which seemed strange because she was a woman. There were two others with her, but they didn't seem to count. Bernard and Marion were there, with Ms. Shaw—who had decided not to sit next to them. They were all behind a glass screen at the back. I couldn't really turn round to wave at them in case Her

Honorness didn't like it. I wanted to, though, very badly—I wanted to catch Bernard's eye. I needed him. I sat on a bench with a few other kids and had to wait my turn. My palms felt itchy and my mouth dry. One of the kids had nicked a car with some aggravation and was given a custodial sentence. Another was doing drugs and had a whole string of robberies to be taken into account. His case was adjourned. Then I was called.

That was when I was asked for my plea.

I took the stand. "Not guilty," I croaked. I'm sure I said it loud enough.

At that point though, I wasn't sure what I was thinking. My mind had leapt ahead. Would I get off? Deepest down of all I wanted to be acquitted. I didn't do it, you see. They had done it *to* me and I didn't want them to succeed. But if I didn't get off, next deepest down I wanted to go to Ghana. There I'd dig up the truth. Definitely. That would almost make being guilty okay. After that I was afraid. Community service for the whole summer? I never wanted to see another pot of community service paint ever again. Or back to the detention center? I clenched my teeth and swallowed.

The magistrate shook her head sadly at the photos of the crime site. She asked Raphael a few things. The police put their side forward. She didn't whisper for very long to the two others before she nodded her head.

I ran my tongue over my lips and waited.

The whole place seemed to be waiting.

She turned to Raphael. "Do you want him to be committed to the Crown, or can we decide the matter today?"

Raphael looked over at me and raised his eyebrows. I knew what he was asking. She *wasn't* going to acquit me. My heart sank. I could plead guilty or face a trial.

Raphael spoke to her fast and low.

She nodded her head. "Guilty then."

I stood there frozen.

"Can we proceed with sentencing?"

Raphael nodded, and she whispered again to the two others.

"You will be fined eighty pounds and be expected to serve two hundred community service hours."

Raphael stood up and indicated something.

"Defense may approach the bench."

They talked quietly. Raphael passed her some papers. There was more whispering.

I was stunned. I mean I *hadn't* pleaded guilty. I knew of course that if the magistrates weren't ready to acquit me, if the evidence was so much, I'd stand little chance at a full trial—but, hey, even though I knew that, I was NOT guilty. I waited, my legs feeling a little shaky. I chewed my tongue. Would she agree to Ghana?

Seconds crashed.

Ms. Bowdich looked very unconvinced.

"Your defense counsel has proposed that you are ready to agree to humanitarian service overseas. He suggests Ghana. Do you volunteer?"

"Yes, Your Honor."

"The boy is hardly sixteen," she said, shuffling through her papers. "Don't you think he's too young?"

Raphael spoke to her again and I heard the words "community care" and "social services" and "youth project."

"Do you understand that you will have to leave this country and undertake community work in a missionary settlement?" She didn't sound approving.

"Yes," I said, but my voice was harsh and faint.

Again she whispered to the two others.

My mouth was like a desert. The seconds carried on crashing.

"It may work out. I want a psychiatric profile before he goes, and I believe he has spent three days in custody. The eighty pounds will be discounted against this." She turned to me. "Do you understand?"

I nodded. I wasn't brain-dead.

"Your social worker will be contacted." She looked at the papers Raphael had submitted. "You can take advantage of the African Settlement Scheme we have in Ghana. It's specially targeted at people like you. Contact Gloucestershire Social Services and see if they are ready to assess him and set this up." She waved the stuff at an official. "I'd like a full report to the court before he goes." She turned to me. "If I see you before this court again, I shall have no choice but to detain you in a secure juvenile unit. Do you understand?"

I tried not to look happy. I gave her my most sorrowful, repentant, head-hanging routine.

I don't know what happened to not-guilty, but in one way you could say I went for a settlement after all!

Raphael, Mr. Bernard, Marion, and Ms. Shaw met me outside.

"It's not so bad, Zac." Ms. Shaw looked at more papers. "It's part of a pilot project in exposing young offenders to new situations. It may make you reflect on your role in life. It's to help you develop a social conscience. It will assist you in integrating your feelings of displacement, and help with your feelings of anger, and hopefully reduce your antisocial behavior. You have been very lucky to be offered this opportunity."

!

"The prosecution had it in for you," said Mr. Bernard. "We should appeal."

"It is very costly and all funded by taxpayers' money," said Ms. Shaw.

"Oh, Zac," said Marion.

"You will be away for six weeks, during which time you will have to be self-reliant. You'll have to be very strong indeed. You will have to help with the mission's health project, cook your own food, wash your own clothes, and have other community duties that the camp will assign you. You are going to Cabo Corso Missionary Settlement, which is on the coast of the Western Region of Ghana, so once you are there you will have to make a go of it," said Ms. Shaw, as if she'd set it all up for me as a special favor!

Raphael grinned at me and winked.

Cabo Corso!

I winked back.

"You'll be expected to report to the British High Commission every week, but I'll fix up a person locally to perform that role—maybe one of the missionary fathers. On the whole I'm well pleased. You're a nice lad, Zac," said Ms. Shaw.

Mr. Bernard gripped my shoulder. "Are you sure you're happy about this? I'm not. You shouldn't have accepted a guilty plea. It was highly irregular. In fact, I'm surprised it was allowed. I think you were pressured into this overseas service. It should have been given a lot more thought. Just say the word and I'll fight it. It might take time, but—"

"I'm fine," I said. "I need a holiday."

Summer Holidays

I was sent back to Syde, pending my community order, and allowed to finish school, while Ms. Shaw made my travel arrangements. I was put on a pink report card, which meant a teacher had to sign me present every lesson, and I was driven to the police station to report every Friday afternoon. There was no chance to visit Pops again, but in my head I promised him I'd find the gold. I promised him a headstone. I promised I'd fight for the justice he wanted. I told him that whoever had dug him up would pay. I sent a text to Raphael before I left. He sent a text back: *U take care—update me—stay out of trouble—trust nobody—r.*

In an odd way it felt quite safe being escorted everywhere—I stopped looking over my shoulder so much. I figured that I'd got my own set of bodyguards. Even though it was kind of disgraceful to be in so much trouble, I felt cheerful. I even put a bit of a skip back into my pimp-limp-gangsta step. Hey—I was going to Africa! *Zac is coming—no hesitating—don't underrate him— he's the meanest—just a genius. . . .* I was going to find all that

treasure and by the time I returned I'd be so important—
Yo! People would have to show respect. Already, in a way,
I was kind of a celebrity, although my pals weren't very
encouraging.

"You're mad," said Maggot. "The maddest I know.
Africa's full of diseases and cockroaches. And no TV."

"Even being in custody must be a lot easier than cooking your own food in some jungle," said Lee.

Maggot outlined the diseases. "There's yellow fever,
scarlet fever, brain fever, black water fever, not to mention
fever-fever. All of which will kill you."

"Plus added hazards like crocodiles and leopards,"
said another.

"The food is the worst," came back Lee. "Slime balls
with snails."

"And the people are all thieves. They'll slit your throat
for a pair of your sneakers," put in a fourth.

Opoku snorted. He was the Ghanaian kid, and pretty
homesick. At last he said, "That's such junk. It's not true—
and you're all stupid. None of you have ever even been
there! You shouldn't believe stuff you see on telly. Ghana's
not like that—it's the best country in the world. But there
is something you won't have thought of, Zac."

Everyone waited.

"You might like it. And then you'll have to come back."

I grinned. Come back—with all that gold! I reckoned
I could live without swaying palms and piercing blue skies
for a while 'cause, boy, when I started the court case I'd get

to be really famous; I might even get put in history books. Then I could go wherever I wanted. I could have a permanent suite of rooms at the Accra Novotel if it was that good! I started thinking of fame and endless wealth and how I'd spend it. But after I'd gone through every new piece of designer kit, enough expensive sneakers, and Sky TV in every room, I got to thinking about Bernard and Marion and my magnolia bedroom. There was a pretty pathetic part of me that would rather be there, staring at the wall paint, than watching Sky anywhere in the world.

Saying good-bye to Ashley wasn't easy. I'm not sure if he wasn't jealous. He kept saying, "So you're ovogovogoff and leaving me." Or, "This place will seem empty when you're gone." Or, "You'll miss me, you know." In fact, he wouldn't speak to me the night before I left. I think he'd been crying. But under my pillow I found a note.

Right, mush—I'll keep the strips and the list. You take the original divagiavagarravagy—I've printed you out a glossary, but I'll translate too, and post it at our e-mail site. Here's a penknife (put it in your main luggage) and a road map. Sorry I couldn't get any of the other stuff on eBay. I'll contact Bernard if I don't hear from you. Send me a text minimum once a week with the code word Susie in it, innit? Then I'll know you're okay, mush. I know we weren't really ready yet, but you can do it, Zed. You can find the gold. You've got to believe it. When you do—don't forget the percentage factor. DESTROY THIS NOTE.

A

The last thing I did was phone Bernard and Marion, but I only got their answer machine. I left a message. I said, "See you soon. Eleven fifty-five p.m. Terminal Three. Keep my room painted magnolia."

Too good to be true, that's what you're thinking. Getting to Ghana, right to Cabo Corso—too neat. That's what I thought—at first.

Poor me. How sweetly I'd been set up. I didn't see that others might want me there, might want me far away from any kind of help. I didn't wonder why Ms. Shaw had raised no objection, or why the magistrate had agreed—before she'd even seen the reports. Why the police had made sure I couldn't do a bunk. Why there just happened to be a health project right at Cabo Corso . . . No, I didn't see it— at least not until I reached the airport.

Only by then it was too late.

PART TWO

Cabo Corso, Ghana

On My Way to Get the Gold

The minute I'd gone through to the boarding gate for Ghana, I knew something was wrong. That old feeling was back. It had nothing to do with cold nights, but it was cold all right.

I think it was because I was inspecting the lineup of fellow travelers that I first noticed him. There he was. His back to me, pacing up and down. His brown CLIPPERS fitted cap turned sideways, wearing *a royal blue tracksuit with white stripes* . . .

We were a bit late, and I hadn't had time to say good-bye properly to Bernard and Marion. Ms. Shaw had hurried me through, pressing papers into my hand, cautioning me, telling me the schedule, instructing the Unaccompanied Minor airline steward who had charge of me. I guess I was excited, taking it all in. And there he was, a distant figure pacing at the end of the queue. For a minute my heart stopped. I couldn't believe what I was seeing. You see, I recognized the clothes. I recognized the movements. I recognized them from the road outside Arrowsmith House, from the orange glow on frosty pavements. I recognized them from the Jamaica Meeting House.

Pacing up and down was the figure of *Uncle Fidelis*.

I stopped. My blood froze. I thought I was going to be sick. Uncle Fidelis was *dead*. He was stabbed repeatedly with a steak knife. He could not be pacing up and down at Gate 25, Terminal 3, Heathrow. Uncle Fidelis was incapable of sprinting down a cold street in a blue tracksuit. He could not be one of the muggers. And yet there he was. I didn't need to see his face. I could see the angle of his shoulders, the slight shuffle, and that awful brown cap. I'm not stupid.

Just as I took courage, just as I was about to step forward to tap his shoulder—he turned and disappeared. I don't mean like a ghost, he just seemed to melt back into the queue and was gone.

I think I panicked. I told the Unaccompanied Minor lady from Ghana Airways that I felt sick. I needed time to think. I couldn't. She took me to a washroom. I turned on the taps. I splashed water on my face. I leaned my head against the mirror and blew steam on it. My heart was banging; my mouth was dry. I gulped some water from the tap and choked. I spluttered, coughing.

You see, I knew what was coming next. They—or maybe just *he*—was going to mug me. He was going to steal my stuff. He was going to plant something on me, maybe more. I don't know. I DON'T KNOW. I was coughing too much to think. Maybe *she* was around too.

Her blank lizard eyes watching me. It couldn't be Uncle Fidelis. He couldn't be one of them. He was dead. He was very steak-knife-stabbed dead. Wasn't he?

My baggage!

It was too late. I'd checked it in. I had a feeling I wasn't going to see my new Nike sneakers again. Mobz and the diary were in my hand luggage. Phew! I swung my rucksack off my back and clutched it. I unzipped it, checked they were still there, zipped it back.

But Uncle Fidelis?

I thought, Zac, you don't have to go through with this. Phone Bernard. Change your mind. He'll do something. You could do more community service. Live at the detention center. Then I thought of Pops and my unpromise. Was I going to be the kind who gave up at the first sniff of danger?

The public address system announced after a long ding: "All passengers for GH 741 should proceed to Boarding Gate 25." I swallowed air, set my backpack straight, and stepped outside.

He *was* one of them. No wonder he'd turned yellow at my picture collection. So all along he'd been betraying Pops. That hurt. Those sneaky questions about whether I'd got the map . . . He was after the *Chamo-me* diary. Had to be. I'd be bound to take it to Ghana. This was going to be like taking candy off a kid.

But how did he know? The flight? The airline?

No reply necessary.

Yes, Big Brother 24-7 was still watching me. Suddenly I longed for Ash, longed to hear him say, "Right, mush, you are a pawn in a deadly game of chess. You can only move in one direction and only a step at a time. But don't be a mug, Doug, a pawn can still win the game." But I wasn't winning. Look at the graveyard incident. Somebody had been following me then, watching me all the time. They'd set me up and here I was—all alone.

I stayed real close to the UM lady. Then it occurred to me that the chip in my phone had not run out. I found it kind of funny that *they* were paying for all my texts. I stopped laughing when I remembered, with a contract line, all the numbers I called would appear on the bill. So I called numbers. So what? They wouldn't know who I called—that is, unless . . . call the numbers back. Simple. But that wouldn't tell them *where* I was.

Unless Mobz was bugged. Unless Mobz was fitted with a tracer. Unless they were tracking me by satellite . . .

Even Ash hadn't thought of that!

I started sweating. I couldn't dump the phone. That was my lifeline. Keep it real, I told myself. Keep it real. If you turn it off as much as possible, that'll help. Keep it really real.

We were approaching the last security sweep. I chucked my rucksack unwillingly on the moving rubber belt and stepped through the security doorway. I never took my eyes off that bag. I saw it go all the way through on the green monitor screen. Then I had an idea.

"Can you see inside everything?" I asked the man.

"Everything."

"Could you tell if I'd planted a device in my phone—you know, like a detonator?"

"Straightaway."

"Check this out," I said. "See if you can detect the bugging device."

The man slung my bag back round onto the rubber belt and watched it go through again.

"You're clean," he said.

"Did you see it?"

"Don't waste my time; there's no bug in your phone."

I picked up my rucksack and, scouring the queue behind me, stepped through to the boarding gate.

I didn't dare sleep on the plane. I sat bolt upright clutching my bag. I didn't put it in the overhead lockers. I didn't put it under the seat in front. I didn't watch the movie. I didn't eat anything. At any moment *he* might appear. What would it be? A quick steak knife in the chest? Throw the airline blanket over the blood? Snatch the bag?

Every quarter of an hour I patrolled the aisles. Bag in hand. I searched every face. Nobody. I checked the loos, one by one. Nothing. But I was too smart to think he wasn't on the plane. There was still club class, the jump seat, maybe other places.

I tried to settle. I tried to think of a plan, but I was well upset. I wasn't going to be safe at the settlement—if I ever made it there. I needed to keep moving—that seemed intelligent. I'd got the map of Ghana Ashley gave me, and knew roughly where Cape Coast Castle was. I'd escape and head for the castle. That was about as far as my plan went. I needed a lot more information on how to get around in Africa. I thought I might try to get there by sea. You know, borrow a boat and paddle down the coast.

I started experiencing a serious sense of humor failure.

I'd need the treasure map. I started to think as hard as I could. It must be something Pops had given me. Wrong. If it wasn't the diaries, or in the flat, it must have been something he'd said. I remembered the newspaper, the quote from him: *"I have tangible proof of where the treasure is buried."* Tangible didn't mean words. I gave up. I had nothing tangible to go on.

I needed to feel safe just for a while, so I locked myself in the washroom.

You know I am really not the kind of character who likes to dwell on the gloomy side of things, so I stayed there and spent the rest of the flight writing my will.

I, Zac Baxter, being of sound mind and body (at the moment) leave my Portuguese diary written by my ancestor, Bartholomew Baktu, and a fortune in gold dust (yet to be collected) to Mr. Bernard Caruthers on the understanding that he gives 50 percent to Ashley Bainbridge, pays for a headstone for Samuel J. Baxter, buys Marion Caruthers a holiday time-share in Barcelona, and sponsors Maggot, Lee, and Opoku for a shopping spree at Cribb's Causeway. He should use as much of the rest of the money as

necessary to start a human rights case to ensure that all the vic-
tims of slavery get compensation from the British government.

Hereto I append my name: ZAC BAXTER

I scribbled it into the back page of my passport in pencil. That way I figured someone would eventually find it. Then the intercom went: "Please fasten your seat belts and return your seats to the upright position. We are approaching Kotoka Airport. Local time is four twenty-three a.m. and the ground temperature is twenty-three degrees Celsius. Please remain seated until the aircraft comes to a complete standstill. Thank you for traveling Ghana Airways. We wish you a pleasant stay in Ghana or onward journey to your final destination."

My Final Destination

When I stepped out of the plane, humid air smelling of dust and fermentation told me straightaway that this was not Weston-super-Mare. I looked around for the courtesy shuttle to carry me to the Arrivals Hall and guessed it had probably got a puncture. I waited—not much longer than it would take you to change all four tires and then I figured it would not hurt to adjust my expectations a little and stretch my legs.

After I'd gone a few meters, it occurred to me that the courtesy shuttle might have been sabotaged by *them*. They might have arranged a little "accident" for me on the quarter-mile stretch of tarmac from the plane to the main airport building. Anxiously, I found the UM lady. I didn't want her to think that I was very tired and very scared, so I chanted rap and did my gangsta walk, but every now and then I speeded up or slowed down, I swapped from behind to in front, from her left side to her right—just in case.

When we got into the Arrivals Hall, I kept under observation all the people nearest to me. They crowded in on me, taller and fatter than I could bear, but that might have been because I was feeling very small and thin. I scanned them all and logged each face, searching for a match with anyone I'd ever known. I was half expecting to see Uncle Fidelis, and half terrified of it. One thing that reassured me was that the passengers and airport staff were nearly all brethren. There were black pilots and air crew trailing their little pullies from the planes, black officials stamping passports, black customs officers—kind of tired-looking—wiping the sweat off their foreheads with folded hankies, black porters in old brown uniforms, black ladies squeezed into bright clothes; boy, the few white passengers stuck out like peeled pink prawns. I figured the enemy wouldn't be quite that obvious, even the flat-faced woman couldn't blend in here; but to be sure I took photos.

I'm not going to give you any credits for guessing whether my luggage arrived. If it made it as far as the baggage claim carousel, I'd be surprised. I didn't waste much time looking. After fifteen minutes of hanging around in that marble-floored baggage hall with the chilly air-con whistling down my back, I gave up. I knew their moves by now. No, instead I kept my eyes open everywhere: my back, my front, my two sides, above my head—the number of places'd surprise you. The UM lady said she'd check for the bags, send them on. She obviously liked a challenge.

By 5:15 a.m. we were through customs and outside. The hot night smothered me in an instant sweat. A sea of dark faces swarmed against the metal barricades, beyond which the continent and what else waited? Nervously I scanned the crowd. Two figures detached themselves from the throng and crossed toward me: an official from the British High Commission and an armed policeman. They signed the UM papers and I had no choice but to go with them. There was no way I could escape. They bundled me straight into a Land Rover.

"It's a four-hour drive," said the official. "There are supplies to be bought for our Cape Coast office, and the vehicle to be checked before it leaves town, but we hope to get you there before sunset. Sunset and sunrise are always at six." And with that he promptly fell asleep and started snoring.

The driver nodded at me. "We are taking you to Father B. Bullingham, a British. You should try to sleep too. When you've been up in the air all night it is very tiring."

I suppose he was right. I should have been sleepy; I should have been a lot of things, including a carefree teenager lying on a sunny beach tuned into my iPod. I dragged my jacket off. Underneath, my T-shirt was already damp with sweat. Apart from noticing that they drove on the right, I saw a car pull out of the airport car park behind us. It was a dark-colored Toyota. I spotted the way it suspiciously dropped back and allowed a family car to pull out in front of it. I kept my eye on the side mirror, wondering when it would turn off.

"So what first, eh driver?" said the policeman.

"Aha! First, I think, we should introduce ourselves.

Good morning. My name is Wisdom K. Gbedemah," said the driver, "driver for the late Dr. Ofori and now employed by British Embassy."

The policeman grinned at me and nodded.

"Zac Baxter," I said.

"We always greet from right to left," he said. "I'm Sergeant Yao Yeboah, Ghana Police Force; YY to my friends." He grinned again and stuck his hand out in an oddly formal way, as if to remind me that I hadn't. We shook hands.

The official carried on snoring.

"So is this your first time in Ghana, Zac Baxter?" asked Wisdom, clicking the K-sounds in my name as if he were tasting them.

"Yep," I said, only lifting my eyes briefly away from the side mirror.

"Ghana is great country," said Wisdom. "We were the first African nation to gain independence. We have the biggest man-made lake in the entire world, Lake Akosombo, and we produce the most cocoa. We have produced more than chocolate. Ha! Ha! Kofi Annan is our best export. He was head of the UN, you know. We are very proud to be Ghanaians and we welcome you, Zac Baxter, to our homeland, Ghana."

"Thanks," I said, and wound down the window. By sticking my head out, I could check the Toyota. Yep, there it was, hiding behind the Peugeot family car. Maybe *they* thought I was stupid; but they were going to have to think again, because nobody was going to follow me, surprise me, and fool me—a fourth time! Feeling pretty clever, I pulled my head back in as we passed the Golden Tulip Hotel.

"That is the Golden Tulip Hotel," said Wisdom, "built on the site of the old Continental by the Dutch and the Libyans. We have many such hotels in Ghana. It has four stars, two hundred and thirty-four rooms, sixteen chalets, and fifty-two executive suites with five-star service! But I have never been inside it, so I cannot tell you if it is worth all those stars."

I could see that Wisdom was a chatty kind of person.

The family car turned in at the hotel, and the two kids on the front seat waved. I realized they'd seen me watching. I resolved to be more sly.

"In fact we have everything we need in Ghana. You can buy French cheese and South African roofing tiles, Chinese watches and Chicken Yassa from Senegal. Everyone in your country thinks we are all trying to get to England, but it is not true. We only go there to buy things like PG Tips to sell back here. We prefer to live in Ghana, but we still like drinking tea!"

"Roofing tiles," said YY, "how do they sell them?"

In front of us a minivan pulled abruptly out. Wisdom blasted the horn, hit the brakes, and swerved. He rolled down his window when we were level with the van and shouted out, "You are not correct! You are a foolish man!" The maroon Toyota caught up, but I couldn't see who was inside it because the windows were tinted.

I noticed the minivan had written on it NO TIME TO DIE

in capital letters. I agreed. It was an excellent motto. Starting with memorizing the number plate of the Toyota, GR598 XL, I was going to do everything I could to stay very much alive.

"What kind of roofing tiles?" asked YY.

"Imported ones, very durable."

"I am building a house in my village on my auntie's plot, and I want economical tiles for the roof."

"If you look at the roofs of all the Goil filling stations, they are using these tiles. Then you will know if you will like your house to look like that," said Wisdom.

YY grinned and looked out of the windows with determination. I watched the Toyota—still behind us. The official grunted and adjusted his position. A kid younger than me threw a set of newspapers in through the driver's window, collected a note from Wisdom, and raced alongside the car with change. The newspaper headlines read: DAILY GRAPHIC: FLUSHED OUT! AMA CLEARS STREETS OF HAWKERS.

For a while it was hard to keep up my surveillance, because we kept weaving away from the road edge. You see, the road had no pavements. That meant everyone walked in the street. And even though it was only just starting to get light, there were a lot of people out walking. Wisdom had to keep swerving to avoid killing someone. I shifted so that I could glance behind.

"Ah, I hope you are comfortable," said Wisdom. "Our roads are still under construction."

I made a mental note to be even less obvious.

YY grinned. "Ghana, Ghana," he said, shaking his head in a fond way. He peeled off his white police gloves and wiped the sweat from his forehead on them. "Sweet Ghana."

Suddenly Wisdom swung over to avoid a particularly large pothole. The Land Rover caught the edge of it and sent a shower of brown water over a fat lady in starchy pink lace. A taxi swerved in front of us, beeping. A man leaned out of its window shouting, "Circle, circle." The official woke up and the lace lady shook her fist at Wisdom. Through the side mirror I saw her step out into the road, forcing the Toyota to slow down. She started waving her arms at all the traffic.

"Why are there so many people in the street?" I said.

"Drop me off at the residences," said the official. "I don't need to go all the bloody way to Cape Coast. You take the boy. Just bring me the petrol receipts and make sure he's signed for."

"That woman was too fat, she could not move quickly," explained Wisdom.

"Yes sir," said YY.

"I mean, where are they all going?" I said. "Or is walking a popular pastime?"

"Are you some kind of smart aleck or what?" snarled the official at me, and then he turned to YY. "Is there anything else? Because I'm tired, and overworked, and now I've got to put up with smart alecks who arrive at obnoxious hours. God! Obnoxious just about sums everything bloody up."

I agreed. Obnoxious was a good summing-up word.

"Just something small, please, Mr. Toseland, sir. I am coming from Nsawam yesterday; I have been detailed to serve you in my line of duty, but I am paying for the transport and lodging myself. I will manage whatever you can give," said YY.

"Aha! They are going to work or the market maybe," said Wisdom, trying to lighten the mood. "In Ghana we like to get up early to enjoy life and also because it is not too hot in the morning."

"Too bloody hot all the time and too bloody early," said the official. He ran a finger round the inside of his tight blue collar and pushed back his thinning hair over his pink bald forehead.

You know, I figured just from looking at him that he probably rationed himself to the one joke a year he found in his Christmas cracker.

We turned off the main road, past a sign that read: *God Is Able carpenters ahead—stop here for your wall wardrobes, all sizes of shelves and fitted cabinets.* YY sighed. "I'm not really ready for the finishing yet."

The fat lady had helped me. I was sorry about her ruined outfit, but she'd stopped the Toyota. All that arm-waving had allowed a tide of people to flood across the road. Through the mirror I could see it marooned, honking its horn and gesticulating out of its windows behind a stream of people.

I breathed deeply and wiped the sweat from my hands on my jeans. YY picked up the newspaper and read: "*Teach*

Pupils in Their Mother Tongue . . . if a Ghanaian language were to replace English, Dr. Nana Frimpong-Aponsahmensah would choose Twi, because it is the most widely spoken in the country. . . ."

"Oh!" said Wisdom. "These Ashanti people!"

The Land Rover reached traffic lights, took a right past a post office with bright red PO boxes covering its outside wall, and then we were alone on a wide leafy street in what looked like a posh part of Accra. The sun was rising and the road ahead was striped with thick yellow light.

Wisdom turned in at a gate that had rolls of barbed wire over the top. It wasn't all that secure, not much more than HMP Broadmoor prison. A uniformed security man peered through the window of a sentry post. Then he came out to open up. The official, Mr. Toseland, got down and dismissed us with a flick of his wrist. Behind the gates I glimpsed a lush garden with sprinklers and palm trees.

Wisdom backed up. I wiped a trickle of sweat off the side of my face.

"He never gave me my transport," said YY.

"Ah, this our man, he likes to complain and likes to keep us waiting," said Wisdom. "He goes to his parties, drinks too much, and forgets we have to get home too—ah, but he cannot give money away easily. Oh! Ah! We will have to help him." He pulled a wad of notes out of his pocket, counted out five, and gave them to YY. "I will get extra receipts from the filling station and we will help him like that."

After Mr. Toseland had gone, the atmosphere in the

Land Rover got almost frisky. YY chatted about his building and Wisdom delivered enough information, like: "Aha! This area is called Cantonments. It is where the colonial masters lived and now all the diplomats live here. It is a very rich area and we are very proud of it—although some Ghanaians who think they are better than others live here too, like that thief, the Minister for Energy, Justice H.T. Adipuigah. Can you believe he wanted to turn all our rain forests into barbecue charcoal!"

Cantonments looked paranoid to me—high walls and fancy railings topped by jagged spikes, boxes on gates which read things like: *Securicom Alarm System; Golden Panther Protection Unit; Safe Tec Surveillance*. Even the trees had been trimmed and chopped so that offending branches didn't stick into anybody's space. Their nice big houses were no better off for sidewalks either. Instead, clipped lawns edged the walls and sloped down to dangerously deep storm gutters, through which four feet of swilling water enclosed the residences like a medieval moat.

We passed a big advert that read:

• MASSIGUARD •

Built-to-protect collapsible security grilles, tougher, heavier, very dependable. Razor-ripper wire, slasher-sharp fences, chain link and electric coils— we make your security our problem.

It looked to me as if diplomats lived here under siege from the outside world. I thought of Arrowsmith House and the walkways into Tuffley estate. I guess life is dangerous everywhere. There are always others who want what you've got. Right now, out there, there were people who wanted what I'd got.

I slid the rucksack off my back and furtively stuck my hand inside, just to reassure myself. YY glanced at me, so I pulled out my phone. I was being very careful. Only Ashley knew for sure I'd got the diary.

The phone screen lit up and read: *searching*. For a minute I was worried. Was the chip on roaming? At the airport it hadn't picked up a local signal. Then it cued into Spacefon. Almost immediately it buzzed and a text message came through: *So wots GH like mush? Gotta b beta dan SGCCCH! Txt bac so no u safe—A.*

A wave of relief swept over me and, suddenly, I missed Ashley like crazy. If only he'd been there to talk to. What would he have said about the Toyota? I could almost hear him: "Right, firstly you gotta figure out their next move. Nextly you gotta be a move ahead. Lastly you gotta anticipate the surprise element. It's a three-point plan, mush. Take up playing chess and stay ahead, Fred."

So what would be their next move? If you're tailing someone and you lose them—what do you do? It depends if you know where they're going. If you do, you speed ahead and lie in wait.

I glanced out of the window: taxis, carts, BMWs, people

148

weaving in between. We'd turned back onto the same busy road we'd branched from. There was Mohammed's Auto Electrical shop with the sloping telephone pole and the Amansi Ventures yellow billboard by the roundabout.

"Which way to Cape Coast?" I asked.

"Ah, we must first pass the ring road and get to Kwame Nkrumah Circle. Aha! You should know that Kwame Nkrumah was the greatest leader in the whole of history. He led our homeland Ghana to independence, he had a vision for Africa that—"

A 4x4 honked and Wisdom waved it on.

"How many different routes are there to Cape Coast?"

"Ah, sadly there is only one road—that is because we are still developing. It is not a good road, and that is because some of our politicians are greedy men—not all, you understand, but there are a few and they spend all the money for tarmacadam on their fat girlfriends. Take Justice H.T. Adipuigah, for example. He was the opposite to Nkrumah. He was supposed to . . . Oh! I cannot repeat it. . . . Oh! Such a disgrace—and his mother is one of my countrymen too. Ah!"

A Leyland tipper-truck with sand trickling from the back overtook, forcing us to climb onto the dirt shoulder. I checked the side mirror. Yep, we'd lost the Toyota.

"Look, a Goil filling station!" said YY. "But you cannot see the roof. Is it that blue color?"

"You can get it in any color-oh," said Wisdom.

"So there is only one road?"

"Yes. It is a very beautiful road. You will see the coast. In Ghana we are very lucky to have a wonderful coast and a big fishing industry. . . ."

So if they knew where I was going, they'd hit the coast road and lie in wait. I could almost hear Ashley say, "Right, now that tells us something too. If they know where you're going, it shows that they have been informed accurately by someone. That's logic. So to find out exactly who the someone is, you gotta make a list of all the people who knew you were going to Cape Coast and work through it. Process of elimination, my dear Zacson."

I made the list. This is what I got:

Ms. Shaw
Ashley
Bernard
Marion
Raphael
Fidelis
[Maggot & co] (?) (probably not, 'cause they couldn't
even remember the school address when it came to
letter-writing in English)
the Judge
the missionaries
the British High Commission
Wisdom
YY

After that it got a bit hazy. I mean, did the teachers or SGCCCH care workers actually know my exact destination?

We pulled up at traffic lights next to a huge building called Gold House. Three kids waving squeegees rushed out to clean the windshield, and a beggar limped over on his crutches.

Wisdom rolled down the window. "You are a lazy man. You have found the money for crutches and the time to beg. You should go to the handicraft center and earn a decent living, working like everyone else. But no, you want, instead, to beg at the junction and make our country look useless. Shame on you. Even these small boys work harder." He gave the kids some money and bought a sachet of water from a girl crying, "Pure water, pure water."

"Even lazy men must chop," said YY, and gave the beggar a coin. "I am lucky to have a good job protecting the people of Ghana and two reliable legs to do the work with, and I am building a house for my children to live in—but this man will always be limping."

"Gold House," I muttered. I thought of the gold and Bartholomew, and wondered if Ghana still had any.

"Aha! Gold House is the HQ of Ashanti Gold Fields; it was the first gold-mining company in all of West Africa to be listed on the New York Stock Exchange and that is because Ghana produces the purest . . ."

Yep, the gold. I wondered what Pops would have made of Ghana. Would he have liked it? Would he have felt that he'd come home? I stared hard out of the window to see if there was anything out there that made me feel I'd come home.

Here is what I saw:

Animals—chickens, dogs (not so many), goats, sheep (at first I thought they were goats and the goats were a kind of small antelope—duh!), cows with lumps like camels, and lizards.

Stuff—piled up along the side of the road: baskets, carvings, cane-work furniture, and one huge red velvet three-piece suite.

Other stuff—billboards, container stores, kiosks, all crammed with tinned milk, tomato paste, mosquito coils, phone cards, Coca-Cola, sardines, candles, bread, eggs, and ironing boards.

Beyond that was wasteland where green shrubs struggled to grow; and farther off still were rooftops and dust, and the walls of half-finished buildings with iron rods sticking out from them; and in the far distance dirt tracks, and still more walls; so that the whole city seemed to disappear into some giant construction site where it looked like someone was building a sprawling shopping center in dusty concrete, and all the things to stock it with had arrived ahead of time and were stacked for sale on the roadside.

But farthest of all, beyond everything else, were the vast white-hot skies of Africa.

As I gazed into the dusty distance thinking of Pops and his dreams, of my life without him, something sharp and painful seemed to crack inside me. I was the last descendant of the Lost Prince. It was three hundred years since he had left this continent. I cupped the immense sky above the city in my hand. This was the same sky that had been there in Bartholomew's time. Africa didn't feel much like home to me, but then nowhere felt like home since Pops had died. . . . Maybe home is as much about people as places. But, Pops, you *are* home, I whispered to him. Wherever I am, you are too. I'll get your gold and I'll sue the whole British nation for taking Bartholomew away from *his* home, because a home is precious. It is where you belong, and if you have it and then you lose it, you could spend eternity searching to find it again.

I dragged my eyes away from the window and that sharp something stopped cracking. I thought about food instead, and then I noticed that the color of that vast sky was very like the color magnolia.

Move Number Two

Macarthy Hill filling station was the last outpost for supplies before the police barrier and the open road. We spent a long time there. Wisdom had to eat and YY said he didn't mind if he did too. We sat down on white chairs in a shady fore-court in front of a spot painted in Guinness colors. In front of us there was a huge billboard of Michael Power diving into an outsize pint of Guinness. Wisdom explained, "That is because they sell Guinness here." Papery bougainvillea leaves rustled, and I could smell something frying and wood smoke. Boy, was I going to eat!

When I saw the huge gray balls of kenke, and the fish fried with their eyes in and heads on, I didn't feel so hungry. Wisdom must have guessed 'cause he laughed, and after telling me that, "Aha! Kenke was the food of the Ga peoples who had fished and farmed the coastal plains and savagely resisted the British and the Ashanti nations—and all of them grew strong on kenke, which was made from fermented maize dough and cooked in corn leaf," he ordered me chicken and chips.

It was a good job I ate them before I saw the Toyota.

Suddenly I felt sick. There was GR598 XL, neatly parked at the side of the Shell shop under an almond tree. I tried hard not to stare. YY thought I was looking for the waiter and called him over. "What mineral do you take?" said the man as he wiped the table with something that smelled like kerosene.

"I'm fine," I said, knowing I was not.

"You must take, Ghana is a very hot country and you must drink plenty," said YY. "Bring me Fanta—cold one," he added to the waiter. And then he put his hand into the side bowl of water to wash off the kenke that had stuck to his fingers. "Fingers were invented before forks," he said, grinning.

So Ashley was right. Someone out there knew exactly where I was going. What were they up to? Were they going to ambush us?

Almost as if he could sense what I was thinking, Wisdom said, "We had better get moving. There are armed robbers on the road after dark and plenty of drivers who don't have proper headlights."

"Not so," said YY. "The Ghana Police Force have caught all of the armed robbers—who were Nigerians, by the way, and not from our country—and anyway you have me with you, so you are very safe."

I glanced again at the Toyota and I was pretty sure that from behind the tinted window someone was looking at us through binoculars. Instinctively I gripped my rucksack. I reran through the list in my head and started the process of elimination:

Ms. Shaw

~~*Ashley*~~

~~*Bernard*~~

~~*Marion*~~

~~*Raphael*~~

Fidelis

~~*[Maggot & co] (?) (probably not 'cause they couldn't even remember the school address when it came to letter-writing in English)*~~

the Judge

the missionaries

the British High Commission

~~*Wisdom*~~

~~*YY*~~

(I was pretty sure it couldn't be Wisdom or YY, because they had already had all the time and opportunity to take my rucksack off me. Also I'd decided I liked them, but I only gave them a single strikethrough because I didn't know them that well.)

I mentally put the list in order.

Fidelis

Ms. Shaw

the Judge

the missionaries

the High Commissioner's man (Toseland)

I wasn't too sure about the High Commissioner's man because it struck me that he:

1) represented the British interests
2) knew where I was going
3) was obnoxious
4) might have been instructed by *them* to get the diary and stop any chance of a compensation court case
5) had decided NOT to come with us and might therefore be waiting ahead of us somewhere so that we'd be sandwiched
6) hadn't come with us because he knew we'd be held up.

So I shifted him up to second place.

Wisdom paid and we went back to the car. Suddenly he stopped. "Eh! Did you leave your door open, Zac?"

"What?"

The back door of the Land Rover was slightly ajar. YY straightened up and, holding me aside, opened it. After lifting the cloth cover off the yams, plantain, garden eggs, okra, oranges, and paw paws, and then opening the cool box to check the iced water, he said, "Everything is correct, nobody has touched anything— but you can't be too careful, Ghana is not like before, when you could sleep in your house with the doors open. We are lucky, we could have lost everything—

these thieves will steal the slippers from your feet. Next time, you, Zac Baxter, be more careful."

"It wasn't me," I said.

"It's okay—it's okay," said Wisdom.

But it was not okay. I hadn't left the back door open. I'm not stupid. In the middle of that tropical heat, that old cold feeling was back. I didn't need to see the orange glow on frozen tarmac. Did I?

No.

Once safely inside the Land Rover, I locked my door. I watched the side mirror. *They* were out there behind the steering wheel of a Toyota with tinted windows, out there planning something that I didn't want to be a part of. Already they were two moves ahead, they'd got my cases, searched my Land Rover, and now—out there—I knew they were discussing move number three: how best to get me.

4×4

We passed the police barrier where we waited in a queue, passed the Liberian refugee camp, which Wisdom pointed out, passed Kasoa, passed the long-distance taxi ranks, the last half-finished building, the last game of draughts under the last mango tree, and we were alone on the Cape Coast road. Wisdom drove slowly. He explained, "The Tro-tro drivers chew cola nut to stay awake and earn more. They drive their vans too fast, to do two trips in a day. They overtake on the wrong side to save time. All this makes this road very dangerous. Ah, poverty is a great evil in our country. It forces people to do things that they don't want to. We will drive slowly. We want to arrive alive, eh, Zac Baxter!"

I nodded. Arriving alive was definitely one of my preferred choices. I didn't mention it to Wisdom, but it wasn't the Tro-tros that worried me, although it began with a T all right.

The Cape Coast road from Accra to Winneba and beyond was unusual. I didn't have much experience of

African roads in general to compare it with, but it was different. I can say that.

We had a four-hour drive before us. Four hours of what? The safety of Accra behind, the uncertainty of the road ahead—anything could happen. Africa is a big place. Did you know you can fit the whole of Europe and India and the USA into it in one go and still have space left? On the map I had, the distance from Accra to Cape Coast was about four inches. I positioned myself near the door. I was going to give myself the best chance.

A ribbon of tarmac stretched out ahead and merged into dust. From time to time we swerved onto the wrong side to avoid potholes. Dusty banks of grass rose on either side. On the right was the rain forest, massive trees with brilliant climbers. From beneath them a shape would sometimes spring out to flag us down, a cloud of birds would rise vertically, my heart would start thumping—until I saw it was just a leather-sandaled old man hoping for a lift. On the left, beyond a fringe of palm trees, the Atlantic Ocean bashed down on holiday brochure beaches. Above everything the vast sky scorched on.

For a while we passed things for sale on the roadside: a hunter flourishing the carcass of a duiker; women holding up baskets of tomatoes piled in towers, and children who tried to wave to us to buy the tomatoes; signs that read: *Tomorrow Be Tomorrow* BLOCK FACTORY—*get your hollow design and quality solid blocks here guaranteed.* And YY would say, "Yes, I need design blocks for my garden walls. I like the Gye Nyame ones."

But soon there was nothing except the occasional twisted wreck of an old car.

Nothing? Nope, we were not alone. Just like before when we left the airport, there was a car following. It stayed a long way behind, so I couldn't be sure it was the Toyota, but I was pretty certain; the exact distance it maintained was a dead giveaway. My palms started to sweat. I wondered how they'd stage it. A blockade up ahead? The friendly offer of help from behind? And if that didn't work?

I tied my shoelaces up tight in case I'd have to run for it. I wondered how far I could run in this heat and where I'd run to. I got out my coast plan. I put my rucksack on. Both shoulders. I needed to find out where we were. I questioned Wisdom.

"Where are we?"

"Aha! We are approaching the stool lands of the Acron peoples. In the seventeenth century they were sandwiched between the Agona and the Fante, both allies of the British, and they wanted to build a . . ."

I vaguely wondered if Wisdom had ever considered taking up a different career.

"A fort, of course . . ."

I wondered if it was one of the slave forts marked on my map—if so, I could track exactly where we were. "Has it got a name?"

"Aha! It is Fort Leydsaamheid, which means patience. It was built by the Dutch in 1698, who also hated the British. Now the Dutch . . ."

I looked for the first or second castle sign after Accra on my map, and found Fort Good Hope at Senya Beraku, and, yes, Fort Leydsaamheid at Apam. There was one track to the fort from the coast road. Nothing else.

"Ah, now you need to know, in November alone of 1705, Dutch ships loaded more than nine hundred slaves from Fort Patience. . . ."

I was not sure if I really did need to know that, but Wisdom seemed to like telling me, so I said, "Interesting." I thought of slave ships and castles and dungeons, and I thought of Bartholomew. I suppose up until then I'd never really considered how the slave trade was organized. Suddenly it was all too obvious: different local clans selling off their neighboring local enemies to the Dutch, who exploited one group, while the British exploited the other . . . competition . . . wealth . . . profit . . . with continual fighting, capture, and slavery for the locals. Only the Europeans left Africa laughing.

I ticked off the fort at Apam and checked the mirror. The car was still there. Still maintaining that particular distance, almost out of sight but not quite—where you can't see the make, you can't see the number. Every time you curl a corner it ducks out of view. But it hasn't gone.

On the left we passed a break in the foliage. Someone had tried a bit of farming. There were ridges of red earth and spindly cassava stems. It must have been a pretty thankless task, and the farmer must have thought so too, because about half a mile farther on was a small shack and a pile of old car tires over which was a sign: *Try Anything Once Vulcanizers*. A chubby kid about my age waved happily at us as we passed.

"If we get a flat tire we will be okay," YY said, laughing. "But better watch out he didn't put nails on the road!"

"Ah, you think like a policeman, always suspecting a crime," said Wisdom. "They are only trying to make a living."

I was still wondering what exactly a Vulcanizer was. Sounded to me like a cross between Superman and vampires; still, if they had sprinkled nails on the road, I sure hoped the Toyota would pop one. I checked my map. If we did get a puncture, where would I run to?

Between the two inches that separated Apam and the next town coming up, Mankessim, there wasn't much. On my map there was a red road, two turnoffs that led to nowhere on the coast, a palm tree, and an umbrella. The legend said that the umbrella meant Festive Town, but it didn't say anything about the palm tree. On this stretch, the road veered away from the coast, crossed one river and a yellow circle before the shoreline swept round to meet it again at a place called Saltpond. It was on this section I figured they would make a move.

It was about time for my three-point plan.

I stared out of the window, thinking about it. My hands

were sticky. Sweat was trickling into my eyes. The map was getting soggy and offered me no ideas. Dust from the open window rasped against my face. I can't say that I was feeling inspired.

My three-point plan:

1) I'd run. If for any reason between now and Saltpond we stopped, I'd yank the car door open and be gone. I'd hide in the long grass, and the comment about nails on the road had given me an idea.
2) I'd hole up. If they lurked around, I'd wait till dark—they'd have to sleep at some point.
3) I'd puncture their tires. I wouldn't even have to puncture them. I was quite an expert at letting air out of tires.

What I'd do after that, I hadn't worked out. Still, grounding them would make me a whole lot safer. For some reason I didn't worry about what Wisdom or YY would do, or if YY'd get into trouble for losing me. I'm glad now I didn't have to put my plan into action. Good jobs are not easy to get in Ghana, and if he'd lost his, he'd never have been able to get his house finished—and that was his dream. Everybody needs something to keep them going.

No, they did not ambush us. We drove all the way to Saltpond without even slowing, and the Toyota followed. We overtook a lorry with huge tree trunks roped to its trailer. We dodged an oncoming State Transport Corporation bus, which drove in the middle of the road and forced us to the side. We swerved to avoid a broken-down truck on a blind corner—and that was as dangerous as it got. I spent a miserable two hours gripping the back of the seat in front of me and sweating.

I suppose I was glad. I could imagine Ash laughing. "So, Joe, if they didn't attack, it means three things. One, they don't know you have the diary; two, they do know but they have another plan; three, they messed up."

To the left, in silhouette against the sea, framed by palms, was the ruined outline of another fort, its white walls blackened by sea damp and mold. I checked the coast plan. "That fort?"

"Ahh! Now that is Fort Amsterdam. It is sometimes called Fort Abandze, and it was built by the . . ."

"Dutch?"

"No, British. Ah, now when you compare the Dutch to the British in the terms of slave-trading . . ."

I switched off. Wisdom lived up to his name so well, it got irritating. I consulted the map. "We're at Kormantse then."

"Ah yes, Kormanste is the modern way to say Cormantin. That hill there," he pointed to the right, "is the Cormantin hill where this village put up a good fight against the white man—but sadly they lost, so this fort supplied the West with the toughest fellows. . . . In 1661 it was transferred to the Royal African Company and it became the HQ of the English on the Gold Coast. . . ."

So this was Cormantin, this small hill with its few jumbled houses and dusty tracks. I thought of Pops and the Cormantin Club, of all the Cormantins sold from the Slave Coast; how from this one village, that had resisted capture, a movement of revolt had sprung, until all slaves were proud to call themselves Cormantin.

"Would you like to see the fort?" said Wisdom.

Suddenly that seemed a good idea. I mean, I did want to see it, but I also wanted to get off the road and lose that car. I checked the map.

We pulled off the main road where a sign said: *Abandze Fort*, with an arrow that pointed to the coast. The Toyota was out of view. I let go of the chair back in front of me and wiped my sticky palms on my jeans again. Looked like getting one step ahead was not going to be too difficult.

"You know, Zac Baxter," said Wisdom, "I am enjoying driving you to Cape Coast. I should have gone to Legon University to study history, but my father died and I had six brothers and sisters to take care of, so I could not complete. I wanted to have my own company and drive a tourist bus, but it was not to be. Well, I must not complain, because here I am, the driver of a very sturdy Land Rover, and you are a passenger from over who is interested in my country. . . ."

We parked up under a huge shade tree. The sea crashed

in front of us and the spray sparkled in the afternoon sun. Down that perfect beach there was not a person, ice-cream van, deck chair, or beach hut—just shimmering miles of paradise. Beside us, the fort rose dark and gloomy. It perched on a headland where one solitary palm tree battered its fronds on the blackened stone of the southern bastion. A crowd of little kids collected around the Land Rover. They tapped on the windows and pulled silly faces at me through the glass. I pulled some back and they giggled.

"We can alight," said YY, "and you can view the fort."

We all climbed the long flight of steps up to the summit of the headland: Wisdom, YY, the little kids, and me. A custodian showed us around. Apart from the staggering view, it wasn't much: damp salty air, a few ruined walls, the smell of mold and bats, one window repaired by an African-American charity, weeds, broken gutters, and neglect. There were two interesting things though. Firstly, Wisdom said, "Look, there is the Door of No Return." I jumped. I mean I wasn't somehow expecting it to show up at Abandze Fort.

"Door of No Return?" I said.

"Ah, yes, all the forts and castles have the Door of No Return. It is through that door they shipped out the slaves."

I nodded, trying to take that in. So there was more than one Door of No Return. I imagined a long line of doors, a bit like in *Monsters, Inc.*, all leading to some weird unknown place.

We signed the visitors' book. That was when I discovered

the other funny thing. I noticed that the last name in it was Raphael Dery of London, UK, dated March 15.

Was that my Raphael? He'd said he had contacts at Cabo Corso. He'd said he'd set something up if things went badly for me. I mean, it could have been him. But I didn't remember him telling me of any trip to Ghana, and the date was before Easter, before SGCCCH, before I'd visited Uncle Fidelis.

Maybe it was a different Raphael. Wisdom saw me staring at the entry. "Ah, sadly we do not have many visitors to Ghana. No one comes here. It is just as well I didn't set up a tourist bus; maybe by now I would be down broken."

"These walls are very solid," said YY. "It must have been very costive to build."

The place was oppressive, and I was happy to climb back down the steps again into the balmy air of Abandze seafront. Before we climbed into the Land Rover, YY gave the kids some oranges. Smiling, they waved us off.

I was not so happy to see the Toyota, though, parked up on the roadside on the outskirts of Kormanste.

300 Miles and 300 Years

I was too tired to panic any more. Instead, a dogged kind of vigilance took over and I started operating on auto-alert. The Toyota pulled out behind us, but it kept a respectful distance, and slowly sank far behind. I ticked off the fort at Kormantse. We were three inches along the map from Accra, and Cape Coast was the next-but-one place coming up. I double-checked with Wisdom.

"What is the next fort?"

"Aha! Yes! Now that will be Fort William at Anomabu. . . ."

"That must be British."

"Ah, no. That one is Dutch."

It was a bit confusing. Much later I learned that the Europeans were constantly fighting over the forts. They changed hands and names so often it would make you dizzy. Take Fort William, for example. It changed owners four times, from the Dutch to the Swedes, to the Danes, back to the Dutch, and only finally became British when the Dutch moved west.

Boy, I'm beginning to sound like Wisdom! But you see, this open road was steering a course along a coast littered with ruins of the past. It was like driving through a history textbook. You'd have to be stupid not to be interested.

"How many forts are there?" I asked Wisdom, because it struck me that I'd never actually seen so many forts and castles all together before.

"Aha! There used to be fifty: Fort Appolonia, Fort St. Anthony, Fort Groot Friedrichsburg, Fort Metal Cross . . ."

"*Okay, okay,* allow it," I said, as we passed two huge termite hills. "I believe you. How long is the coast then?"

"Aha! Nearly three hundred miles, from Aflao to the Ivorian border. There is no coast in all of Africa as famous as the Gold Coast. . . ."

"Infamous, you mean." Because boy, that meant there was a slave-trading fort every six miles. You'd have thought there wouldn't have been enough slaves to fill them.

At a tiny village motor park, we pulled in to refuel. The fuel pump looked like it belonged in a museum and the car workshop boasted: *Hope for Future Generations Engine Works.* A cheerful greasy-overalled mechanic served us and stroked the Land Rover lovingly. "Eh-ye, I like your car-oh," he said. "The Land Rover has a strong engine; I am fitting my car with one too." He pointed at a vehicle on a concrete ramp. "I am the owner," he said proudly.

The Toyota did not pass us. I got out and stood in the shade of a mango tree, while the mechanic served a round-faced man on a motorbike and checked our oil and water. Allowing two minutes, I started timing—just to see how long it would take the Toyota to overtake us: thirty seconds, forty, fifty? No. On to the next minute. Nothing. An Opel estate taxi passed and then a VW Golf. I timed another minute, and got a pickup with a goat roped down in the back, and a new Audi being driven fast by a flashy guy in sunglasses, but no Toyota. It wasn't anywhere. Had it turned off? Do not congratulate yourself for guessing the answer.

The mechanic slammed the hood down and washed the windshield. He beamed happily at us and filled in three different receipts for Wisdom, and then we left.

"Have we reached Fort William yet?" I asked. You see, I was suddenly worried that I might mix up Cape Coast Castle with one of the others. I needed to be sure I went back through the right Door of No Return.

"Long passed, we are nearly through Anomabu. Aha! It's got a famous beach, but don't swim there."

Up until then I hadn't considered swimming. But hey—you never know—I might have to swim for it! I ticked off Anomabu Fort. By my calculation, Cape Coast Castle had to be the next fort coming up.

"Why not?"

"Ahh, the surf has got tricks. In the old days, the English Royal African Company licensed ship captains at ten percent to slave trade here. The Ten Percenters during one spring alone took 30,141 slaves from Anomabu. They were very lax and slaves had the chance to fling themselves into the foam trying to escape. Many didn't survive. The undercurrent pulls you out to sea. If you float for long enough you arrive back on Anomabu beach. If you fight, you get too exhausted. Don't fight the surf, especially at Anomabu."

"Thanks for telling me." That's what knowledge can do for you. It's the difference between life and death.

"Anything else I should know?"

"Aha, yes, any fisherman can tell you, never jump out of a canoe in the surf to the leeward side. The boat will turn and strike you under and then you'll have to deal with the injuries, too. A broken back is not a good start to surf-floating for half a day."

"I'll try to remember that, too," I said.

Twenty minutes later, the sun started to sink. It was directly ahead of us and we were blinded. I thought of Ashley. I could almost hear him giving out advice, "Right, mush, that means you are heading due west and it is nearly six o'clock, Jock. You can always read direction from a wristwatch. You point the hour hand at the sun. It's like a sundial but backward. It's useful to know these things if you have to go across country on your own, Joan. Take your bearings and make sure you locate a good source of drinking water. Moss always grows on the north side of trees and spiderwebs face south. You can survive for four weeks without food, Jude, but only four days without fluids."

Thanks, Ash, I muttered to myself. I didn't have the kind of wristwatch he meant. And I figured if there wasn't water I preferred Coke anyway.

The road widened and became a dual carriageway. On

one side we passed two old colonial houses with generous verandas, and a new place with brick cladding and arches. On the other there were trestle tables one after the other, loaded with stuff wrapped in blue plastic. Each table had a name painted on it. We passed tables: Vida, Evelyn, Agartha, Mabel, and Gifty. The tin roofs started, and the road developed a fringe of kiosks, and suddenly there were people—a carpenter carrying his saw on his head, guys like me in baseball caps and earphones (one of them had a Miami Dolphins T-shirt on too!), ladies in bright wax prints, schoolkids in cream and brown uniforms playing some kind of clapping game, girls in tight skirts—all on their way home, piling into yellow tooting taxis, flagging down minivans, shouting out greetings, waving, smiling, and I knew we were on the outskirts of Cape Coast.

Soon we turned right and took a dirt road toward the forest.

It was getting dark fast. The sun hovered like a burning red football over the horizon. The clouds turned pink, the edges of the sky sank into shadow, and I stared. I'd never really seen a sunset so bright and so close up before. Then the track twisted and the sun dipped behind the trees. Even though it was gone, the Toyota was still there. I could tell by the dust clouds swirling up far behind.

We passed through a small village. A little family was already sitting around on wooden stools outside their hut. Two men chatting, three kids: one with a baby on her knee, another carrying a little aluminium covered pot on his head. Their mum was pounding something. In front of her, over a charcoal fire, a huge blackened cauldron bubbled with something that smelled good. Yum! Supper. This is sad, but I began to think of coming home from school, helping Marion peel potatoes, and setting the table—funny the things you miss.

Then we arrived.

I was not sure what the word "Leprosarium" meant. I crossed my fingers, crossed my legs, crossed my eyes, and prayed it didn't mean what I thought it did. YY pulled on his white police gloves and stuck his nose deep into his uniform collar. Wisdom looked like he was holding his breath. He slammed on the brakes.

I uncrossed everything. It looked like God was asleep.

We bumped over a few more potholes. "This is as far as I go," said Wisdom. Now what was going to happen?

YY grinned at me. "I am not going to embarrass our-selves by signing you in, so please go straight—you will find the mission through those gates."

Wisdom added, "You see, from here YY and I return. We will lodge in Cape Coast and deliver the supplies. We leave for Accra first thing. But you take care, Zac Baxter, and we see you later." He smiled, but not with the same open teeth like before. Something was up. He looked kind of sorry for me, as if he'd like to say more but couldn't.

YY eased the door open. "Good-bye, Zac," he said. He stuck his hand out. As usual I hadn't thought of shaking hands. "Sorry," he added, his grin fading.

Gripping my rucksack, I stumbled forward through the gap and slammed the door. All around me was dark forest. A few birds chirped sadly. Sweet, thick, fermenting air hung heavy. I turned and hammered on the metal.

"Where do I go?" I looked back down the track to see if that Toyota was creeping up with its lights off.

Wisdom gestured farther on, while YY hung his head. In front of me were huge iron gates, and on them was written: *Cabo Corso Missionary Settlement and Leprosarium.*

Enter Badu

Once outside the Land Rover, a wave of humid air washed over me. There was nowhere to run; believe me, I looked. On every side towered tangled rain forest. The orange sky was streaked with gloomy clouds and it was getting dark. Fast.

Even though the sun was gone, the heat continued. I could feel my clothes sticking to me. Sweat trickled down my neck. Reluctantly, I turned toward the gates. Behind me the Land Rover waited, just long enough to see me sound the knocker, just long enough to see a small figure shamble forward and struggle with the locks. Then it turned and sped off, leaving a column of dust behind.

I kept as far away from the boy as I could. If I was right, touching him could be fatal. I waited until the gates were as wide as they would go and stepped in at the very edge. The boy struggled to close them. They were twelve feet tall and must have weighed a ton. I didn't offer to help. I clutched my rucksack, wiped sweat off my face, and tried to breathe sideways.

"I'm Badu," said the boy, and offered his hand. I ignored it.

"Please yourself," said Badu, "you don't have to come in. You can go out there." He pointed to the jungle beyond. "There's leopards out there, they've got an L and an E and a P and an R and an O and an S, and no Y, but they kill you a lot quicker." Then he turned his back on me and shuffled off into the darkness.

I held my bag tight. With a banging heart, I headed down a track toward a low building far away across a flat open area. It was the only building with a light on, so I figured someone might be in. Every now and then I paused to see if I could hear a car engine. I tried to remind myself of the reasons why I was there—the muggings, the deaths, the setups, the court case, the diary, the lost treasure, justice, compensation, Ashley's enthusiasm, Bernard's worried smile—but I was so hot I couldn't think straight. I tried to imagine Bartholomew in Africa, but somehow he didn't fit. I knew him better in the cold dormitories of Gloucester Center. I tried to convince myself that this was all part of my promise to Pops. But, I swear, none of it made sense.

Not even Pops.

The last ray of pink faded. The moon rose over the canopy of the forest and at its floor fireflies flickered. I think if I'd been feeling happier, I would have seen how beautiful it was. But right then everything seemed menacing.

Yellow moonshine, eerily bright, seeped onto the grass. From somewhere far away I could smell charcoal fires. A cockerel crowed and a distant car horn tooted. Sounds of a world just out there, just out of reach.

In front of me a vast space loomed. To my right, high buildings towered—the first of which had *JNR Staff BLK A* stenciled on it in white letters five feet high. Apart from those letters shining in the moonlight, everywhere was horribly dark. I strained my eyes to see if there was anyone around, but after a few minutes I figured the junior staff had been promoted to the senior blocks because the buildings were definitely empty. I passed JNR Staff BLK A, B, and C and was predicting the next two might be D and E when from the corner of my eye I saw Badu shuffling along a different path toward me again.

Badu was carrying a flashlight, but I quickened my pace anyway. Maybe there were blocks where the okay kids lived. Surely nobody would expect me to live with a leper?

Raphael should have told me. This was not the kind of surprise I liked. I thought about texting him right there and then, but I needed to save my batteries. Electricity didn't look like it was much of a big deal at Cabo Corso.

"You're gonna need all the friends you can get here," said Badu, catching up and offering me the flashlight.

I turned my back on him.

"What did you do, anyway?"

"Nothing."

Badu laughed. "You only come to this place when nobody else wants you. This is a place of no return."

I was beginning to get a little worried about this whole No Return thing. "I didn't do anything," I said.

"Where do you come from then, Mr. Didn't-do-anything?"

"England—Gloucester."

Only eighteen hours ago I'd stood in Terminal 3, Heathrow Airport. I'd been Zac Baxter, in search of buried treasure; Zac Baxter—whatever. But somehow that all felt like it had happened to someone else. Here in Ghana I was raw, a beginner all over again. Boy, I was a whole lot more than eighteen hours away from anything I knew.

"They can cure leprosy in England, can't they?"

"Guess so."

"You'd better bank on it if you ever get back." Badu lunged forward and deliberately laid his hand on my arm. Then he laughed.

I swallowed a scream and ran forward. I passed D, E, F, G, and H, and kept on running until I was gagging for breath. I stopped, drenched in sweat, bent down and pulled handfuls of grass; I scrubbed at my arm, pulled more grass and scrubbed again. I looked behind. Badu was standing there—a dark shape against the immense rain forest—laughing. Up ahead I heard a car door slam. I froze. I heard the unmistakeable rev of a Toyota engine.

Welcome to Cabo Corso.

Lesson Number One

BUNG 1 was probably half a mile from the gates: It just felt like ten. For some reason, I was approaching it from the back. It must have had a front entrance somewhere, but right then I wasn't in the mood for exploring. If the front garden was anything like the backyard though, I'd hazard a guess that the nearest home base was in Accra. I picked my way over broken concrete paving slabs, ducked under washing on a line, and could smell chickens—not the Kentucky Fried kind either. As I got nearer, I heard the hum of a generator.

It seemed kind of odd that nobody (Badu didn't count) had come out to receive me. Here I was, a grave robber, juvenile delinquent, on a weird community service plan, sent at taxpayers' expense; met by diplomats, armed police; educated by a driver, chased by criminals; in need of a rolled crust, deep pan, spicy chicken supreme with added toppings—and now nothing! I stopped for a moment to catch my appetite and look around. Apart from the bungalow, on my far right was a collection of broken-down buildings. A large collection. They could have been JNR Staff BLK J and K, but somehow I didn't think so. In the moonlight they looked like the ruins of a ghost town.

It was a good job I'd stopped. Silently out of the darkness bounded two shadows. They came straight at me.

Ice has got nothing on the way I froze.

Two meters away the dogs slithered to a halt. They leaned toward me, hackles raised, teeth bared. They were both huge. They started growling.

"Here, boy, nice doggy." I tried inching one foot forward.

The nearest dog leapt at me. His teeth, razor sharp, clicked to, just millimeters from my hand. I'd obviously got his name wrong. I thought about trying Rover or Fido or Prince or Caesar, but I didn't want to get it wrong a second time. Out of the darkness more dogs arrived. Cold sweat trickled somewhere down my back. My throat dried up.

By the time a light had flicked on outside the back door of the bungalow, ten dogs surrounded me. There were more, but that was all I wanted to count. At last, the figure of a large man stepped out toward me. "Down!" His voice was harsh and deep. Most of the dogs slunk away, but one zipped forward and ripped my rucksack. That was a mistake. Yelling "DOWN" again, the large man stooped and picked up a rock. The rock hit the dog on the leg. The dog squealed. The leg made a horrid cracking sound. It wasn't that I'd developed a man's-best-friend feeling for it or anything, but it sent a chill down my legs and I winced.

After that, even though the dog couldn't move, I

could—but not far. I got inside the bungalow, that was about it. I could tell at a glance I was already in trouble. I had to stand in the center of an open hall while the large man went and called others. They came in chatting carelessly, as if leprosy colonies and ferocious dogs were commonplace. They seated themselves around me in comfy chairs. In all there were four people. There was the large white man, who introduced himself as Father Bullingham; he could have easily passed for two people. It would have been nice to have imagined him as a gentle giant, but I've never believed in fairy stories. There was a husband and a wife who were introduced as Dr. and Mrs. Sniddon—they looked completely ordinary—and a bony-faced boy not much older than me. In fact, they all looked exactly like missionaries. For some reason though, I shuddered; there was something—a feeling—a tingling down my spine and a sudden dread that gripped my stomach.

"I'm Boss Boy," said the boy, standing up.

"Wow," I said.

"You call me 'Chief Boss Boy' every time you speak to me."

"Don't worry," I said, "I won't."

Boss Boy's mouth sagged a bit like he was trying to work out exactly how I'd managed to insult him. A sudden brain wave told me he might not be considering going on to sixth form.

Talking about school . . .

"You've got a lot to learn," said Father Bullingham,

"and you can start right now." Despite the coldness in my stomach, I think I smiled. I should have known better, after the dog incident.

Father Bullingham signaled Boss Boy to the only empty chair.

I stood on the gray terrazzo floor and waited.

Father Bullingham picked up a bowl of toffees from a side table, took a fistful, and passed them round to everyone except me.

Being polite, I waited.

"Like toffees?" Father Bullingham asked.

"Yep." I nodded. Like I said, I'd have preferred a pizza, but, hey! Toffees were okay.

Father Bullingham got up and went out of the room. He came back with a crate of Coca-Cola. On the way, he tipped all the rest of the toffees in the trash can.

"Like Coke?"

"No." I was thirsty, but not stupid.

Father Bullingham got up again and opened all the windows; he opened the door too, and passed the mosquito repellent to everyone—except me. I think I was beginning to get the lesson.

As Dr. and Mrs. Sniddon, Boss Boy, and Father Bullingham rubbed on the repellent, the room began to zing with mosquitoes. I began to zing with anger. I mean! I might be doing a community order, but this was taking liberties—even in the police station they'd fed me. . . .

"You see, God gives to those he loves." Father Bullingham

chewed his toffee and took a long swig of Coke. "God showers his favorites with riches. On Earth, as it is in Heaven."

What was this lesson called then? Next Time Use the Front Door? Father Bullingham Is God? You Better Make Sure You Do What I Say or I'll Starve You to Death? Was that why the Sniddons were playing along? I mean, why didn't they do something?

A mosquito bit me over my anklebone. It itched.

"But beware the wrath of God," Father Bullingham said sadly.

There was something in his voice that stopped me bending down to scratch the bite. A knot of fear started to tighten in my stomach.

"Here at Cabo Corso, you will see how God punishes sinners."

I'm not a hasty sort of person, but I decided I didn't like Father Bullingham.

"But—," said Mrs. Sniddon.

"Sssh." Dr. Sniddon laid a heavy hand on her arm. There was something about his heavy hand and his small head. I was sure I'd seen him before.

Another mosquito bit my other ankle.

Boss Boy looked at the trash can.

"This is a wonderful project." Mrs. Sniddon smiled at me. "We're going to rebuild this hospital and treat leprosy—"

"NO, madam! We will treat *lepers*." Father Bullingham had jumped to his feet. He thumped the table and pointed to a religious print by the door on which was written: *The Wages of Sin Are Death.* The Coke bottles rattled and Dr. Sniddon looked a bit alarmed.

I was thinking: What's going on? Why aren't they doing the usual stuff—you know: "Hello, Zac. Welcome to our humble abode. How was your journey? I expect you're a bit tired and hungry. We'll just sign you in, collect your passport—you know, for safekeeping. . . . Look, here's your room—cute wallpaper, huh? Okay, the rules: breakfast at seven, lunch at one—you've missed supper but we'll fix you a snack. Full induction is tomorrow—ask if you need anything. . . ."

"But surely . . . ," started Dr. Sniddon, as if he was going to object.

"Would you *dare* interfere with God's justice?" Father Bullingham slammed his Coke down.

The fear twisted into my chest. I'd stepped three thousand miles down the Prime Meridian to be with a complete nutter!

Then he smiled. (A horrible experience.) He pointed to another poster of two outsize hands clasped in prayer. Under them was written: *Repentance Is the Best Cure.* He smiled again (shudder) and nodded straight at me.

The guy was plainly cracked. I swallowed and looked through the open door to the space beyond. Was Badu still standing there, small against the rain forest? Was this what he'd meant about needing friends? I'm not a coward, but I was scared all right; my knees weren't shaking because I suddenly felt the urge to salsa. I tried to tilt my head into an Up Yours angle, first perfected by Maggot during away soccer matches; but even as I got my lower jaw into position I realized there was something phony about this whole little welcome committee. Father Bullingham wasn't nuts—he was an actor! And his character was called the Religious Fanatic. Someone had made a cunning plan called: "How to Receive Zac Baxter When He Arrives at Cabo Corso So as to Scare the Pants Off Him." I mean that poster! *Repentance Is the Best Cure.* (Was it some kind of obscure hint?) Even if it was—it was too cheesy to be true!

Suddenly somewhere at the other end of the bungalow I heard noises. I heard a door shut and the sound of heavy cases being dragged across a floor. A light flicked on. I saw the square of yellow on the yard outside. I heard a car door slam and then that same rev of a Toyota engine. I think I started to twitch.

"But I was trying to tell Zac about the work he'll be undertaking, the mission we're building, why he's here ...," said Mrs. Sniddon. I figured her character was called the Voice of Reason.

Uncle Fidelis had arrived. He was in this bungalow. He must know Father Bullingham!

"And the medical care we'll offer," continued Dr. Sniddon (Mr. Suck Up?). Yes, I *had* seen that small head before. Where?

"Down on your knees, boy, and pray for God's mercy," snapped Father Bullingham.

If Fidelis knew Father Bullingham, then FB must know him. . . .

"Down on your knees, boy."

If FB knew him, then they were both in it together. . . .

"DOWN."

Cheesy or not, I remembered the dog, and figured it wouldn't hurt to move my ankles a bit.

"May God bless you." Father Bullingham unwrapped another toffee.

Like I said, I'm not stupid.

"And you better call me 'Chief,'" added Boss Boy.

The New Block
and Other Blocks

At least I didn't have to sleep in the same block as Badu. I was taken to Room CCH/1 in the New Block and given a mat and a candle. The New Block was not one of the JNR Staff BLK alphabets, but it was just as dark. It was two stories of concrete floors and whitewashed walls. It still smelled of cement. After I'd bolted my door, I sat for a while trying to work it out.

Ashley had once told me about a book he'd read called: *Terror Tactics, Brainwashing, & Interrogation Techniques*. "It's all about breaking you, mush," he explained. "The aim is to create a feeling of madness, where you no longer trust reality. They search for the cracks in you and widen them. They make you feel they are the only ones who can make sense of the world; so you see, Lee, you do what they want, because that's the only sane thing left to do. They use tricks to confuse you like intimidation, humiliation, and starvation. From the very start they try to disorientate you—and somebody always volunteers to be your friend. If they try this on you, Zac, for real, hang on to simple ideas like brushing your teeth, and think of something worth living for. It's the only way—you gotta have a purpose. Remember that—right?"

I thought of Pops and his dream. I reminded myself of my promise to him. I brushed my teeth. But humiliation and starvation were already working. I lay there and thought of the evening meal at SGCCCH: fish fingers, mash and peas—that's how desperate I was. I thought of Boss Boy and his stupid sneering face. I imagined punching it. *Get a grip,* I told myself. *Think, analyze who and why and what . . .*

Who? And why? And what? Okay, first—if Father Bullingham was one of them, then Ashley was right about interrogation techniques; that toffee routine was classic. Next—the ordinary-looking Dr. and Mrs.? Were they in on it? Ordinary was suspicious: indifferent age, average height. Very suspicious. I checked my door was locked. What if Mrs. Sniddon was that woman? That's when I sat down and started to panic. You see, she could be! All those disguises! I'd walked into a trap. This was another setup. I started to swallow air. . . . There was somebody else in that bungalow too! Somebody who had arrived at the same time as me, in a Toyota, with a load of cases—my cases! That meant Enemies 1, 2, and 3 were all there—plus a giant-size sadistic lunatic!

Hang on to simple ideas. Hang on to a purpose. Get a grip. Use logic.

How could it be Uncle Fidelis? I must have made a

mistake. First of all, he was dead. And by my reckoning he'd been dead long enough to rule him out. Second, he was a stuffy old man who didn't want to go as far as Bristol, let alone Africa. But what about the blue tracksuit and the brown cap? That hadn't been a mistake. Maybe normal logic didn't work.

He *was* dead, wasn't he?

Suddenly I wasn't sure. Had he faked his own death? The article Ashley had shown me had said ". . . *the unidentified body . . .*" Maybe it *hadn't* been him; maybe all that time he'd been working for them. Uncle Unfaithful. The more I thought about it the more certain I became. Fidelis had double-crossed Pops. He knew everything there was to know. He'd nearly all the documents he needed. All he lacked was Bartholomew's diary—and the map. He'd probably told Raphael about this place. He'd set us all up.

With my fingers crossed, I emptied the rucksack. The translation glossary was pretty mangled, but *Chamo-me* was safe. For how long? Maybe right now they were searching my luggage. What would they do when they didn't find anything? Would they come here? I was shaking badly, so I lay down for a bit until the trembling stopped. I sent Raphael a text: *Arrived sumhow—ware did u dig dis plce up from d old testament? Was it Uncle Fidelis who tld u bout it? U c my baggage is gone n I think dis is another trap—uv got 2 get me out—still wrking on da map—z.*

Then I sent Ashley one: *Listen mush, we bin tricked think ICU1 an ff woman r here—ICU3 cud be uncle fidelis hang on*

4 pics 2 b sure—ps no luv 2 susie. Boy, how I wished Ashley were there. I imagined him thumping down beside me saying, "Right, mush, normal logic does work and you gotta use it. Either Fidelis is dead or he's not. You can't be both. Either he's after you or he isn't. Choose the worst scenario and make a plan, Stan."

I chose.

"So he's alive and well and out to get you. So why hasn't he got you yet? That is the question: to be got or not to be got? Hamlet, my dear Zacspeare."

I guessed I hadn't been "got" yet because they still needed me to show them the way to the treasure.

"Dead right, mush," said my imaginary Ashley, "and you will not be got so long as you don't hand over the diary or the map. They are your life insurance! Now what you need to do is translate the rest of the diary and find the clue, Sue. So I suggest you go to sleep and ask your subconscious some very tough questions. Like firstly, where is the map? Secondly, where is the map? Thirdly, where is the map? Until you get an answer."

I smiled a little and decided to take his advice.

Before I slept, I reread that one entry on the loose page from Bartholomew's diary, the one I'd memorized in the churchyard. I was hoping, praying, that that might help me figure it out. Suddenly I felt my life depended on it. "*. . . they told me the secret. I can't tell you, because I promised not to—until I die.*"

I'd heard those words before, hadn't I? Where had I?

If only I could crack it! ". . . until I die . . ." That was so typical of the Baxters—stubborn to the end. Just like Pops, even as he lay bleeding on the pavement, keeping on about the diaries.

In many ways I was very like him. I just hoped my end was a long way off.

Keeping On
About the Diaries

I suppose I should have worked on *Chamo-me* straightaway. If I had, this next section would have cheered me up. It's about the bond. It proves how right Pops was. Here it is.

Case for the Prosecution
Exhibit 01 Attached

Form MG 14
(CJ Act 1967, s. 9; MC Act 1980, ss. 5A(3) (a) and 5B; MC Rules 1981, r. 70)

EXTRACT: *From the alleged diary of Bartholomew Baktu Page eleven*

This exhibit (consisting of *case for the prosecution one (1) pamphlet written in Portuguese ———certified translation Lisbon University——verified against accounts of the Royal African Company——considered authentic. Professor Braithwaite, British Museum.* ~~page(s)~~ each page signed by me) is true to the best of my knowledge and I make it knowingly, if it is tendered in evidence, I shall be liable to prosecution if I have wilfully stated in it anything which I know to be false or do not believe to be true.

Signature *N/A——see subsection* Date *November 5th DC Hesketh*

I was standing in the middle of a flat open area, where the sea crashed beside me and a gigantic rain forest rose to my right. I looked back down that beach and saw in the distance the white towers of Cape Coast Castle. It was night, and I was afraid. In front of me stood Senhor Dias. I longed to run to him, but the guards held me back. He was reading from a paper. He uncurled it and read:

"I, King of the Mighty Baktu People, send fifteen of my finest sons, in the care of my Ambassador, Senhor Bartolomeu Dias the VII, descended of the Navigator and Overlord of Cabo Corso, to greet the British government agent, Mr. Gorman Fergus Stafford Durward, and Lord of the Castle of Carolusberg. With them I send fifteen thousand Dambas of the purest Gold Dust and a lock cut from the head of every Man, Woman, and Child of my people, so that the English shall know them by their shaved heads and not wage capture against them. All this gold I freely give as a gift in greetings.

"By this Bond, delivered unto ye by the same Ambassadors, I pledge the Land upon which ye have built your Castle to be deemed the property of your Crown. And by this Indenture, enclosed, sign over the said Parcel of Land and all such Structures that lie upon it. All this I exchange for my Dearest Son and Prince of my Kingdom, Bartholomew, also known as Nii Babila Tita Sakwaa Dzamaa of the Ga Stool Accession, named for the Queen Mother's delight, and Teki Kartu VIII of the Baktu Royal line and who is Best Beloved of the Baktu Peoples and for the Word of the English that Me and my Peoples shall be Honored by them. . . ."

One of the guards started laughing. I saw Akonor drop his hand to the long spear that stood beside him. "No," I whispered, and then stopped my mouth, because he was right. To laugh at the King's honor was something that must be punished by death. I must not put my hope before the honor of my people. And then I whispered, "Yes."

But Senhor Dias turned and laid his hand on Akonor's shoulder and held him with his eyes.

"Bring the gold," demanded the English lord.

"Not until you sign the bond," said Senhor Dias.

"Puh!" said the Englishman, but Senhor Dias stood forward with his quill and pushed the parchment toward him.

"There!" said the Englishman as he scratched on the bond. "Now the gold."

"Place your fingerprint beneath and write your name, then use your seal, for this is a binding document," insisted Senhor Dias.

With much disdain the Englishman printed the bond and drew from his bag the wax, which he heated a little from one of the flaming torches held by his men and dripped it onto the bond. Then he pressed his ring from off his right hand into the warmed wax upon the parchment.

"Thank you," said Senhor Dias, but I noticed that with his left hand he made the warning sign to my people, and all their hands fell onto the long spears which stood in ranks beside them.

"And now show me the gold," said the Englishman.

Senhor Dias motioned for Tendia and Gabriel to step forward. I smiled then, for Tendia is short and fat and very, very strong, yet he is forever smiling. As they stepped toward us, bent beneath the weight of the chest, which they dragged behind them on a small cart, Tendia wrinkled up his nose in the way that the old women do when they have noticed something that smells bad. Tendia fell on one knee dramatically and flipped back the top of the casket.

There, even in the dim moonlight, in the dull flame of the English torches, sparkled the yellow gold that I knew so well. How many times had I not panned the great Pra River and returned home with a twist of bright yellow tied inside my tunic. Yes, my people were rich in yellow gold, but the quantity I saw in that iron box would have taken a hundred and fifty boys more than ten years to pan.

The Englishman stepped forward, arms oustretched.

"No," Senhor Dias's voice rang out.

The Englishman stopped with a curse. "What! Do you still not trust my bond? You Spanish Cur!"

"Portuguese," murmured Senhor Dias. "Remember— Portuguese Cur."

There was a light in the eyes of the Englishman, and I saw my brothers gently lift their spears.

"Unchain the boy and let him stand forward," said Senhor Dias in the same mocking tone.

One of the guards undid my shackles then pushed me, and I stumbled.

"Stand off," demanded Senhor Dias. There was an edge in his voice.

The Englishman and the guards backed away from me. At this, Tendia stepped forward and placed my hands on the chest. "You turkey," he whispered, "you'll get us all killed." Then he started clucking like a guinea fowl.

"Tendia, Gabriel, go with Bartholomew to the water's edge, drag the chest, then walk back toward us," ordered Senhor Dias. He turned then and spoke to the

Englishman. "When they reach the water's edge the gold is yours and the boy ours. Do not try any treachery. Where the land ends and the seas begin, there must the bond be honored. Do you agree or not?"

"Puh!" said the Englishman again.

"These are the terms written here." Senhor Dias held up the paper. "Any treachery and the gold is forfeit. It is written thus. May I have your word?"

"Have it and be damned," cursed the Englishman, as if he was not used to being confronted so plainly.

I did as Uncle Senhor asked; I turned to face the great Atlantic Ocean and stepped out with my brothers toward it. The chest of gold was heavy, so heavy that even Tendia—who was the strongest of all my clan—sweated. Gabriel grunted with the effort, and I too used my strength to pull that chest. My heart was banging, and the sand shifted beneath my feet, until I reached the hard sand where the water swept the shores. There, just where the surf ended in its ripples of foam, we stopped. Then I ran. I ran as if I was chased by the leopard, back toward Akonor's arms. And as I ran it seemed to me that the stars exploded above me and the earth was lit up by their flames.

I turned. No. It was not the heavens. It was not the earth aflame. It was the guns of the English.

They were firing upon me and my brothers!

Mina

Sweating, I awoke to the sound of a football whistle. For a moment I wondered where I was, and if someone had scored a goal. Then I remembered.

Panic.

Outside I heard a radio on. "*. . . specially dedicated for the listening pleasure of our African-American cousins who are down here in Cape Coast for PANAFEST. . . . Let's welcome them with a little Kodjo Entwi. . . .*" Seeing as I'd slept in my clothes, it didn't take long to get up. I put the loose page into the diary and shoved everything into my back pocket. How was I going to play this? I was in a trap. Panic × 2. Think of simple things.

Okay, breakfast at seven.

Should I take my eggs scrambled or sunny-side up? "*. . . Yo cuzzes, this is yo ol' dog Lantei Quaarcopome celebrating da African Art and Culture Rock on Soundz Live from . . .*" Luckily, I was spared the difficult egg choice. 'Cause when I got to the restaurant section of the mission I realized it hadn't been built yet, so figuring that breakfast was only another of those repetitive daily things, I paid particular attention to my screwface-gangsta-walk-with-attitude and sauntered over toward where the music was coming from. All the time I was thinking: What if Mrs. Sniddon is the flat-faced woman? What if this is a trap? Think about simple things. Food. Eggs. Food. The sun shining through the palm trees. Food. What am I going to do?

About five kids had already collected in the center of the yard ("... *sweet sounds . . . from Rocky Dawuni . . .*"), and more were emerging from concrete BUNGs squared round an open compound.

In the center of them, Boss Boy was sitting on top of a pile of broken masonry. He was wearing a designer T-shirt and a pair of green army trousers. He was eating a sandwich and holding a transistor, which was tuned up to full blast. "*. . . kick off your charle-whatte and prepare for some smooth lovers' rock tonight at the Meet-Me-There at Oyster Bay on the Takoradi road. . . .*" I noticed that all the blocks in the pile had numbers scratched on the sides of them, and the sandwich was tuna mayo.

"New Boy," he yelled, "fetch the tool sack."

He was well out of order, so I stuck my hands in my pockets and eyeballed him. He picked up a chunk of stonework and flung it at a large bag propped up against the New Block wall. Then he picked up another chunk. His radio crooned "*. . . I said I loved you but I lied . . .*"

A girl came out of the last BUNG and strolled over.

"Fetch the sack, New Boy," he yelled again.

I saw the girl looking at me, so I leaned up against the doorframe. "Fetch it yourself."

It was quite easy to sidestep Boss Boy's second shot. The girl came forward. "I'll get it, dummy," she said.

"I'll help *you*," I said. ("*. . . this is more than love I feel inside . . .*")

"You're lucky I'm wearing this T-shirt," yelled Boss Boy, "or I'd get down and sort you out."

"Yeah, yeah, sure, sure, whatever, whatever." I could deal with Boss Boy, blindfolded, but I scoped the area well, in case Mrs. Sniddon was about.

"Better do as he asks," warned the girl.

"Only because you ask." I smiled at her—maybe mixed race, thick dark hair, sweet nose . . .

We dragged the tool sack into the center of the compound. It was heavy. The girl untied the string around its top and began to pull out a large assortment of hammers and chisels.

"Today you're demolishing House Twelve. I want to see the rest of the west wall down, numbered, and stacked there."

"*. . . and now the news: fuel prices set to rise . . . one thousand children at Ledzokuku to be given free screening . . . Mpasaso projects inaugurated . . . and clashes on the Togo border . . .*"

Boss Boy looked straight at me and pointed to a spot right beside the pile he sat on. While we kids collected tools, he ate his way through another three sandwiches. When he finally climbed down from the pile, he walked up to me. "Next time I tell you to do something, you do it."

I looked him over, slowly, from bottom to top and back again. No competition. "Then next time," I said, "I suggest you wear a different T-shirt."

You'll be wondering what Cabo Corso was like. You wouldn't be alone, I was wondering myself. From an aerial view it must have looked like acres of dry savannah dotted with buildings and teak trees—huge leaves, straight trunks. The buildings were either lined up like the alphabet BLKs, or grouped in a little residential area like the numbered BUNGs, or arranged in a cobweb that was linked by roofed walkways like the WARDs. That was the hospital part. Next to the hospital and stretching for a few hundred meters into a dense tangled rain forest were the ruined stone houses of an ancient settlement. I learned that Kwame Nkrumah, the first president of Ghana, had built the Leprosarium in the fifties, on the same site that the Portuguese had built their settlement in the fifteen hundreds. A scruffy hedge with wilting, trumpet-shaped, yellow flowers ringed the Leprosarium. A solid stone perimeter wall two feet thick ringed the ancient town. That was a significant difference. You can tell a lot about places from their security. (No prizes for guessing why I was interested.) Everybody must have wanted to get into the Portuguese town, whereas nobody wanted to get into the Leprosarium.

In fact, nobody wanted to get into the Leprosarium so badly, it was empty. The huge compound was empty; the JNR Staff BLKs were empty; the WARDs were empty, and except for BUNG 1 and those we were using, all the other BUNGs were empty. The chalkboard over the RECENT INTAKES WARD told it all:

Patients in total	Male	Female
Voluntary	0	2
Court Order	3	0
Family request	20	4
WHO	14	0
Away	37	6

It was dated September 1998. You may think I'm slow, but I began to wonder if there were any patients left, and how exactly the health project was going to work.

Anyway, after having done my recce round the place, disguised as an athletic jog, and found out that escape was rather easy if only you knew where to go, I lined up next to the girl by the west wall of House Twelve in the Old Portuguese ruins. It was still early, but already the sun was beating down, and even though I'd only done one lap, I was drenched in sweat.

"What have we got to do?" I said.

"Well, to start with—be careful of Boss Boy."

"He'd better be careful of me." Maybe it's a boy thing, but you know straight off, there are some guys that are going to end up getting punched. I could feel that nice springy feeling as I balled my fist.

"You can't win against them."

"Oh yeah?" I said. Then from the corner of my eye I saw Mrs. Sniddon. She came out of BUNG 1 and stood on the veranda. A cold feeling wrapped itself into my stomach, and I lowered my hammer.

"You can't," said the girl.

"What are they gonna do then?"

"I don't know," she said. Her voice trembled. "I don't want to find out."

I swallowed. I looked at the girl. She was definitely scared. Mrs. Sniddon turned and went back into the bungalow. The cold feeling stayed.

"We've got to chip the blocks out of this wall. We better get started, New Boy."

Far away a car with a loudspeaker blared: "*Vote for Akweli, your NPP election candidate . . .*" I thought of Akweli, whoever he/she was. I thought of a world out there, of folks doing their daily rounds, thinking about their futures, who they'd vote for—while I was here, with the flat-faced woman, and the muggers. . . . The sound faded. Dust hung in the still air. I shook myself. "My name's Zac, not New Boy," I said.

"Hi," she said. "Zac's a cool name."

I grinned a bit, but I was still thinking, out there, beyond the hospital, maybe folks were having breakfast . . . getting off to work . . . hugging their kids good-bye . . .

"I'm Mina."

I turned to her. "So what are you doing here?"

"Well, I volunteered my summer holiday to help rebuild the Leprosarium. It's good to give your time to charity, and I'll get the credits I need for my community service after I've done one hundred and fifty hours."

"Wow," I said. Although I didn't have a clue what kind of rehab order she was on. "What did you do?"

"Omigod!" she said. "You thought I was one of those people who get sent here, didn't you?"

I gave a funky shoulder toss and looked at her.

"It's for my school, dummy, SOS Tema, for my IB Diploma."

"SOS Tema?"

"Save Our Souls, you know, the Swiss organization for kids who—you know . . ."

"No," I said, "I don't."

"Orphans."

"Oh," I said, "sorry."

"To graduate you have to do community service. I'm—well, my parents were—from around here. Elmina, actually."

"So are all the other kids here doing their diplomas too?"

"I don't really know—I think all of them are volunteers, but they're not from my school. Some of them could be from local churches, some of them could be problem kids sent over here to be booted into shape. When Father

Bullingham started the mission, he said he was going to take all the help that was offered, including help from druggies and weirdos! Why are you here?"

"Ahh," I said. "So tell me about Father Bullingham and the mission." You will notice the clever way I changed the topic.

"Well, he negotiated for this place from the government. He's going to build a clinic that will take people with leprosy from all over West Africa. He says it's going to be a 'monument to human charity' and will be built on 'good will'! You get a certificate for donating your time and stuff. I think that's great, don't you? We've got to clear the grounds for the building. All these old ruins have to GO! And today is House Twelve's turn. Then we dig out the foundations of the new clinic. Father Bullingham's got the Sniddons as consultants: Mrs. Sniddon's an architect and Dr. Sniddon's a skin specialist. They're with some organization or other—something like the Peace Corps. They're going to design the new medical center."

That's what you think, I thought, but all I said was, "So you mean it's a kind of cheap summer camp for bored kids who like smashing things up?"

"Dummy! If you don't fill your quota they won't keep you for nothing."

"I see: no work, no food. So what do I need to do to fill my quota?"

"Chip out these blocks."

For half an hour I worked very hard—just in case she

was looking, of course. I've got nice definition, specially on my flexors. Sadly I only succeeded in loosening one block. Every time I got the chisel nuzzled into a crack and hit it with the hammer, it skidded out. And then there was the matter of the sharp bits of flying stone. I had to squeeze my eyes, aim for the chisel head, swing, and then close my eyes tight. Apart from the jarring on my left hand as the hammer landed, twice I hit my thumb.

"Boy," I said, "this is mad. Talk about doing things the hard way!"

Mina just smiled and carried on.

"I mean, what's the point?"

"Well, we've got to clear the place, dummy. You can't build a clinic on top of these ruins. And anyway, Father Bullingham says we're helping ourselves, too. That hard work and discipline is character building—it'll make us better people."

"Then why isn't he out here? Or Boss Boy—they could both do with major improvements."

She giggled. "You'll get used to it. It's not sooo bad after the first week."

"I don't intend to stay that long," I said. "I've just decided, I need to share my good will with some of the more exciting places around here."

"Well, that's not very charitable, is it? And it will be harder than you think. We're ages away from anywhere." Suddenly she looked worried again and glanced behind us. "Best not to cross them," she said.

"They don't scare me," I lied. "Which way to the nearest McDonald's?"

"Dummy."

"Well, these ain't my favorite kind of chips." I tossed a handful of gravel in the air. "It's not a prison, is it? They can't keep you against your will; if they tried to, someone would complain."

"Like who?" said Mina.

"Anyone—like parents."

"Have you got someone who'll complain?"

It was a good point. I thought of Marion and Bernard. I swatted at flies and wiped my face on my T-shirt. Yep, it was a very good point.

At eleven o'clock the football whistle went. The sun was high overhead. An onshore breeze had started, but that was like being fanned by a hairdryer. I had loosened four blocks and turned my thumbnail black. Sweat trickled down my face. My clothes stuck to me. My stomach felt like it had digested itself, and I still didn't know what to do about the diary. All the kids dumped their tools when they heard the whistle and headed back to the main compound.

"Number your blocks before you go," said Mina. "If you don't, someone else might put their numbers on them and you'll have to start over."

That was not as easy to do as you might think. I started scratching Z1 on the first one. It was like trying to scratch railings with a toothpick.

"What are these blocks made out of, cast iron?"

"Granite," said Mina, "most of it from here, but some of it was brought from Portugal in the fourteenth century."

"How d'you know that?"

"That's where I come from—well, part of me comes from. The whole Iberian Peninsula is granite—at least underneath. Don't I *look* Portuguese?"

"Who'd want to bring lumps of rock here?"

"Dummy, this is the ruins of Cabo Corso. Portuguese traders built this town to defend themselves from the Africans."

"That explains everything." I was trying to sound casual, but as soon as she said, "*the ruins of Cabo Corso. Portuguese traders built this town*," my heart skipped a thud or three. These ruins must be the Cabo Corso that Bartholomew had referred to. The Leprosarium must have been named after it! Boy, I was hot in more ways than one.

"'Cabo Corso' means short cape—it's the original name for Cape Coast. If you climb up to the top of this wall and squint, you can see the castle; it's one of the earliest slave castles in the whole world."

I stopped scratching. "What did you say?"

"Cape Coast Castle, dummy!"

I put down my chisel. Quickly I climbed the wall, my heart beating and my hands trembling. The granite blocks shifted slightly and I grazed my elbow. It hurt and I caught my breath. The coast must have been three miles away, but I could still smell salt on the breeze. Screwing up my eyes,

I searched the white sky. Then I saw it. There, squat against the brightness, shone the walls of Cape Coast Castle. Even at that distance, it was much bigger than any of the forts I'd seen. It rose huge, glowing strange and pale, flanked by turrets on either side. The sea at its back, crashing on rocks.

Despite the heat, a part of me shivered.

Cape Coast Castle.

I climbed down, picked up the chisel. I was still shivering.

"You okay?"

"Definitely," I said.

But I was not okay. I was far from okay—I was afraid. And there it was—Cape Coast Castle! I didn't want to believe that Bartholomew had really been chained inside it. And I felt I was him in another life, and I didn't want to go back there. And I knew I had to. I knew I was going to. I was going to go back through the Door of No Return, back into the darkness of the slave labyrinth—and I wanted someone to stop me, but no one knew I was going, so they couldn't.

"Definitely, definitely," I said again.

"You know something?" she said.

I pulled my mind away from the darkness underneath the castle, away from the fear germinating in those empty dungeons.

"You've got me thinking—I mean about this place."

"Yeah?"

"If this," she waved her hand around at the ruined walls, the broken paving, the ancient houses that straggled out toward the rain forest, "I mean, if this is the Old Portuguese town—why are we knocking it down?"

"Easy. To clear space for the clinic, so we can have Nando's chicken and chips with peri-peri sauce and one side order every evening."

"Dummy. It's a historical place. It's a bit like knocking down the pyramids—sort of."

"That might be a bit harder." I looked at my bruised thumb. "Although maybe not."

"It doesn't make sense. With all this space, why do they have to build the clinic right where the old town is? We could easily clear a huge area over there and then we could rebuild the old town, too—you know, restore original houses. It could be a tourist attraction and that would bring in money for the Leprosarium. I mean, that would be just as much hard work and just as good for us."

"You're right," I said. I liked her logic. "They should put you in charge of the development plan."

"We'd be better citizens if we were concerned about conservation. I think someone should say something."

"If you like," I said, "I'll take it up with Boss Boy right now."

"No," she said, her eyes suddenly scared.

"Why not?"

"Please, Zac, forget everything I said."

I looked at her, puzzled.

"Don't you see?" she hissed. "You can't win against them."

The Deal

Back at the compound, the other kids were already queuing up for breakfast. Before joining them, I nipped back to my room. It'd been nice talking to Mina, but I was wary. Don't get me wrong, as soon as I heard she was part Portuguese the same idea occurred to me. I'd almost pulled out *Chamo-me* to see if she could translate it. But you know, already I was suspicious. Cute as she was, why should I trust her? Maybe it was just too convenient for me to be befriended by a Portuguese person.

At first I didn't notice anything strange. The same smell of cement, the same whitewashed walls. The mat lay in the same corner. I squatted down by my rucksack and, holding the ripped place together, unzipped it. The first thing I saw was two rolled-up pairs of Adidas socks. I frowned. That was odd. I tipped everything out. When I saw my wash bag at the bottom, I knew something was wrong. You see, inside my wash bag was a bottle of CK cologne and I always made sure that something soft, like socks, were packed under it.

I sat down. Someone had been through my stuff. I ran my hand over my face. Then, slowly, I repacked everything. Battery or not, I sent another text straight to Raphael. I told him I'd been searched. I told him about the leprosy. He sent a text straight back: *Things seem 2 b hotting up don't worry they wont do n e thing until they have d map leprosy can b caught by close contact avoid sharing clothes it's a v nasty disease—r.*

I joined the breakfast queue with the diary still in my back pocket. Even though I was starving, I felt sick. I'd been right. This was a trap. They *were* here. What was I going to do? Some of the kids were unloading bread from a van. It had *Auntie Ester's Blessed Touch Bakery—all your catering needs, bread dough, and birthday cakes undertaken, PO Box 1135 Mfantsipim Hill, Cape Coast* written on the side of it. I wondered if I could sneak round, get inside it, and escape. I figured I'd like Auntie Ester. But then I saw Boss Boy sitting on the tailboard, chewing a meat pie.

Breakfast was a hunk of bread, with something like margarine smeared on it, and a dollop of omelette. That solved the egg decision anyway. There were no plates, so I copied the other kids and folded the egg inside the bread and bit into it. Focus on simple things. Chew. Swallow. What was I going to do? The whistle blew again. Mina found me. "Morning prayers," she whispered, "at the meeting place. I'll show you."

Outside the front of BUNG 1, under the shade of a spreading flamboyant tree, Father Bullingham, the Sniddons, and

Boss Boy sat on white plastic chairs. Everyone else had to sit on the ground, and as there was not enough shade, some of us ended up in direct sunlight. Me, for example.

"Our Father, who art in Heaven . . ." I snuck out Mobz and Nokiad them. Then I kept my head down, thinking fast. My baggage gone, Land Rover and rucksack searched. It didn't take a whole lot of GCSEs to work out that I would be next. In fact, I was surprised that they hadn't strip-searched me already. Okay, maybe they didn't want any up-front confrontation yet, maybe they were hoping I was brain-dead and would lead them straight to the treasure, but they weren't going to be patient forever. Averaging out their timing, I reckoned I had till midday. What was I going to do?

The Lord's Prayer ended. Father Bullingham stood up and started clapping. "The Lord will provide," he bellowed. "Today we are clapping for Mr. Sackity. He has donated ten chickens to the mission and a sack of yams. Praise the Lord! We are clapping for the Ankerful Women's Project, who will come and hoe a vegetable garden and plant it with corn. Praise the Lord! We are clapping for Chief Nana Gyan Barimah, who has sent six bags of cement and donated a piece of land on the other side of the river for a nurses' hostel. Praise the Lord! Clap for them! May angels follow them home!"

I was sitting right next to one of the other kids from the New Block. "Hey bro," I hissed, "mind if I ask you a question?" He turned and smiled. "Does anyone here actually have leprosy?"

"Eh! You are funny," he said. "You are a joker."

I grinned. "Only sometimes," I said. "Right now I'm serious."

"Nobody has leprosy here. We are all volunteers helping Father B. Bullingham. I'm Kwabena from the E.P. Church of Djolepo, my father is the pastor. Only that boy, Badu, may have it. He is not a volunteer; he was living in the gatehouse when Father B. Bullingham started the mission."

I nodded. "Hey, nice to meet you, cuz," and I gave him the brotherhood fist twice on my chest and one touch knuckle to knuckle. That cleared up one mystery.

And I suddenly knew what I was going to do.

Father Bullingham and the Sniddons left. Mina was waiting for me, but I'd figured it out.

I had to hide the diary.

Excusing myself, I made my way back to the New Block, but instead of going in, after checking that nobody was watching, I slipped round the side instead. At the back of the block rose the beginnings of the rain forest. Just old stranglers and young shrubs that had been hacked away.

Keeping well inside the edge of the undergrowth, I worked slowly round toward the main gate. I moved very quietly. I couldn't be sure where the dogs were in the daytime.

It was very hot and sticky inside the forest. Clouds of biting insects hung over my head. Underfoot was leaf mold, dark and damp. From time to time I heard the high whoop of monkeys or some forest bird. My first idea had been to stuff the diary into a tree trunk, but considering how wet everything was and how quickly it might rot, and after talking to Kwabena, I had come up with a better idea. At last I saw what I was looking for.

Badu's gatehouse.

Gatehouse was perhaps too good a word. It was definitely not a house. It was not constructed of stones or cement. It wasn't even a mud block hut. I paused for a while. Suddenly I felt sorry for Badu, but not very sorry. I'd still have liked to punch him for scaring me. But to do that, I realized, I'd have to touch him.

"Hey, Badu," I hissed.

"Told you you'd need all the friends you could get." He was sitting in the tree above me.

"Is the offer still open?"

"Maybe."

"I'll make you a deal."

"I'm listening."

"You help me and I'll help you."

"Is that it?"

"I'll get you a visa. I'll send you to England. I'll pay for the treatment. If that's what you want."

"Oh yeah."

"Definitely, I mean, there's not much career potential here." I pointed at his wooden shack. "Have you ever thought about going to college?"

"You are full of big talk, Mr. Didn't-do-anything."

"Not just talk."

"How?"

I sucked in my breath. There was no time left to be picky. I'd got to trust somebody and Badu was my best bet. "I've got to get out of here and into Cape Coast Castle. I know where to get hold of a whole lot of money." Sometimes you have to talk big.

Badu laughed. Not a very good sign. "First, how you going to escape the dogs? Next, how you going to cross the forest? Next, how you going to get into a fort built to withstand three hundred years of attack? Last, anyone outside here will call the police if they see you. We are a very law-abiding nation when it comes to criminals."

"I'm not a criminal."

"Who cares?" said Badu. "You don't get it, do you? In Ghana everyone knows everybody's business. All the local people know about this project, they know everyone who volunteers to help. They know you were sent here with a policeman, so therefore you are a bad boy from over. If you run away, no Ghanaian will help you do the wrong thing. You, Mr. . . . . Nothing, are on your own."

"But . . ."

"And if you try, Father Bullingham will set the dogs after you. He'll send word out that a hardened criminal from the UK is on the loose—you'll never get away."

"That's where you get to help me." Maybe everything he said was true. I guess he knew, but that didn't mean I was going to listen. "Look," I said, pointing at a woman who'd arrived at the main gate. She had a glass box of something that looked like doughnuts on her head. A baby was tied on her back. He was fast asleep, his little head nodding all comfy against her back. "She got here. It's not impossible. If she can come and go, I can too."

"She is a local woman. Everyone knows her. She sells her food for a living. You, Mr. England, are not like her. You cannot go where she goes. Ah!"

"Okay, I'll work on the dogs thing, I'll find my way through the forest, I'll get into the castle—just say you'll help."

"Okay, I'll help." He said it like it didn't make any difference if he did or not.

"So it's a deal?"

"Do you want to shake on it?" He held out his hand. I mean, I wasn't sure. I felt embarrassed—then scared—then not scared at all.

"Okay."

Badu laughed. "You really mean it, don't you?"

"Yep."

"Okay, I'll help."

"I want you to look after this. It's important—if they get it, I'm dead."

"Okay."

I held up the diary. Badu leaned down and took it. I liked him. He didn't ask unnecessary questions.

"By the way, why are you sitting in a tree?"

"That's why." Badu pointed over my shoulder. Hardly fifty meters behind me sat a ring of dogs.

Lesson Number Two

Doberman and Alsatian with a touch of local is probably the worst combination you could wish to meet in Africa. The Doberman bit is unstable, the Alsatian bit very large and foul-tempered, and the local part makes them probably rabid.

Badu must have seen me thinking.

"They breed them like that for hunting leopards," he said. "As long as you don't run, they won't attack. That is unless one of them starts. Then they'll all join in."

"What do I do?"

"Stand very still."

"I am."

"Good."

"For how long?"

"Until someone comes. Boss Boy will miss you soon. He's probably on his way already."

As if to speed Boss Boy up, the dogs started barking. Horrible. Dead nasty.

"You better think up a story fast."

My mind went blank. *Moi*, Zac Baxter, had run out of lines.

By the time Boss Boy arrived with his radio blaring out (. . . *we have a request from Maami Bentsi-Enschill of Wesley Girls, congratulating her year group on their great efforts in their SSS exams—she's praying for God's guidance and success—may there be more grease to your elbows . . .*), rivers of sweat were running between my shoulder blades and my knees were shaky. When I'd first spoken to Badu I'd made a mad plan to make friends with the dogs. I could see now that would be difficult. They weren't friends with anyone; they probably even hated each other. The only way Boss Boy got to me was by shooting rocks at them and waving a big stick. They cowered away from him, watching, waiting for him to make a false move. (. . . *with a special thank-you to their biology teacher, known to them as Slow Lane Motorway . . .*) When he finally got near, he blew the football whistle and Father Bullingham had to come to escort us back to the bungalow. The dogs kept well away from him.

By the time I was standing back inside the hall again, I didn't know which was worse, the dogs or Father Bullingham.

"You've got a lot to learn," he said.

I didn't answer. I was wondering what kind of lesson he had in store for me. Somehow I didn't think it would be more toffees and Coca-Cola.

"We could start with a little history."

There was something in the way he spoke, all breathy, as if there were holes in his windpipe.

"Very recent European history might include why decent law-abiding people pay taxes to help reform delinquent vandals who think it's fun to desecrate graveyards."

Boy, did I nearly knock him out. Believe me, it wasn't his six and a half feet or his two hundred and forty pounds. It was that I'd promised Pops I'd finish his business. I had to stay alive to do that.

"More distant history might include the days of slavery. When male slaves tried to escape, they were put in the condemned cell as an example to others. The cell had only standing room and there was no window. When the cell door was shut, it was airless and dark. The door remained shut for as long as it took the slave to die. Three days? Four days? Longer if it was the rainy season and he could lick a little condensation off the walls. Who knows—maybe two weeks."

He was joking. Had to be.

"They could always tell when he was dead, by the smell."

My stomach turned. I felt like vomiting.

"It was a good lesson for the other slaves. They could listen to his screaming."

"I wasn't trying to escape."

"You were visiting Badu?"

"No."

He smiled. "You were admiring the front gates?"

"I was exploring."

"How can I know what you were doing? You were entrusted to me by the British courts. If you try to run away or fail to complete your hours here, you will be given a custodial sentence. You will also spoil the chances of other young offenders who might actually want to help this mission. I found you with a leper. That gives me a little idea. I shall have to isolate you, put you in solitary confinement until I know God's will."

"But I didn't even touch him."

"We have no proper isolation unit here at Cabo Corso, but the old condemned cell in the Portuguese ruins will offer us the right kind of security."

"You're joking," I said.

He didn't look like he was joking.

"Empty your pockets."

As he searched me, I thought, you know, sometimes it's nice to be one step ahead . . . but, hey—don't think I was feeling smug. I wasn't. I was wondering what he'd do to me when he didn't find anything. Boy, was he gonna be jarred off! Worse still, I was worried Mrs. Sniddon would show up. I was hoping things weren't going to get painful.

So there I was, arms raised, unsmugly one step ahead, when I saw an open file on his desk—the last e-mail printout right under my nose. It was upside down, but when you are as good as I am at cheating in exams, that is no obstacle. This is what it said.

From: Harold Reeves <reevesh@MI5.gov.uk>
To: GCHQ Cheltenham <bullinghamb@gchq.gov.uk>
Subject: Cormantin Club
Date: Fri, 08 Aug 09:62:78 +0100

Bullingham

Okay, good job in getting the boy down to Ghana, and selling the aid idea, but I think the time has come to cut our losses. Tempting as the gold may be, it is not worth losing an election over. It is all taking too much time and that is worrying. It makes me edgy and the PM doesn't like it. The Ghana government is beginning to ask questions too—nothing worrying, you understand, just paperwork over the aid money going into revamping their health sector. More worrying is that LEPRA are asking to get involved—it's all too much. Get on with the job you went over for, get that settlement demolished so there is no evidence of this whole affair in Ghana, destroy the bond, and get the hell out of there. LEPRA can take it on if we work quickly, and we can come out smelling sweet.

Reeves

Oh boy. My eyes bulged. My mouth fell open. . . . The mission was a front! Oh boy. GCHQ!

I read it again. My eyes bulged more. My mouth went dry. I started swallowing air. *Get a grip, Zac,* I told myself.

This is not a surprise. This is what you already worked out. Read it again. Try to think. GCHQ. Government Communications Headquarters. MI5. The guys who do all the dirty work . . .

I reread it.

"Worrying" seemed to be a key word. Yes, a key word! And the PM (which I don't think meant later in the afternoon) wasn't the only one who was doing it. I didn't need to read it a fourth time. I knew exactly what it meant.

DEEP TROUBLE.

Here's the script: Good Guy takes on the system, Good Guy has a bad time. Someone dies—and (even though the scriptwriter is on his side) Good Guy gets hurt. Hey, I had no scriptwriter to help me out! And boy, getting hurt was not one of my fave activities.

Like I said, DEEP TROUBLE.

One ray of hope only. The Prime Minister put the demolition of the buildings one step before demolishing me—although it was obvious Father Bullingham thought differently. I could tell by his snorting. He'd have demolished me there and then if he could have. He couldn't seem to believe the only thing in my pockets was my phone. It put him in a very bad mood. He was definitely jarred off, times plenty. He twisted my arm behind my back and didn't seem to care that I didn't like being hurt.

Still more worrying, I was marched out of the bungalow, surrounded by a pack of howling dogs, and into the Portuguese ruins.

My Second Night

The condemned cell was a deep chamber built into the ringed wall of the old ruins. It had a gruesome skull and crossbones carved above its entrance. Inside was hot and dark. It smelled bad, of mold and stone. The walls were uneven and the floor the same. There was just about space for me to squat down and jam my feet against one side, my back on the other. For a while I groped at the walls, determined to find something that would give me hope. I kept thinking: This must be a joke, nobody nowadays can get away with locking you in an airless cell until you starve to death . . . ? But as the minutes turned into hours, I started to get scared. Badly scared.

I had plenty of time to rerun the e-mail through in my mind. Ashley was right, I was a pawn in some game way bigger than even Pops imagined. Of course, it would be quite easy for them to starve me to death. I thought sadly of Bernard and his passion for human rights, his passion for the rules. Huh, different rules applied now. Rules that Father Bullingham had the power to make up as he went along.

I decided to text Raphael. I knew that any minute my battery might run out, but the sooner he knew what was happening, the better. I wondered how long it would take him to get to Cabo Corso, and if I'd last. I reckoned I could manage two days. Surely he'd get here by then? I copied the text to Ashley too, although there was no hope he'd be able to do anything. I guess I just wanted him to know. I didn't want to vanish from the face of the earth without somebody knowing. I've still got the text; I keep it as a reminder of how comforting the little green light of a mobile can be. Here it is: *Dis cud b my last txt father bullingham as locked me in d condemned cell i don't tink es joking—av discvred e is a uk gov agent n dis plce is fake—u shd no dat an b v careful—uv got 2 help me widout water i don't tink il last long im in d portuguese ruins at cabo corso pls pls cum quickly i still dont av a clue where d map is but it seems u r wrong about dem dey r quite happy 2 let me die—help me—zac.*

Sometimes I wonder if I'm slow or what? Instead of hoping for rescue, I should have been wondering why Father B hadn't taken Mobz off me. He wasn't well known for being generous. If I'd thought about it, I might have suspected something. That might have saved me a lot of trouble. But I didn't. I just sent my texts, got the report back that they were delivered, and like a nursery kid began waiting.

Being in the dark, in a cramped stuffy space, in solitary confinement, does things to your head. Soon I began thinking about all the other people who had died in that cell. It seemed like I could hear their voices whispering and their dead bodies heavy against me. I started thinking about Bartholomew and how he'd been captured and imprisoned. He was a child, seven years old. That's hard. Then to dream of release, to dream that his father's gold could rescue him . . . I had no father to pay a ransom for me. I don't think my father even knew I was his. See, Pops had only a daughter, my mum, and she'd died having me. Like I said, it had always been just Pops and me. I shifted my mind away from Pops. I didn't want to cry. I carried on feeling sorry for Bartholomew instead. To hope, to dream of release! And then to be cheated and the gold gone, to be sent in shackles to another world. I think I might have cried a bit. I'm not sure.

Perhaps these ruins were where Senhor Dias had lived. Maybe House Number Twelve had been the Dias house. Then I started thinking maybe they'd buried the treasure here. I mean, they could have. I didn't care about the treasure anymore. I think I must have fallen asleep at some point; it's hard to tell when all around you is forever night.

Forever Night

Case for the Prosecution
Exhibit 02 Attached

Form MG 14
(CJ Act 1967, s. 9; MC Act 1980, ss. 5A(3) (a) and 5B; MC Rules 1981, r. 70)

EXTRACT: *From the alleged diary of Bartholomew Baktu*

This exhibit (consisting of *case for the prosecution two (2) pamphlets written in Portuguese . . . —certified translation Lisbon University—verified against accounts of the Royal African Company—considered authentic. Professor Braithwaite, British Museum* ~~page(s) each page signed by me~~) is true to the best of my knowledge ~~and I make it knowingly, if it is tendered in evidence, I shall be liable to prosecution if I have wilfully stated in it anything which I know to be false or do not believe to be true.~~

Signature *N/A—see above* Date *November 5th* *DL Hesketh*

We were running, my brothers and me. The air smelled thick with gunpowder, and cries, terrible cries, filled the night. Men were dying. Behind us I saw five of my brothers standing and throwing their spears, and when the spears were thrown I saw them draw the Afena swords that only the King's sons may carry. Akonor, Tendia, and Gabriel were pulling the cart with the gold dust. Akonor was wounded. I could hear his breath coming in rattles, but he touched my arm and whispered, "Courage, little Prince, courage. We run for you, or I would turn and fight the White Death like a man."

Dias led the way and I longed to hear his voice. Uncle Senhor Dias was so clever, I knew he'd find a way. Then I heard the dogs. The hounds of the white man. It was the same baying that I'd heard on the night they'd taken me. It was the sound of the dogs that had stopped me from running into the bush where I could have hid.

"I'm sorry," I said.

"Sorry no help," whispered Akonor. "Run fast, little antelope."

We ran until my legs felt strange and painful. The sores from the shackles hurt and my chest was on fire. I saw ahead the white walls of the Portuguese town. I heard Uncle Senhor calling to his people. I heard bolts slotted back and raised voices. I heard muskets fire and booming from the great cannons that sleep on the city walls of my uncle's settlement. I must have fainted, for the food they had given me since my capture had made me sick and weak. I awoke, held in Akonor's arms in front of a small fire. Uncle Senhor's wife was holding a bowl of soup under my chin.

"Drink," she said, "for you are thin and ill."

I drank the soup and it was warm and good, but the fear of the white man was still in my heart and I vomited it out again.

I heard Uncle Senhor Dias's voice. "We must rest tonight, but tomorrow we cannot stay here. I fear for the people of this town. The English will burn them in their beds. Tomorrow we must leave, by first light. See to the boy."

I turned to look up into Akonor's face. He was smiling. "Courage, little lionheart. You see, here is your gold. They shall have neither it, nor you." I fell asleep again cradled in my brother's arms, and did not feel the slow drip of his blood throughout the night.

I awoke to the darkness of my cell. Shivering in the heat of that tropical night, I thought about Bartholomew. Maybe Akonor had rescued him. I hung on to that thought as long as I could. The word "rescue" had shot to number one in my top ten of words. If Bartholomew could be rescued, I could too.

I had no brother. I shook myself. Akonor and Bartholomew had been dead for three hundred years. Get a grip. Things could be worse—although not much: I could be Badu. Then it hit me, Badu, Baktu, Baxter. I grinned. Maybe I did have a brother after all.

It was morning when Boss Boy let me out.

"Sleep well?" He was grinning all over his stupid face.

I'd have punched him, straight—but boy, I didn't want to go back into that cell again.

Emergency Escape Plan No. 2

After that, I kept my head down. Same stuff, different day. Work on House Number Twelve, clap for Auntie Tina, work on House Number Thirteen. Prayers. Stack and remove the blocks. Prayers. Wash your own clothes. Work on House Number Fourteen. Iron your own clothes (with a heavy charcoal box iron) and—guess what—more prayers. Kitchen duty, fetching water duty, sweeping compound duty, cleaning kerosene lamps duty—until I lost count of duties and days.

I kept away from Mina and the others, and they kept away from me. I was afraid they might be spies. Hey, maybe they were all genuine volunteers, but I wondered how long they'd stay that way, if I got close to them—you know!

I soon realized that even though the security at the settlement was weak, the chances of getting away from it were weak too. We were miles from anywhere, and any runaway would quickly be rounded up. Also, Father Bullingham was waiting for me to try. For example: Whenever we got a trip to the beach, or a Saturday afternoon in town, I'd know the event was staged, like a prison door left unlocked, and I was being invited to make a run for it. Perhaps he was hoping I'd lead him straight to the treasure, or perhaps he wanted an excuse to start on me. I didn't take the bait anyway. I was not yet brain-dead, and I still did not know where to run to.

Sometimes, when the Hausa boys drove their hump-backed cattle past the bakery-van gate, I toyed with the idea of slipping unseen among their muddy hooves, but I wasn't too comfortable around cows (and these ones were definitely bulls, with wicked long horns). I tried to make friends with the boys anyway, hoping they'd help me, but they just grinned and waved their sticks, shouting, "Salaam alikum," and didn't seem to get my point.

However, time was running out, even though I wasn't. At any moment, Father Bullingham might start cutting his losses, and I was beginning to get jumpy. If I couldn't work out how to escape and where to go to pretty quickly, I'd be not only brain-dead. I reckoned most of my other major organs would end up deceased too.

I imagined Ashley saying, "You see, Lee, if you had the snakebite kit, and the cigarette lighter (which can spark in a monsoon), the Neat Deet (for lepidopterists), the waterproof flashlight, and the emergency high protein capsules, not forgetting the Swiss Army knife, the wristwatch, and the instruction manual on how to find water in the wild—you'd be fine. You could gap it on a nice moonlit night and live in the jungle for weeks." And I had to admit he was dead right. "DEAD" being a word continually on my mind.

So I started a second emergency escape plan in my head. If they did start on me, I tried to imagine what they might do first, and I figured at some point they would put me back in the condemned cell. The next time it might be for longer, so every morning I worked hard until the football whistle went, then when Boss Boy had his break, I moved to the perimeter wall.

I'd figured out where the back of the condemned cell was and I'd started a scheme to loosen the blocks. I only had about five minutes to suss all this out while the other kids finished up signing their stones, or I'd have been missed. I was being watched, of course—but only by Boss Boy in the mornings. He was greedy and thought about food first.

By the third day I'd managed to hide a chisel and a hammer in the shrubs by the wall. This meant that when I was sure everyone was asleep, I could creep out of the New Block, skirt the settlement walls, and very quietly chip away at the ancient cement between the blocks.

On one of those nights, a fresh evening, when the moon was just over three-quarters full, I set out for the wall. I slid past the BUNGs and into the ruined ghost town. Moon shadows cast dark uneven patches on the ground and a deliciously warm wind blew. I found my tools and crouched down in the darkness. With my fingertips I felt for the niche I'd already excavated. I started scratching. I was working very low on the wall where the grass hid everything, so when I heard the footsteps, it was easy to press myself flat against the ground.

"You shouldn't be out," said a voice that I recognized as Father Bullingham's. For a moment I thought he meant *me* and my heart jumped into my throat.

"I can't hide all the time," said another. It was faint, but familiar.

"Patience and perseverance," said Father Bullingham, "he'll give himself away soon."

"He's smarter than you think. I told you he's onto us, we should make our next move."

I strained through the shadows to see if I could see them. All the time my heart was pounding. What did they mean, "*our next move*"?

Father Bullingham spoke again. "Put your faith in God. (*Cough.*) We have him here—that is the key." He broke into a round of hoarse coughing. "Whatever he knows, we will—soon enough. Let the work break him. Give him plenty of rope and when he ties the noose, *then* we'll strangle him." His voice was breathless and urgent, and disappeared beneath another bout of dry coughing.

"You should have taken that mobile off him. Don't forget there's that lawyer friend of his. He'd love to be all over us like a ton of bricks."

"Ah—the little mobile . . . Ho, I like *that* soupçon—it gives him a fighting chance . . . and don't forget it's useful for us, too. As for his friend—how long will it take him to get here? First the visa, then the vaccinations, then the Embassy, then the forms . . . and who will meet him and drive him to Cabo Corso? You forget *I* arranged all that— even the nice little Toyota. Oh no, I don't think anyone will get here in a hurry."

Father Bullingham sounded almost mournful—as if he'd have welcomed a challenge. "I'm always telling you, cross each bridge as you come to it. You were so sure he had the map, but we haven't found it on him, have we? Let us give him a little longer—and then, you know, I don't think there's a lawyer born who can help him."

I lay trembling in the grass as their footsteps faded. I gripped the chisel tight and pressed it against me. I thought wildly of running off, straight. But where could I run to? I'd made no preparations. I tried to tell myself that I had a "little longer," that I should loosen the blocks and at least figure out the right direction to run in. I stayed there, unable to move. At length my reason won, and I scratched feverishly away at the old mortar of the condemned cell for the rest of the night.

After that it was like old times. Yours truly running scared, looking over his shoulder, on guard 24-7. I covered my back, I covered my front, I tried never to be alone, tried to stay a step ahead. Each night, after restless sleep, I'd wake to creep out and scratch stubbornly away at the perimeter wall; and during the day I'd toil for long hot hours demolishing the settlement walls. In the evening I'd sink exhausted onto the mat of the New Block and there was no Ashley to cheer me up. Instead, I'd imagine him saying, "You've just gotta admit it, mush, you are not cracking this fast enough. What are you doing still there? You need to make a serious one-point plan, Stan. Get out of Cabo Corso. Get out of Cabo Corso. Get out of Cabo Corso. Fast."

My calculations were pretty good, anyway. Three nights later, I broke through into the damp of the condemned cell. After that—when the first block had been loosened— it was a bit easier to get at the others. I wasn't so success- ful at discovering which direction to run in though. Once I slunk round through the undergrowth to the front gates looking for Badu, but I couldn't find him, and the dogs nearly found me. I didn't try again. I couldn't send any messages, either. I'd been hoping to text Ashley, to get him to research Cabo Corso, to tell me where to escape to, advise me how to navigate the forest—anything. But my battery went flat.

That meant I'd have to take the road I'd come by, where I was sure to be spotted.

And that *really* worried me—I was more on my own than even *I* realized. Badu was right, if anything went wrong, I'd be wasting my time hoping for rescue.

Murder, Conspiracy, and Skeletons from the Past

I think it was when we were first detailed to start on House Twenty that it happened. Like I said, I'd been avoiding Mina. On more than one occasion she'd tried to talk, but I'd answered in the stiffest way and she'd turned that puzzled look on me. She got the message. She stopped trying to be friendly.

That morning on House Twenty was hot. I mean *hot*. The metal on the chisel was too hot to touch. (I had to pull one of my socks over my hand to hold it in place.) The wall was hot and seemed to radiate heat back from its surface. The air was hot. The breeze was hot. It was the kind of heat that bruised. My head was pounding. Soon I was drenched, my eyes stung from sweat, and I had a serious headache.

Mina came up to me.

"I don't know what I've done," she said.

"You ain't done nothing."

"I've figured out why we're doing this. I just wanted to tell you."

"Yeah? I thought we're doing it to stop getting on the wrong side of Father Bullingham, to help him build his mission for free." I nodded toward Boss Boy, who was sitting on a half-broken wall, watching, his radio as ever blasting. (. . . *it's Naa for Joy FM News . . . the Ghana delegation will travel to Abuja to meet the Nigerian . . .*)

"Well, for a start, we're not building anything. How can a bunch of kids build a mission? We haven't even got a builder here to supervise. It's a joke."

"Nobody's laughing."

"You know what I think. I think they're hiding a body . . ."

They say heat can make you go mad, don't they? I looked at Mina and felt sorry.

"I think we're burying the evidence."

Boss Boy got down off the wall (. . . *Jasikan Training College marks its Golden Jubilee . . .*) and settled a bit closer. Duh! I thought, if you want to hear our conversation, why not turn your stupid radio off?

I turned and shook my head—gently. "Mina," I said, "you read too many mysteries. The only dead bodies around here are going to be ours."

"No," she said, "that's what I'm trying to tell you."

I'd been meaning to blank her again, but there was this earnestness in her voice. She looked at me and suddenly I saw a scared little girl. "Okay, what?" I said.

"My family were Portuguese—well, mulatto: mixed. We lived in a big old house in Elmina. The Portuguese

House, that's what it was called. It had this above the door—" Mina bent down and drew a crest in the dust. "When I was really little, I remember my mum telling me that our family was special. I guess all mums say that, don't they?"

"I dunno."

"I think they may have murdered him."

(. . . and Ghana's Black Stars are set to play Germany in the next round of the World Cup . . .) I mentally crossed my fingers for Ghana. "Hold on," I said, "who murdered who?"

"Chris Barnett, the man who came to find out."

"Mina," I said, "I have a headache and I don't follow. Start at the beginning and don't jump around."

"Dummy," she said, and I knew I was forgiven. "This man came from Britain. He came to find out about the Portuguese; he was measuring all these buildings. He had lots of papers, and though Father Bullingham wasn't pleased about it, he wouldn't go away. Then one day he disappeared. I didn't think about it at the time, but yesterday I found this—look . . ."

Mina held up a round disc of glass. I looked at it—mostly to please her.

"So? He lost his camera lens."

"He wouldn't have. He wasn't the type, dummy! I know. One afternoon when I was on cooking duty, I came down here to find him. I was going to invite him, you know—he'd bought some shrimps from Cape Coast and

I'd made a stir fry. . . . Anyway, he was here taking close-ups of these walls.

"'Mina, Mina,' he said, 'just the girl I need—stand right there so I can get a sense of scale.'

"I stood by the wall and asked him, 'What are the photos for?'

"'Big story,' he said. 'Big mysteries about to be solved. The world is about to understand the secrets of Cabo Corso!'

"'Ooooow,' I said.

"'Not big ooowws, big NE-OOO-WS! This place was the first Portuguese settlement in all of the Guinea Coast. Bartolomeu Dias, the greatest navigator Portugal ever produced, founded this place in 1488. It's a historical wonder! The navigators were given stone pillars—padrões—to stake the claims of the Portuguese Crown. His is here—somewhere!'

"I laughed because he was making it sound so exciting. Maybe that's when I first started thinking about history and being Portuguese. . . . Anyway, he took my photo and he used *this* lens. I remember it because he had to change the one that was on the camera."

"Lenses look pretty alike," I said.

"No, look, this one has a small scratch—here. He made me stand in a bit, because of the scratch. He showed it to me. I saw him wipe it carefully and put it away. He said, 'If I get another scratch on this, it'll be big trouble! I'll have to replace it and that costs big money!'

"Well, for a start, he wasn't rich. He was a journalist. He was making a program—he told me, 'I've got a secret source! And if the BBC likes this idea, I'll be in the money! Crazee! This is a story of big betrayal—of terrible savagery and of dreadful horror! This is where it all started before *The Heart of Darkness*. Wikked! The British tricked a local chief, massacred amazing numbers of Portuguese settlers— here in this *very* village—and went on to annex the whole of the Gold Coast. My story will hit the big, big time—if I'm lucky I'll get a nine p.m. slot!'

"He was wonderful. Nobody had ever made me feel special about being Portuguese before. In fact I'd even stopped speaking it. After that, I tried to find ways to talk to him, to learn more about my history. . . . I guess I hoped I'd find a link between me and the greatest navigator the world has ever known—does that sound stupid?"

Mina paused. I shook my head.

"Then he left. Just like that. No good-bye. No 'Mina, Mina, I'll make you a big, big star,' or anything. No photo in the post—although he promised. Then yesterday I found his lens. He'd *never* have dropped it. *Never*."

"So?"

"Since yesterday I can't get it out of my head. Little things that don't add up . . . They don't want any BBC camera crew here—they want to hide everything. That's why we're knocking these walls down. . . ."

I was stunned. Firstly, I'd underestimated Mina. Secondly, I remembered the words of the e-mail: "*Get on *with the job you went over for, get that settlement demolished, and get the hell out of there."* So that was why they'd wanted to demolish Cabo Corso. The diaries, the gold, illegal slavery, massacres, annexing the Gold Coast, colonization, broken bonds, a whole empire and civilization built on crime— and Pops, my bright-eyed grandfather, burrowing away like a deathwatch beetle into forbidden history: starting the Cormantin Club; airing his views about compensation and treasure hunts and court cases—not once, not just to family, but on the radio . . . and often. I looked hard at Mina. "Okay, what exactly are we hiding?"

"Well, the Portuguese man had been working for the English, helping them against the Dutch with trade. Then, *something* happened and all the Portuguese at Cabo Corso disappeared—just like that. The man, one of the descendants of the navigator actually, was blamed for it. Back in Portugal, they excommunicated him."

"What was his name—this Portuguese guy?"

"Bartolomeu Dias the Fifth or Sixth or something."

(. . . *over to Enyo Dagadu for a financial update on the Ghana Stock Exchange* . . .) Boss Boy snapped off the radio and sat up.

I looked at her. *Bartolomeu Dias VI*—the sixth descendant of the navigator. That would make it about . . . two hundred and fifty years later.

"But you see, it wasn't *him*—I mean Dias. It was the English. . . ."

Two hundred and fifty years later would make it exactly

the time that King Baktu had sent the gold with a Portuguese ambassador named Senhor Dias. I wonder.

"This sounds stupid, but I think that Father Bullingham is knocking the place down so that if it ever came out that the English had done massacres and stuff—"

"Sssshhhhh," I said.

"There'll be no evidence left," Mina whispered. "Look, see that—even after three hundred years the soot is still there. Smell it—go on!" Mina ran her hand over a piece of stone.

Boss Boy got down off the broken blocks and stood up. To tell the truth, it *did* still smell of burning.

She was right.

I leaned up against the wall and then jumped back. It was scalding. Maybe she was right about the murder, too. Pops had been murdered—why not some nobody freelance journalist? Had he been following up Pops's story—all those records Pops had unearthed? I had a sudden strong feeling that he had—that maybe even Pops had put him up to it. . . . I decided to trust Mina—was I wrong? I told her about the Cormantin Club, the compensation plan, the investigations, the diaries, my community order, and the e-mail I'd read in Father Bullingham's study—right down to the missing map.

She listened, her eyes growing wide and her face pale. At last she said, "This is bad. They killed him. Do you realize it's to do with politics—and that's very, very dangerous. . . . It's to do with your ancestor and this Senhor Dias. And now it's to do with us!"

T-shirts

She was right.

"I'm scared," said Mina.

I was too angry to be scared.

They'd messed up my life, slammed Pops on the pavement. Broken me. They'd tricked me into coming here, set me up, hunted me—all so that I could end up in this nasty place covering their tracks for *them*, so that I could end up being the next mug in the next body bag? The veins on my neck felt tight. My face burnt. My headache evaporated. I paced up and down. Mina stood there looking frightened. My eyes stung. I could feel my face getting ugly. Was I stupid? Was I turning my thumbnails black, sweating in the sun, stinking like an animal, to make them sleep easy, to provide them with the clues to *my* treasure, and then to obligingly die?

I pulled off my T-shirt and flung it against the wall. I picked up the chisel again and set about hammering the hell out of House Number Twenty, with each blow wishing it were someone's head.

Mina worked away beside me; I think she was saying, "What are we going to do? What if they work out we know?" If she was, I didn't listen. Instead I thought: *How ironic—the only dead bodies around here really* are *going to be ours.*

I hammered until my hand trembled, and carried on hammering long into the morning. Boss Boy moved closer, smirking away to himself. He turned his radio back on and started singing along (irritatingly) to "Gangsta's Paradise."

I ignored him, but when my temper was worked out and I stood in a mess of stone chips, he stepped out toward me. There he stood, fancied up in some yesterday designer gear. Stuff I wouldn't be seen dead in. Stupid girlie labels.

"Enjoying the work, New Boy?"

He'd just picked the wrong person at the wrong time. "You starting?" I said.

"Starting and finishing," he said.

I laughed. Funnily enough, that exact phrase was running through *my* mind. Pops had always told me, "*Don't start what you can't finish.*" If ever I was going to finish anything, it was right now!

"Then you better take off your T-shirt too."

He backed away. He blew the whistle.

Let him blow till he bursts, I thought. I'll do him before anyone gets here.

I guess I looked pretty fierce. Bare-chested and sweaty. I was leaner and meaner than I'd ever been. A hammer in one hand and a chisel in the other. I sized him up. Pops had always told me: "*If you can't run away and it's you or them, hit first and hit hard. Don't hesitate and don't leave any chance for any bugger to ever get up.*"

He backed away and fumbled for a block of stone to throw at me.

I took a small step to the left and dummied another; meanwhile I was coiled inside ready to spring. As he bent to pick up the stone, I went for him. I aimed the hammer straight at his shinbone and, at the same time, kick-boxed his chin.

Boy, he went down like a bowling pin. He started howling. Then I was on him, punching. I don't know how far I'd have gone if Father Bullingham hadn't pulled me off. I was still holding the chisel, but I didn't use it. One blow and he'd have been as dead as Pops. But I didn't. Father Bullingham grabbed my arms. I was a mass of sweat and his grip slipped. I kicked backward. I think I got him, but he didn't let go. By the time he'd pulled me off Boss Boy, we were standing in a ring of kids. They looked scared. None of them tried to help me. At the time I thought: What cowards, this is what it must have been like three hundred years ago—a bunch of scared stupid faces. No wonder the English did as they liked. I didn't care. Boss Boy was moaning on the ground. I looked him in the eye and smiled. Then I turned on the kids. "You're stupid!" I yelled at them. "STUPID. Look at you. Doing their dirty work." It wasn't fair, really. They didn't know. That only goes to show something about never knowing the whole picture, I guess.

"Do something!" I screamed.

As if in answer, the dogs started howling. The kids backed away. Only Mina stood still.

One Door Closes—
Another Opens

After that it was back in the bungalow and "You've got a lot to learn."

I had.

I wasn't prepared for the lesson. Nothing could have prepared me for it.

I stood stripped to the waist, covered in dust. Father Bullingham circled me. I think he was shocked. I know I was. The look on his face was surprise—no, disbelief. He'd let the dogs into the front hall, otherwise I might have tried taking him on. Instead, I scanned the study for a weapon and kept backing away. He called Dr. and Mrs. Sniddon.

"What do you think?" he said.

They circled me too, and smiled.

There was an old wine bottle with a candle in it on the desk. With that, I figured if I had to I could take out one of them. I edged toward it, my heart thumping.

Suddenly, the three of them left the room. I heard the key turn and then hushed voices. I supposed they were seeing to Boss Boy. I picked up the bottle and tried the door—just in case. It was locked. I saw an encyclopedia on the table. I moved across to pick it up.

It was open at the word "LEPROSY." I scanned it.

Leprosy (Hansen's disease)

Leprosy is one of the most feared diseases, the leper being considered as "unclean." Yet it is not a highly infectious disease, prolonged contact being needed for its spread.

The disease is caused by the leprosy (or Hansen) bacillus, and has two principal forms.

In one form, body cells crowd into the area in an attempt to seal off the invader. This form of leprosy is known as tuberculoid leprosy because of the hard nodules that form in the skin.

The progress of leprosy is slow. It may be years before the first sign of the disease, often a vague, scarcely noticed spot on the skin . . .

Here the page ended. I didn't turn it over. It looked pretty boring. Wondering why it had been open in the first place, I slammed the book shut and picked it up. It was nice and heavy. I positioned it where I could grab it quick. If I could smack the book into Father Bullingham's face, I'd use the bottle on the dogs. Then I'd go. I'd get far away, as fast as I could.

That was when I saw the file. The Government Communications Headquarters file. Anyone who's grown up in Gloucester knows about them! Their buildings stretch from Cheltenham right down the Golden Valley bypass. Their stranglehold stretches right around the globe. GCHQ, otherwise known as MI5!

There it was! The same file that I'd first read the upside-down e-mail in. I could tell by the gray and black cover. I picked it up. I removed these two pages. Here they are. Read them. They're a year old and not the sort of thing you'd normally bother to read, but they completely change the picture.

The Picture Changes

Case for the Prosecution
Exhibit 03 Attached

Form MG 14
(CJ Act 1967, s. 9; MC Act 1980, ss. 5A(3) (a) and 5B; MC Rules 1981, r. 70)

E-mail and attachment ....

This exhibit (consisting of................*case for the prosecution: an e-mail sent from* *Whitehall to GCHQ detailing a plan to suppress evidence and commit* *murder* ~~page(s) each page signed by me~~) is true to the best of my knowledge ~~and I make it knowingly, if it is tendered in evidence, I shall be liable to prosecution if I have wilfully stated in it anything which I know to be false or do not believe to be true.~~

Signature *N/A — see above* Date *November 5th* *DC Hesketh*

From: Harold Reeves <reevesh@MI5.gov.uk>
To: GCHQ Cheltenham <bullinghamb@gchq.gov.uk>
Subject: Cormantin Club
Date: Fri, 05 June 12:59:35 +0100

Listen, Bullingham, you better get this sorted out. With the general election coming up we need the black vote. Never underestimate how much damage insignificant things like this cause. Imagine this Cormantin Club can recover the gold and the bond. Imagine that they get someone to sue. Imagine there is some nosy-parker human rights lawyer around—add in a journalist and we have got trouble.

Imagine the front pages three weeks before the elections: BRITISH GOVERNMENT SUED FOR COMPENSATION OVER SLAVERY. BRITISH GOVERNMENT INVOLVED SINCE 1701 IN MASS KILLING OF FOREIGNERS.

It's not just the damage a lawsuit like this could cause the party—it's a national issue. The cost of backing out of it graciously would be astronomical. International affairs would be compromised and we could lose the election. We can't afford to alienate the ethnic communities, and it could cause real problems with America. The White House is definitely NOT going to like this. We've got our work cut out to stabilize the Muslim affair—we DON'T NEED this.

Make sure it is buried.

Do I make myself clear? I want this whole Cormantin issue six feet.

I do not want to hear of any bond, I do not want to see one ounce of gold dust in the hands of that Baxter boy, I do not want that Portuguese settlement to have one stone left in it. All of it never existed. If I could demolish the castle as well, I would.

See attachment STRATEGIC PLAN OPERATION WHITEWASH. Do what you have to. I think you understand what I mean.

Reeves

ATTACHMENT

Operation Whitewash

Target Statement: By September 20 there will be no remaining peoples or evidence in the Cormantin Matter.

Background

It has come to our attention that a group calling itself the Cormantin Club has enough evidence to bring a slavery compensation case against the government. The situation needs resolving.

Strategic Plan

Stage 1

Objective:	Seize evidence currently held by S. Baxter/Cormantin Club
Start date:	1st Sept.
Completion date:	31st Jan.
Responsibility:	Ingleworth/Mason/Dery

1. Collect the evidence—currently believed to be papers and diaries—from the chairman of the club, Samuel Baxter, 13 Arrowsmith House, Tuffley, Glos.
2. Clear the dwelling and pass contents over to special unit.
3. Snooze key litigants.
4. Watch the activities of the club and remove all their files—apparently they have a lawyer.
5. Contact the lawyer and defuse.
6. Keep surveillance on all members and the activities of their relatives.

Stage 2

Objective: Remove evidence in Ghana
Start date: 1st Sept.
Completion date: 31st Aug.
Responsibility: Bullingham

1. Contact Ghana government, liaise to set up mission/ NGO for Cabo Corso Leprosarium.
2. Offer aid package for control of ancient settlement site; be very careful not to alert the Ministry of Museums and Monuments as to proposed objective. [Suggest using manpower, as demolition contractors will draw attention to the project.]
3. Set up Head Office at the leprosarium.
4. Make sure the project receives local support.
5. Demolish the Portuguese settlement presently in ruins, ensuring that each block is examined for evidence which may lead to recovery of the gold/bond.
6. Erase any records of Bartolomeu Dias VI from national archives.

Stage 3

Objective: Erase evidence in the West Indies
Start date: 1st Sept.
Completion date: 31st Aug.
Responsibility: Forrester/Usher/Hannah/Watts

1. Set up subsidiary office in Jamaica, Montego Bay.
2. Remove and destroy births, marriages, and deaths registry and all documents relating to slaves of the name Baktu/Baxter at Rose Hall, Montego Bay area.

3. Locate public records in Bristol and remove any references to Baktu/Baxter and trading between Gloucester, Bristol, and Cape Coast between 1701 and 1702.

Stage 4

Objective:	Resolve the Zachariah Baxter problem
Start date:	1st Jan.
Completion date:	1st Sept.
Responsibility:	Ingleworth/Mason/Bowdich/Dery (Team Leader Ms. Ingleworth)

1. Isolate.
2. Watch.
3. Create a criminal record and destroy credibility/defame.
4. Penetrate social welfare system, exert control over case worker(s), etc.
5. Remove to State home.
6. Seize any documents in his possession.
7. Seize any map.
8. Try to relocate to Cabo Corso—if he knows anything it will then become apparent.
9. Collect all evidence, including if possible the bond.*
10. Destroy all evidence collected/confiscate gold dust if found.
11. Keep significant others he may contact under surveillance.
12. Snooze Zac Baxter.

* Key

SNOOZE ZAC BAXTER! That is what it said! I didn't need to ask what "snoozing" was. It didn't sound pleasant.

Stage one, objective three—snooze key litigants . . . Poor old Pops—he just hadn't known what was coming. . . . I looked again at the wine bottle and the dictionary. What kind of a chance did I stand?

I should text someone, phone the police, photo it, and e-mail it to Raphael. . . . I should PHONE someone. . . . No battery. I could soon change that. I pulled out my phone and charger and plugged it into a socket. . . . 0044797606087 . . . *pip pip pip* . . . *"All lines are currently engaged. Please try later. . . ."* Send text: *listen ash, hang on 4 a call—*

My text was cut short when they reentered.

They circled me again, staring. I waited, ready to act. Finally Dr. Sniddon touched my back and said, "Can you feel that?" I jumped, startled.

Now I wonder whether he touched me at all, but at the time I thought: Duh—how can I feel through scar tissue?

"Nope," I said. I'd have said a lot more, but suddenly the heat of my anger was gone and I was beginning to feel shivery.

Dr. Sniddon touched me again. I felt that. He traced my scar marks. Up and across; left, right. His fingertip moving over my scars, tracing patterns.

I wheeled round, bottle in hand.

"Definitely leprosy," he said.

Was he mad? I'd just read how it takes years for a skin patch to form.

Father Bullingham grabbed me from behind. He gripped

my shoulders and pulled the skin taut. He used all his weight to keep me still, while Mrs. Sniddon—or should we call her Ms. Ingleworth now?—twisted the bottle out of my hand and put it back on the table. Dr. Sniddon traced the pattern again. Up, left, right, up. Then back again—up, left, right, up . . . Look, I wasn't just kneeling there! I was trying to get away. I was writhing and yelling and kicking. My heart was going so hard, I thought it would pop up out of my chest and I'd bleed to death. I was too young to be snoozed; I had a lot of living left to do. I hadn't even been to a nightclub in Ibiza, I hadn't driven a Ferrari. I had promises to keep and—I didn't want to die. . . .

Dr. Sniddon traced over my back again. There was something feverish in the way he was trying to work out the scar marks.

"The wrath of God," declared Father Bullingham. His voice was fast, breathy. I jerked and thrashed about, but he pushed his thumbs in just above my shoulder blades. It hurt and I whimpered.

"Complete amputation," said Mrs. Sniddon. "It's the only way."

"I think so," said Dr. Sniddon.

"Let me go!" I screamed.

"The whole of this skin area looks infected," said Dr. Sniddon, and drew a circle around the marks on my back. "It will all have to come off." Then he ran his finger *again* over my scars—the scar marks put there by Pops— up, left, right, working the pattern out.

The door inside my head began to swing open.

The pattern. The scars.

The tangible evidence.

"If you touch me," I said, "if you just try to—my barrister will have the whole lot of you. He'll clean you out of this godforsaken place. I'm warning you—just try."

"Godforsaken—oh dear," said Father Bullingham, coughing.

"I've got people, you know. I'm not like those other kids you fool here—I know what you're up to. I know about the government. Don't mess with me. . . ."

"Oh! So you think your barrister will come and save you, is that it? Is that the sum of your threats? And do you think I will sit here and wait for him? Oh dear. Let me teach *you* a little geography lesson, Mr. Baxter. You are not in England now. Oh no, you are in Africa, and you are on *my* territory where *I* make the rules. And I change the rules just—as—often—and—as—*suddenly* as I like." He punctuated his words with sharp digs, and then jabbed his thumbs cruelly into my pressure points. I shuddered to the floor. "Oh dear, oh dear," he said. "Such a lot to learn."

Dr. Sniddon prodded my back again, ran his fingers over my scars.

The scars. The evidence.

All the time, it had been there.

The door in my head swung wide open. Light streamed through.

Oh my God.

"You'll never get it!" I screamed. "I'll never let you ..."

Of course—*that* was the thing Pops had given me. The one thing he'd had too. That he'd carried for the whole of his life. *That was the secret.* That was what he'd planned on showing the Cormantin Club on that terrible evening before Christmas—the diary entry had said it all. . . .

"*When the cutting was finished, they told me the secret. I can't tell you, because I promised not to—until I die.*"

The secret. The scars.

Until I die.

That was it.

It seemed that the room rocked. I had to press on the floor to steady it.

These were no tribal marks. Akonor and the brothers must have carved the map into Bartholomew's flesh, and he into his son's, and so on, and so on—until me.

I started trembling.

The map was on my back.

My back, my skin. *My back.* I tried to look like I didn't understand.

"But those are just tribal marks."

"We can take no risks," said Father Bullingham, almost as if he was sorry for me.

"I think you must go into isolation while we prepare."

The condemned cell? I cringed. "No! Not the cell!" I put on my most sorrowful, repentant, head-hanging routine. "I was angry . . . I'm sorry . . . I'll be good . . .

Please . . . I didn't mean to hurt Boss Boy, but don't put me in the cell. . . ." Believe me, Brer Rabbit would have been jealous.

But Father Bullingham and the Sniddons left the study, locking the door behind them. There were bars on the window, and no way out. I paced the floor. The map was on my back. My skin was going to be amputated. I wasn't going to survive. I tried to call. No lines. I sent Ash the text. Not delivered. I screamed and screamed and no one came.

Did I say no one came? Sorry. As soon as it was dark, Father Bullingham came. I was terrified. I attacked him. The bottle splintered into a thousand bits, the dictionary caught him full in the face, but it was no use. He twisted my arm until I could bear the pain no more, then he pushed me from the bungalow across the space to the perimeter wall. He opened the condemned-cell door. I struggled as he shoved me in. Then he turned the key.

But in the musty darkness I smiled. Then I laughed. I laughed and laughed. Before I leaned sideways and started my escape, I sent another text to Raphael and Ashley: *found d map dey r people called harold reeves, father bullingham, boss boy (maybe hired locally), n a dr. n mrs. sniddon—gov officials ingleworth, bowdich, an dery check dem out I tink ull cum up wit sumting call up d cormantin club 2 ders sum funny biz der cum out 2 help me ive got 2 escape dis is serious—zac.*

I sent Ashley an added line: *contact mr. bernard immediately.*

Then I leaned sideways, I scrabbled low down with my

fingers—had I loosened the stones enough? I dug into the cracks, the lime powder clogged up my nails . . . It wasn't loose enough. . . . Hell . . . my nails ripped, the lime stung. I would have crossed my fingers, but I needed them. . . . I forced—and—yes, it moved! Yes, air, yes, moonlight!

And, YES, the wall crumbled out.

Good-bye to Cabo Corso

The first thing I did was head for Mina's BUNG. Badu had been right. I needed all the friends I could get. Number one, I couldn't read a map that was scarred into my back. Number two, she hadn't stepped backward at the fight with Boss Boy. A small step, but as Armstrong said, "A giant step for mankind." Sort of.

Waking her was easy. She wasn't asleep. I think she was worried. I think she liked me and was worried about me. Anyway, she was ready, dressed, and so relieved to see me.

"Don't ask anything—just give me a T-shirt; pack useful stuff. I've got the map. I need you, but I need to get out of this place fast."

She didn't say a word; she chucked me a T-shirt, grabbed her rucksack, and followed.

"They want the skin off my back—that's the map."

"Okay."

There were the dogs to think about. And I needed to get Badu, too. After all, we had a deal; he had the diary, and I had the feeling he was a brother.

Just like before, I stayed inside the edge of the rain forest until we made our way round to Badu's shelter. I didn't want to make any noises that would alert the dogs. I figured they stayed near the bungalow at night. But boy, I wasn't taking any chances.

Badu was harder to rouse. He was truly asleep, and as much as I wanted to shake him awake, I wasn't ready to touch him yet. Then it took at least five minutes to get him to understand what had happened. Five minutes is a long time when at any moment you might be discovered. I figured we'd have only the night to escape, with maybe a ten-hour start.

Ten hours wasn't long. We had the rain forest to get through and we'd have to cover our trail. Dogs can track anything—especially trained hunting dogs. We had to find a river to throw them off the scent. I tried to forget about the added hazards of leopards and crocodiles.

I was on my way to get the gold.

PART THREE

Cape Coast Castle,
The White Man's Grave

High Jungle

I haven't told you much about the castle, have I? You'll think I'm making it up, but I'm not.

These are the essentials.

For nearly a century the Portuguese, Dutch, Swedes, and English fought to gain control of Carolusberg Castle. The English won. The English Chartered Company of Royal Adventurers, who controlled it, wrote: "*The lodgings within the castle are very large and well built. Three fronts face the sea around a very handsome quadrangle—a place of arms, well paved—under which is a place to keep the slaves. Cut out of the rocky ground, arched and divided into several chambers so that it will conveniently keep a thousand blacks—let down through an opening made for that purpose. From these chambers through long passages cut into the rock, the slaves pass to the Door of No Return.*

"*Once through the Door no slave ever again sets foot on African soil. The Door is a stone opening which is passed through in single file. It leads straight out to the Atlantic surf. There the boats of the middle passage wait. From there the journey to the New World begins. After long imprisonment in the dark labyrinths, the sunshine is often too much for their weak eyes, and many leave without even setting sight again on their motherland."*

It was back through the Door of No Return I planned to pass. In some ways, I suppose it was fancy. Hadn't Pops said, *"Until my son, the Lost Prince, comes back through the Door of No Return and claims his ransom, my soul will never rest in the land of my ancestors."* But it was not just fancy. I knew *that* was another clue from Pops; the treasure was inside, and the Door of No Return was the castle's weakest point. If I could get out beyond the surf and approach the castle by sea, I stood a reasonable chance of getting into the slave labyrinth unnoticed.

I hadn't worked it all out, of course. In fact I hadn't worked very much of it out. There was still the matter of getting there.

At last Badu sat up. He shook his head, then smiled. "So you really meant it?"

"Yep," I said.

"The deal is still on?"

"Definitely."

"You take me to England?"

"Absolutely."

He nodded. "I also keep my side. I will help you."

He pulled on his tattered shorts over his equally ragged boxers, and groped around for his shirt. He was very thin. His shoulder blades stuck out at sharp angles, but his feet were what scared me most. Three of his toes were missing.

"What happened?" I said, stupidly.

"Life," he said.

Mina stood there watching. That was one of the things I liked about her. Nothing made her back off.

"Listen, I can give you my life history as we go, but we'd better get moving if you don't want to end up as dogs' dinner."

He was right. I started out toward the main gate.

"Not that way," Badu hissed. "Follow me."

He led us down a track into the rain forest. It was very dark inside and hard to avoid the scratchy creepers. When we had gone about two hundred meters, Badu gave us both a twist of paper. "Hold this," he said. "We will climb now up and over the wall. We will stay in the trees for as long as we can. From time to time rub the pepper in this paper over your feet. Put some on now. The dogs hate hot pepper; it will get in their eyes and nose and confuse them. It will cover our scent, too. I've been thinking about this and I have made preparations. Since you told me of the plan, I've been over the wall many times. Don't think a deal is not a deal. I took the flashlight, some tools. I've hidden water for us, and fresh coconuts, so that we will not starve or thirst on our way through the jungle. I have been as far as the coast, and know where the canoes are kept. It was easy for me, nobody cares what I do, I can come and go; but tomorrow they will fire the old cannons and all my people will know that a criminal is out. They will not hesitate to tell the police, so we must become invisible."

I smiled. I stretched out my hand. I laid it on his shoulder. "I'm not afraid. And thanks."

I could feel his happiness through the darkness between us. I wondered how long it had been since someone touched him in friendliness. "Great," I said. "You lead the way, you know it."

"It is important that we go in silence. The animals of the forest are easily scared and they will give us away if we disturb them."

I remembered the clouds of birds that rose from the forest when the Land Rover had passed. "Good thinking," I said.

"So we will whisper, and if I raise my hand and make this sign of alarm, then you freeze and keep as quiet as the grave. It will need much concentration and we will move very slowly. You do not know what you are doing—only I know. So tonight I am Boss Boy—okay?"

"Deal," I said. "Can we get a boat and make it to the front of the castle?"

"Maybe, the moon is nearly full so the tide will be high. Maybe if we are lucky the surf will let us through."

"Tell me about the castle—have you been there?"

"Yes. It's a museum now. It's set up like in the slave days."

"And the Door of No Return?"

"The sea has gone down since the days when men passed through. Now rocks guard the way for maybe ten meters."

"Is it possible to get through?"

"Yes. There is a door of old wood that is shut after the opening hours of the museum. It is not durable; we can pass it."

Inside I was cheering. Yep. I wriggled my scar marks against the inside of Mina's T-shirt. I planned on keeping them right where they were.

Just as we reached the first giant tree and scrambled up into its fork, we heard the baying of the dogs.

"Quickly now," hissed Badu. "They'll soon find this tree, but nobody will notice the dogs till morning."

He reached his hand down past Mina to help me and, I'm pleased to say, I didn't flinch. I grasped his hand firmly and hoisted myself up.

Higher and higher we climbed, up into the huge tree. Beneath was a sea of darkness. I didn't look down. Badu led the way, Mina followed, and I brought up the rear. I heard the first dog arrive at the foot of the trunk. I heard a coughing and a hideous whining. Pepper up your nose must be very nasty.

Life's funny, isn't it? There we were escaping from the Old Portuguese settlement, Mina, Badu, and me. Later, when I read the diaries, I thought of how Bartholomew and his brothers and Uncle Senhor had escaped too. How old do trees get? I figure trees can live for over a thousand years. So if those trees could talk, what would they say?

For what seemed like half the night we crept along branches, onto other great limbs of ancient trees. Badu never faltered, never seemed scared. At times he hissed directions, but he backed them up with help—holding a bough aside, showing us a foothold. At one point I saw the wall of the Old Portuguese settlement below us, then we were over it and into unmarked rain forest. In some ways it was the scariest thing I've ever done, in others it was the most glorious. I hope you never have to go through a night like that, but if you do, you will feel the forest air against your skin and smell the sweet perfume of Lady of the Night, you will see the moon high above set in a vast starry sky, you will hear wild things and know that Africa is the most wonderful continent in the world. I think I would almost be ready to go through it all again. Maybe not all. Maybe not the next bits . . .

Just as I felt done in and Mina crept slower and slower, Badu halted.

"We rest here," he said. "We have not covered much distance. It is always like that in the trees. We become invisible by staying where we are." I looked around in the dead of night. Everywhere was dim. We were fifty feet high. Rest—was he mad?

But Badu led the way into the trunk of a giant silk cotton tree. There, carved out by time and rain, was a hollow that would just about take the three of us. We settled, knees bent and elbows cramped, into the trunk. No one would ever think of looking there! From deep in the cavity, Badu pulled out coconuts and an old cutlass.

"See, I keep my deal," he said.

In seconds we had slashed the tops off them. Boy, if ever coconut juice tasted sweet! As the water slipped down our throats and we chewed the jelly, I mentally cut Badu in with a take of the treasure. Then, surrounded by the husks—for we dare not cast them out—we slept curled up. Leprosy or not, we were all in it together.

All In It Together

Case for the Prosecution
Exhibit 04 Attached

Form MG 14
(CJ Act 1967, s. 9; MC Act 1980, ss. 5A(3) (a) and 5B; MC Rules 1981, r. 70)

EXTRACT: *From the alleged diary of Bartholomew Baktu*

This exhibit (consisting of *case for the prosecution two (2) pamphlets written in Portuguese — certified translation Lisbon University — verified against accounts of the Royal African Company — considered authentic; Professor Braithwaite, British Museum* ~~page(s) each page signed by me~~) is true to the best of my knowledge ~~and I make it knowingly, if it is tendered in evidence, I shall be liable to prosecution if I have wilfully stated in it anything which I know to be false or do not believe to be true.~~

Signature *N/A — see above* Date *November 5th* *DL Hesketh*

Akonor's arms were still round me. Uncle Senhor was shaking us. It wasn't dawn yet, but the door of the house was open and a pink blush was spreading through it.

"We must go," he said slowly, as if to mask the urgency in the rosy glow around him. "All the others are waiting in the forest, you can rest no longer."

Akonor had bound his chest during the night with swathes of cloth, but I could see the dried blood, a dense black staining outward. He didn't say anything. He tried to smile, then he was on his feet pulling me gently up.

"Imagine we are going hunting," he said. "The forest is quiet and we will track the duiker. Let us move silently so they will not hear us."

I smiled as I remembered those mornings when he had taken me deep into the forest. Armed only with our spears we had crept together, full of hope. Often we found nothing, maybe a grass cutter, or some other small bush meat. But sometimes we found the tracks of large deer, the red one with the horns. Then we would hunt! I squeezed his hand. "I will catch the red one today, and the white man will not catch me again."

We left Cabo Corso by the forest wall, and soon we entered into the high jungle. There, even the sun could not send our shadows out to betray us. My elder brother, Baidoo, led the way, but soon I realized that we were traveling in a huge curve.

"Why are we not going to the red deer's lair?" I asked Akonor.

"Today we are the red ones, little frog, and the White Death hunts us. We will try to reach the coast again, near the castle, and if we can take the canoes from there we shall escape him."

"But the white ones have the dogs, they will track us down?"

"Sssh, then we must move fast. Once we take the canoes the dogs cannot follow, and the white man does not know the canoe craft. He will drown if he tries."

"Yes, he will drown," I repeated. For to sail the canoe is very difficult and the surf is very dangerous.

We traveled for a long time, stepping softer than a leopard over the twigs. Already I was tired, my waist was paining, and I felt much like vomiting again. But always when I stumbled, Akonor was there to lift me up and press me forward. Only once did I complain and he stopped, lifted my chin upward, and said, "You are the son of King Baktu. The blood of princes runs through your heart. Let not the ancestors hear that you would whine like a woman." I felt ashamed and hung my head. From then on I made no complaint again.

And indeed I should not have, for my brothers took turns carrying the gold chest on a palanquin and never once asked me to help. How long we crept for, I do not know. From inside the forest it is hard to tell how high the sun climbs. Far away I could hear the sound of the dogs, but it was very far away, so at first I was not afraid. But even though we did not stop to rest or drink water, the sound of the dogs gradually became louder. I tried not to be afraid. My brothers were there. Uncle Senhor was there. I was very safe. At least this is what I told myself. But my drops of blood that beat sometimes at the top of my chest did not want to listen. I could feel them pounding over my heart and they wouldn't stop. My legs too were cowards and sometimes they trembled so much I was sure Akonor would notice. I didn't want him to see how the fear made my legs shake.

At last we broke from the forest to the shrublands that led down to the beaches, but at the same moment the undergrowth burst open behind us and one of the largest dogs broke through. When it saw us, it doubled speed and set up a baying that froze all the drops of blood from my chest down to my shaking knees.

"Run!" screamed Baidoo. "Run for your lives!"

I knew we shouldn't run in front of the dog. I knew that was the worst thing to do. "No!" I said, but nobody listened.

And my legs, those shaking cowards, did not listen either.

Routes A, B, & C

It seemed that the howling of dogs in my dreams had broken through into my waking up. I lay still, cramped and stiff, fifty feet in the air, snuggled tight to Badu. It was not a dream; I could hear the dogs howling in the forest below. Suddenly, the forest seemed to shake. The boom of a cannon roared through the morning. It was so loud I had to cover my ears with my hands and grit my teeth. For one minute it seemed like every animal in the forest squawked—and then there was silence. I opened my eyes and there were Badu and Mina staring back at me.

Cautiously, I peered over the edge of the tree hole. Below, endless space stretched downward. Even sitting down, it made my legs weak. My head swam and my heart started to thump wildly. How on earth had we crept along branches in the dark so easily? The whole of my chest sort of seized up. How were we going to get down? Or go on?

"Hold it there," whispered Mina.

But I didn't. I pulled my head right back round and twisted toward them again. Badu was smiling.

"We don't move now. They will see the canopy shake and we will be discovered."

"So what do we do?"

"We wait until night. We sleep. We will need much strength to finish the journey."

"You need to know exactly what we're up against," I said. "You can back out now if you don't like the odds." I told them about the papers I'd seen in Father Bullingham's study. "GCHQ means Government Communications Headquarters. It's not a joke. One of my school friends' dads worked in the new Carillion building and he said that his dad had signed so many Official Secrets Act papers, he'd stopped talking altogether. They don't mess around. If they wanted, they could just bomb the hell out of this forest and us with it."

"But they won't," said Mina, "because for a start, Father Bullingham would have to admit he failed—which he won't. He'll try to get us first and tidy up the loose ends."

"Thanks," I said. "I've never been called a loose end before."

"Dummy!"

"You cannot bomb this forest," said Badu. "The God of Kakum lives here and he will not allow that."

"It would be a shame, too," I said, for in the dawn the forest was magnificent. The world seemed to arch over us while we snuggled down in the arms of our giant tree. All the spaces in the canopy above were filled with golden sunshine, and when I breathed in, it was like drinking something strong and sweet. "Yeah," I continued, "I bet this tree likes us, she'll put in a good word with the Kakum God." I figured we needed all the help we could get.

"And if you'll just turn round again, like before, I'll try and work out the map, dummy," said Mina.

I could think of a few other things I'd rather do than hang headfirst out of a tree hole, but I didn't want to upset myself; so I turned round, rolled up my shirt, and leaned outward as before—only this time I kept my eyes closed. I felt Mina's fingers tracing over the scar marks on my back.

"It must mark the entrance somewhere. If I could figure out where they started in, then I'd know where they got to. What do you think, Badu?"

He too started prodding over my scar marks, while I held my position, eyes tight shut.

"They might have got in from the Door," I said. "Pops was always so certain about going back through the Door."

"Top to bottom, or bottom to top?" said Mina.

"Let's imagine they started at the bottom and marked the way upward." Badu prodded the lower part of my back. "Say, here."

"In that case . . ." Mina started jabbing somewhere beneath my left shoulder blade.

"Yes, but this bit is confusing." I felt Badu trace a jagged line over my ribs.

"It looks like they forced a way into some lower passage, or . . . ?"

"Hard to tell," said Badu.

"Well, for a start, how many times would you guess this map has been copied?"

"Maybe five," I said.

"It could have changed a lot."

"I dunno," I said. "I didn't know it was a treasure map."

Mina sighed. But at least she didn't say "dummy."

"How old were you when it was done?"

"Seven. Pops said scar marks were always done on your seventh birthday." I thought of seven-year-old Bartholomew.

Suddenly, the horror of the first cutting seized me, and I think I trembled. I imagined little Bartholomew lying face-down on the clammy floor of an underground chamber, and Akonor bending over him with a splinter of broken glass, sawing at his back in the shuddering light of a candle.

"We needn't worry now," said Mina, "because when we get there the passages will probably only go in one direction anyway."

"I don't think so," said Badu. "The dungeons are close together and built one after the other; they run in every direction."

"You better figure it out," I said. "When we get down there, we won't have much time and it might be dark."

"Then," said Mina, "I think you go down first, then there's a choice: You turn left and go through a wider space, at the end of which is a passageway, then you go through a small gap or down to a lower dungeon and continue halfway, then the treasure is buried in the wall. Well, that's what I think, anyway."

"Not bad," said Badu.

"I agree," I said.

"But," she continued, "I'll figure out route B and C as well in case I'm wrong, and if none of those is right, well . . ."

"Yes?" I said.

"I'll think again."

So that was it. For at least an hour, Mina figured out routes B and C and probably more. I grew tired of leaning out of the hole and tried opening my eyes. The same giddy feeling swept over me, but I forced myself to feel the solid trunk and the enclosed walls of the nest. Then I focused way down on the forest floor. Beneath the branches I could see movement. "Shh," I whispered.

The leaves and creepers and overgrowth obscured almost everything—but every now and then I caught sight of a band of people moving over the forest floor. They seemed to be doing something that involved a lot of crouching and digging. At last I turned and beckoned to Badu. "What are they up to?"

He took my place and peered down. At last he turned to face us. "Traps," he whispered. "They are setting mantraps."

Ground Flaw

The three of us looked at each other. I know I was thinking: mantraps—kidtraps—Zactraps. We had to get down fifty feet of tree trunk, outrun hunting dogs, dodge murderous MI5 agents disguised as missionaries, avoid being caught by the local police—not to mention leopards—and now the whole forest floor was riddled with steel mantraps. Traps that could snap through the bones of your leg—like dry spaghetti.

Badu nodded and closed his eyes. "Worry," he said. "Worry plenty—then worry some more. I have set such traps to catch big bush meat. I know them. I know how to see them, but we can only move at night and down there it's going to be very dark."

"The flashlight?" I suggested.

"The batteries are weak. We should save them as much as possible."

"That is really reassuring," I said.

For the rest of the day we stayed crushed up, very depressed. I longed to stretch out; I was hungry and even coconut jelly gets boring after a while. I imagined Big Macs—super-, extra-, double-size, big meal deals, with doughnuts and chocolate milkshakes. . . . I wanted to take my mind off everything. I turned my phone on, wondering if I could get away with a game of Snake before I *really* rationed the battery.

There were two messages on the phone: *stay calm mush u can do it am v worried have foned mr. b he will pick me up later n will tell u what he says cant get r—ash.* That message had been sent yesterday. The next one said: *Mr. b not happy chappy is going 2 come n get u take ur time if its done by d rules may take another 300 yrs—ash.* I smiled a little. At least Badu was wrong—there *was* someone who cared enough to come and help me, even though he'd probably arrive in time to fly my body home.

I'd been thinking about bodies. I had begun to wonder how long "sustained body contact" was needed to get leprosy. I tried not to, but I couldn't help it. I wriggled a bit, and wrapped my phone and the diary in a piece of plastic bag so tightly you'd have thought they might catch it too.

At last the sun began to dip below the canopy and dusk seeped into the pink across the sky. I began to feel quite poetic about that sunset. It might very well be my last.

"Before we move, rub your muscles well," said Badu. "Sudden exercise after being cramped up can make your legs go hard. The pain will hold you and you might fall."

It was difficult to bend and rub our own legs, so we rubbed each other's.

"In the bottom of this hole I put a rope. It was the washing line from the bungalow." Badu giggled softly and so did we. We were tense, I guess. "We must go down now and try to make the big river before morning. The dogs will go back to the house after dark, because that is when they are fed. Afterward they'll sleep and we'll move. I don't think they will come back to the forest before dawn, so we'll move fast. The big river is ten miles away—it's in the wrong direction, but that is to confuse them. Once we reach the river I've hidden a small canoe and paddles. It's mine; don't worry. The dogs cannot follow through the water, but men can, so we must go downstream at dawn. My island is five miles as the water flows and I know a place where we can hide. The big river runs all the way to the sea. From there we will take a long canoe and cross the surf to the castle."

"Yo!" I said, and upped his percentage.

"It will be hard, the leopard hunts at night and the river has many crocodiles—and now we cannot take the straight path because of the traps. We must cut through the forest with only the moon to show us the way, and down there little moonshine will reach us."

All of it sounded a lot better than plastic surgery.

"I have been to the river, and kept more coconuts there, but after that we must tighten our belts and take our chances."

"Wow," I said, "you've done well." Actually I was surprised that he had done so much. Still, a deal is a deal. I peered at him in the dim light, punched him gently. "Don't worry, we'll make it. And when we've got the gold you're going to get a private suite at the best BUPA."

"Bupa?"

"Hospital—private, Sky TV, lots of drinks, better food, lovely nurses!"

"Tie the rope around your waist and cling to the tree. We will lower you."

"Let Mina go first." I thought the two of us were strong and that would be the safest way.

"No, you are the heaviest. Mina will help me. She is small—I can manage her alone."

"What about you?"

"I'll climb."

"But—"

"Don't worry about me—how do you think I left the rope up here?"

"'Cause you went back along the branches? 'Cause your real identity is Spiderman? I dunno, I give up. How did you?"

Badu didn't answer. He snorted, as if I was a little kid who didn't understand anything.

"Well you better be careful, 'cause if you slip we're finished."

"Because of you I will be very careful," said Badu, all serious.

I thumped him. He laughed. I laughed too and tried not to think of the yawning space below.

"Just cling tight to the tree. If you swing around too much, the bark will take the skin off you and then the flies will come. You will suffer."

I didn't answer. If we started talking, we'd stay up there all night. There was no point in wasting time. So instead I tied the washing line with a reef knot around my waist. Starting out was very scary.

"Here." I passed the line to Badu and watched while he passed it over a branch just higher than the nest and then wound it around his waist. He took Mina's hands and placed them on his shoulders. "Steady me," he said.

Then, trying not to think of anything, I climbed out of the hole onto the lower branch and slid off into the darkness below. I clung for a moment to the branch until I felt the jerk of my body-weight in my shoulders, then reached for the trunk with my feet. The next bit was the worst. One moment I was suspended, toes outstretched, arms aching, then I felt the trunk, the tug at my waist, and I let go. The tree was smooth and I was grateful. Like a lizard I clung to it, legs wide, arms not long enough to go around its girth, line taut again. Then the line slackened, just a foot, and I slid down the trunk slowly. But not slowly enough to stop the bark taking the skin off my palms. "Mina," I hissed, "wear socks on your hands." Then the line slackened again and I slid another foot.

I guess I was too tense to notice the pain. It wasn't until my feet touched the ground that I realized my hands were badly grazed. My legs crumpled beneath me and for a moment I lay there, heart pounding. As soon as my trembling fingers would work, I undid the knot and tugged sharply on the line. With a slight hiss it snaked upward into the dim canopy above.

As I lay there spread-eagled on the floor, trying to stabilize my pulse, the seriousness of it all hit me. Here I was in the African jungle, no food, no money, no Tangfastics sour jelly chews, and running for my life. There was no one out there who knew exactly where I was—hey, even I didn't! And behind me was more danger than before. Boy, I lay there afraid to be myself.

I heard a faint thud and Mina was beside me. I think she took the climb down better; soon she was kneeling up and whispering, "Thanks for the tip about the socks. It was quite fun, wasn't it? You okay?"

To tell the truth, I wasn't feeling too absolutely fabulous. I flopped back again on the leaf mold. I think I might have fainted. I'm not sure. I don't remember waiting for Badu to get down. The next thing I knew, he was beside me coiling up the rope. How he'd got down with it I don't know. At the time he just said, "Leave no clues, no trash, no footprints. Rub pepper now and follow me."

For hours we dodged through the thick undergrowth, weaving our way, single file, in silence, breathing in damp air and sneezing. Everywhere was rotting and smelled kind of sweet. Badu led the way, swiping at the undergrowth with his cutlass.

It was very slow going, and I got to remembering how

Tarzan had swung across Africa on nothing but a few creepers, but although I looked up to see if that was a good idea, I could only see splotches of inky blackness.

Beneath us twigs crumbled like soggy cornflakes and our feet sank into centuries of leaf mold. In places where the ground was flat, tiny clay cones erupted. Some of them had holes bored right through, and I knew just from the feel as they squidged underfoot that inside nasty biting insects waited. Between the insect cones rose ant hills, squiggled and soft like those lugworm piles you see on the beach in England. On either side were twisted stranglers, dripping leaves, and straight supple shoots. From time to time Badu flashed on the flashlight and swung the cutlass—then we continued in darkness.

On we journeyed, curving round huge buttress roots, stepping over mossy fallen trunks with roots upended, as if a giant hand had plucked them like straws from the ground. Keeping always away from the beaten tracks, we crept— scratched and weary. From time to time a night bird called "Hoo Hoo Hah!" and I shivered inside, thinking of witches and witch doctors and wondering what else was out there in the forest. And as I listened, more noises. The "*peep-peeping*," high and distant like an impatient taxi, and the "*tickety-ticky-tick*," like a strange animal Morse code, punched and metallic. But worst of all I felt rather than heard the soft padding of a heavy thing behind us.

"Badu," I whispered at last, "I think something is out there. It's not an echo, I'm sure—listen." Obediently he stopped and listened, but the heavy creeping thing stopped too, and soon Badu moved on.

"But Badu . . . ," I said again.

"I heard it long ago," he said. "It is the leopard; he hunts at night." He said it with such composure that for a moment I didn't believe him—that is, until I heard the distinct padding again.

The Added Hazards

It wasn't even a pad, now I come to think of it. It was the swish of a stem twisted back and let loose, the snap of a twig under a great weight, and the faint push of shoots forced apart. I was bringing up the rear, and I'd been trying to imagine myself in a movie, as if I were a hero creeping through the tropical jungle. Something a bit like Tarzan after he'd stopped swinging. It'd helped. But now I realized that the guy at the rear always gets it first. You know! And then there were two! So for a while I kept pushing at Mina, until she turned round and snapped at me, "What's up with you, dumster? I can't go any faster."

I didn't want to scare her so I just said, "Well, you've got to." But the whispering scared me as much as the swishing behind, and when she tried to hurry she made so much noise that I snapped again, "Can't you be quiet?" She replied something that I won't repeat, and then it was all too much noise to stand.

Somehow I kept my legs moving. Stumbling past tangled stems, bunches of black fruits, spiked branches and thin creepers meshed together like a sail ship's riggings, all the time my heart was banging. Which part of you does a leopard bite first?

Someone screamed. Was that me?

Was that the "Hoo Hoo" bird? His "Ha Ha!" out of control?

Badu stopped; he turned. "The leopard has marked us; he screams like a girl. Now we must be very careful."

I have to tell you that Mina doesn't scream. She can get high-pitched, but right then she didn't even gasp—but she did walk faster. "That's it, babes," I said. "Now you're moving." I went faster too, but something else was controlling my legs, and they weren't doing a very good job. I kept tripping on stranglers and stubbing my foot on spikes. My breathing had gone all wrong as well. I just seemed to be gasping all the time. Air was going in, but not coming out. Breathe, I told myself; for God's sake, breathe.

We came to a huge bamboo grove. Thick shadowy poles arched over us, like the nave of some amazing cathedral. On the floor: dried pointed leaves curled like wood shavings, straight like knife blades.

"Hurry," whispered Badu.

It's funny how some things stick in your memory; those bamboo poles were tufted as if they were wearing grass skirts!

"He can only attack where there is space."

The arc of bamboo spanned fifty feet across and forty up. It was the kind of place where you could have a great party. But even though it was Friday night I didn't feel much like raving. I didn't feel much like sprinting, either, so I didn't go much faster than Concorde. Still, that was the longest bamboo grove I ever ran across. We must have disturbed frogs, for suddenly there was a loud chorus of croaking. Running, croaking, and running, all the time expecting the pounce and the slice of teeth . . .

At last Badu dived into the undergrowth, and Mina and I sardined in after him.

"The traps have helped us," said Badu.

"Helped?"

"If not for the traps we would have taken the pathways."

"Well, that would have been easier."

"Then the leopard will already be in his tree."

"Meaning?"

"The leopard uses his speed to hunt. He must have a space to spring in, or he sits in the trees and pounces. This way we give him no space, no tree, so he only follows, waiting for the grove or the pathway. After the leopard has made his kill, he drags his meat into the tree and eats."

"Will he get tired—give up?"

"No, he is hungry. He will follow us till dawn."

"And then?"

"He knows we go to the river. This is his jungle and he knows all directions."

"Are there more than one?"

"No, he hunts alone."

"Anyway, so what if he knows where we're going?"

"He will circle us and find the next open space. He will be waiting."

"Then we might as well give up."

"No."

"The trees—yeah, what about climbing again?"

"No, he is better in the trees than in the bush. He likes to eat baboons. . . . Wait—I have an idea. . . ."

We waited, trembling there in the spiky undergrowth; waiting while the unseen leopard circled us.

"The dogs."

I'd forgotten about them, and I can tell you, I wasn't pleased to be reminded.

"The leopard likes to eat dogs as well. He likes dog meat very much; twice he has come into the settlement and taken a dog."

I could see what he was thinking. As far as I was concerned the leopard was welcome to the whole pack.

"These dogs are his old enemies, for they are hunting dogs—but he will not attack them all. If only we can get him one . . ."

I kept quiet. If it had been Tuffley Park—but here?

"It is a risk. We must travel on in this bush and reach near the river. At dawn the dogs will follow us—two hours they will be here, well before the trackers. Then we must cross out into the open path and let the leopard come. When the dogs run for us maybe one of them will spring a trap. The leopard will want the trapped dog—for even now you see he is uneasy about hunting humans. Then we must stick together and run for the river before the other dogs get us."

"Sounds like a piece of cake, Badu," I said.

"What if there is no trap?" said Mina.

"Babes," I said, "have no fear. You are with the Forest Rangers."

"Dummy," she said, and this time I think she meant it.

"The dogs will confuse the leopard anyway, so we should still run. Maybe we will be lucky."

It was a rubbish plan, but at the time, I figured it might work. It's useful sometimes not to have too much imagination. For a while we struggled on through denser and denser undergrowth.

Sometimes do you ever think "How did I get here?" And your mind flashes back to you as a little kid watching telly, eating crisps? What happened? How did the chain of events start? How did it lead to this? You woke up each morning and thought, "Another day." So how had the days led on until I found myself here—in this dark jungle with its overpowering smell of animal and undergrowth?

I started this account with the diaries, but the story didn't start there, did it? Did it even start with Bartholomew on that afternoon when the white men hunted him? I think when you are faced by the end of your bit in the story, you realize how long history is. If it had ended for me that next morning, I knew the whole story wouldn't end there—that somehow all this was bigger than me. And that even now thinking about each bit of that journey, I know the story won't end here. No. And when you put this down and go to bed, that won't be the end either. Suddenly, seeing life like that makes you feel very small, although not unimportant.

I'm tempted to write that I wasn't scared at all. You know, big up myself. Superman stuff. But I was. I was so deeply afraid that I had the urge to pee all the time, although there was no liquid left in my body. It would be hard to say what scared me most, the leopard catching me or catching Mina or Badu—and it shows what a coward I am, because I secretly, *desperately*, hoped that it would get one of them first. Or was I more scared of the dogs with their razor teeth, or Father Bullingham—my skin crawled—or the police and capture? But there was another kind of fear too. The fear of failing, of returning to Gloucester without the gold. Returning back to SGCCCH. Returning to that meaning-less life with no dream. It's ridiculous, but I was scared of what Ashley would think if I came back empty-handed. "Right, mush," he'd say, "can't be helped, you've got to look at this logically. You did your best and it wasn't good enough."

How would I tell Pops that I'd reached the very place where the treasure lay hidden, found the map, and failed to bring it back? What would I text Raphael? I think I decided there in the darkness of that night that if I failed to get the gold, I wasn't going back. The dogs or the leopard could have me—but not Father Bullingham.

Maybe it got a bit easier. Maybe it's always easier when

you know what you can stand and what you can't. For some silly reason being part of the story made the fear of dying go away. It would be just the end of a chapter. A chapter in which Zac Baxter died. Just like the other sad chapters in the diary. Like this one.

The Fear of Dying

Case for the Prosecution
Exhibit 05 Attached

Form MG 14
(CJ Act 1967, s. 9; MC Act 1980, ss. 5A(3) (a) and 5B; MC Rules 1981, r. 70)

EXTRACT:..*From the alleged diary of Bartholomew Baktu*................................

This exhibit (consisting of ....*case for the prosecution two (2)*
pamphlets written in Portuguese........................certified translation Lisbon
University......certified against accounts of the Royal African Company......
considered authentic: Professor Braithwaite, British Museum...........................
~~page(s) each page signed by me~~) is true to the best of my knowledge ~~and I make it knowingly, if it is tendered in evidence, I shall be liable to prosecution if I have wilfully stated in it anything which I know to be false or do not believe to be true.~~

Signature *N/A—see above*... Date...*November 5th* *DC Hesketh*

I was running and my chest was hurting. I had fallen far behind my brothers. I could see that Tendia, short and fat as he was, had already reached the canoe and was dragging it alone toward the surf. Soon Baidoo was with him and Kafui and Senhor Dias and the gold. I tried to cry out, but no sound came from my throat, and then I stumbled. My nose hit the sand and I breathed it in, choking. My chin slammed my teeth together and I bit

295

my tongue. As I lay there, winded, I expected to feel the fangs of the hunting dog rip into my back, and I closed my eyes. But even as I closed them, I saw Akonor stop and look behind him, and when I opened them again, he was standing over me.

I heard the dog spring. I heard Akonor grunt and the dog howl, and then they fell on me—the dog and my brother.

I do not know how he defeated the dog, for it was of a great size and with terrible teeth. Later he said, "I waited until it sprang at my throat and then I grasped its forepaws. I wrenched them apart, for that is how to defeat the dog. His chest is narrow and his ribs will crack."

Akonor slung the dog aside and picked me up. "Do you want to crawl like the turtle to the water?"

I spat out the sand and the blood and hung my head. Akonor took my hand and led me forward. We reached the canoe before three more dogs broke through to the beach and, close behind them, the first of the white men's native trackers. He was holding a firing gun and he dropped to one knee.

The blast of the gun screamed past me. A puff of smoke swept down the beach to the water's edge. My brother Tendia seemed to sway. He caught at his side. He hovered for a while on the bows of the canoe. It seemed that he grew taller and thinner, that suddenly there was less of him, as if he had aged terribly. Then he tottered and pitched. He landed in the froth at the water's edge and the foam around him turned red.

Blood Runs Thicker

I would like to tell you that it all went according to plan, that the leopard got the dog and we escaped into a very comfy boat and sailed downstream and had lunch (preferably chicken tikka masala with pilau rice and Peshwari naan) somewhere in a safe place. But it did not go according to plan. There was a trap all right, but it didn't get a dog. It got me.

In some ways I was lucky. It didn't splinter my shinbone. It didn't drive three holes straight through the major muscles of my calf. It seemed I couldn't even spring a trap shut properly. No, I tripped over it and went sprawling.

The pain was proper though. I don't think at that moment I worried at all about the leopard or the dogs. As I hit the pathway, my chin snapped shut on my tongue.

By the way, dawn had already dawned. And we'd been listening to its chorus of dogs for too long (like two hours). We were near the river and it was time for the rubbish plan not to work. And like I said, it didn't. I fell into the trap. The dogs appeared. I knew what they were thinking. Yum. Breakfast. Zacfood.

Before I closed my eyes, I saw Badu look back.

The dogs stopped. Mina told me afterward that they seemed confused because we weren't running. Badu came back to help me. The lead dog was huge. He eyed Badu. Badu eyed him. They were not strangers. Then Badu bent down as if to pick up a rock just like Father Bullingham did on that first night. That was when the dog did something weird. It rushed forward, bit my leg, then turned and bolted.

Badu straightened up.

There were no rocks on the path.

There was also no sign of the leopard, either. Then I heard the mangled yell of a dog away back in the bush. Wild animals are more cunning than you can predict. I mean, imagine that the leopard had tracked us all night, but when he'd heard the dogs he'd circled back and picked off the last one.

For some reason, maybe because we weren't running, maybe because of the screaming, the rest of the dogs turned and, baying horribly, started back toward the leopard. Maybe that's how it is. You can be trained to go for what seems like the next thing, but your history calls. Your blood is moved by the things your ancestors did.

After all, they were leopard-hunting dogs.

At the time I can't say that I thought much about the psychology of dogs. I was just glad they didn't finish me off. When I asked Badu later why the lead hound hadn't attacked him, he said, "You must fix it with your eyes. Its eyes can't hold you because they aren't set completely at the front of its head, and then you pick up a rock. It understands that you will hurl it—and that's the way to defeat the dog."

I didn't bother pointing out that there were no rocks. It was irrelevant.

Badu pulled me up and helped me to the edge of the river. I was losing a lot of blood. That worried me. What worried Badu was the trail it left. He dumped me, bleeding, in a small boat that he pulled out from under some overhanging tree; and, after saying, "Leave no trail, no trash, and no blood," he went back and scuffed over the bleeding and sprinkled leaves on the path. "That will not fool the dogs," he said, "but it may fool their owners."

Then he pushed the small coracle out, down the small stream, which led into the pounding waters of a vast river.

Hydrophobia

I don't know which hurt worse, my tongue or my leg. Mina suggested bandages, although we had none. Badu insisted I hang my leg over the side of the boat, so that the wound would be washed by river water.

"Well, for a start, that's not hygienic," Mina said.

"Painful," I said.

"Dog bite is very serious," Badu said. "More people die of dog bite than fever."

"Crocodiles," I said.

Badu sucked air between his teeth in disgust, and grabbed my leg and dragged it—with me following—until he could hang it from the knee joint over the side of the coracle.

I screamed.

"You, Mr. Didn't-do-anything, are foolish. If you don't do anything right now, you will die of this dog bite."

I didn't have the strength to resist. Mina tried a bit harder.

"Badu, dog bite doesn't kill, you know—it's the germs,

you know, infections that kill. I bet this river water is full of every kind of bacteria known to science—and a lot more not even discovered yet."

Badu gave her a withering look. "The dog-bite sickness hates water. That is why you must wash the leg. It will chase the poison out. If you leave the dog-bite sickness inside it will make the whole body hate water, and you will die of thirst, frothing at your mouth."

I didn't know what the hell he was talking about, and I was in too much pain to care. Mina shifted slightly, then she leaned over the side and started splashing my leg like crazy. At last she sat back and turned to me. "He's right as usual."

"Well, has the dog-bite sickness gone for a dip yet?" I asked.

"It's not funny, Zac. He's talking about rabies."

After that I just lay back in the boat and let the water swill over the gash above my ankle. Rabies wasn't one of the diseases I was an expert on. I guess in England we don't see a lot of it. Mina filled me in on the details.

"It's carried in the saliva glands, especially of dogs. We get outbreaks, but most dogs are vaccinated against it."

"Why don't you mop my brow?"

"It has no cure; if you get bitten you've got to scrub the wound immediately. There are injections, but they're tricky."

"Or hold my hand?"

"Stop it, dummy."

"Or give me the kiss of life?"

"If it gets you, you die—mad, running round in circles, of hydrophobia."

"Finished?"

"Dogs with rabies act weird."

"Like the dog that bit me?"

"Yeah. All the vaccines have to be kept at controlled temperatures. If they freeze or go above ten degrees Celsius they're useless."

"Like in a fridge?"

"Yeah."

"I see."

I seemed to remember that at Cabo Corso electricity wasn't much of a big deal. It would be tricky to keep anything at a controlled temperature there. I pulled out my mobile and untied the plastic. "Better update the rescue team then," I said. *Am in a little boat on a big scary river bring vaccine have probably got rabies but at least im with d girl of my dreams wish u were here and I wasn't—z.*

The King of the Baktus

As much as we could, we kept the coracle close to the banks of the great river. You didn't have to be Einstein to figure out why. Center river was swift and dangerous. Center river was easily visible for miles around. That didn't mean to say skirting the banks came with a safety certificate. Badu said, in his matter-of-fact way, "The crocodile stays near the land."

"What if they smell my blood?" I said. "I mean—no offense, cuz, but I'd like to hang on to as many toes as I can."

"Eh! You do not understand the crocodile," said Badu. "He is not like the shark that is excited by the smell of blood. He just doesn't like anyone in his territory."

"How do you know, anyway?" said Mina.

"The crocodile waits in the shallow waters and sights you, and then he knocks you into the water with his tail. He's very proud of his cunning," said Badu. "This is the estuary where I grew up; all these waters are called Pra. My people are the Badus and once we were mighty. From here to the castle and beyond used to belong to us. Then the white men came."

I notice he pronounced Badu in two parts, "Ba—too," with a slight click in the middle.

"My mother and father were sick."

I didn't know what to say. I felt I should say something, but I figured from my angle on the bottom of the boat with my leg cocked over its shallow side, my silence could be forgiven.

"I don't know what happened to them. They took me to the island, to my grandfather, when I was born and then they left."

I tried swishing my ankle a bit to really flush out the DB sickness.

"They had to leave me so that I didn't get it too—you can understand that, can't you?"

He sounded like *he* was still trying to understand it.

"Nunu told me I should never leave the island, and when I was really little I never tried, but you know, an island is a small place. I used to persuade Nunu to bring me here into this jungle—we'd hunt for the red deer. I was okay on the island, but I didn't like it when Nunu left. I'd have to stay with Stick Mummy. 'You stay here, Badu,' he'd say, 'hold on to Stick Mummy's hand till I get back.' He had to go sometimes to get food—you can understand that, can't you?"

I think Mina had fallen asleep. If I hadn't been in so much pain I might have too.

"They came and took me off the island and left me at Cabo Corso. Nunu wasn't there and I couldn't fight all of them."

"What about Stick Mummy—didn't she tell Nunu? Why didn't he come for you?"

"Stick Mummy was only a stick."

I thought about it. Pops and me in Arrowsmith House, Badu and Nunu on an island. Both of us growing up and not knowing about each other.

"Soon Father Bullingham will find the dogs and figure out we have gone downstream. He will tell all the villages around and it will not be possible for us to land anywhere. We are tired, so if you will not mind I'll take you to my island. Nunu will be there, but you must not laugh."

"But won't your folks figure you'll go to the island?"

"Yes, but you do not understand my people. They want to do the right thing, but they don't want to do the wrong one. So, they will say, 'Yes sir,' but in their hearts they will not know the best thing to do. If they see us they will have to tell the police, but if they don't see us they will say, 'Aha! It is not meant to be. Those bad boys may have escaped for a purpose that we will not know today, so we must wait and see how it is.' Sometimes a good thing can come from a bad one. *Batiri nna baabi na woatwa wo ba-bone ti akoto ho*—there is no other person's shoulder anywhere on which you can put the head of your own bad child after you have cut it off."

I didn't understand. I couldn't work out how they

could take both sides at the same time. I think I said so.

"They are not on anyone's side. They are on their own side. They want to do the right thing for all time, that is all."

Not much, eh! The right thing for all time. "But they took you to Cabo Corso—was that the right thing?"

"No, it was the whites who took me there, the ones who come to give the children polio medicine. They heard of me and decided to fetch me. I tried to tell them not to, but they wouldn't listen. Now I'm not sure if I caught the sickness at the settlement, or if I was infected all along."

I wanted to ask him details but I figured this might not be a good time.

"I went there before the days of Father Bullingham. Leprosy exists, you know. There has always been a colony at Cabo Corso. First, they hid from the world in the ruins of the old houses. The people used to call the place 'Lazar Houses.' They said that the place was a bad-luck place, that evil spirits lived there. Fifty years ago, Kwame Nkrumah had the gate built and started a clinic. It was a good hospital. He was a very great man and made us all very happy to be Ghanaians. Of course I wasn't born then, but all Ghanaians know this. He built workshops to train poor people how to help themselves; but afterward when our own beloved Nkrumah was overthrown, the new government didn't care much and the hospital suffered. When Father Bullingham came we were happy."

"But—"

"Father Bullingham is nobody. He is not a big man. At first I thought he would help, but I soon learned. He had his own plan. He wanted to just knock down the old town. He was not serious."

"Why?"

"In Ghana we have much respect for a pastor, but there were rumors . . ."

"What?"

"They said he was an American, a CIA, a spy! That he was not a reverend father at all. Now when you tell me of this paper you saw, I am not surprised. He was just clearing our old Lazar Houses so his country wouldn't have to admit to what they did in ours."

Imagine that, local folks had sussed him out straightaway! Like Bob Marley says, "*You can fool some people sometimes, but you can't fool all the people all the time.*"

"Did you ever hear stories about lost treasure?"

"The story of the lost gold is known here. But we know—I mean, the Badu people know—that the treasure was lost at sea."

It hadn't been lost at sea, that much I knew, or why would I be carrying a map?

"What do people say about Cabo Corso—the bad-luck stuff. The evil spirits, what happened there?"

"They say it was treachery. The Portuguese at Cabo Corso were betrayed and murdered. They say the English cut them into little pieces and fed them to their dogs.

They say that the English sat around laughing as they burnt the children alive in the houses. They say the English stole the land by the castle. They say many things."

I smiled. I'd remembered another of Pops's sayings: "*You can demolish buildings, but you can't demolish history.*" Even if MI5 snoozed me, they could not snooze the truth. I don't know if that made me feel any better, but at least it exercised my cheek muscles.

Badu dragged two coconuts from the bottom of the boat and topped one and handed it to me.

"We will go to Nunu. Don't worry, we will be quite safe with him; he is the last of the royal Badus; he is a chief really, but he is a bit different."

"Different?"

"Yes, he is off senses, you know."

"You mean how?"

"You know—not correct. He hears voices—he has dreams."

"Have you seen him then—since you went to Cabo Corso?"

"Plenty. I make this journey, I bring him food from the settlement and T-shirts when I can."

"Then why do you stay there?"

"Where else shall I stay? With Nunu on the small island? Nunu is old now and cannot get food for himself. I don't want him to get leprosy. And if I don't help him he will die."

He said it so simply, as if there was no other choice. Maybe there wasn't.

The island was very small, a clump of rushes and forest, long and thin in the estuary of the Pra River. In the evening light it floated on a bed of misty water. If I were an artist, I expect I could have won a prize with a painting of that island. We docked under an overhanging almond tree, while petrol blue–flecked kingfishers darted overhead. On a fine flat rock above the shingled bank was Nunu's hut, all green with climbing vines.

My leg was very sore and the DB was white where the flesh bulged out from inside my lower calf, but Badu seemed satisfied with it. "When the meat inside pushes out, then the sickness cannot hide," he said. "It likes to hide inside a wound where there is no air."

We were all exhausted. Mina was in the best shape, because she'd slept some, but Badu and I were almost beyond talking.

Nunu was there. He was a very tall man and I guess if he'd been eating right he would have weighed in at two hundred pounds, but he was thin. You could see the blood vessels over his rib cage where they poked out from the T-shirts that he had wound around him. I guess he was crazy, but he looked kind. His hair was thick. Thick? I've never seen dreads like them. They tufted out of his head at right angles, bleached almost blond by the sun. They fell to his waist, faded and wild.

When he saw me though, he held his arms out, and if

I could have run into them, I would have. As it was, I hopped. He strode forward and embraced me. He picked me up and carried me into his home. He would not let me move. Every time I struggled to sit up, he would stroke my hand or face and say, "No," with such gentle force that I was glad to give in and lie back.

Inside, Nunu's house was amazing. He had woven furniture from cane and bamboo and had covered the floor with fresh matting. It smelled good—of rushes and coconut—and it was wonderfully clean. Outside, on a small neat veranda, were three round stones, a large jerrican of water and a stack of firewood. "The kitchen," said Nunu, with a proud nod.

I know I slept. In fact I must have passed out probably round about the time I saw Nunu stand up and greet Badu. All I know was that it was dark by the time I woke. It must have been late, too, because the moon was already high. Yes, I awoke to one of those great clear tropical nights that now when I sit here, I remember and long for.

Mina was cooking something over a charcoal fire in the "kitchen," and Badu was fast asleep.

"So you are awake," said Nunu.

I smiled.

"My voices told me you were coming."

I tried to flex my foot a little, but it was very sore.

"I have been waiting for you for a long time."

Mina flashed a grin at me. Maybe he'd said the same to her.

"First they sent Badu to me, but they told me he would be the one to bring you."

I nodded. My tongue felt swollen.

"I have been waiting for you for a very long time."

I nodded again and smiled. He took my hand.

"I've been waiting for you for three hundred years."

I could see what Badu meant.

"They told me that I would know you by the wounds on your back."

Definitely touched.

"My son has come back." Nunu shook my hand vigorously.

"Mr. Nunu, can I use that can of corned beef?" asked Mina.

Nunu nodded rather too long. Mina opened the can with the little key and emptied it into her cooking pot. My mouth began to water. I never knew I could get so excited about corned beef. Badu must have smelled it too, for he stirred and opened his eyes.

"Both my sons are back," said Nunu, clapping his hands.

"We can't stay," said Badu.

Nunu nodded again. Timing still all wrong. "No, no, no, you must go for the ransom."

At this I sat up.

Nunu raised his hand dramatically. "Until my son, the Lost Prince, comes back through the Door of No Return, and claims his ransom, the ancestors will not know peace. No, no, no, the voices have told me."

I don't know what I thought. Was it the way he said it? Or was it the words? Suddenly it seemed to me that I was back in Tuffley with Pops. I stared at Nunu, his ridiculous twisted sheath of T-shirts, his mad hair. But it was his eyes, his face, his smile; I saw Pops's eyes and Pops's smile and I heard Pops's voice.

"Yes, yes, yes," he said, smiling at me, as if he read my mind.

"It's the old prophecy," said Badu, winking. "Nunu used to say that that was why he was mad—that until the prophecy is fulfilled, no Baktu chief can ever know peace. Why do you think I was so ready to help you?"

"Because of my stunning good looks," I suggested.

"Dummy," said Mina.

"For three hundred years the chiefs of the Baktu peoples have said this," explained Badu. "You see when the Baktus lost their best beloved prince they never had a king again— just a set of chiefs. Nunu is the last of them."

It seemed a rational explanation, but that didn't explain why he looked like Pops, why he talked with Pops's voice, and why—yes, it's stupid, but I've got to say it—why I felt that I had at last come home.

You'll laugh. Home—after all my adventures! A shack made of bamboo and palm leaves.

It was laughable. It was certainly not the palace I'd imagined lost princes return to—but like I said, turrets and marble floors are about houses, home is about people. I'd rather have come from that neat little bamboo house with

312

its curious cane furniture—and Nunu inside—than all the mansions of England.

What I did next was even more laughable.

I took Nunu's hand and pressed it. I laid my cheek on it and I think my eyes got a bit soggy. I'm beyond embarrassment. You have to realize. Bartholomew might have said a prince may not weep, but I disagree. If you can't weep for three hundred years of separation, then I guess you can't weep for anything.

Nunu allowed it. He was crying too. Hey, look—it was a lot to cry about. Luckily, Mina was just about done with the cooking. She was sorting around, looking for bowls to serve the stew up in. Hot stew and tears don't really go together.

Boy, we ate well. That food was the best I ever tasted. It was kind of difficult to eat though, with only my left hand—but right then I didn't want to let go of Nunu's hand. His palms were rough and hard, just like Pops's. Holding on to him made the food taste better than best.

Now, when I think back, I realize that I'd just been through a bad time, that my emotions may have been unsettled, that I may have overreacted. That's how I'd explain it. I don't want you to get the idea that I'm soft. It's just that the situation wasn't quite normal. But then, what is normal? Was what happened to Bartholomew normal? I don't know. I don't know much at all about normal things.

After supper Mina needed some attention, I guess. She proposed to read the diary and translate it as she read. I was glad. I'd been on the verge of asking her to do just that.

Normal Things?

Case for the Prosecution
Exhibit 06 Attached

Form MG 14
(CJ Act 1967, s. 9; MC Act 1980, ss. 5A(3) (a) and 5B; MC Rules 1981, r. 70)

EXTRACT: *From the alleged diary of Bartholomew Baktu*

This exhibit (consisting of .... *case for the prosecution two (2) pamphlets written in Portuguese : : certified translation Lisbon University verified against accounts of the Royal African Company considered authentic: Professor Braithwaite, British Museum* page(s) each page signed by me) is true to the best of my knowledge and I make it knowingly, if it is tendered in evidence, I shall be liable to prosecution if I have wilfully stated in it anything which I know to be false or do not believe to be true.

Signature *N/A see above* Date *November 5th* *DC Hesketh*

Tendia tried to hold the wound in his side, but it was bigger than the fists of ten men. He reached out his hand at last and smiled. That is how I will remember him, forever smiling. The canoe took to the surf and we left him behind. For this I think all of us were guilty. But scarcely had we turned upon the tide than gunpowder filled the heavens again. The canoe shuddered and a terrible sound splintered the air. Beneath our feet the water sprang, and I saw that the canoe had shattered.

"In nomine Domini!" cursed Senhor Dias.

"Pull," commanded Akonor. And all my remaining brothers took the oars that lay in the canoe hull and pulled against the surf. A solid wall of water towered above us. It was so huge and so dark it swallowed the sky. We dipped into the undertow and then started to climb. For one terrible minute it seemed like we rose vertically and the waters were about to break right over us. The chest of gold dragged us down like an anchor.

"Steer to the cape, where the castle stands," yelled Senhor Dias. "We must sink or make the rocks."

It must have been God who guided us, for our canoe was breached right down the windward side. But our people choose the forest trees well, and even a breached canoe cannot sink easily. We clung to the spars that straddled the hull as wave after wave crashed upon us. And all my brothers pulled, even though there were only eight left. The current took us after my brothers were spent, and we foundered upon the rock they call Diablo Filius. There the waters swelled calm in the lee of the great rock. There we were washed up: nine men, a boy, and a fortune in gold dust beyond the dreams of men. But what can I say of the price? That one of my brothers should fall for my sake? And now seven of them were lost. Oh Tendia, my best, most cheerful of childhood companions! I tried to cast myself forth into the waters for I could bear it no longer. Yet ere I tried, Senhor Dias held me and commanded me with his eyes.

"Do not sin against the will of God," he said. "Let not your brothers fall in vain."

And I was ashamed and trembled in those cold seas. And then I saw that he was badly hurt.

"Father," I said, "Teacher, Uncle—"

"Hush, little one, I would rather die like this, than live knowing I had abandoned you to the English." He laid his hand on me. "I am not dead yet," he said. "There is still a way. My fathers' fathers built this place, long before the British came, and in all the great fortresses of the Portuguese we blasted shipping canals and rainwater passages through the rock bed underneath the walls. Here at Carolusberg it was no different. Less than ten paces to the shore, only half a meter below the sea, you will find the entrance to the canals. Let us haul the gold there and wait in the passageways until we are rested and the English gone. Yet may we win the day."

He was a brave man, Senhor Dias, and my brothers, though tired to the bone, hauled that gold under the waves and well into the darkness of the old Portuguese canals. There we slept until the sun rose. There we stayed, in those passageways beneath the castle, which no living man knew of save my teacher, Senhor Dias.

But with the dawn the tide returned and we were forced sharply upward, right under the very dungeons where they held the slave men. And before we could retreat out again to the seas, a terrible shudder passed through that labyrinth and the rocks fell behind us and our way back was sealed.

"Above us, barely twenty-one paces forward, is the slab that will let us into the slave chambers," said Senhor Dias. "But once there, we will never again be free men. For my own part, I do not wish to end my days a captive; neither do I think your father, King Baktu, would wish his gold to be so easily taken. Let someone among you judge the matter."

And so my brother Akonor spoke. "Let us pledge an oath. We will hide the gold and each among us must swear not to speak of it—whatever comes—until death. As long as we are true to each other, the English shall not gain by our misfortune. This I ask of you all. Whatever the happening. Do you swear?"

I looked at him, for I was not sure that I would be able to withstand the tortures of the English. "Please," I said, "Akonor, do not then tell me where the gold shall be hid, for I am afraid."

In the darkness he laid his hand upon me. "No, little leopard, I will not tell you. Lie upon the stone and we shall hide it. Close your eyes. You shall not know where it is."

Senhor Dias passed around his water hide, and all my brothers drank to their pledge. I lay still upon the cold stone and covered my eyes. Then with the last flickering light of the tallow candles Uncle Senhor always carried, my brothers buried the gold a long way off in one of the many passageways of the old Portuguese canals.

At length Akonor returned and, taking the sharp edge of the flint for striking fire, cut the flesh of my back. I was happy to bear the pain for it meant I could never see it. I would never be able to tell.

"These are our people's markings," said Akonor. "They are scar marks only, do you hear, little one?"

"I hear," I said.

"They are secret markings. Do you swear never to tell?"

"Until I die," I said.

The kerosene light flickered. Mina stopped reading. I sat very still. What had happened to them after that?

"I don't think I . . ." Mina sniffed. "I don't want to read the last bit in the dark." She folded the manuscript up and handed it back to me.

"They didn't make it, did they?" said Badu.

"Course they did," I said. "It was just Bartholomew

317

who got sent to Jamaica. The others must have escaped somehow. They couldn't carry the gold, that's all."

"Then why didn't they go back for it?"

"Nobody went back for it," said Nunu.

So the gold was still there, under Cape Coast Castle, hidden somewhere in the maze of secret passages.

"Maybe they didn't escape," said Mina.

Suddenly I felt very tired. I'd worry about them tomorrow. It seemed to me there were a lot of other things to worry about, starting with whether *we'd* escape.

Before I slept, Nunu said something that didn't comfort me either. I saw the whites of his eyes as he bent down. I felt the breath of his words on my neck.

"The voices have just told me something; they say it's very important. They say it's a special message—for *you*."

"What?"

"They say the English men are not *only* after the treasure and the bond, you should know that, and someone who is your friend will betray you."

"Who?" I said.

"Someone," whispered Nunu.

"No name?"

"No. I wait and see if they speak again."

I started to mentally calculate all the friends I'd ever had . . . then I wondered what *they* were after—if it wasn't *only* the treasure or the bond.

I came to the *only* obvious conclusion.

Me.

The Pra River

We slept pretty much throughout the whole of the next day. I remember waking once and finding Nunu sitting beside me holding my hand. In some strange way it reminded me of the nights I'd spent holding Bartholomew's hand at night in SGCCCH. I smiled at him and he smiled back, still Pops's mouth, Pops's way of crinkling up his eyes.

By dusk we were awake. The rest of the stew, with some added stuff, was simmering away, and after a calabashful each, we were about as ready as we were going to be. My leg was a lot better. While I'd slept, Nunu had made a paste of herbs and smeared it over the wounds. The swelling had reduced and it was dry and clean. My tongue was healing too. We were pretty filthy, but it didn't seem to be the right time to start washing.

After last night's story, Mina was quick to figure out that if Senhor Dias had found the old canal entrance under the castle, then the map would need rereading; so I lay for a while on my stomach while she tried to figure out route D.

After about fifteen minutes, during which Badu and she quarreled, Nunu came over.

"The treasure is here," he said, and pointed out a place somewhere in the middle of my back. "This is where they entered through the rock, and this is the Door of No Return. This is the way you must go." He ran his finger lightly across my scars. "Go back through the Door and into the main slave dungeons. Then down," he said, "down into the secret passageways. The man is buried here, and the gold here."

"Man?" I said, suddenly afraid.

"How do you know?" challenged Mina.

"The voices never lie," said Nunu.

"It's true," said Badu. "His voices have never lied."

Grudgingly, Mina retraced the route he'd taken over my back. "O-*kay*," she said.

After that we left. I hugged Nunu hard. I asked him if his voices had said anything else, but he shook his head. Badu didn't hug him; he just looked like he wanted to. Mina was still a bit vexed about route E, but she squeezed his hand and shook it about as many times as he did.

Once again the coracle slipped into the vast waters of the Pra River. Badu told me that the Pra was very wild and very wonderful. "The river is full of diamonds and gold," he said, "but you cannot get them easily, you cannot travel most of it—even by canoe."

I nodded.

"The water goes mainly toward Shama—there the river empties into the Atlantic. It is very dangerous."

I nodded again. I didn't have a clue how dangerous.

"So I will find one of the other streams where the waters from Kakum forest drain into a big lagoon; sometimes during this season, when the rains have been plenty, there is a way. We must paddle, though, and watch out for small rapids."

"Sure," I said, like small rapids were toothpaste.

So for most of the evening we sailed, drawn on by the river. Once we heard the sound of a cutlass on wood and we ducked down as far as we could into the hull of the coracle. "It is only a woman hewing some firewood," said Badu, "but it is good we do not let her see us." And once we hid among the reeds while a bigger boat sailed past. "They are bringing palm wine home—see the calabashes," pointed out Badu. "Maybe there is a funeral wake-keeping tonight, where they will drink." But even though they did not see us, we kept cover for more than an hour.

Certain at last that we were alone, we slid out into the current. All around was a wide black highway of water. The sound of frogs played through the air like weird music. Badu and I paddled hard to keep the coracle out of the treacherous stream toward the center. I could hear it slapping away off to my right. I could see it too, a line of white that marked the fast lane where river waves crested and broke.

"The tide is ebbing. It is not good," said Badu.

The banks of the river were crowded in mangrove and swamp trees. In the darkness, I could see their tangle of roots stretching into the water like bony fingers. We kept as close to them as we dared, searching for any tiny exit. At last Badu found a cutting, which he hoped would take us left—back toward Elmina and Cape Coast. I thought of Ashley and heard him say, "Time to play Spot the Croc, mush, and use your compass. If you don't have one you can use the North Star—it's the one that is straight above the Little Bear, Claire, and marks true north. Sailors safely navigated the entire globe with it, and lived on ships' weevils." I didn't have a compass. The swamps were too dense to see the sky—and why live on weevils? Frankly I preferred special fried rice with black bean sauce, and when I got back, I'd tell Ashley, too.

At some point we must have passed near to the funeral. We could hear drums and women wailing—but they did not hear us. Silently we paddled past. The night made us invisible, and the splish of water over the canoe sides and the slosh as Mina bailed it back out merged with the slapping of the river against the edges of the shallow coracle.

It wasn't really a proper coracle made of canes and hides; it was more like a dugout base with a woven rim. I had a feeling that Badu might have made it himself. Sadly, the rim let in a lot of water. "This boat cannot go to the surf," sighed Badu.

All around us was a high curtain of trailing branches. Dangling roots fell from trunks to either side. They seemed to clutch the water and snake out toward us, as if trying to entangle our small canoe. Mosquitoes swarmed in dark clouds. Badu found the matches and fuel he'd taken from Nunu and set fire to dried lemongrass in an old tin can to help keep them off. The smell of kerosene and raw citronella clogged our noses, so the silence was punctuated by our sneezing. After we had navigated many miles of dense, over-hung waterways, Badu put the fire out. "Sometimes people go out at night to visit the shrine of Mammy Water," he explained. "Maybe this smoke is a bad idea."

We tried as much as possible to keep to the middle of the narrow tributary, away from the stretching roots and the hanging curtain. But even there, from time to time we were all forced to lie down on the dugout base, while we glided under branches that swept almost down to the surface of the water. But as we neared the sea, the river widened. High above us shone the full moon and we sailed on a silver ribbon of moonshine. At one point Badu made the alarm sign and we kept very still.

"Listen," he said. "Can you hear it?"

I listened, but apart from the croaking of frogs and the *tickety-ticky-tick* of the crickets I could hear nothing.

"Listen," he said again. "Listen to the roaring."

I strained my ears. I didn't know quite what kind of roaring to listen for. I hoped it wasn't more leopards.

"There now."

I strained again.

"I hear it," said Mina.

At last I heard something, the dull tearing roar of something very distant and very terrible.

"That is the Atlantic," said Badu.

I listened to it intently after that. It was as if it was trying to tell me something—and long before I could see the white surf, the sound of it grew and filled my ears, until I swear I could almost feel the crash of each monstrous wave as it hit the shores of Africa.

"If it's a bad ebb tide, what does that mean?" I asked Badu.

"We are bound for the Door of No Return, so we must take any tide."

"But—I mean, how dangerous is it going to be?"

"As bad and yet no worse than the slave men suffered."

"Oh come *on*," I said.

"It doesn't help," said Badu, "to imagine problems. The surf is always terrible and always wonderful. Just do what I tell you. It can't be any different for us than for our ancestors."

"You made that point," I said, but I thought about it anyway—the sky and the sea. How some things stay the same. I guess I was afraid. I wanted Badu to tell me that it was going to be easy, that somehow, magically, things would be different. I wondered if there was any other way to the Door. A way that didn't involve the breakers.

"I wonder if my ancestors feared the surf," said Mina. "I mean the Portuguese part of me. I don't know, but I always imagined the navigators were fearless."

"Even they, I'm sure," said Badu, "shook at the sight of the Atlantic. You know, the fishermen cross the surf every day, and yet whenever they go they say good-bye, in case it is their last time."

So all three of us sat there—imagining the past, fearing the future.

At last, after stretches of dense overgrowth that left me hot and breathless—for the air in that place was filled with a kind of dull heaviness—the coracle slid out of the tangled swamp ways. There ahead of us was a wide open expanse of water, which I guessed was the lagoon. Immediately, the sound of the Atlantic was far fiercer. In the distance I could see a huge wild sky.

"Just beyond this lagoon is the harbor of Elmina. We must hide the small boat now. To cross the surf we must steal a long canoe. In case you don't know, stealing is a terrible thing; these fishermen depend upon their canoes for everything. They live each day trusting themselves to the sea so they can bring in many fishes to feed their families. To lose a canoe may be the straw that will break their shoulders—if they catch us, they will not be merciful."

"When I get the gold, I'll buy the owner a whole fleet," I said. "Any fisherman'll be real pleased we chose his boat."

Mina giggled. "Dummy," she said.

"The fishermen sleep early, because they go to the sea at dawn. It is already late for them and few are awake—but it will only take one dog to smell us, and one shout to bring out the whole village. So we must be quick and quiet."

We pulled the coracle in under the leafy curtain that clothed the exit of the swamp way. Then we slid into the water and struck out, swimming silently. The lagoon water was strangely warm and thick and brackish. It was very buoyant. It was like swimming in lukewarm syrup. I wasn't too sure just what ingredients went into that syrupy lagoon, so I made really sure I didn't swallow any.

Swimming abreast in the moonshine was one of the most awesome things that I have ever done. I thought of Pops and his stories of romantic deeds of daring and of peril. And at last I felt that I was truly living. I could be anyone and do anything, and the Cormantin spirit in me was strong.

We made for a thin metal bridge, which spanned the lagoon neck before the sand bar. Beyond that I could see the canoes.

Of all the things I've nicked—and once I nicked a covered ride-inside lawn mower from Brockworth Golf Course—I think that long canoe was the weirdest.

High Seas

Stealing the canoe was much easier than I thought. We didn't have to drag it onto logs and roll it down the beach. I think we would have had a hard time doing that. You see, the fishing canoes that go out on the surf are HUGE. They are carved out of the single trunk of a forest giant, over fifty feet long, although only about five wide. All of them are painted with symbols: "To drive away Mammy Water," said Badu. And all of them have names.

We chose one called *Ten Against Eleven*. Partly because it amused us, the idea of a canoe being named after a football match; partly because it seemed that the odds were unfairly stacked against us too; mostly because it was moored farthest from the beach, almost out at sea. We could reach near it by climbing over the rocks at the end of the curved headland that sheltered the bay.

I won't forget the first time I saw that canoe. The huge wild sky, the full moon afloat on a scary sea, the dark arm of headland, the white line of surf, and there in the starlight, *Ten Against Eleven* rocking on the black water. That was some canoe.

Over the rocks we scrambled. Although the sky was shining, underfoot it was very dark. More than once I skinned my shin and heard Mina stifle a cry. On the far reach of the headland stood another slave fort. It was just as dark and dismal as Cape Coast Castle. The moon shone down on its white walls. Beyond crashed the surf.

"You know that is Elmina," said Mina.

"Correct," said Badu.

"The Castle of São Jorge da Mina."

"Yes."

"I am named after this place. It was here that the first Portuguese explorer, Diogo Cão, set a post—and the first Bartolomeu Dias landed after leaving Vasco da Gama."

"You don't say," remarked Badu.

"It's true—Chris, the journalist, told me. Dias's ship, the *São Cristóvão*, carried the padrões, 'the pillars to set up the claims of the Portugese Crown and act as marks of discovery and overlordship.'"

"Overlordship!"

I kind of felt sorry for Mina. She couldn't help being sort of descended from Portuguese navigators, but she could have shut up about it. If I'd been named after a slave-trading fort, I wouldn't be gagging to tell the world.

My wet clothes clung to me and a sea breeze started. I felt a bit cold, and I think I trembled. The darkness pressed close around me too, and I had a strange feeling, as if I were turning in my own grave. I couldn't understand how Elmina Castle could thrill anyone, namesake or not. It was vast and sinister. I thought of all the slave forts stalking the borders of Africa. I thought of all the Doors of No Return and all the unreturned. I thought of Cape Coast Castle and saw it again—as in my nightmare, its long shadow falling across my mind, drowning me. I remembered the sweating and the screaming, and I shuddered at the thought of going back into the slave labyrinth.

"There are many forts and castles." Badu turned to Mina, his voice much softer. "All of them sold my ancestors."

With that he dived silently into the seawater and struck out for *Ten Against Eleven*. I followed. Mina stood there. Maybe she was imagining the *São Cristóvão* docking in the bay by the headland, dipping beside palm green shores. Maybe she saw Dias the explorer striding up the beach. Maybe she was reconsidering whether she wanted to belong to them or not. Maybe she was trying to come to terms with the glory of the navigators and the horror they'd brought. . . . Within ten minutes, anyway, she'd caught us up and we'd all scrambled aboard the long canoe. We cut the mooring rope with the coconut cutlass and were drawn on the ebb tide out toward the barrier of surf.

Although Gloucester was once famed for its docks and did a roaring trade in most things on the high seas from the West Indies to Calcutta, I knew nothing about sailing. As it turned out, that was fine.

"Three of us cannot sail this canoe," said Badu, when we were well and truly clear of the headland.

"Brilliant," I said. "Now you tell us."

"I chose this fishing fleet because at full moon we will be pulled out to sea and the current will take us east. There are no more headlands between Cape Coast and us. Soon we will see the Cape—it's only eight miles away. As we are pulled past, we will bail out and swim to the rocks. We must try not to let the canoe get too far out to sea—or stay too near the shore where the rocks are."

"What?" I yelled. The canoe was beginning to sway wildly and against the din of the surf his voice was hard to catch.

"Cape Coast . . . eight miles . . . watch out . . . then we jump."

"Okay," I yelled. "What about the canoe?"

"*Ten Against Eleven* . . . must take . . . chance."

"Okay."

"Break up . . . or lost."

"Okay."

"Or wash up . . . Anomabu beach . . . in God's hand now."

I clung on to the gunwales. *Ten Against Eleven* wasn't the only one in God's hands. The canoe sides were slippery wet and my fingers slid along them, fastening on nothing but splinters. On either side, the sea leapt up and smashed at my hands wherever I grabbed. My knuckles grew pale and numb. I hoped God had got a better grip than I had.

Through the hull, beneath my feet, I felt how *Ten Against Eleven* was being dragged toward the long line of surf. I started swallowing air in panic. I could see the waves clearly now. Twenty feet high and a quarter of a mile wide.

"The surf breaks . . . underwater . . . ," yelled Badu.

He wasn't making sense, but I nodded anyway. The closer we got to the break line, the faster my heart pounded. I started holding my breath and swallowing more air.

"The seabed . . . narrow . . . beyond the breakers . . . drops hundreds of feet . . . deep . . . undertow . . ."

I stared at the white line ahead. All around those booming crests was dark water, endless miles of swirling, choppy, dark water. The sea snarled at every side, the wind raced, and under everything the relentless tide ebbed away. I could barely hear Badu. He was shouting, but the wind snatched his voice and drowned it under the crashing.

"We must take the surf head on . . . if we go broadside . . . will roll."

"O-kay," I yelled again.

Badu was still shouting and shouting at the helm. He waved one arm wildly. "HELP . . . NEED HELP . . ." Very cautiously, I stood up and tried to maneuver toward him. The canoe pitched dreadfully. I shifted weight. It pitched again. Spray smashed into my face, everything went black. I sat down, blinking—crying—wiping my eyes. Then I inched my way on my bum toward him along the wet bottom of the boat. It was terribly difficult to get over the planks that spared the hull. I had to sit on them one at a time and swing my legs over, knees together, while the whole hull rolled. When I reached him, he motioned Mina to move farther down the canoe to balance out the weight. "HELP ME," he yelled. I could see he was struggling to hold a large wooden lever, which seemed to be pulling to the right. I grabbed hold of it and pulled too. It slipped in my hands.

Slowly, the bow turned to face the surf. When we were ninety degrees on, Badu and I did our best to hold her steady. Mina had found some rope at the front and was busy tying herself down. Great, I thought, if we don't roll she won't be washed overboard. Not so great if we do.

Ten Against Eleven set a course for the horizon, although I couldn't see the horizon from one minute to the next. It plunged up and down under my eyes until I began to feel sick. All the time I could feel the undertow, feel it dragging us out to sea, sucking us down, as if the Atlantic were some vast hungry monster. Seventy feet away were the breakers. Now I know why breakers are called breakers.

The first was the worst. A solid wall of water rushed right at us. It towered high, like a cliff. It was so huge and so dark it blotted out the moon. I held my breath. I swallowed air. I gritted my teeth. I prayed to God: *Oh God, help me . . . Only help me and I will believe—I'll always believe, I'll give to charity. . . .* My breath didn't come back. I closed my eyes. I bit my lip. My heart stopped.

Ten Against Eleven dipped into the underwash and then started to climb. For one horrible minute it seemed like we were perpendicular and the wave was about to crash right over us. . . . Like a pessimist I renamed the boat *A Million to One.*

The wave crested, but I don't think it got us head on. I think we managed to peak before she broke. It was a good job we didn't wash at Nunu's though, it would have wasted time. Before the churning foam closed over me, I saw the entire canoe disappear into a wall of black water. Salty seawater smacked into my face. It went up my nose. The back of my throat burnt and ached. I spluttered and spat, eyes closed tight, and I coughed and coughed. I couldn't wipe my face. I didn't dare to let go of the wooden handle for fear I'd be washed overboard, for fear the canoe would spin. When I did open my eyes, they stung, they watered, and I had to close them fast and stay blind. I guess my heart must have started beating again, but I wasn't sure when.

Minute after minute we battled against the surf. The hardest part was righting the canoe and getting her to sit square on before the next breaker hit. Each wave was as monstrous as the last. Again and again we dipped and climbed into the fury of black water. Sometimes an Atlantic roller came in from the west, and although they were easier to navigate, they turned her bows, and we'd be sitting wrong for the next wave. I didn't have much time to be scared. My arms ached from holding the handle, and my bad ankle kept slipping on the wet boards at the base of the hull. Sometimes I was thrown against Badu, and we both almost lost hold and were swept away. But Badu twisted a piece of mooring rope around our wrists, and as the sea smashed us from left to right, he lashed us to the rudder.

Ten Against Eleven did well. I was sorry I'd doubted her. She took each titanic wave; and although she groaned and creaked until I felt sure she'd break up, she didn't.

At last we crossed the surf.

Once out beyond the break line the sea swelled gently and was reasonably calm. It took some time for me to get calm, though!

Our next challenge was to set a course for the Cape. This time we had to keep the handle tilted shoreside, but even though we rode the calm well and were dragged eastward, we were also being dragged relentlessly out to sea.

Countercurrent

In the starlight we could see the ramparts of Cape Coast Castle. Square low towers that looked odd in the African night. Did I say odd? I can still feel the shivers they sent through me. I hope one day the sea will grow mad and wash them away.

Still, keeping our eyes fixed on them we pulled our weight against the rudder, and the westward rollers helped us. They carried the canoe back toward the shore, before the undertow kicked in. If we kept a steady course I could see that we'd pass the headland near the rocks.

It was a beautiful night. The full moon sailing on a bank of midnight blue, a steamship way away on the horizon. "It is a Korean trawler," said Badu, "heading for Tema. They catch big tuna, which the market women smoke. It is very nice."

I figured I could use a tuna sandwich right then, but even though I tried waving, the Korean sailors didn't see me.

You gotta keep a sense of humor, you know, 'cause it was far more likely that the tunas would be getting a Zac sandwich, but as Pops used to say, "*You're better off laughing than crying!*" We had no sail and no paddles. That was worth a good laugh. And we had no life jackets. Ha ha.

I realize now we were crazy. Later I found out that the only reason it worked was due to the Atlantic Equatorial Countercurrent, which is strongest off the coast of Ghana. Funnily enough, it's called the Guinea Current. Mina told us it was the same current that landed Bartolomeu Dias at Cabo Corso in 1486.

I bet he had a smoother landing than we did. We loosened our safety ropes and waited for the right minute to bail out. That's when I learned the hard way that you should never jump a canoe to the leeward side. At the time it seemed the most sensible thing. You know, jump with the wind rather than into it? It was only because I was in the very stern that I escaped being mown over by the hull of the boat. I realized my mistake the minute my feet left the gunwale. The canoe was traveling a lot quicker than me.

I hit the water twisting sideways and dived as deep as I could. I started remembering everything that Wisdom had told me—fast. I was lucky. Mina and Badu did the sensible thing and leapt into the wind. We all surfaced to see *Ten Against Eleven* swing wildly out to sea. At the time I didn't care much what happened to her. Later I learned that she made the arc and ran aground on Anomabu beach. Nowadays when I watch football I never worry when my team gets a red card.

If you ever get the chance, take a look at the rocky cape

that Cape Coast Castle is built on. When you see the size of the rocks and the strength of the swell against them you may get some idea of how stupid we were. Then add a full moon and high tide. How we ever survived being smashed to bits, I still can't work out.

"Link arms," yelled Badu.

We struggled to stay together. Inside, the sea was dark and vast. Wave after wave broke over me and I started swallowing seawater. It was hard to link up and swim with one arm. And I was on the wing. But as usual Badu was right. Somehow the span of us slowed our progress toward the rocks. It made sure we weren't separated. I guess three pairs of thrashing legs are better than one. Badu was in the middle. It was toughest for him with no free arm, and he was weighed down by the tool bag. We'd dip and the underwater fight began, then we'd surface—gasping, trying to hold each other up. Once a huge breaker swamped us all and I thought, this is it. But Badu held on to me so hard, my wrist was bruised for weeks.

Down there, deep below the booming surf in the black seawater, everything is eerily silent. You're sure you're drowning. A strange hum presses on your ears and everywhere is so dark, so very dark. Then—*bam*—you surface to noise and spluttering, to eyes smarting and the taste of salt.

At last a roller gently took us. We missed Bad Lad, the biggest rock of the Cape (thank God), and were swept into its lee. There the sea was deep and calm. It was just a slimy breathless scramble and then—there we were, twenty feet from the Door of No Return.

Back Through the Door

Don't think for one minute that I'd forgotten about Father Bullingham and the Sniddons. You can be sure as soon as I hauled myself up on the rocks at the back of the Door, I remembered. It worried me that they always seemed to know every move I made. Nunu may have heard voices, but I didn't somehow think that they had psychic tabs on me. So how did they always know? I scanned the dark coast, searching for any shadows. There was nothing, only a green-lit veranda far away across the bay. I hadn't forgotten Nunu's last voice, either: "Someone who is a friend will betray you." Did that mean someone who *is* a friend *had* betrayed me? Or was it future tense? There were only the three of us plus Nunu who knew where we were going. I relaxed. Looked like this time I'd outwitted them. *Nobody* could follow me now.

So, shivering like water rats, we started out for the Return of the Lost Prince. The English had positioned the Door well. It was almost unreachable from the land. Three hundred years ago it would have been impossible either for a slave to bolt, or for a rescue to be successful. Nowadays they've put a little jetty nearer to the Door, but it still looked weird. A door that leads nowhere, except onto a wild ocean.

I must say, though, I was kind of disappointed with the Door. In my imagination it had become a huge portal, more symbolic than the Pearly Gates and far more beautiful. In reality it was nothing, not even a properly arched entrance. It wasn't even a door actually. It was a door*way*, wide, low, and hewn in stone.

I felt somehow that I should commemorate the moment anyway, if only for Pops. I mean, here I was, the last true descendant of King Baktu, about to step back through the Door of No Return, after three hundred years. I was about to fulfill the prophecy of my forefathers and right the wrongs of the past. No—I couldn't right those wrongs. Still, I felt it needed a bit of ceremony. I remembered the camera on my mobile phone, and even though I had been saving the battery as much as possible by turning it off, I reckoned a photo of the three of us by the door would be in order. Luckily, my packaging of the phone had been sea-proof.

I don't think I got the best shot ever. I held it at arm's length and got mostly my head and the door behind. Mina and Badu didn't figure at all. I sent it to Raphael and Ashley with this text: *About 2 go in thro d door, no where d t is, wish me luck—z.*

Almost immediately I got a reply: *WELL DONE*

ZACMAN, I new u wud do it. Bernard already left—only 299 yrs 364 days til e gets der. So dont w8 4 him, Kim. Good Luck an cum home soon mush. A. I smiled and imagined Ashley's face when I showed up with all that gold. Boy, were we going to go on a shopping binge! Starting at Bluewater and continuing on to every retail supercenter in the south of England. We'd become consumer legends. I tried to improve on the "shop till you drop" theme. We could graffiti up each line like a tag as we careered through the malls. This is what I invented:

> "BUY TILL U DIE
> GET TILL U FORGET
> SPEND TO THE END
> SPLASH OUT TILL U CRASH OUT
> ACQUIRE TILL U EXPIRE . . ."
> ZAC'N'ASH'N' LOADZA CASH WUZ 'ERE

The cutlass easily prised the rotten wood of the door a good foot open. It appeared to be held by some bent iron clasp or hinge, but it was quite wide enough for the three of us to squeeze through.

Inside, everything was quiet. Even the crashing surf seemed dim and far away. It was pitch dark. Immediately, we knew we'd never be able to navigate the labyrinth of chambers without some kind of light. Of course we had thought about it, we (Badu) had brought along the chisel, hammer, and cutlass—he'd even packed the flashlight, but seawater doesn't go too well with batteries. For a while the three of us stood there huddled together in the passageway behind the Door.

"We can't give up," I said.

Mina's "No-oo," was not definite enough.

"Now what?"

"You tell me."

There, in the darkness of Cape Coast Castle, our voices whispered up and under the ceiling. The whisperings seemed to multiply and soon the whole air around us shuddered with unintelligible murmurs. My old fear flooded back. How many feet had passed this way? How many voices had moaned and sighed into these walls? How many had longed for their families, wept, and passed on uncounted? How many? The place smelled dank and moldy, the same stench of cold stone that I'd first smelled in the condemned cell. I shivered, suddenly freezing.

"As for you," said Badu, "you think that all Africa is like the bush where Nunu stays. This castle belongs to Ghana Museums and Monuments Board. This town was called Oguaa and was once the capital of all Ghana, and now it is the provincial capital of this region. We have everything here—famous schools and grand government offices, and this is a museum. Even the famous English poetess, Laetitia Elizabeth Landon, is buried here! You think they will not have electricity to illuminate the dungeons for the tourists who come?"

For some reason, I hadn't thought so. For some reason,

it seemed to me that this place would stay forever fixed in the past. As if nothing could wipe out its darkness. Of course, now he pointed it out, it was obvious that there must be some lighting system. Nobody could expect tourists to fumble around.

"So find the switch, dummy."

With that, it seemed that the air temperature rose slightly and we spread out, groping the walls around us. Under my touch they seemed to be made of lozengelike stones or bricks coated with a brittle surface that crumbled chalkily into my nails. They were curved, as if we were standing in the crypt of a cathedral. I worked my way from beside the Door, palms flat, sweeping the wall to my right. I think Mina was on the other side of the passageway; Badu had gone ahead into the darkness.

Suddenly there was a slight click and a light flickered on. It was very dim, probably only a forty-watt bulb, but hey—I wasn't planning on reading any small print. It hung suspended from a carelessly nailed plank at the top of what I could see was the arched roof. From it trailed a wire pinned at places to the stones. But hey again—I wasn't complaining about the workmanship!

"The map," whispered Mina.

Obligingly, I knelt down and pulled off my sopping T-shirt.

"Now," she said, "for a start we must find a way to go right—then underground."

An entrance on the right led into a small vaulted

chamber, which had *Male Slave Loading Prison* written on an information plaque. We followed the thin electricity wire into the Loading Prison and found another switch. More dim light. The bulb swayed slightly and shadows swiveled round the walls. At the far wall was a doorway. It was bricked up. The chamber was a dead end.

"What now?"

"We've got to get through there. If Nunu is right— that's the way."

"We chisel?"

"Wait," said Badu. "Look at that." He was pointing to another plaque, half pulled off the wall. It read:

> *Passageways leading to the male slave dungeons.*
> *Slaves brought here were held for up to one month*
> *awaiting transportation. These passageways were*
> *converted into rainwater cisterns in 1810.*

"Good job we didn't bust a hole in it," I said.

"Don't need to," said Mina. "There's a vent of some kind, an overflow maybe—look."

Above the bricked-in doorway was a hole barred by a nought-and-crosses affair in rusty iron. By giving Mina a leg up she could look through the barred opening. "Looks like some upper passage, although it smells yuk," she said, "like stagnant water."

"Can you loosen the bars?" I asked.

"Pass up the chisel and hammer. I'll try."

Badu passed them up to her and she struck twice at

the bottom of the bars where they were set in stone. The noise was deafening. It rang round and round the chamber. My heart started banging. What if someone heard?

Badu grinned across at me. "Don't worry, the museum is shut at night, and we're the farthest away from anywhere. You can scream as much as you like down here. They made it like that on purpose."

I nodded and braced myself against the wall. Mina was standing on my shoulders!

Mina must have worked away for more than half an hour, and when I couldn't stand it any longer, she got down and climbed up again on Badu. You'd have thought that after three hundred years of sea air those iron bars would have crumbled into rusty nothingness. You'd have been wrong. After an hour of hammering they were still as firm as the day they were put there. That hour gave me a pretty good picture of how impossible escape in 1665 would have been.

"You know something," said Mina, "I think there's nothing in these passageways. Any water must have been drained or dried up. I've loosened a few chips of masonry and I can't hear them splashing."

"Here." I passed her up a loose chip that had fallen on our side. Mina dropped the stone through the bars. We heard a distinct *plink* as it hit ground on the other side of the bricked-up doorway.

Loosening the bricks was less difficult and much less painful. Mina and I were pretty good at chiseling blocks, and working a sort of shift in which she hammered and I cleared, we soon had a gap in the doorway big enough for us to squeeze through. Whoever had done that bit of work in 1810 hadn't been worrying about escaping prisoners.

I was beginning to get worried about the idea of escaping myself. We'd left Nunu's island in the coracle at dusk the previous evening, and it must have taken us at least four hours to navigate to Elmina. If our encounter with the surf had been another three, and our time in the castle two, that made it about 3:00 a.m. I checked it on my phone. 3:10 a.m. We had another three hours till dawn, by which time we had to have found the treasure and be out of there.

I realized that we had made no plan for our getaway.

The Male Slave Dungeon

The passageway behind the bricked-up doorway might have once been used for water storage, although the quantities must have been small. The floor was slippery with an oozing kind of slime, and it stank. Mina figured we had to pass down it to the central male slave dungeons. I hoped there wouldn't be another bricked-up doorway ahead.

Luck was on our side. We groped our way down the passage in pitch-dark, expecting at any moment to come to a full stop. But whoever had drained the cisterns had done so from the far end. The sealed doorway there had been dismantled and the bricks were piled along one wall. When we emerged through it, we could tell by the dryer floor underfoot and the echo that we were now in a much larger chamber.

We began sweeping the walls again for a light switch. As usual it was Badu who found it. We were standing in a wide double-vaulted chamber. The ceiling was quite high and the one lightbulb threw a dreary yellow flush over it.

"If the diaries and Nunu are right," said Mina, "the

346

secret passageways start below this floor. There must be an area of flooring that is hollow, where the Old Portuguese drainage canal was built over."

We started tapping on the floor, listening for anything that sounded hollow. At first our tappings were random, but when we did not immediately strike lucky we began to work systematically across the chamber.

At this point I have to tell you something that still makes my flesh creep. The floor was covered with a hard layer of something very black. At first I thought it was some kind of flooring material, like felt or tarmac. In places where we thought the floor sounded promising we chipped through it. It was hard and more than two inches deep. It wasn't until I found something smooth and white embedded in it that I realized what I was digging through. The feltlike coating on the floor of the male slave dungeons was nothing less than packed and hardened excrement. In other words, I was cutting through the shit of thousands of male slaves that had been trampled flat over nearly three hundred years of slavery. The white object I found—a human tooth.

Something inside me shuddered and sank. I didn't want to believe it. I'd been afraid all along that it was true. Afraid that every story I'd heard was accurate. Afraid that people could really have done that to others. Afraid that the world wasn't a good place, not a nice place, not a safe place. Afraid that even my worst imaginings would not be bad enough.

They weren't.

My people had been imprisoned here, forced to lie in their own soil, forced to wait hour after day after month in darkness. Forced to die here or live, when life had no dignity, no hope. My people. Little kids. Little seven-year-old kids. I sat down on the dirt floor and hung my head. Oh my God. What had happened down here in these chambers? Crush—degradation—filth—despair . . . While the British agent and all his crew sat above, sipping sherry?

My people.

I think I clutched my knees.

Little kids.

It's funny the things you think of. I remembered a school trip to France. One of the only holidays I'd ever been on. We visited a château. It had a hunting lodge and stables. Seems like the French liked stag hunting. It had been built in the seventeenth century—fifty years before Bartholomew was transported. You know, the stables were spotless. Spotless! The guide had told us how the lord had them mucked out three times a day, what pride he had in his horses, how he could "not abide for his animals to be neglected."

My family.

I don't know—I started to feel angry. I smashed with my hammer at the floor. Chips of it flew up, hard like pieces of glass. Somebody should be forced to clear this shit up. Somebody had a shit lot to answer for, and when the shit hit the fan the whole world had better watch out, because somebody somewhere was going to pay. . . .

My hammer hit stone.

The stone rang out clear like a bell. No, not a bell—a drum, a hollow drum.

I'd found the Old Portuguese canal.

Digging Up History

We excavated a square three feet by three feet through the flooring. We loosened the cobbles beneath and prised them out with the chisel and the cutlass. Beneath them was a small flagstone about the same size as a paving slab. There was no mortar around it, only the dirt of centuries wedging it in.

We levered it up, sweating in the chill of that dank chamber. Beneath it was a drop of about five feet. It sloped down toward the sea. The Old Portuguese rock canal was still there!

"Be careful," warned Badu. "Take the rope—it may shoot down. The sea may have leaked in."

I tied the washing line around my waist and lowered myself into the canal. There was no handy forty-watt bulb down there, and the dim light of the one in the main male slave dungeon was hardly more than wishful thinking. I felt my way along some of its length. It was just as Bartholomew had written. Three feet wide, blasted through rock with many, many passageways leading off it.

It seemed strange to think that since he and his brothers had been there, maybe no one had stood in that canal since. I started getting quite upset just thinking about that, until I realized that it had better be true. There was only one reason why someone else might have been there!

How much longer did we have? An hour? I didn't know what time the castle opened, or when the first bunch of tourists would arrive in the dungeons—certainly not till 8:00 a.m., maybe. But that wouldn't help our getaway. We couldn't afford to be seen. Okay, I guessed in Cape Coast town there would be loads of people all doing their thing early in the morning. And I could see that at first they might not really notice us—wrong! Mina was drop-dead gorgeous. That was a dead giveaway. But pretty soon I reckoned two and two would add up and some bright spark would say: "Those kids look like the escaped criminals!" Then there was the matter of carrying around a treasure chest with fifteen thousand dambas of gold dust inside. . . .

No, we had to get out of the castle and the town before sunup. Either that or we'd better hole up in the old canal, like Bartholomew had done, for another twelve hours.

I thought about it. Twelve hours without food or water. One hour till sunup. We were all tired. I guess the treasure had lain there for three hundred years—another day wouldn't hurt.

My plan wasn't very well received until Badu made some fine-tuning.

"You and Mina get into the canal; I'll put the slab back and the cobbles and pack the dirt down. I'll repair the bricked-up wall—at least as best I can. I'll turn off the lights and slip back out the Door. I'll take your shoes, Zac—no one will think twice about me if they don't see my feet. I'll swim to the bay and try to get some water and food for you. I'll lie low all day and be back after dark."

"Leave the tools," said Mina, "in case you don't make it."

"Thanks," said Badu.

Baktu Voices

After Mina and I had crept into the old canal and Badu had sealed the entrance over our heads, we whispered a little. We tried not to think of twelve hours without water or food. We lay down on the rocky floor and made an effort to sleep.

It would have been nice if we could have read some more of the diaries, but you need light to read.

Maybe it's a good job it was so dark. This is the next extract. It is not exactly cheering.

So Dark

Case for the Prosecution
Exhibit 07 Attached

Form MG 14
(CJ Act 1967, s. 9; MC Act 1980, ss. 5A(3) (a) and 5B; MC Rules 1981, r. 70)

EXTRACT: *From the alleged diary of Bartholomew Baktu*

This exhibit (consisting of *case for the prosecution two (2) pamphlets written in Portuguese . . . —certified translation Lisbon University—verified against accounts of the Royal African Company—considered authentic; Professor Braithwaite, British Museum* ~~page(s) each page signed by me~~) is true to the best of my knowledge ~~and I make it knowingly, if it is tendered in evidence, I shall be liable to prosecution if I have wilfully stated in it anything which I know to be false or do not believe to be true.~~

Signature *N/A—see above* Date *November 5th* *DC Hesketh*

How long we stayed there in the old canal I cannot say. At first we talked. We tried to believe that we would survive. I clung to Akonor and while he held me, my heart was not afraid. It was not until Baidoo, my senior brother, asked what had become of Gabriel? Then we went over all our adventures and yet could not account either for his death or escape. I think it was Senhor Dias who said, "Gold and slavery are powerful things, a man can betray his own mother for less."

354

After that we did not talk of Gabriel again, for each
of us knew in our hearts that he must have turned back
somehow when we took to the surf and made a deal with
the English. Hope died then, for Gabriel knew all the
waters of the coast, and even if the rocks shifted and we
could make our escape, there would be no safe haven
again, no port that Gabriel would not tell the English of.
I wept much after that, for it seemed to me that I had
caused my brother to turn to the devil, and that sin
weighed as heavily on me as all the lives given in love for
my sake.

I couldn't tell if it was halfway through the morning or
late afternoon when I woke up. But suddenly I was bolt
upright and scared stiff. Nunu's words *"Your friend will
betray you"* drummed in my head. I shook Mina. "What if
Badu tells?" I said.

"Don't be a dummy."

"I'm not," I said. "There's a lot of gold stashed away
down here."

"Well, for a start, I don't think Badu would."

On the streets your crew are your brethren. Nobody
tells. But I wasn't sure how the street code worked here.
What if Badu was the "friend" the voice meant? I didn't
tell Mina about Nunu's voice. I didn't want her to think I
was beginning to get schizo, but I pushed my point. "Let's
dig the treasure up and move it. I'm feeling freaked out."

"It'll make too much noise."

"Now you're being a dummy; you can make as much
noise as you want down here. Nobody will hear a thing.

C'mon." I figured if he had to get back to Cabo Corso and call out Father Bullingham, cut his own deal and return, we had a few hours to shift the treasure and get out after the last bunch of tourists.

"Why would Badu do that?" insisted Mina.

"Just a feeling," I said. "If we move it and I'm wrong, so what?"

"Huh! If that's what you think of your friends," said Mina.

It was too hard to explain to her that it wasn't my idea to not trust him, so I just said, "You don't know anything. Ever since this thing started *they've* always known every step I've made. Maybe Badu was a plant all along. Maybe that's why he made our escape so easy—all those coconuts and stuff. Maybe that's why the dog didn't go for him; maybe that's why nobody's caught us. They're waiting for us to find the gold, 'cause they can't. Isn't it rather convenient that now we're actually sitting on top of it—Badu's not here?"

"But it was your idea to hole up."

Suddenly I was held by the conviction that right now Badu and Father Bullingham were plotting out how to come back into the castle and take the treasure. Boy, if I was correct, my life was about to come to a big full stop.

I started frantically groping around in the dark canal. "If you don't want to help me," I snapped, "then maybe you're in with them too."

When I think back, I realize how cruel that was. Mina may have said some stupid stuff, but she was as trusty as her navigators. After months of persecution, I guess I was near break point. In fact, add paranoid to the schizo and you wouldn't be far wrong.

I know she was upset. She didn't say anything and I couldn't see her, but I knew. I thought about saying sorry, really I did. I thought about putting my arm round her and giving her a big kiss. I'd have liked to have done that. I'd like to be the kind of guy who *could* have done that. But I wasn't, I didn't. I heard her stand up and start feeling around the walls. I guess I'm a bully.

In the darkness we measured the canal as accurately as we could. The diaries had said that the gold had been buried in one of the passageways off the canal. Mina ran her hands over my back, and said she could work it out. She traced Nunu's route—and route E seemed correct. Every now and then I flashed my mobile on and in its brief light we double-checked. By moving our hands, which I guessed to be about four inches wide, repeatedly over the wall, we marked out the way foot by foot, hand by hand. Mina said we were as spot on as any map scarred into six generations of skin tissue could make us. Although she didn't see me, I smiled at her through the darkness. After we had navigated two passageways and about fifty feet, we found the place. A blank rocky wall, the same as all the tunnel walls around it, save for a slight unevenness. We started scratching with the chisel and cutlass. The wall seemed strangely soft. We didn't even need the tools. It came away in handfuls.

"Weird," I said. "It's like this place has been dug out before."

"I'm not just a pretty face, you know."

"No," I said, wanting to say more.

The wall started to crumble. I touched something hard. Something hard and smooth. "Hey Mina, I've found something. . . ."

Despite everything I had been through, I nearly yelped with joy. Of course, I couldn't see what I was doing. I didn't want my battery to go completely flat. So we worked away a little longer in darkness on that smooth object. But with every fistful of dirt we removed, it began to feel less and less like a treasure chest. I ran my fingers over its curves and felt a strange array of bumps and ridges. My joy started to turn to horror.

I flashed on my mobile. There staring up at me was the empty eye socket of an ancient skull. "Oh my God," I said.

Mina backed away. "Cover it up."

With trembling fingers we collected the dirt we'd piled around our feet and pushed it back over the skull. Shaken, we retreated toward the canal exit.

That was when Badu and Father Bullingham pulled back the flagstone and shone a flashlight right at us.

In the Land of My Ancestors

"Well, what a pretty hiding place," said Father Bullingham, his face sagging through the hole above us. "You could hide a body down here and nobody would ever know. Two bodies, three even."

"Badu," whispered Mina, her voice hoarse.

I didn't say *I told you so*. I just gasped. You see, I hadn't really believed it.

"It wasn't my fault," said Badu. He looked straight down at us, chewing at his lip, his face tense, his eyes wide, his voice trembling.

I still couldn't believe it. And looking at him did nothing to convince me. How can you look so innocent? How can your chin quiver so? How can you be so rotten and look so sorry? I turned my back on him. I wasn't going to let him see me hurt. Somehow all that gold suddenly meant nothing. I'd made a big mistake. I should have listened to him a lot more closely. Hadn't he said, *"You do not understand my people. . . . They are not on anyone's side. They are on their own side."* So Badu, like Gabriel, was on his own side. So much for the brotherhood.

When I turned back again, Father Bullingham was lowering himself into the rocky canal. There were some others standing behind him. One of them handed down a pickaxe and a shovel. Another shone a huge bright flashlight straight down on us.

"You've got a lot to learn," said Father Bullingham. "Start by digging." He shoved the pick at me.

I thought about teaching *him* a lesson right then, with a heavy pickaxe. But he coughed his dry little cough and I saw his hand glide toward his pocket. I had no desire to dig up the skull again, so what made me move into the same passage-way? Sometimes I believe there's a weird fate that makes you do stuff. I stepped past the bit Mina and I had scratched out—a few feet back from it, just where the toe bones might be—drawn to a curious ridge on the passageway wall.

I couldn't have chosen a worse place.

My first swing uncovered the edge of something hard and metallic. My next swing cracked open the whole wall and the rock and soil crumbled away. There before my eyes was a metal box, the side of which—about three feet high by five wide—was now completely exposed.

I can't tell you how disappointed I was. To think I'd been planning and hoping and suffering to find that box, and just when I didn't want to find it at all, boy, there it was as bright and real as a bad dream.

"Dig it out," ordered Father Bullingham.

I thought for a moment about refusing. Then I remembered

the dog on that night I'd first met him. I remembered all about his little lessons. I remembered Badu's guilty face. I thought about Bartholomew trapped down here. The gold wasn't worth it. I stopped thinking. I guess I'm a coward.

I dug out the trunk. That's not true, I dug *round* the trunk; it was too heavy to lift. In the end, Father Bullingham had to help me. As I said, he was a very big man and even he had trouble. We could only drag it a bit and manhandle it to the floor. The people outside, upside, whereverside, slung down ropes. Reluctantly, I helped fix them onto the handles of the chest; but it was no use, the chest didn't shift, and anyway even if we could have got it out of the passageway and into the shipping canal the flagstone entrance was too small. For a horrible moment I thought that they were going to smash in the arched roof and widen the hole above us. I imagined it falling in huge chunks of masonry onto Mina and me. I backed off down the passageway, pulling Mina with me. At length, they hoisted Father Bullingham back out and replaced the flagstone.

For about a quarter of an hour we waited in the darkness. Mina was trembling. I put my arm around her and we sat on the treasure chest, scared and miserable.

"What are they going to do?" she said.

"Dunno. Go to the Bahamas, buy a Rolls. What would you do?"

"I mean, to us?"

"Thought you did," I said. "I was trying not to."

"Can't believe that Badu . . ."

I squeezed her shoulders. "Sorry."

But I *was* thinking about what they were going to do. And I had come up with an answer. They were going to leave us here, buried alive in the old passageways. They were going to "snooze" us. And we'd scream and scream and no one would hear, and no one would come, and we'd scream some more, and cry, and still no one would come. And I'd text everyone I could think of—no, I'd phone everyone, but that would kill the battery, so I'd text—in fact I started texting everyone right there and then: *uv got 2 help me this is 4 real im going 2 b buried alive in a canal under d main slave dungeon uv got 2 rescue me*, and still no one would come.

"See," I said, "help is on its way." And I kissed Mina. It was a pretty pathetic kiss, more like a peck on the cheek, but at least I did it. At least when it mattered I'd tried to be the kind of guy I could admire. It sucked, really. For three hundred years the Baktu Baxters had kept to their pledge and the English had not "profited by their misfortune." And now? Yes, it really sucked.

They raised the flagstone again. Without thinking, we crowded toward the hole. I was almost glad to see the flashlight.

"Open the chest," ordered Father Bullingham. He dropped the pickaxe back through the hole. Luckily it missed Mina and me—but only just. "Shovel the gold into the buckets." More things dropped down the hole. Two shovels and galvanized metal buckets. They were new. They still had the prices chalked on them.

"Don't make me come down there to insist!" said Father Bullingham, coughing. "Oh dear. Oh dear . . ." He leaned through the hole above us. "Open the chest."

Back in the passageway, I hooked the sharp end of the pick under the rusty lock on the front of the chest. One yank and I levered it off. It didn't break. The wood and metal around it splintered. From a thousand tiny cracks along the length of the chest, streams of golden dust suddenly burst through. Like sand from an hourglass, like water from a cracked container. I dropped the pick and cupped my hands under the largest flow, until even my hands couldn't contain it.

Here was the gold that Pops had dreamed of. Here was the ransom to free Bartholomew.

Here it was—the Baktu treasure!

I don't know what I thought. I don't know if I was happy or sad. They should make a new word to describe the feeling of finding a vast fortune in gold dust just when you are about to die.

"Shovel it into the buckets, and pass them up."

The next half hour was crazy. I wrenched the lid off the chest. Gold dust spilled everywhere. Gold stuck to my clothes, gold coated my fingers. I got gold in my hair. I slopped gold into buckets, which tipped and poured gold back over me. I trailed gold across the rocky floor, down the passageways in shining tracks—each probably worth a million pounds. And I filled bucket after bucket after bucket, until I lost count and my arms ached and I wished the gold would come to an end—but the chest hardly seemed any emptier.

At one point Father Bullingham lowered himself down into the canal and, pushing me aside, dug away at the gold in the chest. He seemed angry and then, with the help of those above, hoisted himself out again.

"What about us?" I said, following him.

Bad question.

The flashlight swung out of the hole, and from my position at the foot of the opening five feet down, it was hard to tell what was going on up there. I heard the sounds of metal against metal. Then I heard someone say, "Where is it then?"

The flashlight reappeared through the hole.

"Where have you put it?" demanded Father Bullingham.

"Put what?" I said.

"Oh dear, dear," he sighed.

"What?" I said.

"If I have to come back down . . ."

Maybe it was the way he said it. Or maybe I thought there was no point in hanging on to battery power if you were going to die. Anyway, I switched the phone on to video record. Who knows, maybe one day, in another three hundred years' time, somebody would get to know about the last minutes of Zac Baxter.

"Steady on," said a voice that was vaguely familiar. "Get the boy up here."

Two pairs of arms descended through the hole, and for the

first time since Father Bullingham and Badu had appeared, I felt a bit happier. Once out of that hole, I was NOT going back in it. I'd fight. I'd die fighting. I'd look for a way to bolt. If I could get away, I reasoned, I'd come back for Mina. They replaced the flagstone over the hole. Mina was down there in the dark. I didn't want to leave her there, alone in the Old Portuguese canal with only a skull for company.

Back in the dim light of the male slave dungeon, I saw four people. Badu definitely didn't count. Father Bullingham was towering over me. Behind him were Dr. and Mrs. Sniddon. To his left stood a man. I looked at him. He was black, not too tall, with a thin wiry frame. He was wearing khaki safari shorts and a safari jacket. He was not Uncle Fidelis, but that was about all I could see, for Father Bullingham suddenly shone the flashlight full in my face and blinded me.

"Don't frighten him," said the man. There was something about his voice. Something familiar.

Father Bullingham did not remove the flashlight. The man spoke again.

"This is irregular, sir. I want to remind you that I have had to come out all the way from the UK to satisfy myself that my client, Mr. Zac Baxter, is being fairly treated. And what do I find? If you do not put that flashlight away, sir, I shall file a full report to the courts."

Father Bullingham swung the torch away from my face, and in the dazzle of bright spots still wiggling in front of my eyes, I saw—could it really be? How could my text have brought him so quickly?

"Zac, my boy," the man said, and stepped nearer to me. As he put his hand out, I saw Badu make the alarm sign that we'd planned when we first left Cabo Corso.

"Raphael, remember? Look a bit different out of my black suit, don't I?"

Raphael—here? How my heart began to sing! I smiled. The smile stayed on my face—until I was grinning like a complete idiot, until it started to hurt behind my ears.

"I got your texts and I was very relieved to get the last one, I can tell you. Father Bullingham has got a lot of explaining to do, when we get all this mess sorted out."

Raphael! My mind did a backflip. My heart raced. Raphael had come to rescue me!

I must have looked weird. I was just standing there, grinning.

"Now tell me, Zac, we've got the gold here. (Nod, nod. Well done, well done.) Was the bond with the gold?"

I shook my head.

"Are you sure?"

"Maybe the—" I was about to tell him about the skull, but something stopped me. I mean, don't get me wrong. I was very, very, very—a million billion zillion times—glad to see him. I figured that bar any accident it meant I would be seeing my next birthday too. But there was something . . .

Suddenly Ashley flashed into my mind. I imagined him standing there, his stupid haircut and his big grin saying, "*The Hitchhiker's Guide to the British Intelligence Manual* indicates that someone will pose as your friend—and you can't be sure who it will be. (Hey, it could be ME, AshLEY!) But never, ever, Mr. Clever, trust the guy who asks you for the bond."

"Yes?" he said.

"Mina's still down there," I said.

"What else, Zac?"

"Raphael . . . *Mina—is—still—down—there*," I repeated. "We need to get her out. And that woman is THE woman." I pointed at Mrs. Sniddon, aka Ingleworth, who looked back at me from her pale blank face. "Don't let her get near me . . . ," I shouted.

Raphael stood there still nodding his head, and I waited for him to do something. I shook his arm a little. I admit, I was nervous, I was scared. I couldn't swallow, and deep down in my stomach the old spiral of fear was back. From the corner of my eye I could still see Badu secretly, *frantically* making the alarm sign with his hands. There was something I didn't understand. I turned away from Badu. He wasn't going to trick me a second time.

"Yes, Zac, you were about to say—'maybe the . . .'?"

"I didn't find the bond," I said. I couldn't work out why he wasn't worried about Mina. You may think I'm very slow. You would be right.

In the distance away back through the vaulted slave chambers another light flashed. I saw it bounce dimly off the wall. I heard footsteps and voices far, far away.

"Someone's coming," said Mrs. Sniddon.

"Can't be anyone. Maybe the museum attendant. You paid him enough, didn't you?" said Dr. Sniddon.

"The boy's a liar," said Father Bullingham. "He's got the bond! Put him back down in the hole, until he hands it over."

What did he mean? Raphael was my barrister, wasn't he? Suddenly it seemed weird that my barrister should be here right at this crucial point. How come Raphael *was* here?

"I will not have my client put in any hole," said Raphael. "If he has the bond he will give it to me and . . ."

Badu made the warning sign *again*, and this time I looked at him. The message written all over his face was as loud as the Atlantic surf: DANGER.

I was confused. I backed away from Raphael.

"Oh dear, oh dear, dear," said Father Bullingham, coughing. "I think he's twizzled you, my dear fellow."

I eyed Raphael. Wasn't he the barrister employed by the Cormantin Club, the same that had defended me? The barrister who had got me sent to Cabo Corso? Where *did* he know Father Bullingham from? How come he was *here*? He hadn't come from England as a response to my texts; he would have told me, texted me he was coming. So why had he come? I stared at him from his black face down to his khaki shorts, to his thin thighs. That's when I saw the scar over his knee. A jagged dark line.

I stared. I laughed. My mind flashed back to cold orange pavements and frosty nights. I saw again two shadows sprinting down the street, one an old woman who might not have been . . . the other limping, holding his knee. . . .

Raphael, with all his friendly texts, knowing my every

move. Raphael, who had a copy of all the diaries—except mine. Raphael, feeding me information . . .

He took a step forward. There it was—the angle of the shoulder, the slight shuffle. I'm not stupid.

It was *Raphael* who had betrayed me—*not* Badu, *not* Uncle Fidelis. It was Raphael who Nunu's voices had spoken of. I clutched at my stomach, feeling suddenly like vomiting. It must have been Raphael who had mugged Pops, Raphael who had murdered Uncle Fidelis, Raphael who had followed me to Cabo Corso. . . .

"It was you all along," I whispered.

Raphael's smile vanished. His voice changed, hardened. "So you finally worked it out, did you, Zac? A bit too late. Just like Fidelis. Just like the real Raphael. Slow. And you'll die like them, I promise—slowly. Unless you hand over the bond, of course."

"It wasn't my fault," whispered Badu. "They were waiting by the Door when I came out. I held out as long as I could. . . . They forced me . . ."

"Oh, do shut up." Father Bullingham brought his thick leather boot down hard on Badu's damaged foot. I don't know if it was that, or shock, but I twisted away from Raphael and leapt to Badu's side.

"Fight!" I yelled. "Fight, Badu. Scream. Run!"

"From the slave dungeon there is no escape," he whispered, his voice full of pain, already weak.

I pushed him behind me and stood there, fists raised, heart racing.

"You messed up." Raphael swung round angrily at Father Bullingham. "I could have got all the information out of him, no trouble. I don't think he's got a clue where it is. The bond probably doesn't even exist anymore. Even if it does, it's going to be incarcerated with the three of them in that hole for another three hundred years, by which time there'll be nobody left to sue you with any bond for any compensation at all. We've got the gold—it'll have to do."

"I have my orders," said Father Bullingham.

"That's right," said Mrs. Sniddon. "Whitehall was very firm about the bond. Reeves said, 'No evidence, no court case.' I was there when he said it." She swept a pair of lizard-like eyes over me and started pushing back the cuticles of her left hand.

Deep down in my stomach the old icy grip tightened.

I frantically scoured the dungeon for help. What I needed was the entire student body of my kickboxing class, plus a dozen black belt karate experts. I imagined Ashley encouraging me. "Go get 'em, Zackie Chan!"

"You work it out then. You go down there and search," said Raphael. "They never told me anything about digging."

"Ho, believe me, we've done our share of digging," said Mrs. Sniddon. "We dug that grave up, you know, we didn't even get the right one first time. Imagine having to dig up two because they both had no gravestones! But Whitehall insisted, 'Leave no stone unturned.' Ooo, I made a funny!" She smirked at her own stupid joke. "Although digging up a dead body isn't my idea of treasure hunting."

I thought about community service, thousand-pound fines, prison sentences, and public disgrace, but I couldn't think of anything nasty enough for flat-faced Mrs. Sniddon.

The footsteps in the next chamber grew louder. The flashlight swung across the far dungeon wall ahead of me.

"It's probably just the attendant bringing more buckets," said Dr. Sniddon.

Father Bullingham yanked the slab back off the entrance to the shipping canal and with all his bulk came straight at me. I bent low and timed him. I heard Pops's voice, "*When taking on a bigger guy use his weight against him. Big guys can't move fast. Time him—wait—go for the knees or the throat.*" I waited, every second counted. Then, when he was within an arm's length, I doubled down and kick-slammed my foot straight into his knee. He tottered and staggered back.

"Help me, Badu," I hissed. "*For God's sake help me*, or we'll be down that hole for a long time."

Badu limped round to my left and tried bravely to make a stand, but I could see that he had no stomach for it and was in a lot of pain. "Come on," I said to them. "Come—right—on." That was another defense fighting trick Pops had taught me. "*Always take the fight to them. Start first and start mean. Grab any advantage and use it—fast. Remember, it's only about winning.*" I edged over to where I'd located the gold buckets. I leaned down and grabbed a handful of gold dust.

I turned toward the blackness beneath the entrance slab and yelled, "Hang on in there, Mina! The rescue team is coming in!"

Father Bullingham seemed to be deciding what to do. That was a good sign. Pops had said, *"Confuse them, don't give them time to think; never hesitate; take whatever you can get."* I rushed at Dr. Sniddon and flung the gold dust in his face. He screamed, clawed at his eyes, stumbled and fell, hitting his head on the stone floor. Not much, but *that was for you, Pops, for digging you up.*

The footsteps in the outer chamber grew louder. I could almost hear voices.

"It's going to be okay, Badu," I said. "I'm going to kill them all, or die trying." I smiled at him, but I could already see that Raphael, at least, had figured out he was dealing with a street kid from Tuffley.

He pulled Father Bullingham aside. "It's no use, Zac," he said with that low tone of certainty, "I can take you out."

I sized him up and I knew it was true. When it comes to your brethren, you just know. That was something else Pops had said, *"Don't be arrogant. Like Bob Marley says, 'He who fights and runs away lives to fight another day.'"*

Only there was nowhere to run. And no other day.

It was quick. There was really nothing I could do. Raphael just grabbed me and twisted my arm behind my back. It was so embarrassingly simple. I whimpered in pain. "Just say the wrong word and I'll break it." He thrust me forward toward the hole. Father Bullingham grabbed Badu, and suddenly it looked like it was all over.

"Say good-bye," said Father Bullingham. "We'll be back for the rest of the gold and we'll find that bond, but

I don't think somehow you'll be in any shape to help us."

Was this it? Was this how it all ended? Buried alive in the slave labyrinths with a fortune in gold dust. Just like Bartholomew, like Akonor? The footsteps in the next chamber grew louder. Father Bullingham nodded at Mrs. Sniddon. "Just deal with that museum attendant; pay him some more; send him away. We don't want to have to put him down the hole too." Raphael almost looked sorry, like for half a second he accepted he was on the wrong side; then he smiled and shoved me sideways toward the hole.

Pops had said: "*But if it comes to the crunch, use everything you've got. They say madmen have the strength of ten. Get mad and stay mad—because if you don't stand for something, you'll fall for anything.*" I was not going to fall into that hole for the next three hundred years. I *was* going to stand for something. The Baktu ancestors demanded it. . . .

I twisted. Pain shot through my upper arm. I screamed. I kicked. I bit down on Raphael's hand. I dug my teeth in, determined never to let go. If I was pushed down that hole I'd drag him with me, teeth first. He lurched and swore.

And there we all dangled when Bernard and Marion and the British High Commissioner's man, Toseland, with YY from the Ghana Police, and Wisdom K. Gbedemah, pushed past Mrs. Sniddon and came stumbling under the low arch into the male slave dungeon.

"What was that I heard about things getting nasty?" said Bernard in his magnolia voice.

"Help me!" came Mina's voice through the hole.

Beep! went something in my pocket.

"Catch!" I yelled at Bernard. With my free hand I tossed him my mobile phone. "Press stop and playback."

"And you'll die like them, I promise—slowly . . . ," said the tinny voice from my mobile.

Everything was on tape.

"I say!" said the High Commissioner's man.

"Red-handed!" said YY, smiling like he'd always wanted to say that. Then he raised his Kalashnikov (not the M version—but hey, it did the job!). "Good afternoon, Zac Baxter, very glad to meet you again! Sorry I can't shake right now. My hands are a bit busy!"

"Eh! Shame on you, Father B. Bullingham!" said Wisdom. "I used to be proud to drive you in my embassy Land Rover when you came to Accra on British government business, but I am resigning right now! You can find another driver, Father B. Bullingham!"

"I can explain everything," purred Raphael, releasing my arm. "Now my client, Zac Baxter . . ."

Mrs. Sniddon stepped over the moaning Dr. Sniddon and tried sidling toward the exit.

She was not going to escape. So—despite that feeling she gave me in the pit of my stomach—I gave her my personal best ever savate classic back heel to the stomach and a double mule in the face. Forget the wheels of justice—that sorted her! Then I cartwheeled back and brought the back of my hand round hard, very hard—so hard it hurt me for weeks after—but boy oh boy, did I smile as it hit home on Raphael's nose.

Ouch.

"No, Zac, we'll play this by the rules," said Bernard.

"Sure," I said. You wanted Zackie Chan, Ash? No prob, Bob. I leaned over the slab and stuck my head into the slave labyrinth hole. "The police are here, Mina, everything is okay."

"And the rule number one is handcuffs," said Toseland.

"Wha-d abou-d my righ-dd-s . . . ," started Raphael, wiping blood from his face. I flexed my fist happily.

"You have the right to remain silent," said YY, pointing the Kalashnikov in Raphael's face. "But I rather think you've said too much already."

"You cannot arrest me," said Father Bullingham. "I claim diplomatic immunity. I work for GCHQ. I have special status at the High Commission. You should know the drill," he spat out at Toseland.

"I'll check when I get back to Accra," said Toseland. "I'm not in my office now, am I? And you can't expect me to know bloody everything. I'm overworked and short-staffed. How the bloody hell do I know MI5 drills?"

But Ashley did. I imagined him saying, "Watch out, scout, MI5 agents always have backup technology—like micro guns disguised as a shoelace. . . ." I snatched the handcuffs from Toseland and snapped them on Father Bullingham before he could go for his cufflinks.

"I'd like to remind you, sir, that you are on Ghanaian soil," said YY, "and until I get orders from my superiors, you will be detained under provisions laid down by the Constitution of Ghana, which empowers the Ghana Police Force to detain *any* nonnational acting suspiciously. Please be aware and don't resist arrest or obstruct me in my line of duty—that is the law here, if you don't know." And he made them lie on the floor while he searched pockets and removed sunglasses, shoes, ballpoint pens, and masses of other stuff from all four of them!

"Yes," I said sadly, shaking my head. "You've got such a lot to learn!"

"Oh! Oh! Oh!" said Wisdom. "Father B. Bullingham, you are a big disgrace."

I jumped over to hug Marion. "How did you know? How did you get here so quickly?"

"Ashley," she said. "We're fostering him. He lent us his phone; all your texts are here. We were on our way to Cabo Corso when we got the one you sent from the underground passages—so we turned round and came straight here. And you know Bernard is a very eminent man—just because he does things by the rules doesn't mean he can't pull rank when he has to. It only took one phone call and we've had VIP treatment all the way!"

"I am taking them out to the Land Rover," said YY, seizing the car keys from Wisdom. "I am commandeering this vehicle in my line of duty."

The Sniddons weren't dead, worst luck. Handcuffed and searched, they stumbled out after the others.

"Mina!" I shouted.

Bail Bonds, Bad Blood, and Bones

We soon got Mina out of the Old Portuguese canal. She was fine. I think she was glad to have missed the scene above. Anyway, she'd made discoveries of her own.

"Please come down with a flashlight," she said.

Bernard, Wisdom, Badu, Mina, and I squeezed back into the passageway. Marion thought it better for someone to stay up in the dungeon while YY and Toseland took the others out to the car.

Mina led the way. There, lying on the narrow shelf, was the skeleton of a tall man.

"I scratched all the dirt off him," said Mina. "Look, he's holding something."

Clutched between the bones of his forearm, with his finger curled over the top, was a long cylindrical tube. It seemed to be made out of something like leather, water-proofed leather, as if it had once been a wine bag or a water carrier. The leather was still strong and good and not at all rotten, and inside it was a rolled parchment.

"Do you think this is it?" she asked.

"Yep," I said. "This is what Father Bullingham wanted. This is it—why Pops was murdered and why we've all spent far too long bashing down walls at Cabo Corso." I turned to Bernard, but he patted my head and nodded.

"If I gather right," said Bernard, "from what I understand from Ashley, from some papers he showed me, this bond documents a treaty, a contract between a Baktu chief and the British government. It's still a legal document. Well, as far as I know anything—and I've been a barrister for the best part of my life—a bond is a bond for all eternity. If the British broke their word, then they are liable to be sued."

"Even," I said, "if it was three hundred years ago?"

"Which makes it worse," said Bernard. "Imagine three hundred years of damages to countless Baktu peoples all illegally sold into slavery."

"And all their descendants, dummy," said Mina, nudging me.

"Well, they'd be hard to trace," said Bernard.

"No they wouldn't," I said. "King Baktu cut a lock of hair from everyone's head." I pulled the shriveled container open again. "Look! With DNA testing nowadays . . . I mean it'd be long, but it'd be possible—wouldn't it?"

"Interesting," said Bernard. "This is just up my street. I hope, Zac, you will let me get involved. It could open up a completely new chapter in compensation claims."

I didn't say anything. I just hugged him hard.

"There are a few other details that are interesting as well. Did you know that the magistrate who sent you here, Ms. Bowdich, JP, has been suspended from all judicial activities pending an inquiry into a government appointment that would clash with her civic duties? That Father Bullingham, which you probably worked out by now, is not a reverend father at all but a civil servant under the present government? And sadly, Raphael Dery, nephew to your Uncle Fidelis and solicitor for the Cormantin Club, passed away on Tuesday the twelfth of April in a hit-and-run accident. Unsurprisingly, the day after, Fidelis was murdered. . . . When I found *those* things out I was seriously concerned. I *knew* there was something very wrong at your hearing . . . and if Raphael Dery was dead, then who was your Raphael?"

Boy, 2+2 were making mathematical history!

"How much do you think compensation for three hundred years of slavery would be worth?" I asked.

"*A lot*," said Bernard. "An awful lot."

"Bow-wow," I said, smiling.

"Well, these people have been getting away with murder for too long. They think they can make the rules up themselves, and that is a grave mistake. The wheels of justice have caught up with them. Things do catch up with you in the end, you know," said Bernard.

I grinned, a big fat, happy grin.

"It will be a *very* serious embarrassment for the government to be linked to this bond. They'll have to protect the monarchy, but in doing so they'll lose credibility—certainly in the next elections, if they don't handle it fairly—not to mention staggering amounts of monies if the case goes against them." Bernard nodded his head in satisfaction.

"No wonder they wanted to bury it six feet," I said.

"They could be embarrassed internationally, and there will be no end to the claims. It's actually an issue that could polarize the British community. I've been doing my history, and feel pretty sure that we might be able to sue other parties as well. Even though you can't prosecute the Queen, I don't think Crown agents are immune, or the English Chartered Company of Royal Adventurers, or the African Company of Merchants—who continued trading in slaves up until 1800. Think of all those profits that were put into the multinationals that followed! And that's before the government of Ghana start their claims for the destruction of their monuments as a cover-up, for three hundred years of the underdevelopment of their country. . . ."

I remembered Uncle Fidelis's words, "*It's more than just his old story. This one's big.*" I was beginning to realize just how big.

"In fact," continued Bernard, "it's one huge can of worms. Once you start digging it gets worse and worse. I've discovered records of an illegal massacre of a Portuguese mulatto settlement at Cabo Corso in the very same year as Bartholomew was transported! With the proof we've got so far—well . . ."

"D'you hear that?" I said to Mina.

"Who do you think this was?" Mina was stroking the long bones in front of her.

I had started to rearrange the fingers, which had held the leather cylinder. They fell apart. From one of them dropped a ring. Mina bent to the floor and picked it up.

Suddenly she cried out, "Oh, look!"

She was holding out the ring, "It's the *crest*—that was on the front of my old house. . . . Do you think . . . ?"

"Then this must be . . ."

"Yes," she said, "I just knew it. I mean I hoped it . . . I wished it . . . This is our—my?—long-lost and ill-fated ancestor, Senhor Bartolomeu Dias."

Justice

You'll want to know how everything ended up, won't you? Most of it was good, some of it was funny—a big part of it was sad.

Here are the good bits. The gold dust was mine. Okay, Bernard said everything had to be done by the rules. The Ghana government took a share, but not too much. The High Commissioner's man, Toseland, got it done through the Embassy and he said it was fair, but "just another bloody thing to do." We gave the chest to Cape Coast Castle Museum. But they couldn't put it on show without breaking the dungeon floor. They're still thinking about that one. Some of the money went to rebuilding Cabo Corso Leprosarium. Bernard set up a trust for the clinic through LEPRA. We took out loads to finance Pops's compensation case, Zac Baxter vs. the State—suit no. MISC 991/200—justice for all the families of all the Cormantins ever sold into slavery. And I gave YY enough to finish his house. After that, I made sure that Wisdom got his tourist bus and Marion her time-share in Barcelona.

The rest we split four ways: Mina, Badu, Ashley, and me.

Mina took her part and the bones of her ancestor and made her first ever expedition to Portugal. She got herself sponsored by the *Daily Mercury*, which her journalist, Chris Barnett, had worked for. We followed all the articles. Senhor Dias got a regular funeral and a public pardon. Mina e-mailed me the picture that was on the front page of the Lisbon papers. She was so thrilled. She got her IB diploma and now she's planning on going back to campaign for Cabo Corso Old Town to be restored as an ancient monument. One day it might attract tourists. Who knows, maybe Wisdom and Mina will work a visitors' tour out? She's looking for the Dias padrõe now. She says if she finds it, maybe it'll make the BBC 9:00 p.m. slot! Maybe she'll find Chris Barnett in a shallow grave. That wouldn't be so funny. Let's hope he's on a beach somewhere in the South Pacific investigating the life cycle of the loggerhead turtle. Mina shouldn't make carting dead bodies around a habit.

Badu set Nunu up on his island, built on a new wing. Nunu didn't want anything fancy, so Badu only built him a smallish palace. "You're the last chief of the Baktus," he said. "The prophecy has been fulfilled, so your luck's changed—you've got to be ready for a new era." We hated leaving him, but he was cool about it. Come summer we are going to go visit Nunu and check him out. We'll hook up with Mina. I'm looking forward to that. Opoku was right about Ghana. I like it. It probably is the best country in the world.

Me? Well, the charge of digging up Pops's grave was appealed against. In the light of Mrs. Sniddon's comments, I was declared innocent. I got fifty pounds for every day of wrongful remand and community service! Ms. Shaw was so shocked and embarrassed she sorted everything out for me with social services. As for her, Mrs. Sniddon/Ingleworth-whatever, like I said, I sure hope the wheels of justice are going to grind her into a pulp.

Badu came to Gloucester and spent some time at a posh BUPA. He liked the Sky TV and the drinks. He said the nurses were lush. They couldn't fix his toes, but they got everything else under control. We live together now with Ashley, at Bernard and Marion's. My room is still painted magnolia and I must say I like it. Even a quarter of that gold dust is more wealth than I've ever dreamed of.

You can be sure Ashley was pleased about his percentage, and I was pleased to see his spiky haircut and silly grin. "Right, mush," he said, "now we are multi-mega-mega millionaires we've got to get serious. We gotta make a five-year life plan, Stan, starting with GCSEs and ending up at Oxford. Money is nice but being smart is nicer. Oxford is not too far away from here, so we can keep an eye on Bernard in case he speeds up or anything. What d'you think, mush?"

You can be sure, too, that we organized the spending spree, and Maggot and Lee and Opoku never had it so good!

Here are the funny bits. When we left Cape Coast Castle we took the road that runs along the coast. We stopped for a rest at Anomabu. That's how I know *Ten Against Eleven* made it okay. I insisted we go down to speak to the fishermen who were trying to launch *TAE* so that they could sail it back to Elmina. Seeing as the canoe was actually in pretty good shape and I wouldn't get any of the gold for a while, I felt that I should say thanks to them, even if I couldn't buy them a whole fleet right away.

We were all traveling in the same Land Rover. Father Bullingham, the Sniddons, and Raphael were handcuffed in the back section. Father Bullingham said he needed a pee and we should unlock him. Well, we figured he couldn't do much with a Kalashnikov pointed at his back and no cufflinks, so YY took his handcuffs off.

Father Bullingham wandered down the beach at gunpoint. As I was talking to the skipper, he made a run for it. He bolted down to the seashore where the fishermen had anchored the canoe (*Sea Never Dry*) they'd used to come looking for *Ten Against Eleven*. He dived into the foam and scrambled on board. Before YY could get a good shot at him, he'd grabbed one of the fishermen as a body shield. He forced the men to put to sea, and we saw the canoe turn toward the surf. The fisherman I was talking to started laughing. I couldn't see anything funny. Then I noticed the canoe was heading for the surf line broadside. The men on board straightened her up a little, but only enough to stop her capsizing completely. Then they pretended to panic. I saw three of them throw themselves overboard. Father Bullingham let go of his body shield and jumped for it too.

Guess what? He jumped to the leeward side.

The body-shield guy straightened the canoe up and brought her back. He picked up his fellow fishermen. Father Bullingham was never seen again.

Like I said, he had a lot to learn.

It was funny about the mobile, wasn't it? They tried to fix me with it, set me up, trace my movements, but I fixed them—and they paid the bill, too!

I'd been wrong about Fidelis, of course. It never was him at Heathrow, just more cunning disguises, more scare tactics. But after Father Bullingham's exit we didn't get even a "Boo" out of the others. When they made statements in Accra, I learned that ever since Pops had been interviewed in the *Daily Echo*, they'd been employed by Whitehall to sort it out. The government had taken the Cormantin Club, its Return to Africa venture, and its compensation case very seriously, especially after Uncle Fidelis had given Raphael the diary copies. It seems that they had watched with growing alarm while Raphael investigated leads and filed petitions—they'd arranged an accident for him after Fidelis's phone call, but luckily not before he'd sent me that first letter. With Pops and Fidelis and Raphael off the scene, it had been easy to set a bogus "Raphael" on me.

You know, when I think about it, perhaps the scars on the back of the Establishment were deeper than my own. That's what a guilty conscience does to you, I suppose. You're always watching your back, running scared—hey, I almost wrote "running scarred"!—believing that one day the truth will out. I don't know. It's hard to understand. What must it feel like to be always rewriting history?

It seemed a lot of trouble to go to, to bury the wrongs of the past, but then I remember the trouble I'd gone to to dig them up, so I can't comment.

What I can't get over is the bogus Raphael—black brother like that. Imagine he'd turned on his own people. He'd betrayed his roots. He was the assassin. With the flat-faced woman, he'd murdered Pops, murdered poor old quarrelsome Uncle Fidelis, run over the real Raphael, taken his mobile—everything. He'd set me up to be captured. All those texts, I'd played right into his hands—and it was all him. If you like, he'd sold me down the river—a good old slavers' term. Was he so different from Gabriel and all the other Africans who sold us out?

Before, I'd have said that men couldn't be so evil; now, I guess I know better.

Not the End

That brings me back to the diaries, where it all started.
Before we left, Mina translated the last chapter. Here
it is.

The Last Chapter

Case for the Prosecution
Exhibit 08 Attached

Form MG 14

(CJ Act 1967, s. 9; MC Act 1980, ss. 5A(3) (a) and 5B; MC Rules 1981, r. 70)

EXTRACT: *From the alleged diary of Bartholomew Baktu* ....

This exhibit (consisting of .... *case for the prosecution two (2)* *pamphlets written in Portuguese . . . —certified translation Lisbon University— verified against accounts of the Royal African Company—considered authentic: Professor Braithwaite, British Museum* ~~page(s) each page signed by me~~) is true to the best of my knowledge ~~and I make it knowingly, if it is tendered in evidence, I shall be liable to prosecution if I have wilfully stated in it anything which I know to be false or do not believe to be true~~.

Signature *N/A—see above*   Date *November 5th*   *DC Hesketh*

I cannot write of those final hours at the castle without weeping. And as I will not allow myself to weep, then I must write very little. We stayed holed up in the old canal, without food or water, until we were very weak. But it was not until Senhor Dias took ill from his wounds and died that my brothers decided to break through into the chamber above. We buried Uncle Senhor. We put the bond and the locks of my people's hair into the long-dried-up water bag he always carried, and folded it in his arms. He was a brave man. I cannot write now. I will stop until I can control myself.

Yes, where was I? We removed the sealed slab and broke through to the chamber above. As ill luck would have it, it was empty. We had hoped to mingle with the slaves there and seek our futures wherever the boats might take us.

It was an empty hope.

The Englishmen found us. My brothers were not slaves, so they were arrested, tried, condemned, and hung. They made me watch. They told me, if I told them where the gold was, we could all go free.

I told them I didn't know.

I would have given every last twist of that gold to have Akonor back. But I couldn't betray him. That's what I thought at the time. Now I am sure the English lied. I've spent all of my life blaming myself, but they wouldn't free me, so why would they have freed him? But I do not sleep well. I think too much. I pray to Akonor to forgive me.

At least I was not a coward.

At least I watched him hang—yes, every last struggle of life. Every kick.

I looked into his eyes until the very end, and he looked into mine. I can still see him looking. I will hold his eyes with mine forever.

That's it then. Not really the end, because stories don't really have ends, do they? No, this is the beginning of another story, that's why I'm sitting here in this office preparing this document. In a way it's come full circle, back to Gloucester, back to witness statements, back to Pops.

Yes, here I am, two days to Christmas, thinking about his low mound once again. Summer has come and gone but his grave hasn't changed. I guess there are some things you can't change. The place looks just the same. I'm not. I'm not the same boy who sat there last winter—but enough of me. I shall finish this account and add it to the pile. Oh yes, Pops's gravestone. It's granite, brought all the way from Cabo Corso. I had the words carved into it. He'll like that. It's my Christmas present to him. On Christmas Day I've planned a little ceremony.

It'd sound corny if I said I'd give all that treasure to have him back, wouldn't it? I guess that was how King Baktu felt about Bartholomew, how Bartholomew felt about Akonor. Sometimes when I feel like that, I really hope I'm the last of them. History shouldn't carry on repeating itself.

There are different kinds of treasure, though. I was lucky, I found two.

Outside, Bernard and Marion are waiting for me in the car. Bernard says he knows a law firm to take on the compensation case. He's very hopeful that one of them, a "young black radical lawyer," might win. He's sure we have enough evidence. It's never been tried in history before, so I don't know how it will go. One thing is for sure, it'll make the papers! I can just imagine the headline: JUSTICE AT LAST FOR KING BAKTU.

There can be no justice, of course. There never can be; not for Bartholomew, not for Akonor, not for Senhor Dias, not for all the seven million Cormantins sold from the Slave Coast.

And for me?

Author's Note

The Door of No Return borrows its title from an architectural feature of the slave castles and fortresses of Africa: it being the portal through which the slaves passed when they left their prisons to be loaded onto the boats. As you can imagine, it is hugely symbolic and raises all sorts of unanswerable questions about all the unreturned, their journeys, and their stories.

This story, however, was inspired by a mention in Dutch archives of a wealthy person, one Badu, who in 1701 deposited 15,360 dambas of gold dust at Fort St. Sebastian, Shama. Around the same time a child of seven years was sold from the same fort. His memorial stone lies next to the south bastion, facing the sea. If you go to Shama today you will be shown his stone; you will also be shown teeth found in the slave dungeons, and you will be shown the entrance to a shipping canal, which links into an underground passage, which if it had not been flooded by a sudden subsidence would take you far out under the sea to a point where slave ships could rest at anchor.

In short, as far as I know, everything related to the history of Ghana and the slave trade in this story is taken from a true source. I've tried to check that out, to be really sure, from eminent books like those written by Albert van Dantzig and Kwesi Anquandah, and from the curators of various forts, especially Philip Atta-Yawson at Cormantin Abandzi, and from the local oral history told to me under palm trees by the coast.

I haven't changed anything, although I have relocated the story from Shama to Cape Coast Castle partly out of respect for the fact that the castle is now a world heritage site. The dungeons are real and the figures accurate, even understated, for I now believe there were in excess of seventy slaving forts along the Gold Coast. Cape Coast *was* first built by the Portuguese in 1555, *was* fought over, until the British took control of it around 1664. Cape Coast went on to become the capital of the Gold Coast, now Ghana. In addition, the Portuguese were defeated by the British and the Dutch. Towns were burnt, especially in the Komenda wars around the 1700s. The Pra River is still not completely charted, still has a wealth in gold dust and diamonds. Kakum forest is real (although I fear the leopards have long since gone north to find wilder places), and there is a leprosarium very near it. Ankerful Leprosarium is, however, completely unlike Cabo Corso, being a bright, cheerful hospital with very welcoming staff who will be happy to show you around.

But if the places and the history are real (even *Ten Against Eleven* is a real boat), the characters are not.

Nobody in this story is based on any living person.

However, there are some living people who helped to make this story what it is. They are: Minty and Sakky Barnor and Joy Coombes—all faithful fans of Zac; Angela Robson, who believed in my ability to write this story; Guido Quarcoopome, my first young reader to give the story the thumbs-up; Naomi Badu, who "dashed" me the laptop to write it on; Kati Torda, who went with me to Shama in search of inspiration; my writers' group, especially Ruth Eastham, who gave me extensive, important feedback; Jude Mussi, who introduced me to the Jamaica Meeting House in Gloucester; Gabriella Badiani Desusa, who checked out my Portuguese; my agent, Anne Dewe, who never stopped encouraging me; and Beverley Birch, my editor, without whose criticisms and insights this story would not be what it is today. Many thanks, everyone.

So *The Door of No Return* is not just a story, it's a history that did happen with a story that could have happened, even perhaps should have happened, and who knows, maybe one day something like this might happen—and on that day, I sincerely hope the governments of the West will see fit to compensate those whose ancestors were stolen from Africa.